A Constant Love
A Pride & Prejudice Continuation

by Sophie Turner

DEDICATION

For Nona, the kindest, gentlest soul

CONTENTS

Part One
March, 1814

CHAPTER 1

For two beloved sisters who had both recently become engaged to be married, and were betrothed to men who were already particular friends, it was natural that talk would soon turn to the notion of a double wedding. Neither Jane nor Elizabeth Bennet could remember who first brought the idea about, but both preferred an arrangement that would be easiest on the families involved, and as both were of generous dispositions, there were no selfish feelings in sharing such a special day.

Jane broached the idea to Mr. Bingley, Elizabeth to Mr. Darcy, and all agreed that there was great sense in such a plan. It was introduced to the rest of the Bennet family, and after Mrs. Bennet – who had planned for each of them to have a separate, quite extravagant wedding – was brought around to the idea, the couples fixed upon a date. All agreed that most of the guests would stay at the larger Netherfield estate, where exposure to Mrs. Bennet's continuing high spirits at having two more daughters married would be minimised, and that the wedding breakfast would be held there, in Netherfield's spacious ballroom.

Jane and Elizabeth's aunt and uncle Gardiner were among the few guests to be put up at Longbourn, and they arrived a week before the date with the usual tumble of young children emerging from their carriage, running up to the house and then remembering their manners as they greeted the Bennets. Elizabeth felt a sense of relief upon seeing her aunt; her mother had been suffering from increasing fits of nerves and had finally taken to her room, attended by their aunt Phillips, and unable to help with any of the final preparations or provide any advice to her soon-to-be-married daughters. And Mrs. Gardiner, as soon as she had changed from her travelling clothes, asked what she might do to help.

The Netherfield guests began arriving a few days later. Mr. and Mrs. Hurst, who brought in their carriage a sulking Caroline Bingley, were first. They were followed by a train of carriages bearing Andrew and Ellen Fitzwilliam, the Earl and Countess of Brandon; their sons, Andrew, Lord Fitzwilliam, and Edward, Colonel Fitzwilliam; Lord Fitzwilliam's wife Alice, Lady Fitzwilliam; Georgiana Darcy, and her companion, Mrs. Annesley. This accounted for all of the close family of the two grooms, with the exception of some relations of the Bingleys from Scarborough, who could not make the journey, and Lady Catherine de Bourgh and her daughter, Anne, who would not be attending. Lady Catherine firmly told her nephew of this in a letter with a great many underlined words, the second such she had sent to Mr. Darcy on the topic of his "unfortunate engagement." He had not seen fit to favour her with a reply.

Of all the guests, Elizabeth was most looking forward to seeing Miss Darcy again. The Hursts and Miss Bingley she had no care for furthering her acquaintance with, but with her sister marrying Charles Bingley (by far the most amiable person in the family), that would not be an option. She was more apprehensive about meeting the Earl of Brandon and his family. His younger son, Colonel Fitzwilliam, she was already acquainted with, and she enjoyed his company very much. However, she was not sure if the rest of the family would be so amiable, and she was not accustomed to addressing an earl. As the carriage brought her, Jane, and Mr. Bennet up to the entrance to Netherfield, she tried not to dwell on how much influence the guests in the house would have over her future life.

Mr. Darcy and Mr. Bingley were waiting to hand the Bennet ladies out of their carriage, and then the group moved through the entrance-hall and into the drawing room that had become so familiar to Elizabeth over the past few months. She need not have worried about the earl and his family. Mr. Darcy made the introduction, and Elizabeth soon found they were all as pleasant to be in company with as Colonel Fitzwilliam, particularly Lady Brandon, whom Elizabeth was encouraged to call Lady Ellen, when amongst family. Lady Ellen was impeccably dressed, and possessed such elegant manners that Elizabeth found herself thinking that here was a woman she could emulate, as the future Mrs. Darcy. Lord Brandon and his elder son were more reserved, but still contributed periodically to the inquiries on the health of her family and the final wedding preparations.

Civil conversation was soon diverted when Caroline Bingley noted how very tired Eliza Bennet looked from all the wedding planning, and offered her services to the Bennet sisters if there was anything she could do to help. Many of those in the drawing room were already used to Miss Bingley's attacks on Elizabeth Bennet; it was no secret that Caroline had wished to marry Mr. Darcy herself, and the event a few days hence would be the end of several years of fruitless pursuit. Lady Ellen, however, gave Caroline a look of strong reprobation and stated that she should never have thought Miss Elizabeth Bennet tired – she looked every bit as handsome and radiant as a soon-to-be bride should.

It was clear during dinner that, while Charles Bingley had his usual cheerful manners, he had planned, or perhaps overplanned, dinner quite mindful that an earl would be in attendance. The richness of the dishes, and the sheer number of them on the table, meant that much of the conversation was centred around the food, and the party spent much of the dinner's duration dutifully applying themselves to try just a trifle of this or that. Elizabeth did not mind, as with Lord Brandon at the table, precedence had been carefully observed, and so she was seated between her father and Mr. Hurst, with Jane across from her. Mr. Hurst applied himself to the food and wine with such dedication that there was not even any aspect of his behaviour that her father could make her laugh at, and she could think of no new topics that the Bennets had not already discussed throughout the course of the day.

When the seemingly interminable dinner finally reached its end, Elizabeth sought out Miss Darcy's company as the ladies retired to the drawing room. Georgiana Darcy had been exceedingly quiet before and during dinner, hardly speaking at all to anyone other than Mrs. Annesley, and Elizabeth wanted to ensure she was not feeling neglected, so when the young lady chose a sofa on the very edge of the room, Elizabeth joined her.

"You are very quiet this evening, Miss Darcy. Are you well?"

"Thank you, Miss Elizabeth. I am well. It is only – I am not used to being in this much company."

"It is rather a lot of people, is it not?"

Georgiana nodded her agreement.

"Do you spend much time with your aunt and uncle?"

"We visit frequently when all of us are in London. Their estate is about a hundred and twenty miles from Pemberley, so we are only there occasionally."

"That is quite a distance. I do not get to see my aunt and uncle Gardiner nearly so much as I would like, and they are only as far away as London," Elizabeth said. "They arrived at Longbourn three days past, however, so I do at least have their company until the wedding."

"Oh, I remember them – they were so kind and such excellent company. Do you – do you think I might call at Longbourn to see your aunt and uncle, and meet the rest of your family?"

"I think that would be lovely. Please do feel welcome at Longbourn at any time, although I must warn you, my mother is not of the sort of constitution to handle wedding preparations well. We may need to spend much of our time out of doors."

Georgiana smiled. "I should like to be introduced to all of your family.

After all, in a few days they will be my family as well – Miss Elizabeth, I cannot tell you how happy I am to be gaining a sister."

"I am as well, Miss Darcy."

"But you have four already!" Georgiana exclaimed. "One more must not be of much consequence."

"When she is as lovely and as accomplished as you, I assure you, she is," Elizabeth smiled. "I will allow you, though, that it is not the same for a lady who has always had sisters to gain one, as it is for a lady who has never had a sister."

"That is what I meant – I have always wanted a sister, and now finally I shall have one."

Their conversation was soon interrupted by the entry of the gentlemen into the room, and Elizabeth encouraged Georgiana to move with her to chairs closer to the centre of the room, and endeavoured throughout the course of the evening to draw her in to the conversation whenever possible, asking her opinion on some of the topics under discussion. Elizabeth was pleased to see that although Georgiana seemed uncomfortable at first to be singled out to speak, her confidence seemed to grow slightly by the end of the night, and Elizabeth's attentions also made the rest of the party think more about the presence of a young lady who was of a shy demeanour, and not likely to interject herself into a fast-flowing conversation. Jane and Lady Ellen, in particular, sensed what Elizabeth was at, and made their own efforts to draw Georgiana out.

If there was one complaint Elizabeth had, when Mr. Darcy finally handed her back into the carriage, it was that she had spent very little time with him in the course of the evening. In such a group, private conversation was difficult, and she was required to console herself with the thought that in three days, they would be married, and able to spend as much time alone in each other's company as they chose. Mr. Darcy provided further consolation by arriving on horseback, along with Mr. Bingley, early the next morning; the gentleman were to go for a long ride, but they had ridden out in advance of the party so they might call on Jane and Elizabeth.

They all opted for a short walk, although it was still chilly and the frost crunched under Elizabeth's boots as they made their way across Longbourn's grounds. As per unspoken tradition, the couples soon separated – not enough to be improper, but enough that their conversations could not be overheard.

"I wanted to thank you for your attentions to Georgiana last night," Mr. Darcy said. "She has not often been in so much company, and I find she has not been comfortable speaking in such situations."

"Of course. With such a silent, taciturn brother it is not a shock that she does not often speak in groups," she teased. "Perhaps it is hereditary. But do not worry, I will help her as much as ever I can. As for you, you are a grown man and must fend for yourself."

"You speak in jest, Elizabeth, but you are right. My own avoidance of unfamiliar company has likely harmed Georgiana, who has not had the opportunities to *practise* her conversation, as you once indicated I should."

"She is not yet eighteen; she still has plenty of time."

"Not for a woman of her station who has no unmarried sisters. There will be whispers in town that something is the matter with her if she is not out in the next season. There are some her age who will be married already by that time," he said. "I worry about Georgiana. Her demeanour is more positive, now – Mrs. Annesley has worked wonders in that regard – but the event with Wickham seems to have permanently shaken her confidence."

It did not help, Elizabeth knew, that her marriage to Mr. Darcy would bring Wickham into Georgiana's family. She and her betrothed agreed completely that Wickham would never be welcome at Pemberley or his house in town. Lydia herself might, in time, be invited as guest, but only well after her letters had passed the stage where she went more than a few lines without mentioning "my dear Wickham."

"We will just have to work to rebuild it, then. She is a very accomplished young lady (and I mean that even by *your* definition, Mr. Darcy) and quite intelligent. She added much to the conversation once she began speaking."

"You are right in that she will need more opportunities to speak up in company. I had thought about perhaps going to London for the little season this autumn – it will be less pressure for her with fewer people in town and fewer events," he said. "It would mean delaying our taking up residence at Pemberley until at least Christmas, though."

"I do not mind at all, if it would help Georgiana," Elizabeth said. Truly, even more than not minding the idea, she actually preferred it. Although the idea of being mistress of Pemberley had thrilled her at first, and still did in some ways, she was also apprehensive about taking on such a role. Her mother, the only person she had ever been able to observe at length, was an indifferent household manager, and Longbourn certainly could not compare to Pemberley in the size of its operation. Elizabeth knew she would be expected to handle things with the elegance and gracious manners of someone like Lady Brandon, and was not sure she was yet able to the task.

As well, going to London in the little season would allow her as well as Georgiana some time to acclimate to the company Mr. Darcy kept. She would be expected to move in different circles, now, to develop influence and ensure that Georgiana had every possible opportunity for superior company. Superior, marriageable company, if she must come out. Elizabeth understood Darcy's concern fully now – Georgiana was a sweet, shy girl, nowhere near ready to fend off suitors she did not prefer.

"You would be amenable to transferring to London after Weymouth,

5

then?"

"Yes, of course."

Weymouth had been their plan for a honeymoon for some months. Brighton was far more fashionable, but held such negative associations for Elizabeth that she had no desire to visit there. Although Lydia's flight with Wickham and eventual marriage had perhaps been the event that reinforced Mr. Darcy's continued regard for her, and therefore should be seen as having some positive aspects, to Elizabeth, Brighton was still a place where a young girl could run wild and be compromised. They had settled on Weymouth as a suitable alternative, because although Elizabeth had no wish to go to Brighton, she did have a great desire to visit the seaside.

"Thank you, dear Elizabeth. You know how important Georgiana is to me, and to know that you share such concern for her welfare – it means a great deal to me."

She patted his arm as they made their turn back toward the house. "No one who knows Georgiana could not be concerned for her welfare. And do not worry, with practise, as you say, she will become more comfortable with what is required of her in being out in society."

"I suppose it may help that she gains a slightly impertinent sister."

"Why Mr. Darcy, I do believe you are teasing me," she said. "You see, if I can teach you to tease, helping Georgiana speak up in company will be nothing."

Georgiana herself came to call, along with Lady Ellen and Mrs. Annesley, about an hour after the gentlemen had ridden off. Elizabeth was impressed by the condescension Lady Ellen showed, in requesting to be introduced to the rest of her family. Although her mother's nerves had shown rapid improvement upon her hearing a noblewoman was calling, to the point where Mrs. Bennet had dressed and joined them in the drawing room, Elizabeth found her mother rendered so quiet by Lady Ellen's superior manners and appearance that she did little more than curtsey and say she was pleased to make her ladyship's acquaintance. Mary and Catherine, as well, were quiet, answering politely and carefully whenever Lady Ellen asked them a question. Georgiana even ventured a question of her own, Elizabeth noted with satisfaction.

With Elizabeth, Jane, and Mrs. Gardiner helping the conversation along, a half-hour passed quickly, and Lady Ellen rose to take her leave, telling them she was very pleased to make their acquaintance and hoped she might see them again before the wedding. Georgiana rose to follow her, but she looked reluctant to leave, and Elizabeth was reluctant to see her go. She suggested that perhaps her soon-to-be sister might stay to dinner and help them with final preparations. Georgiana said she should like that very much, Lady Ellen offered to inform the Netherfield guests of her plans, and

Mrs. Annesley said she would stay as well, so that she and Georgiana could return together.

Mrs. Bennet retired to her room, to rest, and Mrs. Gardiner was left to explain to Georgiana and Mrs. Annesley that they were finishing the items for the Miss Bennets's trousseaux. The wedding dresses were all complete, but there were still a number of other dresses and items to be finished and trimmed. Georgiana picked up a bonnet from the table and said she should like to try trimming it, while Mrs. Annesley applied herself diligently to embroidering handkerchiefs.

Some time passed in silence, all of the ladies working. Elizabeth looked up periodically to see that Georgiana still had sewn nothing on the bonnet itself, although she seemed to be working carefully on some pieces of fabric. Mrs. Annesley, meanwhile, worked with delicate little stitches. Then Elizabeth found herself concentrating on her own work, embroidering the hem of one of Jane's dresses, and it was only Catherine's exclamation that made her look back up:

"Why, that is the most elegant bonnet I have ever seen! You must teach me how to make the little roses, Miss Darcy, you *must.*"

Georgiana blushed, and Elizabeth could see that her sister's praise was not overdone. The fabric Georgiana had been working on had been turned into tiny little pink roses, arranged artfully around the brim of the bonnet, with a pale green ribbon intertwined around them. Catherine moved to sit beside Georgiana, and Georgiana obliged her with a lesson in gathering and sewing the fabric to look as though it was a rose.

Thus began a somewhat unlikely friendship between Georgiana Darcy and Catherine Bennet. Georgiana had long been lacking in company her own age, and while she would be gaining Elizabeth as a sister, a married sister was not the same as an unattached friend of similar age, however different their expectations might have been. Elizabeth worried about the connection, at first – Kitty had, for several years, been nearly as silly as Lydia. But Kitty received her own private letters from Lydia, and she knew that married life with a man of insufficient income was not nearly the same as what her elder sisters were about to achieve. She had come to understand that a good marriage would be necessary for her future happiness and independence, although she still harboured hope that it might somehow be with a man who wore a red coat. She came to realise that she could no longer be amused by chasing after officers, and a friendship with a well-bred, accomplished young lady was far more desirable to her than it would have been before.

Georgiana, meanwhile, benefited from Catherine's friendly, open manners, and as she visited them in the final days before the wedding, Elizabeth was happy to see that Georgiana had found another person she could speak to so comfortably. Mary, initially aloof, was pulled into their confidences when Georgiana heard that she was accomplished at the pianoforte, and asked to hear her play. As it had been a very long time since someone had actually *asked* to hear Mary play, this endeared Georgiana greatly to Mary, and Georgiana seemed none the worse for listening to Mary speak, sometimes at length, in her pedantic way.

CHAPTER 2

The wedding was generally deemed a success among their acquaintance. Those who were inclined to be happy for the couples thought Jane and Elizabeth looked quite elegant, Mrs. Bennet's histrionics were kept to a minimum, and the vicar spoke well. Those few who were not inclined to be happy for the couples found little audience for their criticisms, and were as such forced into silence.

For Elizabeth, the calm scene within the church belied the hectic early morning preparations at Longbourn, where the cacophony of her mother and younger sisters as they finished packing Jane and Elizabeth's trunks and helped them dress had done away with any sentiment Elizabeth might have had in leaving her childhood home. The only time she had come near tears was when her father had called her into his library the evening before and said: "Well, now, Lizzy, tomorrow you will be Mrs. Darcy. I shall miss you greatly." She had expected him to finish his statement with some witticism about how there would be no sense in the house now, but he could not; there were tears in his own eyes.

The ceremony itself had held a surreal quality for her; it seemed unimaginable that all of those people were there, family and friends, that the events so long hoped and waited for were finally happening. Elizabeth had smiled a small, private smile as she reached the altar on her father's arm, that here he was, handing her away to the man she'd once said was the last man in the world she would marry. Her thoughts were much occupied by the events that had led her and Darcy there, and she only half attended the vicar as he spoke, but managed her lines creditably. She had felt a thrill of anticipation when it came time for the gentlemen to kiss their new wives, but was disappointed when Mr. Darcy placed only a proper little chaste kiss on her lips. With so much anticipation she had looked forward to her first kiss, and it had not been so special as she had always imagined it would be.

But Elizabeth was not inclined to dwell on relatively small disappointments on such a day, and she had nearly forgotten it by the time the couples made a slow procession past their well-wishers, to the waiting carriages. Mr. Darcy handed her in and then sat down beside her, and Elizabeth felt the change in her status keenly, now – to be allowed to be alone with him, nay, to have every right to be alone with him – gave her quite a rush of delight.

"I do apologise, Mrs. Darcy," he said, as the carriage pulled out to follow the now-Bingleys. "You know I must be most careful of observing decorum in front of such an audience, when what I truly wanted to do was this – "

He leaned over and cupped her chin and kissed her deeply, and at that moment everything became perfect. She was thrilled by the sensation; she felt she understood him even better, now, that there would be a public Mr. Darcy, and a private Mr. Darcy, and as much as she had finally come to understand the former, the latter she would now discover.

"Did I truly look that disappointed?" she asked, when she had regained her breath.

"I believe it was more a case of felt, rather than looked."

"Darcy – "

"Are you to call me Darcy, too?" he cried. "Can no one use my Christian name, not even my own wife?"

Elizabeth had spent much time meditating on what she would call him, when they were finally married, and "Fitzwilliam" had seemed too much, but she was surprised by the vehemence of his reaction.

"Darcy, you must own that *Fitzwilliam* has far too many syllables for everyday use. What did your parents call you?"

"Son," he admitted, which filled her with mirth.

"Well, Darcy, what I was going to say was that I find I rather like kissing, and I would have no complaints if – "

He cut her off with another kiss before she could complete her statement, and the couple were still embracing when the carriage pulled up to Netherfield. Elizabeth consoled herself with the thought that they would be alone following the wedding breakfast for an entire month – Georgiana and Mrs. Annesley would return to London at first, to give the newlyweds some time alone, and then join them in Weymouth at the end of April.

Charles Bingley was always a generous host, Elizabeth reflected, as they entered Netherfield's ballroom, but he had outdone himself this time. The ballroom had been filled with long tables – some of them built out of rough wood only a week ago, but tightly covered with tablecloth so that anyone who did not know would never guess at it. Nearly every chair in Netherfield had been pressed into service, and arranged around the tables. To supplement what fresh flowers could be had from Netherfield's hothouse, bunches of dried lavender had been tied up in ribbons and placed about the room, so that the scent wafted about the guests as they took their places. These and so many other details had been attended, and Elizabeth assumed that her sister had been behind many of them, for Caroline Bingley seemed unlikely to be enthusiastic about preparations for such an event, when she was about to be supplanted as mistress of the house by Jane.

The Bingleys, Darcys, and Bennets took up the long table at the end of the room, and from her seat there, Elizabeth gazed with great felicity out over the family and friends taking their seats at the tables, as footmen with the first remove were already beginning to gather at their stations around the edges of the ballroom. For the first time, she felt a hint of sadness in knowing that she would see many of the people in this room but rarely in the future. She caught Charlotte Collins's eye across the room and smiled at her friend; Charlotte had ignored her husband's entreaties to avoid further angering Lady Catherine with her attendance, and come with the Lucases. Even seeing Charlotte again was in question; as long as Darcy refused any further communication with "that woman," they would certainly never visit Rosings, and Elizabeth doubted Mr. Collins would allow her as a guest in his own house, when her presence there would be so objectionable to Lady Catherine.

The meal wound on in a leisurely fashion; the Bingleys were to stay a few days to see all of their guests off, before setting out for Scarborough so that Jane could meet her new relations, and the Darcys would stay the night in London, and from there make their way to Weymouth. When many of the guests had left, and only closer relations remained, Darcy called for their carriage, and Elizabeth was forced to listen to her mother's final cries of regret about losing the daughter she had never favoured, and had, up until now, made it her life's purpose to marry off. Elizabeth waved goodbye from the carriage window until they were well up the lane, and then settled into the seat beside her husband.

So late was their departure from Netherfield that it was already dark by the time the carriage rolled into Mayfair and stopped in front of a large, handsome town house on Curzon Street. By the time Darcy had handed her out of the carriage, an impeccably dressed man and woman were standing on either side of the door, awaiting them.

Darcy introduced them as the housekeeper, Mrs. Wright, and butler, Mr. Miller, and explained that his steward, Mr. Richardson, was at Pemberley and spent most of his time there, managing the estate while Darcy was away. Each greeted her properly, and Mr. Miller held the door as Elizabeth stepped into a grand entrance-hall, sided by much of the rest of the staff. Each of them was introduced to her, such a flood of names that Elizabeth knew she would not remember half of them the next day. She would have to learn them all, but perhaps she would be allowed some lenience until she returned from Weymouth and was in daily contact with all of them.

Mrs. Wright informed them that dinner had been prepared in advance, as their time of arrival was uncertain, but that the stove had been kept hot so the food could be heated in as little as a quarter-hour.

"Very well," Darcy nodded. "I will show Mrs. Darcy to her bedchamber so she may freshen up."

He offered her his arm and they ascended the staircase to the first floor, then into a bedchamber that was finely furnished, although notably out of date. Elizabeth suspected that much, if not all, of the furnishings had been here when the previous Mrs. Darcy lived in the house.

"I had considered having it redecorated before the wedding," Darcy said. "But then I thought you might prefer to oversee the decoration yourself."

"Thank you," Elizabeth smiled. "It is quite nice as it is, but I should like that, eventually." She liked the notion of being able to furnish a room entirely to her own taste, although it might be difficult to bring herself to get rid of the current furniture, all of which was much finer than any piece at Longbourn, even if it was no longer in fashion.

He led her through the room, into her dressing room, showed her the door that adjoined to his own dressing room, and from there into his own bedchamber, decidedly more modern, decorated with the same understated quality as she had seen in the rooms at Pemberley. She expressed her admiration of the style, and shared a lingering kiss with him before making her way back into her own dressing room.

Elizabeth could not yet change out of her travelling dress – her trunk had been placed in the room, but no maid had yet appeared to assist her – but she did wash her face and check her hair. With these things complete, she set about exploring her apartment: sitting on the chaise, then the bed, and opening the drawers of the desk. It was far larger than her room at Longbourn, and it was strange to realise she should have all of this space to herself, and in a town house no less. She was startled by a knock on the door, and Mrs. Wright entered with a deep curtsey.

"I beg your pardon, ma'am," she said. "I wanted to speak to you about your lady's maid."

"Yes, of course," Elizabeth nodded.

"I have a young maid, Miss Sarah Kelly, who has been most conscientious since she's been in our employ here," Mrs. Wright said. "She has occasionally served as a lady's maid for guests in the house, and I have been of a mind to promote her – Mr. Darcy likes to promote from within the household, when people are deserving. I wanted to check with you, however; if you would prefer someone with more experience, you may advertise for the position as soon as you please."

Elizabeth felt all the delicacy of this situation: Mrs. Wright was likely used to making these sorts of decisions on her own, and to overrule her might create an immediate rift with someone whose cooperation would be critical for her to be successful as mistress of the house. Yet to comply might tell Mrs. Wright that the new Mrs. Darcy could be manoeuvred into decisions, and would not stand up for what she wished to be done. It could not be a coincidence that Mrs. Wright had noted how Darcy liked to promote from within the house. Beyond these considerations, her lady's maid would be the woman who dressed and attended her every day; a poor choice for someone in this role must necessarily affect her happiness until a replacement could be found.

"Even if you advertise for a lady's maid, someone will have to attend me before the position is hired," Elizabeth said. "Let us have Miss Kelly do so for now – you said she has served in the role for guests before. She may come with us to Weymouth and I shall see if I like her, and if so, she can be promoted on her return."

"Very well, Mrs. Darcy."

Mrs. Wright looked pleased as she curtsied again and left the room, but Elizabeth also felt pleased with the conversation. She had committed to nothing, but she had also shown herself to be open to considering Mrs. Wright's choice. She left her bedchamber and descended the stairs, realising she did not know where the dining room was as she did so, but Darcy was waiting there in the hall to show her into a room so large it could easily seat twenty.

They sat at the far end of the table, and the empty expanse of table made Elizabeth slightly uncomfortable. She knew Georgiana and Mrs. Annesley spent much of their time living here, and she wondered if they also dined alone in the empty space, or if there was a more comfortable option elsewhere. Two footmen began serving the first remove – simple food that could be prepared earlier and then heated up, but still quite delicious, particularly as Elizabeth found herself hungry after the travel.

"You are quiet, Elizabeth," Darcy said. "Are you tired?"

"No, I am merely afraid to speak," she said. "I fear my voice will echo. Are Georgiana and Mrs. Annesley forced to dine by themselves in such a great cavern of a room?"

He laughed. "Yes, this room is wasted far more often than it should be. Georgiana and Mrs. Annesley often dine in the garden when the weather is nice, unless the Fitzwilliams or Lady Catherine are in town and come to dinner. At Pemberley, at least, we have the option of using the small dining room."

"And what is the relative difference between the small dining room and the large dining room?"

"The small room seats ten comfortably; the large upwards of two and forty. It has been some time since we have used it."

"Well, never worry, soon enough Kitty will force us to have a ball there."

"Once Georgiana is out in society, we will have to hold our share of balls, although most of them would be here."

"Poor Darcy, you will be miserable, standing in the corner and glowering at all of Georgiana's suitors."

"I might take pleasure in dancing with my wife. That would be quite agreeable to me."

He gave her such a look then as made her stomach churn with a combination of nervousness and excitement, and reminded her that tonight would be her first night in the marriage bed. This was not a new topic in her mind; she had been thinking of it periodically throughout the day, and especially when they kissed. Now, however, the event was only a few hours away.

Elizabeth suspected she was as well-prepared as any other young lady for what was to take place. Her mother had shrilled nonsense at her and Jane and rather frightened them, the morning before the wedding. But Mrs. Gardiner had later asked them if they would like to walk in the garden with her, and presented a vague, but more balanced notion of what was to happen. It would hurt, the first time, but then after that it could actually be quite pleasurable, she had said, blushing for the first time Elizabeth had ever known her to do so. Still, Elizabeth found herself drinking more wine than was usual for her in the course of the dinner; it did not help that the wine was a delightful claret that spoke to the quality of the house's wine cellar.

It was late enough by the time they finished dinner that Elizabeth suggested they retire directly to bed, rather than the drawing room, and they ascended the stairs together before going to their separate chambers. Miss Kelly knocked promptly on Elizabeth's door, entered, and curtsied deeply. She was a thin wisp of a girl, clearly of Irish descent, and even more nervous than Elizabeth.

"Sarah Kelly, if you please, Mrs. Darcy."

"I am very pleased to meet you," Elizabeth said. "Has Mrs. Wright informed you that you will be travelling with us to Weymouth?"

"Yes, ma'am, I am looking forward to it very much."

As Sarah helped her undress, Elizabeth reflected that perhaps having a very nervous girl tend to a nervous woman not much her senior in years might not have been the best idea on this night. Yet at the same time, she found herself distracted by trying to make Sarah feel more comfortable; she could see that Mrs. Wright had been most correct in describing the girl as conscientious, and that Sarah wanted very badly to do well. She was, in fact, doing quite well, aside from a very evident trembling of her hands, and dropping a few of Elizabeth's hairpins on the floor.

Soon enough, Elizabeth was dressed in her nightgown, her hair loosely braided, dismissing Sarah and thanking her for her assistance. She walked over to the door to Darcy's dressing room and put her hand on the knob, her heart beating wildly.

CHAPTER 3

The carriage jarred under Elizabeth and she roused, discovering she had been asleep on Darcy's shoulder, but that he had no reason for complaint, as he was asleep himself still. She sat up and stretched, peering out the window. All was unfamiliar to her here, and she had no notion of where they were. They were moving through fields turning green with the first touch of spring, here and there a patch of yellow wildflowers, a flock of sheep or herd of cattle. They were to overnight in Southampton, and a quick check of the time told her they were probably at least fifty miles away from that city.

Elizabeth looked over at Darcy and smiled as she thought about how unfounded her nerves had been. He had been every bit as much the gentleman in the bedchamber as he was elsewhere, offering her another glass of wine when she entered the room, asking if there was anything else he could do to see to her comfort. Then, when she had finished the wine, kissing her until she had forgotten nervousness entirely.

And yet there again was her new private Mr. Darcy, because while her aunt had been accurate as to the pain, there were things he had done before that moment which still made her flush to think about them. Pleasurable indeed, she thought, her face growing so hot that she wished she had thought to put a fan in her reticule instead of packing them all away in her trunks, following them in another, more utilitarian coach than the one she and Darcy rode in, along with Sarah and Darcy's valet, Mr. Mason.

The carriage rolled on along the turnpike road, through the Hampshire fields, and Darcy slept through a change of horses before finally waking.

"Good morning, husband," she smiled.

"Good morning, wife." He reached over and took her hand and clasped it in his, and Elizabeth found she would not have minded if they had five hundred miles to go instead.

Their arrival into Weymouth showed the town to be everything Elizabeth had hoped for. She had been to the seaside only once before, also to Southampton, when she and Jane had accompanied the Gardiners on a trip Mr. Gardiner found necessary to make for business. That city's meagre beach on the Solent was nothing compared to the vast expanse of waves on the channel, sparkling in the sunlight, and the beauty of Chesil Beach, stretching out as far as she could see. She had come expecting to be charmed by the place, and charmed she was.

They had daylight enough upon their arrival to the town that they could take a brief stroll along the esplanade before returning to the hotel, where Darcy had reserved a spacious apartment that would have ample room for Georgiana and Mrs. Annesley, when they arrived. For now, it felt overly large to Elizabeth, particularly as the servants and their trunks had not yet arrived, and so there was little to fill it. Still, she was pleased with the quality of the rooms, and with the fine view of the sea from the sitting room. She was standing at the window, holding the curtain aside and watching the last streaks of twilight disappear over the channel, when Darcy asked:

"Is everything to your liking, Elizabeth?"

"To my liking? It is perfect. It is all perfect," she said, with a sly smile. "You have raised my expectations so high now you will have to labour greatly to always meet them."

"It is a labour I shall have to bear, then," he said, walking over to the window to join her. "I find I do not mind it much, endeavouring to make you happy."

They watched the waves come in under the moonlight for a long while, his arms wrapped comfortably around her, until at last they felt the need to step away for dinner.

What else may be said about their first month in Weymouth that has not been said about so many of the newly wed, on their first trip together, with more than ample wealth to make all things easy? They had no close acquaintances in Weymouth, and so they passed their mornings early in the trip with walks along the beach, returning to the hotel for refreshments and correspondence. Elizabeth found that Darcy was most diligent in any matter of business sent to him, and no less so with his family. She, for her part, wrote to Jane and the rest of her sisters – including Georgiana – regularly, and was surprised to find Catherine a much more dutiful correspondent than she would have expected.

Evenings they spent walking the esplanade, and eating lavish dinners for two, until Elizabeth finally grew desirous of some other society, as well as some dancing, and required him to take her to a ball at the town's assembly rooms. They made many acquaintances there, some of which were actually worth preserving, and this provided them with occasional morning callers, as well as people to greet in their walks along the esplanade.

There were no morning callers, however, on the day Elizabeth received a letter from Georgiana that made her begin to suspect why Catherine had been writing her regular letters filled with apparent rational thought.

"Georgiana writes to ask may we invite Kitty to come to Weymouth as well," she told Darcy. "Kitty has apparently written telling her how wild she is with envy over Georgiana's trip to the seaside."

"I see nothing wrong with the scheme," Darcy said. He had been too long in the care of only one person – Georgiana – to automatically give consideration to Elizabeth's sisters-by-blood, but he had seen that Catherine and Georgiana got on well, and that being around a lady of her age but of a more lively temperament might be beneficial for Georgiana. "We have ample space. Please do write to invite her, and Mary as well, if you so choose. I should have thought of them previously."

"Mary will say she has no interest in such frivolous pursuits as are to be found at the seaside," Elizabeth said. "I will write to Kitty, however. She has been saying these six months that she will never get to go to the seaside because papa will not allow it, and Lydia has ruined everything for her. She will be ecstatic, and I am sure my father will have no objection to her coming with us, so long as we promise not to allow her to elope."

Catherine was indeed ecstatic, bounding out of the carriage and embracing Elizabeth before gazing back at the sea and sighing with happiness. She had gone to London and stayed with the Gardiners for a few days so that she might travel with Georgiana and Mrs. Annesley. Those two ladies were helped out of the carriage by Darcy, and looked far more weary from the travel. Any suspicions Elizabeth had that Catherine had worn them out with a constant stream of chatter, however, were gone when they all dined together; it was clear she and Georgiana had shared many confidences and become better friends in the course of their correspondence and carriage ride to Weymouth. Kitty was more energetic than her companions simply because she had so long wished to travel to such a place, and now she was here, and determined to enjoy her time.

The growing friendship between the two young ladies meant that Elizabeth was not able to bond with her new sister perhaps as much as she would have liked, although she found herself knowing Georgiana better simply for spending more time together as a family. When Georgiana was engaged in conversation with Catherine, Elizabeth attempted to learn more about Mrs. Annesley, whom she knew from Darcy only as a gentlewoman by birth who had suffered a loss of fortune at some point earlier, and who had made great strides with Georgiana since being enlisted as her companion.

The ladies were out walking one morning – Darcy had more business to attend to than usual, and had bade them to go without him – and Georgiana and Catherine were walking on ahead, laughing about some thing or another. Elizabeth, following them with Mrs. Annesley, took the opportunity to ask whether Mrs. Annesley had been much to the seaside before.

"Yes, many times before," Mrs. Annesley said. "Usually to the north, however, particularly to Scarborough. We went there many times when I was a child."

"Oh, my brother and sister are in Scarborough currently," Elizabeth said. "Were your family from the north?"

"Yes, we had an estate in Yorkshire."

"I have never been Yorkshire – what is the country like, there?"

"Beautiful, Mrs. Darcy. I suppose everyone says that about the land where they were raised, but I never knew anyone to visit who did not comment on how lovely the country was."

"Perhaps someday I shall be able to visit there." Elizabeth felt it, hanging in the air between them, that she had been elevated in fortune and rank, to the ability to travel wherever and whenever she wished, while Mrs. Annesley had suffered a loss in status. She wondered what had caused it, but knew it would be impertinent to ask, and so they walked on silently for a while.

"I suppose you have a curiosity as to how I came to be here," Mrs. Annesley said.

"No, I would never – "

"It is no worry, Mrs. Darcy. I can understand such a curiosity, as I am a companion to your new sister. You would have a right to ask, although I appreciate that you did not. It is not the happiest of tales, but I do not mind telling it."

They walked down, closer to the water, the stones rolling under Elizabeth's half boots, and Mrs. Annesley began:

"I was born on a small estate, Werchfield Manor, in Yorkshire, as I said. I was an only child, and my father set aside a respectable portion for me, so that I was able to marry well, or so I thought. My husband was a kindly man, but I also learned he was a foolish man, and any means that he could use to part himself from his fortune, he used to their fullest extent. Speculation did the most damage, and he died of typhus in a debtor's prison."

Elizabeth made such expressions of sympathy as she could, and could not but help thinking of her sister Lydia, and wondering if her sister would suffer the grief of seeing Wickham eventually meet a similar end.

"It was less than a year after my husband died that my father also died," Mrs. Annesley continued. "The estate had been doing poorly, more poorly than my mother or I realised, and although I inherited it on his death, by the time I had sold the estate and paid the debts of my father and husband, there was barely enough of a portion to keep my mother in a small cottage. So I chose to make my own way in the world; I was fortunate that a friend of our family was in need of a companion for his daughter. I do not possess all of the skills of a governess – I was never musically inclined."

"You may not have those skills," Elizabeth said. "But I know Mr. Darcy has been exceedingly happy with the progress you have made with Georgiana."

"Ah, yes, well, manners, deportment, helping a girl gain confidence, these are all things I at least feel I may attempt. If Georgiana asks for help with a piano concerto, however, I am at a loss."

Elizabeth laughed, and considered Mrs. Annesley, whom she estimated to be at least five-and-thirty years of age. "How many girls have you been companion to, if you do not mind my asking?"

"I do not mind at all. I was companion to three young ladies before Georgiana. They are all of them married now, and I expect we'll see Georgiana do the same before long. I understand from Mr. Darcy that she is to come out in the autumn."

"Yes, we are for London for the little season," Elizabeth said. "We thought it would be better to ease her into society."

"Certainly. It should not take long for a girl like her to make a good match. She has all the accomplishments that could ever be asked of a young lady, and fortune. There should be nothing to hold her back."

"She is so shy, though."

"Give her time in society, and that will go away soon enough."

"You do not think the – setback – she had when she was fifteen will affect her?"

"If anything, perhaps it will make her cautious and prudent, which I believe to be a good thing. I see a great many girls during the season fall in love with the first handsome man they dance with."

CHAPTER 4

Before Georgiana could dance with any men in London, handsome or otherwise, she had to be presented at court. A date for her presentation was applied for while they were still in Weymouth, and granted, so that when they returned to the house on Curzon Street, they had a fortnight to prepare.

At this point, Catherine should have returned to Longbourn, but her presence had become so much a part of their family unit in Weymouth that Elizabeth had dispatched a letter to Longbourn before they left the seaside, requesting that Catherine be allowed to stay in London with them, and she received a response back from her father that he could perhaps attempt a few more months without the level of silliness he had grown used to over the years at Longbourn, which elicited a smile and a few tender moments of homesickness from Elizabeth. She wrote back to invite Mary, as well, wanting to be fair to her other unwed sister, and it was fixed that Mary should join them after Georgiana's presentation at court.

When Elizabeth had been presented at court, it had been a production involving much shrilling from her mother, who, not a gentlewoman herself, had never been through such a process, and the calmer presence of her aunt Gardiner. Elizabeth remembered little of the actual event itself, and more the ridiculous dress she had been required to wear, side hoops and all, which she suspected to have been handed down from Jane and reworked as much as possible, and knew to have later been handed down to Mary and Catherine, while Lydia had not even been presented at all before being allowed to come out. Their family had not the fortune to have a gown custom-made for each girl for less than a minute of time in front of royalty.

Georgiana, however, had no such blood sisters to provide handed-down gowns, and every expectation that a fortune of thirty thousand pounds could give her. They went, therefore, to a modiste that specialised in court dress, and Elizabeth and Georgiana would have been lost without the presence of Mrs. Annesley, who had been through this three times before, and knew precisely what was required. She requested the gown, made of a rich silk, be produced in a way that it might later be reworked as a ballgown in more of the modern fashion, and ensured that no detail was left undone. Although of less importance, a new gown was also ordered for Elizabeth, who would accompany Georgiana during her presentation.

At this point, the greatest influence Elizabeth could exert over the preparations was to encourage Darcy to re-engage relations with his aunt Catherine. For herself, she would not have minded doing without Lady Catherine's society for the rest of her days, but she knew that Lady Catherine's connexions would be very helpful for Georgiana as she made her debut, and she continually exerted pressure on Darcy as such, until he finally sent a brief letter of contrition to Rosings. He received a prompt response that said nothing at all of his wife but assumed a certain level of Lady Catherine's involvement in Georgiana's coming out. She would not be able to make it to her presentation at court, but would be in town soon enough to make introductions and ease Georgiana's entrance into society.

Elizabeth was fortunate that while Lady Catherine could not attend Georgiana's presentation at court, Lady Ellen had been a part of the plans from the very beginning. She had no blood daughters herself, but had always looked very kindly upon Georgiana, and looked forward with the utmost felicity to seeing her young niece introduced to the world. She called at Curzon Street the day before Georgiana's presentation, noted her gown as being most appropriate, and provided a calming influence over the whole party.

The Lady Ellen of a casual morning call, however, was very different from Lady Ellen attending court. She arrived at Curzon Street in the earl's grandest carriage to attend them to St. James's, and it was not until they all alighted the carriage, with much awkwardness from the hoops of each of their dresses, that her dress was fully visible to Elizabeth. She took it in immediately as the dress of a woman who attended court frequently enough to have no need for such rework as Elizabeth and Georgiana had planned for their gowns. As they approached the palace, Lady Ellen placed a hand each on Elizabeth's and Georgiana's arms and said:

"Do remember to never turn your back on the royal presence. You must curtsey once upon entering the room, once as you approach their highnesses, and then once as you exit. Your presentation will likely be brief; do not be insulted by this."

Elizabeth realised that although Lady Ellen's instructions were ostensibly for Georgiana, they were also meant to benefit her. It had been so long since her presentation at court, and she had never expected to return here as a woman presenting a young lady such as Georgiana. As they entered the palace, Lady Ellen stepped ahead of her and she found herself clutching Georgiana's hand, hoping she herself communicated just a little less terror than she could feel from her sister.

They approached the drawing room and were announced. Elizabeth released Georgiana's hand reluctantly, and they followed after Lady Ellen, who discreetly manoeuvred Georgiana in front of her at the last possible moment.

Lady Ellen had been expecting both of their royal highnesses, but only Queen Charlotte was there to receive them, looking regal, but as tired as a woman in her situation should be expected to look. She examined them all for a moment before stating:

"Lady Brandon, you have somehow been hiding not one, but two elegant young ladies from us. Pray tell, who are they?"

"Your Majesty, they are my nieces, Georgiana and Elizabeth Darcy. Miss Georgiana Darcy is making her introduction to court, and her sister is lately Mrs. Darcy. I understand she was presented a few years previously as Miss Elizabeth Bennet."

Queen Charlotte examined Elizabeth closely for a moment before saying, "Ah, yes, Darcy. Quite an excellent family; I wonder we have not managed to give them some sort of title by now. But then, that is reserved for war heroes, these days. Miss Darcy, did any of your family serve in the war?"

"My cousin – Colonel Fitzwilliam – your Majesty," Georgiana said, her voice quavering.

"Lady Brandon's son, I believe." She looked to Lady Ellen to affirm her statement, and Lady Ellen did so with a decided nod.

"We thank your family for his service," Queen Charlotte said. "We should not have defeated Bonaparte without the contributions of men such as your son."

"I thank you, ma'am," Lady Ellen said.

"Well, Miss Darcy, I look forward to seeing you out in society, as well as your new sister." Her gaze fell on Elizabeth only momentarily this time, but Elizabeth caught in full the question there: Who was she, and how had she managed to marry Mr. Darcy so quietly?

"We thank you, ma'am," Lady Ellen said, taking just the slightest step backward. Elizabeth and Georgiana caught what she as at and stepped backward themselves, until Lady Ellen paused near the doorway and they saw that it was time to curtsey for the last time, Elizabeth dropping down so deeply she could feel the ostrich feathers in her hair bobbing back and forth, so that she felt both ridiculous, and relieved.

When they had exited the drawing room, they had only to make their way out of the waiting room and back out of the palace, to the safety of the carriage. As they left the waiting room, Elizabeth heard something she had no reason to believe her companions overheard, and still it gave her great unease.

"Who are they?" asked an unidentified female voice. "They look quite elegant."

"Oh them," answered another female voice. "One is Miss Georgiana Darcy, who has thirty thousand pounds. The other is the nobody who married Mr. Darcy. I do wonder if she will have an impact on her new sister's prospects."

The carriage returned to the Fitzwilliams's house on Half Moon Street; Lady Ellen had long ago arranged that they should all have dinner there to celebrate Georgiana's presentation, and so Darcy and Catherine were to meet them there. For young Georgiana, there was only relief that the event was over, and that she had made no mistakes, nor said anything that should hamper her entrance into society. For Elizabeth, however, there was a more subtle worry that she must at all times endeavour to be equal to her company; she must prove those who would expect nothing of her wrong.

These things were soon forgotten, though, in the comfort of the Fitzwilliams's home. It was exceedingly well-appointed, to be sure, but even in such noble spaces, to be around family who wished her and Georgiana well was a relief to Elizabeth. Although Colonel Fitzwilliam was still on the continent, helping to complete the final arrangements of Napoleon Bonaparte's abdication and the ensuing peace, Lord Brandon and his elder son and daughter proved to be excellent company. It was clear to Elizabeth that Lord Fitzwilliam had from an early age been groomed to inherit the earldom, and he displayed a thorough knowledge of current affairs and how they might impact the family. If he was not quite as light-hearted or as easy in conversation as his younger brother, she could not find it in herself to hold it against him.

Lady Ellen, as usual, was everything polite, and Lady Fitzwilliam followed her lead. She encouraged both Georgiana and Catherine to join in the conversation, as did Elizabeth, and by the end of the evening Elizabeth felt more assured in having such connexions and allies. She was especially proud of both sisters for making confident and well-informed contributions to the conversation. If anyone had any regrets on the evening, it was simply that Elizabeth and Georgiana had to remain in far more restrictive corsets than they were used to. And yet Elizabeth could not help but feel a swell of happiness for her new sister as Darcy handed her into the carriage to go home – Georgiana had survived perhaps the most difficult part of coming out into society, and now she would have access to all the more enjoyable aspects.

By the time they returned home to Curzon Street, Elizabeth was exhausted, and barely aware of Sarah's motions to remove the great expanse of dress from her. She felt the increase in air, though, when Sarah removed the corset. Sarah had proved so far to be a most careful and dedicated lady's maid, and Elizabeth resolved she must speak to Mrs. Wright about her promotion soon; she did not know how she could possibly do without Sarah's kind company and melodic Irish accent every day, and Sarah was most diligent in all of her duties.

Although she was terribly sleepy, she still passed into Darcy's chamber – he had made it clear to her early on that he enjoyed her presence even if either of them was too tired for marital relations, and so she was no longer comfortable sleeping without her husband at her side. He pulled her close and kissed her hair as she entered the bed beside him, and she found all the discomforts of the day melting away: she had a husband who loved her, a sister newly out in society, another sister newly reasonable in company, and a well-placed relative who had been nothing but kindness to her so far. She felt the benefit of all of these things, but most of all, of a husband who every day provided her with new caresses, new nuances, of his very private self.

Elizabeth woke late in the morning, to find Darcy already absent from his bedchamber. She made her way back into her own rooms, rang the bell for Sarah, and found her lady's maid prompt as always in entering the room.

"Let us go with something very simple and plain, for my day dress," Elizabeth said to her.

"Yes ma'am," Sarah smiled. "That was rather a lot of dress for you to wear all day yesterday."

Elizabeth laughed softly as she thought back to the two of them, trying to manage the unfamiliar corset and determine how the complex dress was to go on, as Sarah had dressed Elizabeth the previous day.

"Certainly it was – I must say I am glad I should never have to wear such a thing again."

When Sarah had finished dressing Elizabeth in a blue day dress that was very plain indeed, Elizabeth requested that she send Mrs. Wright in if the housekeeper was available. Sarah flushed, and said she certainly would, and Elizabeth realised too late that the young maid might have thought Elizabeth wished to censure her work. Sarah had grown more comfortable in Elizabeth's presence, and more willing to converse, which was partly why Elizabeth enjoyed her company in the morning. Sarah was always very careful to stay within the bounds of propriety, never departing from innocent and appropriate topics, and so she should have had nothing to fear. Elizabeth consoled herself that soon enough Sarah would know of her promotion, and no longer be worried.

Mrs. Wright bustled in a few minutes later and asked what she could do for Mrs. Darcy.

"I wanted to speak to you about Sarah," Elizabeth said. "She has done excellent work as my lady's maid thus far, and if you are still amenable to her promotion, I see no reason to delay it any longer."

"Very well, ma'am," Mrs. Wright said, looking very pleased. "I will let her know."

"Please do inform her as soon as possible," Elizabeth said. "And I thank you for recommending her."

"You are most welcome, ma'am."

"We will soon need to begin preparing for Georgiana's coming-out ball," Elizabeth said. "I would appreciate your assistance in the planning, and I thought perhaps we might also include Mrs. Annesley, as she has helped several other young ladies come out before Georgiana."

"Of course, ma'am."

Elizabeth waited a few moments after Mrs. Wright had left her rooms to go down the stairs to breakfast. She felt satisfied by the interaction, which indicated a growing trust between Mrs. Wright and herself. They had certainly agreed on Sarah's qualifications and skills.

Darcy had already breakfasted and was attending to correspondence, but he sat with Elizabeth, Georgiana, and Catherine as they ate; Mrs. Annesley, knowing Georgiana to have no fixed engagements for the day, had requested permission to visit a friend of hers, and Darcy had sent her off in the carriage. The group went to the drawing room after breakfast, and Elizabeth was delighted when Mr. Miller came in to hand her a letter that had just been delivered.

"A letter from Jane!" she exclaimed, and eagerly opened it. The two sisters continued to correspond frequently, and Elizabeth found that although she very much enjoyed the company of Georgiana and Catherine, she still missed the companionship of her elder sister. They had been together for most of their youth, and although Elizabeth knew that their own sisterly bond and their husbands's friendship would still have them together frequently, it was not quite the same.

"She writes they are to come to London, and will be staying with the Hursts." Elizabeth felt a twinge of disappointment that they would not stay at her home, but with Catherine and now Mary coming to visit, she could hardly begrudge that the guests would be balanced between the two houses. If anything, the greater disappointment was that she would have to spend more time in the company of the Hursts and Caroline Bingley.

Elizabeth did not share the more private parts of the letter, which indicated that the cause for their departure to London was that Mrs. Bennet had finally worn down even the heroic patience possessed by Charles and Jane Bingley, and they desired a break from her daily calls to Netherfield, and frequent requests that they all dine together at Netherfield or Longbourn.

"I cannot criticise my mother too much," Jane wrote. "She has grown used to a house full of daughters and now finds herself lonely. But her constant company has become difficult to bear."

Jane wrote on to say that she missed Elizabeth greatly, and would have the added advantage of being able to convey Mary with them in the carriage, as they were to remove from Netherfield quite quickly. Elizabeth hurried to get her writing things and pen a response to Jane, telling her of Georgiana's presentation at court, and how delighted she was to soon be able to see Jane and Mary.

The family passed the day in this quiet way until Darcy suggested they all take a stroll in Hyde Park. They agreed to this scheme readily; Elizabeth was desirous of fresh air and the opportunity to walk a little, and she also knew it to be one of the things done by the circles she would now be moving in during the season. A fine day was not complete without a stroll or a ride through Hyde Park, for those who most mattered in town.

Everyone went upstairs to change into suitable attire for a promenade, and Elizabeth found Sarah seemed even more nervous upon entering her dressing room, curtseying deeply and approaching Elizabeth with shaking hands. Had Mrs. Wright not yet informed her of her promotion?

"Ma'am," Sarah said. "I hope I do not speak out of turn, but I wished to convey my deepest gratitude on my promotion. I cannot thank you enough."

"You need not thank me, Sarah, you have earned it yourself. You have done very well in your work and I am very glad to have you. Although I find I have addressed you incorrectly; now that you are a lady's maid, you are Miss Kelly. Please accept my apology."

"Oh, but ma'am, I feel so odd not being called Sarah. I would prefer it if we continued on as before, at least in private."

"Very well, but then you must also call me Elizabeth, in private."

"It might take me some time to adjust to that, ma'am," Sarah said, in a tone indicating she might never adjust to it. Still, she seemed to relax, and helped Elizabeth change with even more than her usual cheer.

The house on Curzon Street had the advantage of being very close to the park, and once parasols had been found and spencers donned, the group made the short walk there. Elizabeth had spent much of the past week inside, preparing for Georgiana's presentation and learning the ways of the household, and the vast expanse of the park made her realise how much she had missed being out of doors. It was the fashionable hour, and the park was filled with walkers, but it did not feel at all crowded.

They had been walking for a while when Georgiana recognised an acquaintance, Miss Harriett Grantley, and introduced her and her companion to the group. Miss Grantley was a delicate young girl, nearly the same age as Georgiana, but about to enter her second season. Elizabeth could not recall Georgiana mentioning Miss Grantley before, and realised even before they had said their goodbyes and walked on that Georgiana must not have favoured the young lady's company.

Once they were far enough away, Georgiana confessed to Catherine and Elizabeth that Miss Grantley was fiercely competitive, always wanting to be the most accomplished lady in the room, and Georgiana did not care much for her company. Georgiana had once looked upon Miss Grantley as a potential friend, but had realised her overtures of friendship were only to find someone to compare herself against, and so now they were only polite acquaintances.

Catherine felt a certain, but healthy, amount of pride in hearing this; *she* had sought Georgiana's friendship because she liked the lady, *she* had no desire to be competitive for accomplishments, although she realised that it would be better for her to be more accomplished. It might help her find the sort of husband she wished to find. For the time it was but a momentary thought, gone soon enough, and she took up her friend's arm and patted it in sympathy, as the two young ladies walked on ahead of Elizabeth and Darcy.

CHAPTER 5

The first few days leading up to the Bingleys's arrival with Mary passed with nothing more eventful than a few morning calls between the Darcys, Fitzwilliams, and Gardiners. As Lady Catherine was to arrive at nearly the same time as Elizabeth's more-preferred family, Elizabeth had suggested to Darcy that perhaps they should have them all over to dine; he agreed, and so with equal parts anticipation and trepidation, Elizabeth went calling to deliver the invitations. She had taken on the planning of the family dinners with little difficulty and helpful assistance from Mrs. Wright, but had never planned a meal on such a large scale. Still, she looked forward to the idea of hosting so many people whose company she enjoyed, and had been most pleased when Darcy suggested she include the Gardiners in the invitation before she could even ask about them herself.

To one household, however, Elizabeth went with only trepidation, and a great deal of reluctance. Lady Catherine received her with apparent disgust, and proceeded to ignore her and Mrs. Annesley, whom she had brought along with Georgiana. That young lady was the entire focus of Lady Catherine's conversation: what balls she must attend, whom she must be introduced to. Lady Catherine seemed to already have an entire string of young gentlemen for Georgiana to meet, and Elizabeth watched her sister's discomfort grow increasingly throughout the course of the visit. Elizabeth and Mrs. Annesley both attempted to deflect some of the conversation from Georgiana, but Lady Catherine would not have it.

Elizabeth did feel the slightest twinge of sympathy for Lady Catherine; it was clear her daughter Anne, who had stayed behind at Rosings due to her ill health, would never come out into society, and so Lady Catherine could only help a niece through this process, instead of a daughter. She would be in a position to do so frequently, as well; Rosings Park was an easy distance to London, and so she might come and go throughout the entire little

29

season and full season whenever she felt herself needed.

When they returned to Curzon Street, Darcy informed Elizabeth that he had learned another friend of his family, the Dowager Viscountess Tonbridge, was in town, and asked Elizabeth if she might like to include the viscountess in the invite. He described her as a woman of great sense, powerful enough to keep very liberal company, and someone who could be a very helpful acquaintance for her and Georgiana. With such a recommendation from a man who generally did not favour company, Elizabeth readily agreed to going with him for a morning call. Viscountess Tonbridge was a broad woman with a happy countenance and yet very good manners, readily welcoming to Elizabeth and desirous of being introduced to those acquaintances she had not already met. She had no children of her own and enjoyed the company of young people, and as she had no engagements for the evening of the dinner party, would be delighted to attend.

Elizabeth came away from the introduction pleased that she now knew another person with a noble title who had readily welcomed her into an acquaintance. She might still be a *nobody*, and certainly everyone would not receive her so well, but she was not without friends.

The next day brought the Bingleys's carriage to the front door shortly after the noon hour, and with great joy, Elizabeth welcomed her sisters into the house. Jane and Charles agreed to stay for some refreshment before heading on to the Hursts's house, and soon enough Elizabeth and Jane had sequestered themselves in a private corner of the drawing room so that Jane could tell her of news from home, and they could exchange their impressions of married life. Jane was clearly every bit as happy as Elizabeth, and the two sisters's felicity increased even more as each heard how content the other was.

They were interrupted by the sound of the pianoforte. Mary and Georgiana had been corresponding occasionally, and upon learning that Mary was to join them in London, Georgiana had written to suggest they play duets together. They had landed upon a few selections that pleased them both, and had been practising their parts independently. Now, they were eager to play together, and they did so with much delight. It was clear to Elizabeth that Georgiana was the superior player, but she was such a modest girl that she continually complimented Mary on her playing, and only occasionally suggested an easier way to do the fingering on difficult passages. They had mastered one piece by the time Jane and Charles rose to take their leave, and sounded quite well. The wooden, technical sound of Mary's playing was quite softened by playing with a friend, and Georgiana's skill was, as always, delightful.

Elizabeth, Catherine, Mrs. Annesley, and Darcy continued to listen to them after the Bingleys had left. Later as they went upstairs to dress for dinner, Darcy pulled Elizabeth aside.

"Mary and Georgiana play quite well together," Darcy observed. "Perhaps we could ask Mr. Palmer to fit Mary into his schedule either before or after Georgiana, when he comes for her lessons."

"I do not think there is anything Mary would like quite so much as that," Elizabeth said. Her sister had always laboured away at the pianoforte, with no instruction aside from what little help Elizabeth could give her.

"Catherine does not play, is that correct?"

"No, she does not. She has never had an interest."

"Do you think she would like to learn now?"

"I can ask her," Elizabeth said. Perhaps Catherine, with her recent increase in sense and manners, and removed from Lydia's influence towards more frivolous pursuits, would like to reconsider the pianoforte as well. Indeed, Elizabeth had thought she detected a hint of jealousy on Catherine's face in watching Mary and Georgiana take so much enjoyment in their playing earlier.

When she applied to Catherine with the opportunity, though, Catherine felt she was too far behind the other ladies, and still did not have much interest in learning the pianoforte; she was not musically inclined, although she did take a greater enjoyment from hearing others play now. She hesitantly offered that instead she should like to try her hand at drawing and painting.

Elizabeth relayed this to Darcy, and he promised to see if one of Georgiana's former masters in this area would be available to provide her with instruction. Elizabeth did not know which to be more pleased about – that her formerly silly sisters were now growing more fit for company, or that Darcy had made such an effort to treat them as his own sisters.

The morning of the dinner found Elizabeth far more nervous than was usually her nature. She flitted around the house, occasionally calling to Mrs. Wright to ensure some detail or other had been attended to. It was only Mrs. Wright's continuing affirmations that all was set, and the realisation that she was, perhaps, acting a bit like her mother which forced Elizabeth to go to the drawing room and attempt some embroidery while Georgiana and Mary continued practising their duets.

Elizabeth had been very pleased with how all of the dresses in her wedding trousseau had turned out, but among them she had a few favourites, and she was pleased to see when she went upstairs to change that Sarah had set one of them out. It was a lovely pale yellow muslin that flattered her complexion, and Jane – whose patience made her easily the best embroiderer of all the Bennet ladies – had done the trim. Sarah could not have known this, but Elizabeth was pleased her sister would be able to see the results of her handiwork.

There came a knock at the door adjoining Darcy's dressing room just as Sarah was finishing up Elizabeth's hair, which Elizabeth knew to be her husband, for no one else was to use that door while the family were in residence.

"Do come in," she said, and Darcy entered.

He was holding a jeweller's box, and Elizabeth did not look forward to seeing its contents so much as she should have. The last time he had given her some of the Darcy family jewels had been the morning of Georgiana's presentation at court, and he had given over the box with almost a sheepish expression on his face. She had seen why as soon as she opened it. The necklace and earrings had been terribly overset and completely ostentatious – a good choice, perhaps, to suit her court dress, but she knew she would never wear them for any other occasion. It had been a surprise to her, and a source of puzzlement, for her wedding ring, which had belonged to Darcy's grandmother, was a beautiful little delicate piece that she loved very much.

Sarah rushed to finish the last of Elizabeth's curls, curtsied and made her exit, and only then did Darcy approach with the box, although his expression was very different from last time – he seemed to have even the slightest hint of a smile.

"I am glad you are wearing that dress," he said, handing her the box. "I believe these will complement it very well."

Elizabeth prepared herself to make a positive response, regardless of what was in the box, and then opened it.

"Oh!" she gasped, for inside was a most exquisite little sapphire necklace and earrings, with a matching pair of hair combs. "Darcy, they are all so beautiful!"

"Not quite so beautiful as the woman who will wear them, but I am glad you like them," he said, all smiles at her reception of the gift. "I was afraid they would not be done in time, but my jeweller sent them over this morning. You see, Elizabeth, my mother had a bit of a penchant for – what shall I say, substantial – jewellery. What you hold there was only a necklace and earrings, and I do not think the old setting would have suited you."

"This suits me very much – I love them," she said, putting on the earrings, as he picked up the necklace and clasped it behind her neck.

"I am very glad. I fear, though, that it may be some time before we can have all of the pieces re-set," he said. "Hadley's can only take on so much, and I do not like the idea of entrusting the work to someone new."

"It is no worry – I rather like the idea of periodically having jewellery bestowed on me," she said, looking back at him with an arch smile.

"Then you may count on me for periodic bestowal of jewellery. I shall leave you now," he said, tilting her chin up so that he could lean around and kiss her. "I know you will do brilliantly tonight."

The Bingleys were the first to arrive, and Elizabeth found Jane's calm presence a balm to her nerves. The Gardiners came in shortly after them, giving Elizabeth the added benefit of her aunt's being there as well. The drawing room soon filled with their guests, and Elizabeth circulated among them, ensuring they were all comfortable, and it seemed a little silly to her, but she did feel more confident in her new jewels and dress, as though she was properly armoured for the evening.

As she did meandered about the room, Elizabeth observed something that piqued her interest. She had occasionally wondered if Lady Ellen actually approved of her, or whether the lady's manners were simply so impeccable she would never deign to behave improperly to anyone. However, as she watched Lady Ellen's chilly reception of Lady Catherine, she understood that while Lady Ellen would never allow her manners to be anything less than excellent, she would allow just the slightest bit of distaste to show, when she so felt it.

Lady Ellen took her dislike of Lady Catherine to such an extreme that, upon seeing Lady Catherine snub the Gardiners when they were introduced, Lady Ellen encouraged the earl to go over with her and converse with them right up until Elizabeth called them all to dinner. Elizabeth felt a surge of regard that she could call such people family, and noted that the Fitzwilliams and the Gardiners seemed to get on well, which was not such a surprise – despite the difference in their ranks, both couples were intelligent, well-mannered, fashionable people.

The earl offered Elizabeth his arm, noting she was still a new enough bride that she must go in first, with Jane immediately following, a notion that was seconded by both Lady Ellen and Lady Tonbridge. When they all were seated, the dining room was much closer to properly full, and as she had anticipated, Elizabeth felt a great satisfaction in seeing so many friends and family gathered there. The footmen came in with the first remove, and Elizabeth noted happily that everyone seemed to be enjoying the food. She had generally taken Mrs. Wright's recommendations as to which dishes Cook was best at making, and ventured only a few suggestions of her own. All went over well, and it was on the subject of the food that the viscountess first spoke to Elizabeth.

"You, my dear, are not helping my gout with such an excellent array of dishes," she said.

"I do apologise, Lady Tonbridge, would you like me to have something else prepared for you?" Elizabeth responded.

"Oh, no, do nothing of the sort. It is my own fault for refusing to give up good food," the viscountess said. "You have done quite well for yourself here. I would have thought you to be mistress of this house for many years, and yet you are only newly married. When were you wed?"

"I thank you for the compliment, Lady Tonbridge," Elizabeth said. "Mr. Darcy and I were married in March."

"Ah, the flush of young love," the viscountess said. "And I understand there may be more young love in your household soon. I saw in the papers that Miss Darcy has recently come out into society."

"Yes, we presented her at court less than a fortnight ago."

"I will be certain to include your family in my invitations, then. I usually host a few balls over the course of the season. I have half a mind to try to fit one in before Christmas, as well."

"Thank you very much, Lady Tonbridge. I am sure Miss Darcy will be appreciative."

"You will let me know if there is anything I can do to help her," the viscountess said. "And your other sisters, as well. I understand they are also out in society?"

"Yes, Miss Bennet and Miss Catherine Bennet are both out."

"Excellent. I shall have to ensure I drum up plenty of suitable male partners with so many ladies to support."

Elizabeth glanced over at Darcy, caught his eye, and smiled. She understood fully why he had introduced her to the viscountess – the woman must have had the excellent connexions of her rank, but she showed no hauteur at all, only a great friendliness and desire for enjoyment in life.

The dinner continued on through the second remove, and when that was nearly finished, the earl stood with his glass in the air.

"I believe we are still within a reasonable range of time to again toast the Darcys and the Bingleys on their marriages, and especially Mrs. Darcy for hosting such a fine dinner."

The toast was gladly picked up by most of the rest of the table, Lady Catherine excepted, and Elizabeth blushed as his praise was echoed.

"And I would be remiss if I did not also toast Miss Darcy, on her recent presentation at court," the earl continued.

This toast was seconded by all, and Georgiana blushed even more deeply than Elizabeth, looking somewhat mortified to be singled out. She had the good fortune, however, of sitting near Catherine and Mary, and following the comforting glances her friends provided, she was able to gently nod her thanks to her uncle.

The ladies retired to the drawing room soon after, where Mrs. Gardiner chose a safe topic in asking for a description of Georgiana's presentation at court. This was readily provided by Lady Ellen and Elizabeth, both of them periodically applying to Georgiana for her impressions of the event. The time passed quite enjoyably, aside from the occasional interjection from Lady Catherine about how she might have done things differently, had she been in town for Georgiana's presentation, to Lady Ellen's increasing irritation.

"I must hear Georgiana play the pianoforte," Lady Catherine said, not long after the gentleman had re-joined them. "As many of you know, I have an unsurpassed love of music, and I simply must hear how Georgiana gets on."

Georgiana looked to Elizabeth and Mrs. Annesley with terror; she had never performed in front of half this many people before.

"Miss Darcy and Miss Bennet, perhaps you might play us one of your duets," Elizabeth suggested.

Mary, as always, was eager to perform, and all but dragged the more reluctant Georgiana over to the pianoforte. Elizabeth's suggestion had been effective: Georgiana took comfort in sitting down on the bench with a friend. They played delightfully together, and were roundly applauded by all in the room. Mary all but glowed – never before had her playing been met with such reception. Georgiana seemed more relieved than anything else, but Elizabeth hoped this would be the first step in her taking more comfort in playing for an audience. Her musical accomplishments would not be nearly so useful if she was not able to exhibit.

After a second duet, Georgiana was compelled by Mary to play a piece on her own, which she did, a bit shakily at the beginning but beautifully by the end, when she had managed to forget her audience. She then encouraged Mary to play a few pieces, which Mary readily agreed to.

Lady Catherine was in raptures when Mary had finished; she continued to share her love of music with all in the room, and her delight in seeing two young ladies who applied themselves so diligently in practise. Mary sat down next to her and basked in her praise, discussing the frequency of her practises and all the things she did to try to improve herself, and generally deflecting Lady Catherine's attention from everyone else in the room, which all seemed grateful for.

It was only after Lady Catherine's carriage departed Curzon Street that Lady Tonbridge approached Elizabeth and Georgiana, and beckoned Mary to come over and join them as well.

"I too had a great enjoyment of your music tonight, Miss Darcy and Miss Bennet, although perhaps not so effusive as others," the viscountess said. "My gout has settled in my hands and I can no longer play, so I miss it greatly. I have formed a musical club so that I might have music in my house with some frequency, and I should like it greatly if the two of you would join us. We meet for tea and music, every Monday evening."

"That sounds delightful," Georgiana said. "I thank you for thinking to include us."

Mary looked as though she was about to faint; to have such enjoyment of her playing in the course of the evening, and then to be asked by a *viscountess* to join a musical club was nearly more than her spirits could bear.

"I should like that as well," Mary managed, finally. "It is so wonderful to be met with such appreciation of music as I have seen thus far in town."

"Ah yes, Miss Bennet, there is much to feed the soul of a lover of music here. I shall have to have you all to the opera in my box."

The viscountess's carriage was called then, and she took her leave, as did much of the rest of the party. The Bingleys, first to arrive, were also last to leave, but no one had any complaints about this. Charles and Darcy retired to Darcy's study for a final glass of brandy, and Jane sat down with her sisters.

"Lizzy, you have done so wonderfully! To host such a large dinner, and with such nobility, too, in your first attempt."

"It is nothing compared to hosting a wedding breakfast for near on eighty people," Elizabeth teased her sister.

"That is different; all Charles and I had to do was ensure we had enough seating and food."

"Nonsense, Jane, it was quite an event. Since you are too modest to admit that yours was a larger feat, I must put forth that we were both successful. There, now, you cannot argue with that."

"No, I cannot." Jane smiled at her sister before they both dissolved into a fit of giggles not very befitting of two married ladies. At the moment, neither of them cared.

CHAPTER 6

If the Darcys had known what a disturbance Viscountess Tonbridge's invitation to join the musical club would have on their household, they might have discouraged Georgiana's and Mary's participation. Beginning the morning following the dinner, they both began practising so fervently that Darcy was forced to have the ballroom opened so that one or the other could use the pianoforte in there when they were not playing duets, and the house resounded with music every day until they all left to take the promenade in Hyde Park.

Mr. Palmer came for his lesson with Georgiana, and was compelled to add Mary as an additional client. Mary, wild with enthusiasm before her first lesson, was reduced to tears following it; Mr. Palmer had criticised her technique, and her pride, and said they must break everything down before they should build it back up again. After a few hours of quiet reflection, however, she came to see that he was correct, applied herself to his recommendations, and saw enough early improvement to encourage her to continue practising with what he said in mind. He had also, upon hearing her sing, told her she had not the voice for it, and should keep strictly to playing; this was much more difficult for her to accept.

Catherine entered into her first drawing lesson with no such expectations of her own talent. She had tried sketching things on her own from time to time, so it was not the first time she had held a pencil, but she was completely open to all of Mr. Shaw's guidance. With Georgiana and Mary focused so entirely on the piano, she had ample time for practise, and she worked carefully on the exercises Mr. Shaw gave her, only wishing from time to time that they might go shopping, or do something else a bit more lighthearted.

Monday came, and with it the first musical evening at Lady Tonbridge's that Georgiana and Mary were to attend. Mrs. Annesley conveyed them there, and Catherine retired to the conservatory to practise drawing the plants, leaving Elizabeth and Darcy alone in the drawing room after dinner. He sat down beside her and leaned back against the sofa.

"Peace at last," he said. "Do you think perhaps we could start sending them over to Lady Catherine's house to practise? After all, she does have a true love of music."

"I think this amount of practise might test even Lady Catherine's love," Elizabeth laughed. "I only hope their level of talent is equal to the rest of the club, or we will have no peace until it is."

"It does at least give me an opportunity to have an evening alone with my wife," he said.

Elizabeth reflected that for all her teasing, these last few weeks must have been hard on him. To have so many visitors in the house, and to know that their time in company was only to increase as Georgiana's engagements began in earnest, could not be easy for someone who was not by nature fond of society. She resolved to watch him closely and suggest they retire to Pemberley for a few weeks if his discomfort was too great; she expected shy Georgiana would not mind a break from company, either.

"Yes, it has been quite a long time since it has been just the two of us," she said. "What do you say I entertain us on the pianoforte?"

Many of the servants heard the laughter this question prompted, and all that did, smiled. They had always felt grateful to be working for a kind and fair master, and that he had brought to the house an equally kind and fair wife, one who was so clearly a love match, pleased them all very much.

Breakfast in the morning brought a full recounting of all that had occurred at the musical club. The ladies described Sir Robert Morris, who played a surprisingly delicate flute, and Lady Julia Barton, who was quite skilled on the harp, as well as several other young ladies, accomplished on the pianoforte, and a few other gentlemen who played the trumpet, violin, and other instruments that Elizabeth soon lost count of in Mary's excited description.

Georgiana and Mary had been compelled to play a duet and a solo piece each, and on the whole they had found the group to be passionately devoted to music, and very forgiving of mistakes, especially when they were made by a player attempting to stretch his or her capabilities.

Mary conveyed their reception with the utmost enthusiasm, but Elizabeth noticed that Georgiana seemed a little subdued, and wondered if she had been uncomfortable performing in front of such an audience. She intended to apply to Mrs. Annesley at some point during the day to find out how the evening had gone from a more impartial perspective, but found that Mary provided her with all the intelligence she needed in an aside as the ladies were moving to the drawing room.

"Mr. Davis, on the trumpet, paid quite a lot of attention to Georgiana," she said. "He could hardly be persuaded to leave her side the whole evening, and he said she has thirty thousand pounds. Is that true? Could she truly have such a dowry?"

Elizabeth confirmed delicately that it was true, and began to understand why Georgiana had been so subdued. She wished she had gone with them that evening, or at the very least warned Lady Tonbridge that Georgiana was not yet prepared for the fortune hunters that would come her way in society.

Georgiana joined them in the drawing room, but left soon complaining of a headache. Elizabeth followed her to her room, knocking on the door and entering when there was no response.

"Please do tell me to leave if you truly have a headache and do not want the company," Elizabeth said. "But I understand that your headache might go by the name of Mr. Davis."

Georgiana, sitting on the edge of her bed, looked up sharply at Elizabeth. "How did you know?"

"Mary informed me, but please do not blame her. We are both worried about you. Was he at any point inappropriate?"

Georgiana shook her head. "He was indiscreet, but his manners were otherwise unobjectionable. He could talk of nothing else but how great my family were, and how my fortune should be just what he needed to expand his small estate in Wales. He made it sound as though it was certain we would be married and yet I showed him no indication that I favoured his company!"

"Oh, Georgiana," Elizabeth reached out and put her hand over her sister's. "I fear he is not the last man with similar presumptions you will have to face."

"I know," Georgiana sighed. "Mrs. Annesley warned me that I would have many suitors who were only interested in my fortune. It is only – I suppose I did not realise some of them would be such terrible company. I went last night expecting only people who were enthusiasts of music, and I was unprepared. I will not be so in the future."

Elizabeth felt a deep pang of sympathy for her sister. She had grown up facing the challenges that a lack of fortune brought to her potential for marriage, and had only now fully realised that finding a good partner with such a large fortune as Georgiana's could be equally difficult.

"I am sure the viscountess would understand if you did not choose to return for future evenings," Elizabeth said.

"Oh, no!" Georgiana cried. "That is to say, I did truly enjoy the music, and everyone else was so kind. I did not think I would be comfortable performing in a room full of strangers, but I was. I had even thought to ask if we could send back to Pemberley for my harp."

"We certainly can. But how shall you deal with Mr. Davis?"

"I will have to be firm, and tell him that I do not prefer his company," Georgiana said, with enough of her brother's resolve that Elizabeth thought she might just be able to do so.

"I will go with you next time, as well as Mrs. Annesley, so you have more family to support you," Elizabeth said, determined that if Georgiana was unable to do so herself, she would tell the man to stop his overtures. "However for now, if you are feeling well enough for it, let us practise."

"Practise? How does one practise such a thing?"

"Oh, Miss Darcy, you are in possession of such a great fortune," Elizabeth said, taking up her arm. "I am sure you will love my paltry little estate in Wales."

Georgiana giggled at Elizabeth's actions, but finally said: "Sir, I have come for the musical club. I thank you for your interest, but I would ask you to turn your attentions back to the music."

"But Miss Darcy, we are a match made in heaven! Surely our love of music will bring us closer!"

"Mr. Davis, I am sorry, but I must make it clear that I am not interested in your suit."

"There, you did that quite well," Elizabeth said.

"Yes, but I fear it will not be so easy with the real Mr. Davis."

"I think you will manage just fine."

After Elizabeth left the room, Georgiana laid back in the bed, staring at the ceiling. Now that she had feigned a headache, she would have to stay in her room for at least a few hours, and she wished she had thought to ask Elizabeth to bring her a book. She smiled as she thought of her sister; she was feeling much better after her conversation with Elizabeth.

At the very beginning of the evening, she had actually enjoyed Mr. Davis's company. He had sat beside her after she finished her solo piece, and was very complimentary of her playing. But then he had continued to seek her company throughout the rest of the evening, and been increasingly bold about the potential of a connection between the two of them.

The only thing she could take some consolation in was that it had been clear to her he was only interested in her fortune. After her near-elopement with Mr. Wickham – the thought of it even now made her flush with shame – she had realised that he would likely not be the last man to pretend to be in love with her in order to get at her fortune. She had been young, no one had ever paid her such addresses before, and she had thought herself in love so easily. When her brother had first brought up her coming out this year, she had known that he was right, it was time, but she had determined that she must be extremely cautious. She must guard her heart, and she must rule her own feelings so that she would never again allow herself to be persuaded to be in love by such a man.

Georgiana was still in her room when Lady Ellen called on them; expressing concern for her niece and her hopes that she would be recovered a fortnight from Friday. The ladies all expressed their curiosity as to the significance of the date, and Lady Ellen informed them that a particular friend of hers, Lady Ruth Allen, was hosting a ball that evening. Upon hearing that Lady Ellen's nieces were in town, Lady Allen had immediately extended the invitation to include them, and Lady Ellen thought a small, private ball would be a perfect first such outing for Georgiana, whose coming-out ball would not occur until January, when the full season began.

Catherine was disappointed at first, upon hearing this – she had been longing for a ball, and now Elizabeth and Georgiana would attend one, while she would have to stay home. But soon enough, Lady Ellen's statements indicated that both she and Mary were also included in the invitation. Catherine had always liked Lady Ellen, but this condescension to consider her and Mary as her nieces, and for an invitation to a private town ball, of all things, now made Lady Ellen one of her very favourite people.

Elizabeth, too, noted the condescension with satisfaction, and particularly the way Kitty acknowledged it. There was no wild squealing as might have happened had Lydia been around, and instead, Catherine told Lady Ellen that she would look forward to the event with great anticipation; it had been some time since she had danced. Her enthusiasm was evident, but she controlled it carefully.

There was no such condescension, however, when Lady Catherine arrived, so soon after Lady Ellen had departed that Elizabeth wondered if she had seen the carriage with the Brandon arms on it, and ordered her own carriage to circle the block until Lady Ellen left. Lady Catherine had an invitation to deliver to Darcy, his wife, and Georgiana only, for dinner only two days before Lady Allen's ball. She did so despite the presence of Mary, Kitty, and Mrs. Annesley in the drawing room, and Elizabeth had half a mind not to accept it, but knew that Lady Catherine must have invited at least one potential suitor for Georgiana, and she would not harm Georgiana's chances to favour her own indignation.

Kitty had no cares about Lady Catherine's dinner party when she would be attending a ball two days later, but Mary took greater insult; she had thought Lady Catherine favoured her, and she went over to the pianoforte and took up her practise in the hopes of reminding the lady of her diligence. Lady Catherine rose to take her leave soon, however, and so Mary was left to look forward only to the next musical evening with the viscountess, which she did, greatly.

They had a family dinner that evening, having invited only the Bingleys to join them. Everyone was much relieved to see Georgiana recovered, and she was filled in on the callers of the day, and the invitations that had been delivered. Georgiana could not garner much excitement at her aunt's dinner invitation – she had no doubt that Lady Catherine had a suitor in mind for her, someone who matched Lady Catherine's expectations of whom Georgiana should marry, and that they should be introduced at the dinner. The ball, however, she was quite excited for. She knew her aunt Ellen would not have sought the invitation unless she thought it to be a good event for Georgiana's first ball, and she looked forward to it with every anticipation of finally having an opportunity to dance in company.

The gentlemen were not long with their port after dinner, but rather than taking seats in the drawing room, Darcy requested that Elizabeth and Jane join him and Charles in his study. Elizabeth felt all the strangeness of the request; she sometimes joined Darcy in his study during the day to read a book in the comparative quiet of the room, especially when Mary and Georgiana had been practising in earnest. But to request her presence there, and with Jane and Charles, was something else entirely, and she wondered if perhaps he had some bad news to share with them that he wished to keep from the rest of the family at first.

When they were all inside and seated, Darcy seemed at a loss for how to begin whatever it was he was about to broach. Finally, he said:

"Charles and I have made some very fortunate investments in the course of the last year, which brought an exceptional return when the peace was declared. We had been discussing what we might be able to do with the profits, and thought perhaps the best use of the money would be to increase Mary's and Catherine's portions."

"Oh my," Elizabeth said, seeing that Jane still looked too shocked to speak. "That is exceedingly considerate of you."

"Nonsense!" Charles said. "They are our sisters now, too."

"But what of Georgiana and Caroline? Surely as your blood sisters you would want to increase their portions."

"Georgiana and Caroline already have more than sufficient dowries," Darcy said. "Georgiana will be pursued by enough fortune hunters with her current dowry, and it is in part for her that I wish to do this. She, Catherine and Mary have struck up quite a friendship, but the discrepancy in their expectations must certainly colour the relationship."

Darcy did not mention another reason for the decision to contribute to Mary's and Catherine's portions, but he and Charles had discussed at length what should happen if Mrs. Bennet survived Mr. Bennet. Certainly the woman would need to live with one of her daughters, and if one or the other of her unmarried daughters remained so, a sufficient fortune would allow them to set up house in a reasonably sized cottage. If all of her daughters married – and a larger portion would give Mary and Catherine much improved chances – Mrs. Bennet could be shuffled amongst more households, meaning that Darcy and Charles would suffer her company less frequently. This, however, was reasoning he could not offer to Mrs. Bennet's two eldest daughters, so instead he said:

"We had thought to supplement their portions so that each of them should have five thousand pounds. Do you think this would be acceptable to your father?"

In some ways it would be an insult to Mr. Bennet, Elizabeth knew, that what her father had failed to save up over the years could now so easily be provided by his new sons. However, she also knew her father to be selfless enough that he would accept the gift politely. Five thousand pounds, although nowhere near Georgiana's thirty thousand or Miss Bingley's twenty thousand, should be sufficient for them to make a far better match than either of them might have hoped for previously.

"I am certain it would be," Elizabeth said. "I know my entire family will be grateful for the consideration you have given them."

"Oh yes," Jane seconded her. "It is so kind of both of you."

"Good, then we will have the paperwork drawn up, and I will write to your father indicating our intentions," Darcy said. "Would you like to call your sisters in so that we may give them the news?"

"I would like for the two of you to give it to them without us," Elizabeth said, looking to Jane for her assent. "They should know that this was your idea, not ours."

"Very well, then. Please do send them in."

Both Mary and Catherine were mildly terrified to be called into such a conference, and especially without their elder sisters. Mr. Darcy had been nothing but kindness to them as guests, and they had always known Charles as an amiable man, but they could think of no reason why they should be called into the male sanctuary on business.

When the reason for their being called in was explained, and they had absorbed the news that they were each to have five thousand pounds, they were as pleased as can be imagined. Mary did not think it likely that she would find a husband in town; she held out hopes that perhaps she might meet with a country clergyman of the highest moral standard someday. While she already knew she was no longer at risk of being turned out of Longbourn to starve, with two sisters so well married, the idea of having some fortune of her own was greatly pleasing, even if she never did marry.

Catherine, meanwhile, was ecstatic. She had come to London hoping to find a husband, and to go about it much better than Lydia had done, and now in addition to the artistic skills she hoped to acquire, she had some fortune to also recommend her. She looked forward to the ball with even more enthusiasm than before, and looked upon her brothers with nearly as much adoration as she had shown Lady Ellen earlier.

CHAPTER 7

The next morning, the house was once again filled with music, although far livelier than usual. Elizabeth had gone out to call on the Gardiners, and when she returned, she found the drawing room empty. She made her way to the ballroom, and there found Mary at the pianoforte, while Catherine and Georgiana were dancing.

"Lizzy, come join us!" Catherine called out. "Georgiana wanted to practise her dancing before the ball, although she needn't have worried – she dances wonderfully."

Elizabeth took a seat beside Mrs. Annesley in one of the chairs that ringed the ballroom, and watched as they finished the dance.

"If Mary is not too tired for another song, I should like the next dance with Mrs. Darcy." Darcy's voice behind her startled her; Elizabeth had been so focused on Georgiana and Catherine, she had not heard him come into the room.

"I am certainly not too tired," said Mary. "You all will tire before I do; I could play for several hours more."

Darcy led Elizabeth up to where the ladies were dancing, and they all bowed with mock seriousness as Mary launched into the next song. Dancing with another couple allowed Georgiana to better practise all the movements of the dance, and Elizabeth noted that even Darcy seemed to be quite enjoying himself. They all finished the dance in high spirits.

"Mary, can you play a waltz? I should like to practise that as well," Georgiana said.

"A waltz?" Elizabeth, Catherine, and Mary exclaimed, nearly simultaneously.

"It will be some time before it becomes acceptable at country dances," Darcy said. "But yes, the waltz has become quite appropriate at London balls. I would not be at all surprised if it is danced at Lady Allen's ball."

"But I don't know how to waltz!" Catherine exclaimed, although she knew enough of the dance to like the idea of it very much.

"It is actually much easier than the dances you already know," Darcy said. "But I am certain we can get an instructor in before the ball so that you may be taught. There are four parts, but I find the Sauteuse to be the most difficult. Georgiana and I may show you, if Mary has fast waltz she can play."

Mary did indeed have a fast waltz she enjoyed playing, although the thought of dancing it was as abhorrent to her as it was pleasant to Catherine. She launched into it, and Darcy led his sister in a progression all the way down the ballroom, looping about with little hops, and back up to where the ladies were gathered.

Darcy then held out his hand to his wife. "Elizabeth?"

"I do not know how to waltz, either," she admitted.

"Well, then, let us try."

Mary continued playing the song, and after a few early missteps, one of them on Darcy's foot, Elizabeth began to get the motion of the dance, and they worked their way down the ballroom as Georgiana and her brother had done. Elizabeth found that she quite liked dancing such a dance with her husband, but was not sure she could condone the young ladies doing so with just any partner, and from what little she knew of the dance, the Sauteuse was not even supposed to be the most intimate part.

The longing on Catherine's face to try was clear when they returned to the group, as was her gratefulness when Darcy held out his hand to her. She picked it up even faster than Elizabeth had done, with the advantage of having watched the other dancers very carefully. Indeed, she intended to practise the steps on her own as best she could, any time she chanced to be alone.

Elizabeth watched them go around and nearly laughed to think of the first time she had seen her husband at a dance, so uncomfortable and unwilling to dance with anyone he did not know. It was difficult to believe this was the same man before her, encouraging her sister to move her feet just a bit faster. How she had misunderstood him then! And yet, also, he had changed, even since their marriage; he was far more lighthearted, now, and Elizabeth wondered how much of his old serious demeanour had been caused by worry about his sister.

Darcy returned Catherine to the group and held out his hand to Mrs. Annesley, who laughed him off and said she was enjoying watching everyone else dance far more than she would have enjoyed it herself.

An instructor was found, and the ladies spent the next few days alternating between dance practise and the pianoforte, or, for Catherine, with sketching various items around the house in the deliberate fashion of a new student. Now that Mary and Georgiana knew that their level of talent was appropriate for the viscountess's musical club, they felt less pressure to be practising all the time, although they still spent more time at the pianoforte than they had before Lady Tonbridge extended her invitation.

Indeed, for Georgiana, she would have been looking forward to the next musical evening wholeheartedly, if not for the fact that she knew she would have to speak to Mr. Davis. She spent much of Monday in a state of apprehension, thinking of various ways she could politely tell him she did not want his company.

They ate an early dinner, so that the ladies would have ample time to get into the carriage and make their way to the viscountess's house on Grosvenor Square. Elizabeth had worried a bit at leaving Darcy and Catherine alone together – the two people in the house who had perhaps the least to converse about – but Catherine had asked at the end of dinner if he would mind terribly if she went to the conservatory to get some more drawing in before her next lesson. Darcy had told her that he did not mind at all, and that he would be in his study if she needed anything, and Elizabeth left secure in the knowledge that her husband would have what was likely a much-needed evening of solitude.

Elizabeth was roundly welcomed by the group, applied to for any musical skills she might possess, and when she mentioned she played the pianoforte a little, encouraged to join in and play. She demurred; she had not the skill of the others in the room, and she would much rather hear one of the other ladies play than do so herself.

The viscountess pulled her aside as the other ladies made their way into the music room, which had been filled with rows of neat little gilt folding chairs.

"I am glad you are come, Mrs. Darcy," she said. "I did not like the attentions Mr. Davis gave young Miss Darcy in our last session, and an extra set of chaperone's eyes will not go amiss. You do let me know if she is too uncomfortable, and I will ask him not to return. He plays but a mediocre trumpet, anyway."

"Thank you, Lady Tonbridge. I would ask you not to intervene just yet – I should like for Miss Darcy to gain some practise in fending off suitors. It is a skill she will certainly need."

"Ah, there you are correct. Perhaps an even more important thing for her to practise than the pianoforte," the viscountess chuckled. "You do just keep in mind that I will speak to him if it is needed."

Elizabeth thanked her, and they made their way into the music room.

As she had last time, Georgiana took a seat beside Mary up near the front of the room. The seat beside her was empty, and she steeled herself, knowing that Mr. Davis would likely take it. She was correct in her estimation; he sat down beside her just before Lady Julia began a beautiful piece on the harp, so that she had no chance to escape.

"You are looking very well tonight, Miss Darcy," he whispered.

"Thank you, sir," she said coldly, and she made no move to continue the conversation.

"How have you been these last few days?" he said. "I must admit I was so enchanted by our meeting that I have hardly been able to think of anything else."

Georgiana felt it, that this was the moment she must put a stop to his attentions; she trembled for a moment, and then gathered up her courage and spoke.

"Please, sir, I have come here tonight for the music, not for your conversation. I beg you would stop talking and pay Lady Julia the respect of listening to her beautiful playing."

He was silent, following this. Georgiana did not dare look over at him to see his reaction, but she trembled again in the relief of the deed having been done. Following Lady Julia's piece, as Miss Green took her place at the pianoforte, Mary, who had overheard much of the exchange and sensed how awkward it must be for Georgiana to continue to sit next to him, asked Georgiana if she would take a look at the trim on the back of her gown; she thought it had come loose.

Mary stood, and Georgiana – who had never known Mary to care at all about trim – stood with her and inspected the trim, pronouncing it to be fine. Mary indicated her relief, and then, through some manoeuvring, ensured that she sat back down in Georgiana's seat, so that Georgiana was at least one person removed from Mr. Davis. Georgiana gave Mary a look of great relief, and tried to focus her attention on Miss Green's playing.

"Well done, Mary!" Elizabeth said to herself, watching the entire exchange. And well done Georgiana – it was clear the young lady had said something to Mr. Davis that caused him to stop leaning over and whispering into her ear. With such difficulties out of the way, Elizabeth could now sit for the rest of the evening and drink her ladyship's excellent tea, listening to some very beautiful music and seeing her sisters each have the chance to exhibit, which they did, wonderfully.

The next morning found Elizabeth and Darcy reading in his study, Catherine back in the conservatory, and Mary practising the pianoforte in the ballroom, so that only Georgiana and Mrs. Annesley were in the drawing room when Mr. Davis came to call.

"Good morning, ma'am," he said to Mrs. Annesley. "I would like to request a private audience with Miss Darcy."

Georgiana, who had been sitting at the pianoforte in that room, trying to make her way through a new, very difficult piece, heard what he said with mortification, and looked over at Mrs. Annesley, pleading with her eyes not to leave them alone.

"As Georgiana's companion, I am not allowed to leave her unchaperoned with anyone," Mrs. Annesley said.

Georgiana felt a bit of relief at this, but Mr. Davis made it clear that he was not going to leave.

"Fine, then," he said, making his way over to the pianoforte's bench. "I suppose I shall have to say what I have come to say with an audience."

"Miss Darcy," he said, kneeling down before her. "I admire that your love of music did not allow us to speak more last night, and so I have come to tell you today of how deeply I have fallen in love with you. I have come to request you would make me the happiest of men, by consenting to be my wife. You know of my home, in Wales, and I am sure you would give it much grace as its mistress. Certainly it would be difficult for you to be so far away from your family at first, but I have no doubt that our love will make up for such a separation in time. As I have mentioned, your dowry would enable the expansion of the estate such as to make us one of the most powerful families in the area."

Georgiana glanced over at Mrs. Annesley, who gave her a look of deep sympathy, but also made it clear that she must be the one to speak. Only Georgiana could refuse the offer. Her cheeks burned as she listened to him, longing for him to finish and yet unsure of what she would say when he did.

"Sir, I thank you for your proposal," she said, finally. "I do acknowledge the sentiments you have expressed, but I am of a hope that as they arose from less than a fortnight's acquaintance, they may be suppressed in as short a time. I must decline your proposal."

"Oh, of course, the lady demurs on lack of time for acquaintance," Mr. Davis said, reaching out and patting her hand. "I understand, my Georgiana. We should have a long engagement so that you may have more time to get to know me. I am sure you will need time to grow used to the separation from your family, as well."

"Sir, I do not believe you are comprehending me. I have declined your proposal. I do not believe there is any reason to speak any further on the matter."

"Miss Darcy, I can hardly believe you would decline such an offer. Please let me know of your objections so that I may do away with them."

Georgiana could not believe the gall of this man! To continue to press his suit when she had clearly declined him twice spoke of more terrible manners than she had originally suspected of him. She wanted nothing more than to run out of the drawing room; she did not know what she could say to make him leave and end such a horrible discussion. She opened her mouth to speak again, but Mrs. Annesley spoke before her.

"I believe the lady has made her regrets clear enough," Mrs. Annesley said. "I would suggest that you leave now."

When he made no such move to do so, and continued on discussing his merits and those of his estate, particularly when it was enlarged with Georgiana's thirty thousand pounds, Mrs. Annesley rose and walked over to the drawing room door. Georgiana feared for a moment she was going to leave them – how could Mrs. Annesley do such a thing as to abandon her now? Soon enough, though, she saw that Mrs. Annesley was talking to Mr. Miller, who had noticed a tension in the room on announcing Mr. Davis, and stayed near the doorway in case assistance was needed.

After a few painful minutes, Georgiana saw her brother stride through the doorway, his face tight with fury. Georgiana could only remember him looking this way once before, when she had confessed her intent to elope with Mr. Wickham, and he had called Mrs. Younge into the room to speak with her.

Mr. Davis rose to bow to Darcy, perhaps expecting an introduction to be made. None was forthcoming, however.

"You, sir, will leave this house at once, and you will not return," Darcy said. "The lady has made her refusal quite clear."

Under such a command, and with Mr. Miller standing beside her brother, and both of them looking as though they would pick him up and throw him bodily out if necessary, Mr. Davis did finally leave, to Georgiana's extreme relief.

She found herself much caressed by her family in the wake of his exit. She shakily thanked her brother, Mrs. Annesley, and Mr. Miller for their assistance, and felt Elizabeth press a glass of wine into her hand. She overheard Mrs. Annesley telling her brother that there had been nothing lacking in Georgiana's refusal; the man had simply been too stupid and too short of manners to cease. She took some comfort in this – part of her had feared she had not refused him properly, and that was what had made his proposal so interminable. She felt even better when Elizabeth recounted a proposal she had received, before Mr. Darcy had offered for her, that had also seemed to go on without end, no matter what Elizabeth had said.

Georgiana drank the wine, and felt her spirits gradually revive. Catherine and Mary came into the room, as well, offering such support as they could provide. She turned down Mary's offer to practise their duets together, as she was not yet feeling up to the concentration required for music, but when Catherine suggested they go shopping as a diversion, she agreed to the scheme, and if Georgiana's hand was still a bit shaky as her brother helped her into the carriage, the look on her face was complacent enough that he let them go willingly, assured that this would not be so much a setback for his sister as Mr. Wickham had been.

CHAPTER 8

The days before Lady Catherine's dinner passed quietly. Georgiana was relieved to find that Mr. Davis did not attend Lady Tonbridge's next musical evening, and found she could finally enjoy the company and the music to its fullest extent. Everyone continued to take great care around her – Fitzwilliam, Elizabeth, and Mrs. Annesley especially – but she assured them she was fine. She had been discomfited in the moment, but suffered no permanent harm from it.

She did not have any enthusiasm for attending Lady Catherine's dinner, but rather saw it as the final obstacle she must overcome before the ball, which she did have the deepest anticipation for. She and Kitty had been practising their dancing every morning, and she felt quite ready to dance in company.

The object of her aunt's intentions became clear as soon as they arrived, and introductions were made. In attendance were the Duke of Bolton, and his sons: Stephen Mallory, who went by the title Viscount Burnley; and Alfred Mallory, whom, as the second son, was introduced almost as an afterthought by Lady Catherine. Georgiana knew her aunt might have preferred to see her own daughter Anne married to the heir to a dukedom, but as Anne's health had not allowed her to come out, Lady Catherine would focus her efforts instead on seeing whether she could get her niece so married.

She found her aunt steering her to sit beside Viscount Burnley in the drawing room before dinner, although she took an almost immediate dislike of him. His dress showed him to be part of the set of fast young men in town even before his manners did, and all he could speak of was of how he had won or lost at cards on this or that evening, and of nights he had spent in various frivolities with his friends. Georgiana's one consolation was that he did not seem to have any interest in her at all, and so she felt she was in no danger of suffering another proposal of marriage from a man she disliked anytime soon.

Lady Catherine had arranged the seating carefully, so that precedence was generally observed, particularly for the duke and duchess, but Georgiana was forced to sit beside Viscount Burnley through the course of the dinner. Now he spoke of the food, comparing it against other dinners he had been to, before returning to cards. Georgiana was grateful when Elizabeth drew her in to a far livelier conversation about books she was having with Lord Alfred.

Georgiana found herself sought out by the younger son, when the gentlemen had returned to the drawing room after dinner. He took a seat beside her, and said, quietly: "Tell me, did my brother speak of nothing but gambling, or did he perhaps broach the topic of horse racing, as well?"

Georgiana laughed in spite of herself, but could think of no appropriate response.

"Ah, you are too polite to say anything in censure," he said. "I have spent too much time with him to be so discreet. I had hoped perhaps we might be able to continue our conversation from dinner – we had just broached Shakespeare, I believe, and Shakespeare is a topic I would not like to see uncanvassed. But do let me know if you would prefer I talk about cards, or horses. Or perhaps fencing is more to your interest?"

"No, I should much prefer Shakespeare," she said, smiling.

Georgiana considered Lord Alfred. He was a young man of three- or four-and-twenty, perhaps not quite fully handsome, but still very pleasant to look at, and he possessed an amiable air that was nothing like his pompous brother. Like his brother, he was quite tall, but his clothes were conservative, although well-tailored. She realised with a little thrill that he was the first man she had met in quite a while that she would not mind furthering her acquaintance with, although this realisation was followed immediately by the thought that she knew nothing about him, and must still be very careful with her heart.

They talked only with each other for much of the rest of the evening, and this did not go unnoticed by the others in the room. Lady Catherine was disappointed Georgiana had not gone for the first son, but still felt that any connection with a family as powerful as the Duke of Bolton's would be useful, and could help make up for her nephew's unfortunate marriage. Darcy and Elizabeth felt a great deal of relief that she had not shown any interest in the first son, and Darcy intended to tell her as much the next day.

Rather than calling her into his study after breakfast, which he knew would draw attention, he instead asked if she might like to go for a ride in Hyde Park. Georgiana had been raised by a horse-loving father and brother, and riding, to her, was a natural part of life. She realised it had been quite some time since she had ridden – Elizabeth did not like it, and Mary and Catherine were indifferent – and eagerly agreed to the scheme.

They made a handsome pair, the brother on his tall bay stallion and the sister on her lovely grey mare, and were noted as such by more than a few people as they made their way down Rotten Row. Both horses were a bit skittish from want of exercise, and they cantered back and forth along the Row quite a few times before finally slowing to a walk.

"I am glad to see I did not have to warn you away from Viscount Burnley," Darcy said. "That man is clearly a rake."

"I know Lady Catherine would like me to marry the heir to a dukedom," Georgiana said, following the rush of relief brought by her brother's statement. "You and Elizabeth do not feel the same?"

"I should not mind if you married the heir to a dukedom, as long as it was not that particular dukedom," Darcy said. "Georgiana, you know that Elizabeth and I were fortunate enough to make a love match. You have sufficient fortune to do the same, and that is what we would like to see for you. Granted, I would prefer you not fall in love with a chimney sweep if you can help it."

Georgiana laughed and thanked her brother for his reassurance.

"I did find I enjoyed Lord Alfred's company," she ventured to add.

"We noticed that," Darcy said. "He seems to have far more sense than his brother. I could hint to your aunt that it would be good for the two of you to be in company with each other more often, if you would like that."

"Yes, I believe I would. Thank you, Fitzwilliam."

Georgiana spent the day of the ball in a state of nervous excitement. She did not want to practise her dancing, for fear of making herself too tired for the actual event, and she lacked the concentration for music practise or reading. They had no callers, so she resorted to sitting in the conservatory with Catherine while her friend drew a succession of rather well-done ladies outfitted in elegant ballgowns, both of them chattering their anticipation. Would there be a waltz? How many partners would there be? How large was the Allens's ballroom?

It was a relief when Elizabeth finally came into the conservatory and noted they might go upstairs to dress and have their hair done. But Georgiana's lady's maid, Miss Hughes, was both quick and good in her role, and Georgiana found herself rapidly dressed and her hair done up so perfectly that even a nervous debutante could not find fault with it, and she was the first lady to return downstairs. This was the first in a succession of new ball gowns she was to wear, and she enjoyed the way the silk swished around her feet as she walked down the stairs. Her brother was already there, emerging from his study, and he gave her a very strange look as he approached her.

"Brother, is something the matter?" She touched her hair and looked down at her gown, wondering what might be amiss.

"No Georgiana, there is nothing the matter. You look quite lovely. I simply find myself shocked to realise how much you have grown up." Were Darcy of the more expressive sort, he might have noted that Georgiana had finally outgrown the awkwardness of the last few years, and matured into her height, and as such carried herself as a tall, quite pretty young woman. Most would not call her fully beautiful, but then, there was a kindness and good nature in her countenance that most truly beautiful women of Darcy's acquaintance lacked – excepting his wife. His hope was that she would meet with a gentleman who preferred these qualities – if indeed she had not already.

"Thank you, Fitzwilliam." Georgiana stepped forward and embraced her brother. She wanted to thank him for his care of her, since the death of her father, and to tell him she was sorry it had not always been easy – Mr. Wickham and even Mr. Davis came to mind – but she could not think of what to say, and he did not seem to mind that this was all she could manage.

Elizabeth, Catherine, and Mary came down soon enough, with exclamations over Georgiana's dress and how lovely she looked. She returned the compliments, but felt the specialness of her own situation, and how happy they all were for her.

The Allens's ballroom proved slightly smaller than the Darcys's, but was so well-decorated that none of them could find fault with it. Lord and Lady Brandon were the only Fitzwilliams in attendance, their son and daughter-in-law having returned to the family estate at Stradbroke. The elder couple had been waiting to escort the Darcys in and make the introduction to Sir Walter and Lady Allen, and it was clear to all of them that they were the sort of well-mannered company that could be expected to be friends of the Fitzwilliams. The number of male partners, however, was already apologised over by Lady Allen, and after a few remarks among the group about how perhaps there might be more in the coming season, with the peace, they went inside.

Georgiana, at least, had the joy of dancing the first set with her brother, after Elizabeth kindly said she would sit it out; she simply could not see Georgiana not dancing the first dance at her first ball. Elizabeth had not known that this would prompt all the men in the dance to look at Georgiana, and note her to be a quite elegant young lady, worth seeking out for a dance of their own, but this was indeed what happened. Such mental notes by the gentlemen were soon followed by the news that spread quietly through the ballroom that Georgiana was just recently out in society, she had thirty thousand pounds, and her family owned one of the largest estates in Derbyshire. She found her hand requested for every dance, and at first felt all the compliment of such attentions.

By the supper set, however, Georgiana was miserable. Aside from one dance with Lord Brandon, who had kindly asked for a set with each of the ladies in their party, she had been through an array of suitors. One had proved exceedingly clumsy, although nice enough. Another insisted on talking constantly about nothing of great importance, so much that she could not even enjoy the dance. There was Mr. Turner, who was quite good-looking, but seemed to be an enthusiast of horse racing, and little else. And finally there was Mr. Ward, who had claimed the supper set although he had no conversation at all, so that she had spent both the dance and the meal attempting to come up with topics, only to see each of them dissipate after a few minutes of effort.

When supper was mercifully over, Mr. Ward led her back into the ballroom, but noticed an acquaintance and abandoned her before they had reached her party. Georgiana saw Elizabeth across the ballroom and was attempting to make her way over to the only familiar face she could see, when a man stepped up to her.

"Mr. Thomas Simpson," he said. "I understand you are Miss Georgiana Darcy. Might I have your hand in the next set?"

Georgiana was mortified at the nerve of the man – to approach her without her family, to introduce himself!

"Please, Miss Darcy. I assure you I am an excellent dancer. We shall have quite a delightful set together."

She began to better understand the reason for his boldness and unacceptable manners: his eyes were unfocused and his speech was slightly slurred, he had certainly had too much wine or perhaps even stronger spirits.

Georgiana was at a loss for what to say – he had broken all bounds of propriety, but she could not bring herself to do so as well. If she were to refuse him the dance, she would have to sit out the rest of the evening. As miserable as many of her partners had been, she held out hope that someone with at least some skill in dancing and some conversation would ask her for a set, but now she would have to accept that the unfortunate Mr. Ward was to be her last partner of the night.

Just as she was about to open her mouth to speak, afraid that in his drunken state he would not take her refusal well, she heard another voice behind her.

"Miss Darcy! I hope you have not forgotten that you promised me the set after supper."

Georgiana turned around to find that it had been Lord Alfred, calling out to her. She felt such a rush of ecstasy then, such gratitude, such delight; to be saved was a relief in itself, but to be saved by the one person she should most like an opportunity to dance with! How had he come to be here? Certainly she would have noticed him before; the ball was fairly intimate in its attendance.

"Lord Alfred, why yes – I thank you for reminding me," she said.

He held his arm out to her, she left Mr. Simpson with the slightest of curtsies, and they went to take their place among the dancers.

"Miss Darcy, if you did truly want to dance with that man, I apologise exceedingly for the interruption," Lord Alfred said to her. "But I know well the look of a man who has been too much at the card table with too many brandies, and he had it. I did not like the idea of him asking a lady to dance, particularly one I was acquainted with, even if it is but a recent acquaintance."

"Oh no, I certainly did not want to dance with him," she assured him. "He introduced himself to me!"

"He introduced himself? It is even worse than I thought," he said. "I am sorry you had to put up with such abominable manners."

"It is all over, now," she said. "I do not know how to thank you for rescuing me."

"I have the favour of your hand for a dance," he smiled at her as they made their bows and began. "I assure you the rescue was no great sacrifice on my part."

"I did not even realise you were in attendance tonight."

"I was not, earlier. I had a previous dinner engagement this evening, but Lady Allen feared a shortage of male partners, and encouraged me to attend after supper, if I could. I found I was able to break away from my previous party, and so here I am."

Lord Alfred proved to be an excellent dancer – he was graceful, he spoke just enough, but not too much, and he was interested in all she had to say about the ball so far. He was amazed to learn this was her first ball, and assured her she danced beautifully – he should never have known if she had not told him.

When the set was over, he led her back to her family, greeted Mr. and Mrs. Darcy with great enthusiasm at seeing them again so soon after Lady Catherine's dinner, and requested to be introduced to Mary and Catherine, asking them if he might have a dance with each of them. Mary made her regrets, for she had had her fill of dancing and already begun making refusals before supper, but Catherine was relieved. She had already had to sit out one set, and although Lord Alfred seemed to take particular interest in Georgiana, he looked to be an excellent dancer and she would not mind a set with him at all, especially if it kept him from dancing with some other lady who was not her friend.

Elizabeth, who had noted with desperation Georgiana's distance from her before the last dance, and seen the discomfort on her face upon being approached by a man Elizabeth certainly did not know and did not think

Georgiana had been introduced to, was relieved to see her back with them, and intrigued that she had somehow come to be escorted there by Lord Alfred. After Lord Alfred had led Catherine off, Georgiana whispered the story of his coming to her aid, and how he had arrived after supper, and so intense was their conference that no one dared ask for Georgiana's hand for the next dance.

Elizabeth was nearly as thrilled for her sister as her sister was herself; she imagined the joy of the rescue, and noted particularly how it had further endeared the rescuer to Georgiana. She had been asked to dance a few times without introduction by some of the soldiers in Meryton, but they were all of them harmless enough, and she never would have expected such a thing at a private ball in town. She wished to inform her husband of the event, but she had required him to dance every set so long as there were ladies who still wanted to dance, and he was currently leading some young acquaintance of Lady Ellen's up the floor and putting much effort into his countenance, so that he looked only slightly miserable.

After Lord Alfred had escorted Catherine back to the group, Lady Allen let it be known that the next dance was to be the last dance, and it was to be a waltz.

"I realise we just danced recently, Miss Darcy, but I wonder if I might have the favour of your hand again," Lord Alfred said. "I have hardly been here long enough to be introduced to any of the other ladies."

"I would like that," Georgiana said, blushing slightly.

"Mr. and Mrs. Darcy, might I have permission to dance the waltz with Miss Darcy?"

"You may," Darcy said, and Elizabeth nodded her assent as well, secretly thrilled for Georgiana.

Catherine suffered a few moments of agony in thinking that no one should ask her to waltz, but Mr. Turner, who had come their way hoping to ask Georgiana, saw that she was already engaged, and decided Catherine would be a pretty alternative. He asked permission, and Elizabeth, who knew him from Georgiana to be dull, but harmless, and not a bad dancer, murmured to Darcy that he should give it.

They stood there for a little while, watching Mr. Turner lead a delighted Catherine off, and then Darcy held out his hand to Elizabeth.

"You have hardly danced tonight, Mrs. Darcy, and I have had my feet trampled too many times already."

"Mr. Darcy, you forget that I have also stepped on your feet in the course of this dance," she reminded him.

"Well, I would rather have my feet stepped on by my wife than anyone else. Will you never stop punishing me for not dancing enough in the first ball of our acquaintance?"

"I am not inclined to cease punishment yet," she said, allowing him to lead her to the floor anyway. "If I force you to dance with enough young ladies, perhaps you will someday find one that is tolerable."

Elizabeth was fairly certain he stepped on her foot once out of spite, but she found she enjoyed the dance very much anyway.

CHAPTER 9

As was to be expected, they had many callers in the day following the ball. Eager at just the outset of the appropriate hour were no less than three of the men who had danced with Georgiana, and one who had danced with Catherine. They were all of them treated politely, but with no encouragement that any acquaintance should be continued, and Lord Alfred, the one gentleman Georgiana had hoped would call, was not among the early group.

Following later were Jane and, to the surprise of all, Caroline Bingley. Caroline, in anger and embarrassment, had kept her visits to Curzon Street to the minimum that could still be considered proper. She was often indisposed when invited to dine, or had some other engagement that prevented her from calling with Jane. No one in the house minded; they were none of them fond of Caroline's society. Yet here she was today, looking quite happy to be there.

They soon found out the reason for such a change in her countenance and interest in their society. She had lately made the acquaintance of a Sir Sedgewick, and he had become the new target of all her hopes for an advantageous marriage. For a full half-hour, they heard nothing but of what Sir Sedgewick said and did, of his estate in Warwickshire, his divine phaeton, and of course how he simply doted on Caroline.

Well she did to focus her efforts on Sir Sedgewick, who Jane later confessed to Elizabeth was an ill-looking but well-mannered man possessing a knighthood that he had earned some years ago in service to the army. Caroline Bingley had spent too many years chasing after Mr. Darcy; the bloom of youth was beginning to leave her, and if she did not manage to make a match in a year or two, Jane and Charles feared she might never marry. This was Caroline's secret fear as well, and given the choice between compromising on looks, fortune, or a title, she had chosen looks.

Jane finally was able to divert the conversation to the ball, which had been her primary interest in wanting to call. All was related, in great detail, as Elizabeth had refreshments brought in to the sitting room – fresh fruits and the little tarts which were one of Cook's best triumphs. When Jane and Caroline had taken their leave to return to the Hursts's house, Georgiana and Mary took up their practise, so that Georgiana was quite absorbed in learning a new piece when Lord Alfred finally called. Georgiana started when Mr. Miller announced him, and made to get up from her bench, but he encouraged her to finish out her practise – he was quite diverted to listen to her play. Georgiana's practise would otherwise continue on for at least an hour more, so she did not finish, but she did play for another quarter-hour to meet his request. Elizabeth, who had been sitting beside him, conveniently rose to see about more refreshments, in hopes that Lord Alfred would encourage Georgiana sit beside him, and when she returned to the room, found that he had.

"You must all tell me of what happened before I arrived at the ball," Lord Alfred said. "I rely on you for my intelligence since I was unable to be there myself."

He was then told, in far greater detail than any gentleman would have any interest in, of every dance that was danced, the prettiest dresses in the ladies's estimation, and all that had been served at supper. He bore it with patience and good humour, however, and every attention paid to Georgiana. She could not be quiet for long before he would ask her about some thing that had happened, so that any shyness she might have felt in having a suitor – for he must now be considered a suitor – dissipated quite quickly.

They asked if he had been calling elsewhere in the course of the morning, but he replied in the negative. He had been out riding with a friend in Hyde Park.

"Quite an enjoyable way to spend a morning," he said. "Although I do find myself and Gambit longing for open space and a good gallop."

"Oh yes," Georgiana said. "My brother and I went riding two days ago, and it was all I could do to hold poor Grace back. I fear I have been neglecting her – I do not wish her to be always exercised by the grooms."

"So you ride then, Miss Darcy – and your brother?" With this, he looked to Darcy, who had been worn down by the number of callers and all the talk of dress trim and dancing, and merely nodded in the affirmative. "Do any of the others in your party ride?"

The rest of them informed him that they had little interest in riding; Mrs. Annesley had a gentle old cob she could take out if needed to chaperone Georgiana, but she was not nearly to her charge's skill level.

"Well, then, Mr. Darcy, Miss Darcy, I have for the past week been developing a scheme to go with some friends to Richmond Park. We have fixed on Friday next and I hope you might join us."

Darcy had been to Richmond Park many times – any gentleman who was fond of riding and spent much time in town knew it well. Georgiana had never been, but the idea of fresh air and wide open space to in which to gallop would have been delightful to her, even if Lord Alfred had not been making the invitation. Both of them expressed enthusiasm in the scheme, and were glad they had no plans for the day.

The time before the Richmond Park ride passed slowly, with only one event out of the ordinary. Lady Catherine, determined to outdo Lady Ellen, had taken Mr. Darcy's suggestion that Georgiana and Lord Alfred be allowed more opportunities in company with each other, and fixed upon hosting her own ball. She called to deliver the invitation personally, and Georgiana thanked her with deep gratitude, knowing that the ball was held largely for her, and that Lord Alfred would certainly be in attendance. Lady Catherine even deigned to include all of Elizabeth's sisters in the invitation this time, which Elizabeth thought to be either at Darcy's suggestion, or demand.

Elizabeth, Georgiana, and Mrs. Annesley attempted to return Lord Alfred's call in the middle of the week, but found he and his brother were out, and the duke and duchess had returned to the family estate. Georgiana, therefore, had to console herself with knowing she would be in his company during the ride, which she looked forward to with as much eager anticipation as she had her first ball.

Friday dawned with capital weather: crisp in the morning, but with a clear sky. The riders were to assemble at the southwest corner of Hyde Park, and from thence make their way to the much larger Richmond Park, so Georgiana and her brother had the advantage of riding through the park to get to the group's point of rendezvous. Georgiana was wearing her best blue riding habit, and Grace was lively but smooth beneath her – she felt thrilled with all the potential of the day.

Lord Alfred was already there when they arrived, and greeted them with smiles and comments on the quality of the weather. As the rest of the group assembled, Darcy was glad to find that they all seemed to be young men who enjoyed sport, but had sense in reasonable proportion, and he suspected Lord Alfred kept quite different company than his elder brother. Two of the gentlemen had also brought ladies – one a recent wife, the other a sister. This was a relief to Georgiana, who had felt some concern only after accepting the invitation that she might be the only lady in the party.

Two of the gentlemen were to inherit estates, and when they found Darcy, although not much their elder, had already been managing Pemberley for some years, they applied to him for advice as the group set out for Richmond Park. This was a comfortable subject for Darcy, one he could converse on at length, even with new acquaintances, which was a relief to him. The two ladies seemed already acquainted, and rode together, although they had been kind enough to Georgiana when they were all introduced. This left Georgiana free to be joined by Lord Alfred, who rode up beside her as they started onto the streets of London.

"So this is Grace?" he asked. "She moves beautifully."

"Yes, I quite love her. My brother selected her for me when I outgrew my cob."

"Your brother has excellent taste in horses," Lord Alfred said, looking up towards the front of the group, where Darcy was riding.

"Yes, he does. Although, Lord Alfred, I must point out that we are talking about horses." Georgiana blushed as soon as she made the statement; she was teasing him the way Elizabeth teased her brother! She realised how comfortable she was in talking to Lord Alfred – he was so pleasant and had such easy manners that she had just spoken as she never thought she would.

"Ah, Miss Darcy, you refer to our conversation at Lady Catherine's dinner party. You have called me out; I am ashamed," he said, smiling at her. "I beg you to choose another topic for us, although I might point out that talking about horses briefly – whilst actually riding – is a step above talking interminably about racing horses at a dinner party."

Georgiana laughed and returned his smile. "Yes, let us continue on horses for just a little while longer. I have not complimented you on Gambit yet – he is beautiful."

Gambit was indeed beautiful, a chestnut stallion who was clearly of the finest bloodlines, and yet very well-behaved. He seemed pleased to be trotting along next to Georgiana's mare, but was not at all made difficult by her presence.

"Why thank you, I do take great pride in him. You would not think it to look at him now, but he was the smaller of twins born to one of the best mares on our estate. Everyone wanted to put him down so that the larger twin should have all of his mother's milk, so I took him and fed him on goat's milk. That was ten years ago."

"You are correct, sir, I would never have thought it – how honourable of you!"

"I was too young then to think of anything like honour," he said. "I simply could not stand to see him killed. And I have been many times rewarded for my effort – his growth quickly caught him up to his twin brother in size, and I believe he is the finer horse. Since he has known me all his life, his behaviour toward me is much like a young puppy who loves his master."

They did move on to other topics soon enough. On the first night of their acquaintance they had discovered a similar taste in books, but

Georgiana found they also conversed easily on other topics, as well, and she was surprised they reached Richmond Park in what seemed like a very short time.

Georgiana found herself immediately charmed by the place. The great rolling hills and vast expanses of grass, and the wooded areas she could see beyond them, reminded her a bit of Pemberley. A herd of deer, startled by their entrance into the park, took off running, and instantly the riders in the front of their group set off at a gallop to try and chase them; not to hunt, which they could not do on the royal grounds, but simply for the sport of it.

Now the quality of the horses and the courage of their riders began to tell, as gaps formed in the group, and soon enough, Darcy's horse, Kestrel, and Lord Alfred's Gambit were at the head of the group. They moved at an easy gallop, with perhaps just the slightest sense of competition between them, but not so much that they would visibly urge their horses on. Georgiana and Grace stayed comfortably in the middle of the group, although ahead of the other two ladies, Grace quite happy to finally stretch her legs, Georgiana revelling in the wind on her face and the wild beauty of the park. She saw her brother's horse finally move into a clear lead, which did not surprise her. Kestrel was the very best horse that years of careful breeding by her father and then brother had produced at Pemberley, bred for stamina as well as speed, and if her brother had any interest in racing, Kestrel would have been a true contender.

When all in the group had their fill of galloping, they drew back together, and one of the gentlemen suggested they take one of the paths through the woods. Lord Alfred was still at the front of the group, and not near Georgiana, but she received many compliments from the other gentlemen on being quite the young equestrienne, and enjoyed the ride through the trees, with the sunlight making long-fingered rays through the branches. The leaves were full into their change, and many had already fallen, so that they crunched under the horses's hooves as they made their way along.

They rode for another two hours before making their way to a lake, where Lord Alfred had arranged to have servants and grooms meet them with refreshments, and all of the horses could drink, deeply, after such a long ride. It was here that Gambit stood out ahead of Kestrel; while Darcy's horse could have easily gone for another gallop and needed to be held closely by a groom, Lord Alfred simply slipped Gambit's bridle off, so that the horse might follow him and then graze near where his master was sitting. Darcy complimented him on his horse's behaviour, and Lord Alfred gave him an abbreviated version of the horse's history by way of explanation.

Georgiana found she was famished after so much riding, and had to take care to ensure she was eating and drinking like a lady. She was sitting with the other ladies, now, and found them to be intelligent and pleasant, and was glad to see that Lord Alfred kept such good company. For just a moment, she allowed herself to think of what it might be like to be his wife, and spend much time with the people in this group, perhaps going on many more outings like this. However, she soon reminded herself that they were new in their acquaintance, and while she enjoyed his company, and he hers, they still knew very little of each other.

CHAPTER 10

As the weeks passed leading up to Lady Catherine's ball, Georgiana had many more opportunities to get to know Lord Alfred. He called frequently at Curzon Street, and Georgiana and her brother took to more frequent rides in Hyde Park, where they often encountered Lord Alfred and Gambit, and then rode on together.

She began to understand more of his daily life as a second son. He of course had no fortune of his own and no expectations to inherit, but was given a very liberal allowance by his family, and as such could live a life of leisure in London. He was not, however, part of that group of young men with similar means who spent all their time in gambling, dissipation, and drunken all-night routs, although she came to understand that, as she had suspected, his brother went with such a crowd.

Lord Alfred dined at White's frequently, and as Darcy determined he needed at least one night a week away from so much female company, he and Charles Bingley resumed dining there together as they had during their bachelor days, and often invited Lord Alfred to join them, if not for dinner, then at least for a glass or two of brandy or port. Darcy found the young man to be someone of sense and economy, if a bit lacking for purpose in life. Over time, he determined that if the young man's acquaintance with Georgiana deepened further, and Lord Alfred should choose to offer for her, and she to accept, he would readily approve the match.

He discussed this with Elizabeth one day. She had come into his study to take a break from the planning of Georgiana's ball, having just returned from a call to Lady Ellen, who had been helping her determine the best additions to the guest list beyond the family and acquaintances Elizabeth already had in town. Later she was to have another conference with Mrs. Annesley and Mrs. Wright, and she needed a pause in worrying about ensuring that an event of such importance, both to Georgiana and herself, went perfectly.

Elizabeth sat down wearily in the old leather chair she had claimed as her own, and Darcy allowed her some minutes of quietude before broaching his topic.

"I had another satisfactory conversation with Lord Alfred last night at White's," he told her.

"He and Georgiana do seem to enjoy each other's company quite a lot," Elizabeth said readily, for this was a welcome topic to her. She, too, approved of Lord Alfred, and especially the way his easy manners seemed to make Georgiana more comfortable in company, particularly when she conversed with Lord Alfred himself.

"Lord Alfred informed me that he will be staying in town through Christmas; as his brother also intends to stay. He would of course not say so, but I expect his parents may have instructed him to do so, to keep an eye on the elder brother. I told him our plans were not yet fixed. I wanted to discuss with you whether it might make sense to stay here, so that there should be no separation between him and Georgiana. We usually spend Christmas at Pemberley, and I know we continue to keep you away from the estate – believe me, I should much prefer to be there, and were it not for Georgiana's needs, I would have taken you there after Weymouth so that you could take up your rightful position as its mistress."

Once again, when faced with the option of not removing to Pemberley, Elizabeth felt a rush of relief. She had grown comfortable with the servants here – Mrs. Wright, in particular, had been very easy to work with ever since Sarah's promotion – and to go to Pemberley and learn the ways of the house while trying to plan Christmas and a ball back in London seemed an impossibly daunting task.

"I do not mind at all, staying here through Christmas," she said. "I agree they should not be separated by such a distance. As well, it will be much easier to continue planning the ball from this house."

"Very well, then," he said, and then seemed to want to continue to speak, but could not determine just what he wanted to say. Finally, he told her: "Elizabeth, I cannot tell you what a joy it has been to see how you have embraced Georgiana as a sister. I know it means the world to her as well. Before we were acquainted, whenever I turned my mind to marriage, I worried about the effect a new mistress of the household would have on Georgiana – in some ways, it would be to her like gaining a new stepmother. Then I met you and I knew that I should have no such worries, if I could finally manage to win your hand. You would be the sister she never had and always wanted. It pleases me so much to see that my estimation was correct."

Elizabeth did not even consider teasing him after such a tender speech; she demurred, she noted that Georgiana was so lovely that she should have hoped they would have been friends, even if Elizabeth had not married her brother. For her modesty, she found herself rewarded with a kiss rather more appropriate for their bedchamber than his study, one that promised far more when they did retire that evening. She returned the kiss most ardently, but then required herself to leave earlier than she needed to for her meeting with Mrs. Annesley and Mrs. Wright. She feared that if she stayed, a servant might knock too softly and come in, and thus Mr. and Mrs. Darcy would come to be known through the house for having done something most inappropriate in the gentleman's study.

CHAPTER 11

Lady Catherine's ball was precisely what one should imagine of Lady Catherine's ball: overdone in its decorations, and populated with those who made Lady Catherine herself feel more important. The Earl of Brandon was of course there with Lady Ellen, whom Lady Catherine could not very well leave off the guest list without also leaving off her own brother, and – perhaps more importantly – an earl. Both Viscount Burnley and Lord Alfred were in attendance, as well as members of several other noble families and other untitled, but influential guests.

Lord Alfred had already called on them the day before to claim both the first set and the supper set from Georgiana, as well as promises for sets with Elizabeth, Catherine, and Mary. Lady Catherine had also ensured there would be ample male partners at *her* ball, strongly persuading even the slightest of acquaintances to attend, so long as they were of appropriate station and known to be good dancers. Introductions were made, and partners readily found for Catherine and Mary, so that Elizabeth had the fortune of being able to dance the first set with her husband.

Lady Catherine herself led off the first set with the earl, and Elizabeth wondered whom Lady Ellen should dance with. Then she saw her aunt beaming as she was escorted onto the floor by a familiar face – Colonel Fitzwilliam had returned from the continent! She and Darcy both expressed great joy at seeing him returned to England as they took up their places, and indicated their longing to speak with him more over the course of the evening.

Such was the size of the ball that more than half of the guests were unknown to Elizabeth, and she felt for the first time in a while that she was in hostile territory. Whispers followed her as she and Darcy made their way through the dance, and she realised that of course Lady Catherine would move in the same circles as those who had called her *the nobody who married*

Mr. Darcy at court. She felt her cheeks flush, and determined she must hold her head high and try to act as elegant as Lady Ellen. They might find fault with her background, but they would not find fault in her manners.

Georgiana, meanwhile, found nothing but the utmost pleasure in the first dance. Lord Alfred was every bit as good a dancer as she had remembered him to be, and conversation flowed even more easily between them now that they knew each other so well. If it lacked the drama of his rescue before their first dance, she still enjoyed it just as much, and was even more delighted when she discovered that her cousin Edward was among the dancers.

She had the pleasure of dancing the second set with Edward, who congratulated her on her presentation at court and on coming out in society. Edward told her he had just arrived the evening before, and had been happy to learn that so many of his family and friends would be at the ball; he had missed them all dearly. The other dances before the supper set went well enough – Lady Catherine had lined up a few alternatives to Lord Alfred, and continued to introduce them to her niece and suggest strongly that they dance. She danced with Viscount Burnley, as well, and found she did not mind it at all; he was a good dancer, if a bit flashy, and conversed just enough to be polite.

Still, Georgiana was quite happy to be handed over by the viscount to his brother for the supper set. Such a contrast to her last ball, to know she was dancing with a man whose company she would enjoy during supper! She skipped gaily through the dance, and was much commented on, both by her family, and others in the room.

"Georgiana and Lord Alfred seem to get on quite well," said Colonel Fitzwilliam to Elizabeth, whose hand he had claimed for the set.

"Yes, they have been much in each other's company of late," she told him.

"Darcy approves of him?"

"Yes – I cannot speak to what manner of interrogation the poor young man has gone through at White's, but he seems to have passed muster."

"I am sure I will like him as well, then."

"I did not say Darcy *likes* him, Edward. You know my husband well enough to know that it will be some time before he deposits true like upon the young man."

Colonel Fitzwilliam laughed at this, and said, "Oh, Mrs. Darcy, I cannot say how much I have missed you all, not to mention English society."

Supper was also what one would expect of Lady Catherine. No dish that was in fashion was left out, more footmen than were needed attended them all, and Lady Catherine blustered on through its course that no one had a greater love of seeing young people dancing and enjoying themselves than she.

Elizabeth found herself comfortably ensconced in the family group, and not within earshot of any that would whisper about her, so that she could relax a bit, and attempt to apply herself to all of the food before her, and the conversation amongst their group. Georgiana, Lord Alfred, and Viscount Burnley sat somewhat away from the rest of them, and Georgiana began to get a better sense of the dislike both brothers had for each other, which was great indeed. She sided fully with Lord Alfred; the elder brother, although he had been pleasant enough to dance with, she still saw as a rake and a frivolous young man, and to this she added a sense of indignation for Lord Alfred, for it was clear to her that the younger brother would have been a much better estate manager, and the family should suffer that he was not the one who would succeed to the dukedom.

The remainder of the ball passed much as its beginning and middle. Georgiana had not the pleasure of looking forward to any more promised dances with Lord Alfred, although she hoped that perhaps there would be a waltz to close the evening as there had been at Lady Allen's, and he would ask her to dance it again. There was not to be a waltz, however; Lady Catherine was far too conservative for such things. Georgiana was disappointed, Kitty even more so, and although they both closed out their evenings with less-than-ideal partners, in a whispered conference during the carriage ride home, they both agreed that on the whole, the evening had been quite delightful, which was far more than they should have expected for any ball of Lady Catherine's.

CHAPTER 12

Following Lady Catherine's ball, Elizabeth's primary focus became planning for Christmas. Preparations for Georgiana's coming-out ball were already well in hand, save for some families Lady Ellen wished to introduce her to, so that Elizabeth could then invite them.

Elizabeth asked Mrs. Wright to meet with her one morning after breakfast, and informed her that the family were to stay for Christmas. Mrs. Wright was delighted – usually the honour went to Pemberley every year, and it had been some time since the house had hosted the event. Mrs. Wright had been the housekeeper then, however, and she explained to Elizabeth what had been done at that last Christmas in the house. Elizabeth was pleased with most of the decorations, and added only one direction – that they place pine boughs along the stair railing, as had been tradition every year at Longbourn.

The Fitzwilliams and Lady Catherine were to return to their respective family estates, so that the guest list for Christmas dinner was limited to the Bingleys, Hursts, and Gardiners. The menu from the previous Christmas dinner was far more outdated than the decorations, and Elizabeth, Mrs. Wright, and Cook spent quite some time determining the dishes and puddings that should be served.

They were all to remain at Curzon Street, except for Darcy, who determined he must go back to Pemberley for at least a week. Alms must be distributed to the poor in the area, and baskets of delicacies to all of his tenants. Both Elizabeth and Georgiana volunteered to return with him, but he bade them stay, not wishing to see them exhausted with so much travelling, and – as he noted privately to Elizabeth – not wanting even the slightest separation between Georgiana and Lord Alfred, as he suspected the young man would make an offer in the next month or two, and that it would be far better received than Georgiana's first offer of marriage. Mrs.

Reynolds could manage the baskets perfectly well, and he should be back before they even had time to miss him.

On this account, he was most incorrect. Elizabeth had spent every night since their marriage by her husband's side, and she found she was most uncomfortable sleeping by herself, in her own bed. She wrote to him, a tender letter, filled with all she could think to write after so short an absence, and when the post came a few days later, found that he had done the same for her:

"My darling Elizabeth,

"If an acquaintance had told me before our marriage that I should hardly be able to sleep without you by my side, after managing to do so with little difficulty for nine-and-twenty years, I would have thought them to be absurd. Yet last night, after what should have been a most tiring day, filled entirely with visits to as many of the farms as Richardson and I could manage, I found myself unable to do that which had come so easily before. I hope this letter finds you well, and not similarly suffering. It is not as though we have not spent time apart in our acquaintance, but I find I have too quickly come to take for granted that I should always have a last sight of your lovely eyes before I should attempt sleep, that I should wake every morning to your beautiful face. It is, I suppose, in the same way we take the air we breathe for granted, and yet would suffer so immediately were it taken away.

"Pemberley is all disappointment at my not having brought Mrs. Darcy. I believe they assumed you were to accompany me, when I wrote to Mr. Parker to tell him of my coming, and I never saw the faces of the servants fall so much as when they saw me alight the carriage without a Mrs. Darcy to follow. I suspect they have a great curiosity of you, Elizabeth, although they will not ask me anything to alleviate any of it. I have no doubt that you will give them every pleasure, when you finally take your place here. It is not natural for a house such as this to go so long without a mistress, and I fear it would have done so for much longer, had I not had the fortune to fall in love with such a woman, and to eventually become worthy of her affections.

"I must confess to a certain amount of relief at being away from town, and here at Pemberley for a little while. I spent a half-hour before retiring for bed in the library, for no reason other than the simple wish to sit, and to enjoy my favourite surroundings. There is a particular smell to the library, of old books and leather, and it may sound strange to say so, but I crave it when I have been away for too long. It is the place in the world where I feel most comfortable, and yet it is not the same now without my Elizabeth. I think of spring, and a rainy day when perhaps we might sit here together, far from the obligations of town. I cannot wait for the day when you might have the chance to oblige me of such a fantasy. Until then, I shall ask you to give my regards to our sisters, and attempt to tease you by signing this letter,

"FITZWILLIAM

"and reminding you that I think of you with a depth of affection I lack the capacity to describe, and long to be in your presence again."

Elizabeth read these words with the deepest love for their writer, and reread the letter before she would gather her writing things and pen a response that added very little to their correspondence but a repeat of her love, and likely would not even reach him before he had left to return to London.

Georgiana, of course, had more to distract herself with during his absence. She thought often of Lord Alfred, and more and more, she allowed herself to think of what her life might be like, if she were to marry him. After receiving such a strange early proposal of marriage when she had just come out into society, she began to wonder whether Lord Alfred would offer for her, and if so, when. She greatly enjoyed his company, and she preferred him to all other men she had met, and yet she still was not quite sure she was fully in love with him. She feared he might make her an offer before she was certain of her affections, and then she would have a very difficult decision to make.

She confessed as much to Elizabeth one day, while they were alone in the drawing room. Elizabeth looked at her with concern, and then said: "You must never, ever, tell your brother what I am about to tell you."

Georgiana assured Elizabeth of her secrecy, and then listened in surprise as Elizabeth told her that Mr. Darcy had made her an offer of marriage many months before the offer Georgiana knew of, and that Elizabeth had refused him. Georgiana could recall his correspondence of that time, and although she remembered him writing of Miss Elizabeth Bennet with the highest regard, she could recall nothing that indicated such an event had happened.

"He must have been so disappointed!" she exclaimed. "I never knew of any of it."

"Your brother and I had a great deal of misunderstanding between us at the time," Elizabeth said. "I shared the story with you, though, to tell you that even if you are uncertain of your heart when he first offers for you, if he truly loves you, he will wait. Things that are meant to be come out right in the end."

Darcy returned two days before Christmas, and commented, as had much of the rest of the household, including Mrs. Wright, on how nicely the pine boughs made the entrance-hall smell. Elizabeth took some small measure of pride in this, but for her they were less about decoration and more a reminder of Longbourn. Mary and Catherine were to remain with them at least through January, and with Jane coming to Christmas dinner,

Elizabeth wanted only her father with them to eliminate her last remnants of homesickness. He was to stay in Hertfordshire with Mrs. Bennet, however, who wrote regularly to Mary and Catherine and encouraged them to find good husbands while they had such an opportunity as to be in town and in the company of rich men. They had no excuse, now, with such dowries as had been provided them by the extravagant kindness of Mr. Darcy and Mr. Bingley, she counselled.

Christmas came with a light dusting of snow, but nothing that was of concern to those with well-sprung carriages and good horses, and so the Bingleys, Hursts, and Gardiners arrived well in time for dinner. Caroline Bingley arrived with substantial news, as well: Sir Sedgewick had made her a marriage proposal, and she had accepted him, and there could hardly be a lady in town so happy as she was currently. Georgiana felt strange at hearing the news – Caroline had known Sir Sedgewick for about the same amount of time she had known Lord Alfred, and perhaps this did mean Lord Alfred would propose to her soon.

For the rest of the party, the news simply meant that they must all hear far more than they wished to about Sir Sedgewick. If the conversation at dinner was a bit lacking, however, they all assured Elizabeth that the food and wine were not. Cook had felt a great desire to wipe Pemberley's eye, and had outdone herself with every dish. The puddings were universally declared to be even more impressive than the main dishes, and Mr. Hurst, in particular, looked to be in ecstasy.

Before the gentlemen made their way into the drawing room, Mrs. Gardiner sought out her niece and paid her compliments again.

"You have become quite the mistress of this house, Lizzy," she said.

"It is nothing, when I have such a housekeeper and cook," Elizabeth said. "I fear I mostly take credit for their efforts."

"They would not put in such efforts for a mistress they do not like, however. It has been clear to me that you have earned their respect."

"Soon I shall have to do the same at Pemberley. That will be the real challenge. I must admit, although I owe a debt of gratitude to Mrs. Reynolds for vouching so for Mr. Darcy's character that she contributed to my reconsidering him, I still fear taking up residence there with her as the housekeeper. She has been in that role for more than twelve years, and there has been no mistress of the house in all that time."

"You will be fine, Elizabeth," her aunt said. "Use her experience. I assure you it is much preferable to have a housekeeper who overreaches occasionally than one who needs constant monitoring."

Elizabeth continued to think of this conversation as Sarah helped her out of her dress. At least Sarah would be with her, whenever they finally removed to Pemberley. Elizabeth had given the girl a substantial Christmas bonus, and Sarah had been thrilled, sharing that she should be able to send much back to her family in Ireland, before she remembered herself. Elizabeth knew there must be some boundaries between her and Sarah, and yet she still wanted to know more about the girl's family, and resolved she would try to make Sarah feel comfortable sharing such bits and pieces as she could.

Although the guests had stayed late, generally enjoying the conversation of the family group (excepting Mr. Hurst, who had fallen asleep), Elizabeth found that neither she nor Darcy were so very tired when she entered his bedchamber. He needed very little encouragement from her that she desired his attentions, and before her thoughts were thoroughly distracted, she found herself reflecting happily that they were very much matched in this aspect of married life. This led, however, to a reminder of the fear she could not even bring herself to share with her aunt: that they had done this many times, and yet still she was not with child.

CHAPTER 13

When Christmas had passed, all that remained for Elizabeth to do with regards to Georgiana's coming-out ball was to deliver the invitations. This had already been done for those most intimate to the family, including Lord Alfred and his brother, and Lady Tonbridge, who had promised that she herself would be holding her long-promised ball soon. However, there were still the introductions Lady Ellen had wished to make, families with excellent influence and enough sons to ensure there would be ample partners.

As the families began returning to town for the season, Lady Ellen's carriage became a regular fixture outside of the house on Curzon Street. She would call for half-an-hour or so, and then she and Elizabeth would make their way to the house of those chosen for a visit that day. Introductions were made with Lady Ellen's usual standard of elegance, and some families were delighted to receive their invitations; a ball held by the Darcys, so early in the season, gave them something immediate to look forward to.

There were other families, though, where Elizabeth was not so well received. None of them were so ill-mannered as to conduct themselves improperly, especially not with Lady Ellen having made the introduction. However, there were far more of them than should have been possible who claimed a prior engagement for the evening. The ladies of these families did not return her calls in the following days; it was clear they wanted no connexion with her.

Elizabeth was pained by the notion that these ladies – who might, before her marrying Mr. Darcy, have been eager to ally themselves with the Darcys – should choose to shun her. She took heart that some of them *had* chosen to further their acquaintance with her, and that at least there should be no problems with the number of partners. Colonel Fitzwilliam had recruited enough of his comrades-in-arms, returned from the continent, to see to that. This pleased everyone at Curzon Street with the exception of Kitty, who was delighted beyond description, but could not quite bring herself to ask Colonel Fitzwilliam if the gentlemen would attend in uniform.

True to her word, the viscountess called on them a few days before Georgiana's ball to deliver her invitation. Her own ball was to be barely a week after Georgiana's, a sign of the pace the full season promised them. Indeed, their callers and engagements had picked up remarkably; for the week after the ball, between dinners, the theatre, and the viscountess's club, they had plans to be out in society nearly every single evening.

Elizabeth woke the morning of the ball to find her husband had, as usual, already gone downstairs. Beside her on the bed, however, was another jeweller's box, which she opened far more eagerly than the last. It was amethyst, this time, most delicately set, and she showed it to Sarah when her lady's maid came in to dress her.

"Oh, ma'am, those will look so lovely on you!" Sarah exclaimed. "I think we must go with the lilac silk, to match, and I shall talk to Miss Hughes about what I might do with your hair, to show off the hair clip."

"Nothing *too* showy," Elizabeth said. "This is Georgiana's ball, after all."

"Of course, ma'am, although it is your first time hosting a ball, so it is special for you as well. I am sure it will be wonderful."

Elizabeth came down to breakfast to find only Darcy sitting at the table – the young ladies must have chosen to sleep in so that they would be well-rested for the ball.

"I found my present," Elizabeth said, kissing him quickly, in case some one else walked in. "It was not quite so nice as waking up to find you there, but still, very nice. And the jewels are lovely, once again."

"I know it is Georgiana's ball," he said. "But I thought you should have something for all of your efforts in planning it. I am sure Georgiana appreciates all of the work you have put in every bit as much as I do."

"It was good to have a purpose for the ball, otherwise I might have put off hosting my first ball indefinitely. There was so much to attend to."

"Were it not for our sisters, I would be perfectly happy with you indefinitely postponing having any balls here."

Elizabeth laughed, and realised she felt far less anxious about the ball than she might have if she had hosted it a few months ago. By now she trusted Mrs. Wright to ensure that every detail was attended to, and only bring items to Mrs. Darcy's attention if the staff could not, for some reason, handle it themselves.

There were no such issues raised to Elizabeth; the decorations went up and the food was prepared with the efficiency of a well-paid staff who had grown quite used to having their family in residence. Georgiana, however, felt a great trembling nervousness in herself throughout the entire course of the day. She had been to two balls already, and had promised dances to Lord Alfred and all of the Fitzwilliam gentlemen, and so should have felt more complacent about the prospects of the evening. She would rarely be compelled to dance with new acquaintances, and she was at home. Yet one thing was different, and that was that this was to be *her* ball. She would be the centre of attention, leading off the dance with her brother, and although being in company over the course of the autumn and winter had done away with much of her shyness, she felt it returning now.

Her dress for the evening was by far the most magnificent of those that had been made for her coming out, white silk with the most delicate embroidery, and she was much exclaimed over when everyone came down from dressing. Such exclamations continued as they all took up a line in the entrance-hall to receive the guests, and Georgiana blushed furiously to be the centre of the guests' attentions. Caroline arrived with Jane and Charles Bingley, and her betrothed, Sir Sedgewick, and all could see that Jane's estimation of his being an ill-looking man was correct. He did dote on Caroline, however, and no one could find deeper fault with him than wishing to marry her.

There may not have been two other people in the ballroom with less interest in being the centre of attention than Georgiana and her brother, but the pair managed creditably as they led off the dance. They were both of them very good dancers, and it helped Georgiana to know that all the dancers around them were family – Lord and Lady Brandon, Lord and Lady Fitzwilliam, Kitty and Colonel Fitzwilliam, and Elizabeth and Charles Bingley. The latter pairing had been a bit of a surprise to all, but Jane, although in attendance, was feeling a little ill and did not intend to dance that evening.

Georgiana danced the second set with Lord Alfred, Elizabeth with Darcy, and it was only during the third set, which Elizabeth sat out, that she learned the cause of her sister's illness. She had seen her sister in a whispered conference with their aunt Gardiner in a far corner of the ballroom during both the first and second sets, and now Jane told her the nature of their discussion.

"Oh, Lizzy, I am with child!" she whispered to her sister. "I knew only some of the symptoms, but in talking to my aunt, I found that there were more I did not know about, and my condition matches all of them."

"Jane, I am so very happy for you!" Elizabeth mustered as much enthusiasm as she could for her sister, and indeed she was very happy for Jane. But Jane's news brought with it a deep pang of jealousy as well; Elizabeth still had no reason to suspect herself to be pregnant.

"I have not told Charles, yet," Jane said. "I wanted to be certain. Even now it is so early that I wonder if I should wait until the pregnancy is further along."

"Jane, you must tell him tonight," Elizabeth said. "He can hardly dance for looking over at you in worry. The poor man has no cause to think that your illness is perfectly normal and related to such happy news."

Jane looked up, caught her husband's anxious glance, and said: "Lizzy, of course, you are right – I shall tell him as soon as this set is finished."

"There should be no one in the conservatory," Elizabeth said. "Perhaps you might find the air a little stifling in here – it will be much better in there."

When the set ended, Elizabeth watched Jane do exactly that, and as the Bingleys exited the ballroom, she felt such a mixture of happiness for Jane and sadness for herself that for a moment the entire ballroom blurred with the tears in her eyes. She knew many childless couples; some had lost children through sickness, others had never managed to conceive. Only recently had she begun to worry that she and Darcy might be among them, that something might perhaps be wrong with her. Soon enough, though, her duties as hostess distracted her from such unhappy thoughts, and the sight of Georgiana and Catherine dancing every dance and enjoying themselves very much cheered her demeanour, if not her heart.

Mary had obliged them by dancing a few dances, but her heart was not in such things, and all her hopes for the evening were in supper, when Elizabeth had promised her she might entertain them with a few songs on the pianoforte. This she did, and her performance was remarkable in its quality, instead of its silliness. Her lessons with Mr. Palmer and her constant attendance of the viscountess's musical evenings had turned her into a very good performer. She had finally accepted Mr. Palmer's requirement that she no longer sing, and instead of distracting her audience with large, dramatic pieces, she chose works that were complex, but subtle, and well-suited as a backdrop for supper. She played three songs, and was roundly applauded and encouraged to play a fourth, however, a sharp look from Elizabeth made her instead suggest that any other ladies with an interest in exhibiting should come forward.

Other ladies did come forward, and supper passed pleasantly for the majority of those in attendance. All of the dishes came out as Elizabeth had expected, and were praised by most, although Elizabeth did not hear much of the praise. She and Darcy had encouraged those most likely to criticise to sit at the table with them, so that at least some of the other guests would not hear them, and Caroline Bingley, true to form, had not been seated for a quarter-hour before she began speaking of how out-of-fashion the decorations were. It seemed she might go on in this manner throughout the entire supper, but for Sir Sedgewick patting her hand and murmuring something in her ear, after which she smiled and was silent.

This left the brunt of the criticising to Lady Catherine, who took up

Miss Bingley's topic and continued on to others. This dish or that dish was found wanting, the punch was too thin, although she dared not attack the wine, knowing the wine cellar to have been largely stocked during Darcy's bachelor days. Elizabeth bore it all with as much patience as she could muster; it helped her to look around and see Georgiana and Lord Alfred once again engrossed in conversation, and to note that even the Hursts seemed to be quite enjoying themselves. Mr. Hurst even went so far as to compliment her on the food after supper, which allowed her the vindication of knowing that it was likely no one else at the ball had found it at all wanting, for if anyone would have, it was he.

Discussion between Elizabeth and Darcy about whether to include the waltz in the dances for the evening had been short; they both determined that since it allowed Georgiana another opportunity to dance it with Lord Alfred, they must certainly give her such a chance. Thus after several more sets, Elizabeth began making her way around the ballroom and letting it be known that the waltz was to close the evening. She ensured that every young lady who wished to dance it was paired with a suitable partner, one her family approved of. Elizabeth took full advantage of her brother in pairing Charles Bingley with a young lady known to be a bit clumsy; Charles had the countenance of a man who could not possibly be happier, and Elizabeth was fairly certain he would have gladly danced with a horse, had she so suggested.

Kitty, who had been disappointed that none of the officers had appeared in uniform, happily enough accepted Colonel Fitzwilliam's request for the dance; at least she knew him to be in *possession* of a uniform. She had grown wise enough not to consider him a marriage prospect, for even her new dowry was vastly insufficient for the second son of an earl, but knew him to be a fine dancer and very pleasant company.

As this was her ball, all in the room looked to see whom Georgiana should dance with, and none that knew them were surprised to see her on the arm of Lord Alfred as the couples took to the floor. It was much murmured that they looked well together, and that the lady might not long be single following her coming-out ball. Elizabeth, overhearing some of these conversations as she and Darcy made their way along the floor, could not help but wonder if they were correct. Perhaps Lord Alfred had been waiting until after Georgiana's ball to offer for her; perhaps he considered it improper to do so until after this final step towards her being fully out in society was complete.

All in the family were very late to break their fast, the day following the ball, even Mr. Darcy, who was usually up before all of them, attending to correspondence in his study. When they did finally gather, it was with lively recollections of all that had happened in the course of the evening. Kitty teased Georgiana good-naturedly about her *three* dances with Lord Alfred, so that the subject of such teasing coloured nearly as much as she had when he had asked for her hand in the waltz.

Kitty herself was happy for her friend, if a bit jealous. She had danced with many men in the course of three balls, and although many of them were amiable, none who had caught her interest had returned that interest. She consoled herself that with the true season starting up now, she should have even more balls to attend, and even more opportunities to be in company. As well, England was beginning to truly settle into the peace, with officers and naval captains coming into the city in large numbers; many men had died in the war, but at least those who could come home would do so. Kitty had noticed these men on the streets when they went out shopping, and in Hyde Park as they took the promenade, and her spirits still never failed to flutter at the sight of a uniform.

They were all to dine at the Hursts's that evening, and Elizabeth could not even be seated before Jane was speaking of how well the ball had gone off, roundly seconded by her husband. Caroline Bingley said nothing in response to their comments; she merely stared at Elizabeth with a haughty expression on her face, and then made her way over to where Elizabeth and Georgiana were seated.

"Dear Georgiana, how well you looked last night!" Caroline said. "It is such a delight to see you finally out in society. When you did not come out last year, I told everyone it must have been your brother's wishing to wait until you had garnered even more accomplishments."

"Thank you, Caroline," Georgiana said, looking deeply uncomfortable.

"I must tell you, though – you danced too many dances with Lord Alfred Mallory. It would never do for you to settle on a second son so soon!"

Georgiana looked far too embarrassed to respond, so Elizabeth spoke: "A second son of the Duke of Bolton is hardly settling, Caroline."

"But Georgiana can do so much better, with her accomplishments and her dowry. She should not settle for anything less than the heir to a viscountcy and ten thousand pounds a year, in my opinion. And of course he must have his own estate, a house in town, and at least two carriages."

"It sounds as though you have a gentleman in mind," Elizabeth said. "Georgiana, would you be open to the introduction?"

"Yes, I suppose I would," Georgiana said, although her countenance showed little enthusiasm for the idea.

"I do not actually have a gentleman in mind," Caroline said, turning quite red, for as much as Sir Sedgewick doted on her, if she did have such a gentleman among her acquaintances, she would have pursued him herself, instead of a knight with four thousand pounds a year.

"Well, it is no matter," Elizabeth said. "But let us know if you do happen upon such a gentleman."

It was only during dinner that Jane and Charles made the announcement that they were expecting a child; they were roundly congratulated by all, Jane's need to sit out the dancing now made sense to them, and everyone was quite happy that two such good-natured people should soon enough have a baby. Darcy noticed that his wife was not quite so enthusiastic in her congratulations as the rest of them, but determined she must have had the intelligence already, and was still exhausted from hosting the ball.

CHAPTER 14

There began a certain welling impatience within the family when, during the week following Georgiana's coming-out ball, Lord Alfred called almost daily, with nary a marriage proposal. None, however, were quite so impatient as Lady Catherine, who invited the Darcys to dinner one evening so that she might speak of it at length.

"I find it difficult to believe that the young man should wait so long," she said. "If I were his mother, I certainly would have told him that he must not toy with a young lady who possesses thirty thousand pounds."

"I can understand his waiting, if he is not yet sure of his affections," Elizabeth said.

"Pah! Affections! I cannot name one person of my generation who married with any certainty of affection. This foolishness of wanting to marry for love instead of giving precedence to what is due to one's family I shall never understand," Lady Catherine said, with a pointed look at her nephew.

"Aunt, the world is changing, whether you like it or not," Darcy said. "I have no wish to see Georgiana in a marriage without affection."

"And what if these affections never do develop? How long shall we wait for that, might I ask?" Lady Catherine said. "I do not think we should continue to assure ourselves that this young man will make an offer, and if that is the case, Georgiana has not been nearly enough in company so far this season. I will procure her a voucher for Almack's for Wednesday next. Mrs. Darcy *should* have been taking her there already, but of course she does not hold enough sway with the arbiters, and I suppose her *other* aunt did not think to do so, either."

"Aunt, I thank you kindly, but I do not think that is necessary," Georgiana said, hoping to assuage some of the fury on her brother's face.

"It is not about what *you* think is necessary," Lady Catherine said. "You are only just out in society, and you do not know what is needed to ensure that you make a good match."

None of them could point out that Lady Catherine had never before made any sort of match, much less a good one; it would be impolite to draw everyone's thoughts to Anne de Bourgh's health. Only later, during the carriage ride home, did they determine that regardless of how it was delivered, Georgiana should not turn down an invitation to Almack's.

They found themselves inundated with other invitations soon enough; in hosting a ball so early in the season, the Darcys had assured themselves of any number of reciprocal invitations, although few were for something so nice as a ball. Most were not even for dinner, or tea, but rather for at-homes, as Darcy called them, because the invitations usually stated "Mrs. Such-and-So At Home."

Darcy made it clear to Elizabeth that of all the possible social engagements they could participate in, these were the ones he loathed the most. Yet they could not very well turn them down unless they had alternate plans for the evening.

Elizabeth's first experience of an at-home was at the Allens's town house, which at least was a familiar home. However, while it had been perfectly pleasant for a ball, on this night it was horribly crowded, filled with far more people than had been on the ball's invite list. The crowds moved between rooms, drinking port and tea and eating such meagre refreshments as were provided in that space between dinner and supper. There were so many people there that seats were few, and it was so crowded that even a card table could not be made up. Elizabeth stayed close to her husband and could easily see why such an event made him miserable; it was already beginning to do so for her.

As they were moving from one room to another, in the hopes of being seen in attendance by Lady Allen, so that they might then be free to leave, they came across Lady Stewart. She was one of the ladies Elizabeth had invited to Georgiana's coming-out ball, but she had immediately claimed another engagement, and Elizabeth greeted her with some embarrassment.

"How are you this evening, Lady Stewart?"

"Pardon me, Mrs. Darcy, I was just making my way into the dining room to look for Mrs. Chapman," Lady Stewart said, departing without another word.

Elizabeth felt all the sting of the snub; she could not help but think of Lady Ellen, who would never have shown such manners as to greet any acquaintance without utmost politeness. She felt as though she was drowning in the crowd, and only her grip on Darcy's arm gave her any semblance of comfort. These women like Lady Stewart, who would snub her now, and call her *the nobody who married Mr. Darcy* – what would they say about her in a year? That since she was a country nobody, and had brought little fortune and few connexions to the marriage, she should have at least provided Mr. Darcy with an heir.

They pushed on into the ballroom, where there was at least room to move, and a more substantial table of refreshments set out. They made their way there, and with some relief did Elizabeth see Lady Allen, inspecting the table to see that all was well. Lady Allen noticed them, they all made their bows and curtsies, and obligation was thus discharged. Darcy made a few selections from the table; for it was only polite now to also be seen eating Lady Allen's food, but Elizabeth still felt tense from her encounter with Lady Stewart; her stomach was tight, and she would only take a little tea.

"Are you certain you will not have anything, Elizabeth?" Darcy asked her. "The rout-cakes are quite good."

"I am not hungry, but thank you, my dear."

"Are you ready to leave? I was hoping we might see the Fitzwilliams, but they may already have come and gone. We might always call on them instead tomorrow."

"Yes, let us do that," Elizabeth said, quite relieved just at the thought of leaving.

It seemed, impossibly, that there were still more guests arriving than were leaving, but at least this meant that their wait for the carriage was not a long one. Darcy only spoke when they were seated inside, making the short drive back to Curzon Street:

"You must not pay any mind to women like Lady Stewart, Elizabeth. There are any number of women like her in town who seek to elevate themselves by stepping on whomever they can," Darcy said, and then continued on in a tone of some embarrassment: "In her particular case, I believe the discourtesy is more directed at there being a Mrs. Darcy, rather than at you specifically. She set her younger sister at me, some years ago, and Lady Stewart was quite furious that I did not court her."

Elizabeth smiled a little at the thought of Lady Stewart's sister being thrown at an indifferent Darcy. He rarely mentioned such things, and yet she knew a man of his station, particularly one so handsome, must have been pursued by more ladies than just Caroline Bingley. For a man who generally did not prefer society as it was, it must have made him miserable.

"I will try not to pay them any mind," she replied. "And now if I am snubbed, I shall just assume them to be related to some jilted lover of yours."

He laughed heartily at this, and reached over and clasped her hand. "At-homes are not really the best place for you to be, in your first full season in town. I loathe them enough as it is, but I should have thought of that. They are merely a place to see and be seen, and there is little chance for you to converse. If there were, I believe more of them would see why I value you so."

This was not, however, the last at-home invitation they had accepted; there was one evening where they had three separate events to attend, and Elizabeth's weariness with these house parties grew rapidly. They soon began to ensure they had some sort of prior engagement to keep most of their evenings free of the at-homes, and so they frequently endeavoured to have the Bingleys, Gardiners, Fitzwilliams, Lady Tonbridge, Lord Alfred, or some other favoured company over to dine.

There was a prior invitation that one member of their family might have preferred to miss, but Georgiana could hardly avoid attending Almack's with her aunt. The voucher arrived at Curzon Street as promised, together with a note from Lady Catherine as to when she would bring the carriage by for Georgiana, and what the young lady would do best to wear for the evening.

Georgiana was thus ushered into Lady Catherine's carriage by one of her aunt's man-servants later in the evening, and she took a seat across from Lady Catherine, looking blankly at her aunt and wondering how long it should be before the evening was over. Georgiana did not expect that Lord Alfred would be at Almack's, and therefore had no interest in any partners that would be lined up for her. She merely hoped that they would all be pleasant enough for her to enjoy the evening as much as she could. It was, after all, a ball, and there was some enjoyment to be expected out of any opportunity for dancing, if only the partners would be acceptable.

Upon entering the place, however, she felt only discomfort. Lady Catherine first presented her to all of the patronesses, in order to justify their giving her aunt a voucher. What manner of coercion Lady Catherine had gone through to get the voucher so quickly, Georgiana did not know, but all of the ladies greeted her cordially before looking Georgiana carefully up and down, and then welcoming her into the club.

Lady Catherine then ushered her through a rather unimpressive set of rooms, introducing Georgiana to a number of acquaintances, several of whom asked Georgiana for a dance. She quickly began to understand how Almack's had come to earn the reputation of a place where marriages were made; at any moment she felt her aunt might simply sit her down and parade suitors in front of her until she found one she liked. Georgiana felt deeply uncomfortable and wished they might go home already, but knew she must stay, in compliment to the effort her aunt had put in for her.

Georgiana noticed Harriet Grantley standing not so far from them, and, happy just to see a familiar face, made her way over to where Miss Grantley stood, her aunt following behind her.

"Good evening, Miss Grantley."

"Miss Darcy! I did not realise you attended Almack's."

"This is my first time here. I have come with my aunt."

"Who is your acquaintance, Georgiana?" Lady Catherine asked, in too loud a tone. "I should like to be introduced."

"Lady Catherine de Bourgh, please meet Miss Harriet Grantley," Georgiana said. "She and I have been acquainted for many years. Miss Grantley, Lady Catherine is my aunt."

"How pleasant to make your acquaintance, Miss Grantley, is it?" Lady Catherine said.

"Yes, Lady Catherine. I am very pleased to make your acquaintance."

They were saved from any further awkwardness when Mr. Jenkins, whom Georgiana had promised the first dance to, came to escort her to the floor. Mr. Jenkins proved to be a pleasant enough partner – he was young, he was attractive, and he was an excellent dancer. He talked of the weather, and the dance, and gave her some idea of what to expect during the rest of her evening at the club, but it seemed all frivolity to her.

As the evening continued on, Georgiana came to see the usefulness of Almack's for the other young ladies dancing around her, and even admitted that if she had not met Lord Alfred so soon after coming out, it might have been important to her – here, every partner she danced with was quite agreeable. At present, however, her head was full of only one man, and he was not on the premises. Lady Catherine did not dance at all, but lingered at the edges of the ballroom with the other ladies who had accompanied single ladies to the ball, watching all of the dancers and drinking claret cup.

Georgiana felt the eyes of others on her – even in such a crowd, her dowry was substantial – but chose to ignore them. She turned herself over to enjoyment of each dance, and when she began to tire and could not take any more pleasantries from new acquaintances, she informed her aunt that she was not feeling well and was ready to return home. Lady Catherine, who was used to a very ill daughter, saw such maladies as natural and did not question them in the least; she was actually quite sympathetic to her niece as she called for the carriage, and she and Georgiana made their way back to Curzon Street.

CHAPTER 15

The time before Lady Tonbridge's ball passed quickly, and Georgiana went knowing that Lord Alfred would not be there, although not for lack of trying on the viscountess's part. Knowing him to be well-acquainted with Georgiana, Lady Tonbridge had sought an introduction at Georgiana's ball, so that she might invite him. He had an engagement that evening with some old friends of his family, though, that he could not escape, and did not think he would even be able to attend after supper.

They arrived, they were greeted enthusiastically by the hostess, and even moreso than at the musical club, Elizabeth could see what Darcy had meant by the viscountess's liberal company. She was a woman who wanted those who were interesting and good company around her, and it did not matter much if they were of noble blood or only recently elevated through trade. Almost everyone in the room was good-looking and fashionable, but one could hardly tell by looking at a guest if he was a duke, or owned a very successful business. The viscountess ensured that introductions were made, however, so that they had no fear of lacking partners, and the ladies soon found that everyone they danced with danced well and had good conversation.

For Kitty, however, there was one man she particularly wished to dance with. There were some gentlemen from the regulars here, she had learned from dancing with a Lieutenant Worthing, but they were all of them in civilian clothes, as they had been at Georgiana's ball, for they had all grown quite weary of wearing their uniforms. There was one gentleman, however, in a naval uniform, with pleasing dark features and a jovial countenance. Kitty noticed this only after she noticed the golden epaulettes on his shoulders, the gold braid on his coat, and the tall bicorn on his head. Kitty had never had occasion to encounter anyone from the navy in Hertfordshire, so the uniform was still novel to her. She was smitten immediately, and she stared at him with such an expression of longing on her face that the viscountess, upon noticing her, brought him over and made the introduction.

He was Captain Andrew Ramsey, of the Royal Navy, lately of HMS Hyperion and only recently in town. He found Kitty very becoming, and immediately asked if he might have her hand for the next set she had available. As it happened, her next available set was the supper set, and so Kitty was able to learn that he was an excellent dancer and loved to dance, that he also loved the theatre but very rarely was able to go, that his ship had possessed thirty-two guns and he had ended the war on blockade duty, but prior to that had commanded a sloop-of-war in the Mediterranean. He told her tales of balmy breezes, of ruins in Greece, of groves filled with the scent of orange blossoms. If she was smitten simply at the sight of his uniform, she was utterly captivated now, and when he returned her to her family following supper, she knew she should be absolutely devastated if he did not ask her to dance again.

Captain Ramsey was eight-and-twenty, and with the peace was quite interested in finding a wife; he inquired delicately with the viscountess about Miss Catherine Bennet's expectations, found her fortune to be quite compatible with his own, and soon enough did ask her to dance again. Elizabeth watched them happily; Kitty had seemed to be enjoying all of the balls and society of London, but even with her increase in fortune, luck in love did not seem to come her way. She and Darcy agreed that although Captain Ramsey seemed a very light-hearted sort of person – which would suit Kitty very well – he surely must also have a high level of sense, to be able to take responsibility for a ship full of men.

There was no doubt in anyone's mind that the waltz would be danced at the viscountess's ball, and before they had even finished their second set together, Captain Ramsey said:

"I wonder, Miss Bennet, if I would ask too much to be honoured with your hand in the waltz later tonight? With your family's consent, of course."

Kitty enjoyed dancing the waltz very much, but she had never been asked by someone she truly wanted to dance it with. Her spirits were momentarily overcome, but soon enough she was able to answer him: "It would not be too much at all. I should like that greatly."

She was all impatience through the next few sets, but soon enough, it was time. Permission was asked for, permission was granted, and then there she was, in the Marche, with her hand just beside the golden epaulette on his shoulder. They were both of them very good at this dance, transitioning perfectly to the Pirouette, with her stomach fluttering as she looked into his eyes. The viscountess, watching them, could not help but chuckle. "My best introduction on the night, I do believe," she said, to no one in particular.

It was snowing when they left the ball, but not so much that they had any difficulties making the short drive back to Curzon Street. Georgiana did have her revenge, during the carriage ride home, noting that Kitty had danced *three* times with Captain Ramsey.

The snow continued all night and into the morning, so that it was clear by the time the family took to the drawing room that they would not be going out today, and should expect no callers. They were shocked, therefore, when Mr. Miller announced Captain Ramsey, of the navy.

He came into the sitting room having had his boots wiped dry by Mr. Miller, but still with little drops of melted snow on his hat, and they were all amazement. How had he come to get there? He had walked. How far was it from his inn? Only a mile or so, and nice to stretch his legs after being on blockade duty for so long. Was it not quite cold outside? Nothing a man who had been around Cape Horn three times much minded.

Catherine felt all the compliment to herself; she had been disappointed that morning in thinking that he could not possibly call, even if he had wanted to, yet now here he was, having determined to visit despite the snow. He looked well; his cheeks were flushed from the cold, and he wanted only his naval uniform to send Kitty's heart into a complete flutter.

Elizabeth immediately called for refreshments, and asked if he would like something hot to drink. Coffee was his request, if it was not too much trouble, coffee and tea were made, and they all entered into an easy conversation, made easier by his cheerful demeanour, and that he had travelled to so many places unknown to all of them.

Catherine asked where his ship, HMS Hyperion, was now, which pleased him greatly, for there are few things more beloved to a naval captain than his ship, whether she is a swift, elegant frigate or what others would consider a great ugly tub.

"Ah, Miss Bennet, you remembered her name!" he exclaimed, then sobered. "She is to be laid up in ordinary, like so many of our ships."

"Pray, what does *laid up in ordinary* mean?" asked Catherine, who was generally ignorant about anything related to the navy, but now had the deepest desire to learn.

"She will be docked, and all of her stores, masts, and spars removed," Captain Ramsey said, then, remembering his audience and making motions with his hands to explain himself: "Masts are like great trunks of a tree, supporting all of the sail structure. Spars are the pieces of wood we hang the sails from. If you were to go to Portsmouth now, and look up and down the Solent, you would see more ships than you ever could imagine, all tied up there in this state, and still more are coming in."

He rose to take his leave after half-an-hour, but they all begged him to stay; they enjoyed his company, and they were certainly not to have any other diversions on the day. He therefore stayed another half-hour, and then did finally leave, but not before Elizabeth had given him an open invitation to dine with them, once the snow had cleared.

The party in the drawing room broke up not long after he left, and Elizabeth, after listening to Mary struggle with a new song on the pianoforte for a little while, gave her sister some encouraging words and then made her way to Darcy's study. He was inside, reading what looked to be the same paper he had been studying during breakfast.

"Did you not read that already?" she asked. "Or have you taken up a new hobby-horse, to memorise the newspapers?"

"I have not," he said, not even so much as smiling at her teasing. "The *Chronicle* had a very good article this morning about the Corn Bill. I wished to read it again when I might focus better on its contents."

"And now I have come in and interrupted your focus," Elizabeth said, although her interruption was not quite so substantial as the happy chatter Kitty and Georgiana had kept up through the entirety of breakfast, as they recalled all that had happened at the ball. "Let me select a book and then I believe I shall go to the conservatory and read."

"I did not mean to make you leave," he said, making an attempt to smile. "Your presence might be a distraction, but it does not follow that it is ever an unwelcome one."

Elizabeth thought back to what he had said the newspaper article was about, for clearly something was worrying him, and she suspected that to be it. The Corn Bill, he had said. She knew from growing up on the Longbourn estate that "Corn" referred to all grains, including wheat, barley, and oats, and recalled that it had something to do with the price of those grains. She had only skimmed the headlines about it, however, and now wished she had read more.

"You seem worried," she said, taking her seat. "Is it the Corn Bill?"

"It is," he said. "I do not wish to alarm you, but it is of the utmost importance to Pemberley's future. All of the inflation we experienced during the war required me to raise rents on the estate, which was fine so long as the war continued, for it is not as though we were importing grain from France. Now that the peace is here, we will be flooded with cheap grains from abroad, and we will not be able to compete unless Parliament fixes the prices at which all grains are sold."

He had not wished to alarm her, but he certainly had done so. Pemberley had always seemed to her to be an indomitable estate, always assured of success, and that Darcy was worried about what the Corn Bill would to do it meant she should likely be doubly worried for Longbourn.

"Why would they not set the prices?" she asked. "It is not as though the owners of the estates asked for war. It was you who kept the country fed when America and the continent were closed to us."

"Raising the cost of grains will raise the cost of bread, and these new industrialists argue against that. They wish to pay cheap wages for their manufactory workers and they cannot do that without cheap bread. Fortunately, they are not so well-represented in Parliament as those who own land, but still, they make a great deal of noise."

"What will happen if it does not pass?"

"My tenants will have to sell their grains at market cost, and I will have to lower rents so that they can continue to make a living. Our income would be reduced. Some of that will be alleviated by what I have put aside – some of my investments profited from the inflation, and even moreso the peace, as you know."

"Our income could be halved and we would still live very well," she said.

"I am glad you say that, Elizabeth – it is quite a relief to me. I must admit there is a deep feeling of inadequacy, for a man to not be able to provide that which he promised his wife when they were married."

"Darcy, you know that if I had married you for your income, I would have accepted your first proposal, instead of acting like a spiteful creature. Now, the other things you promised – to love and to cherish, for example – those you must continue to provide, and you are not allowed any reduction in that quarter."

He smiled, more genuinely this time, and got up from his chair so that he could come over and kiss her thoroughly. "I do not think you are at any risk of a reduction in this quarter," he said, and was about to kiss her again when there came a knock at the door.

"Come in," he said, taking a few steps away from Elizabeth and looking at her with some reluctance.

It was Kitty who entered, which was quite a surprise, for Elizabeth did not think she had been in the study above once, when Darcy and Charles had informed her and Mary of their portions.

"Pardon the interruption," Kitty said. "I wondered if I might borrow a book."

"Of course, you must always feel welcome to borrow a book. I do not have such a selection here as can be found in Pemberley's library, but there is some variety," Darcy said, making his way over to one of the shelves. "Would I be right in assuming you would like something on naval history?"

"Yes," Kitty said softly, her cheeks a very prominent shade of pink.

"Here it is," Darcy said. "A very good volume on the Trafalgar action. I have more, back at Pemberley. I will have Mr. Miller send for them, when the weather clears."

Kitty took the book from him and made her exit, still looking quite embarrassed, although also pleased.

"I am glad to see Kitty have some potential for romance, although I must admit I find fault with her timing," Darcy said. "Now, where were we?"

"You *should* return to your article, which I did thoroughly distract you from," she said, giving him a wily look. "I will find a book for myself, and then I think we may pick up where we were tonight."

CHAPTER 16

It was three days before the snow melted enough to leave the house, and with great relief did they all walk to Hyde Park to take the promenade. It was cold, but the fresh air was quite welcome, and it was clear by the number of people in the park that at least on this day, many of the fashionable set did not mind the sacrifice of walking through a bit of slush and mud, so long as it meant they could get out of doors for a little while.

Catherine noticed Captain Ramsey first; he was walking along with another naval officer, and she called out a greeting to him, before remembering it was not very ladylike. He did not seem to mind, though, and approached the group with his fellow officer a step behind him, asking if they were all well, but looking particularly at Kitty.

They assured him they were, and Darcy asked if he might introduce them to his friend. The friend stepped forward and bowed; he was Captain Matthew Stanton, he and Captain Ramsey had served as lieutenants together on the Foudroyant, and he had only just come into town that morning after having to stay several nights at a coaching inn due to the snow, and even with the wait, his last miles into town had been a near-run thing. These facts were not so intriguing to the ladies in the group, however, as the observation that he was quite handsome, several inches taller than his brother-officer, and perhaps seven- or eight-and-twenty years of age. They were both of them quite tan, although it was more noticeable on Captain Stanton's fairer features, and he seemed to possess a far more serious countenance. Too serious for Kitty, who appreciated his appearance and uniform, but then returned her attentions to Captain Ramsey. Georgiana, however, was overwhelmed; he soon added good, if reserved, manners to his looks, and she retreated into extreme shyness such as she had not shown in several months.

The group walked on together, Elizabeth on Darcy's arm – Kitty on

Captain Ramsey's, to her great delight – and Georgiana, Mary, and Mrs. Annesley behind them, with Georgiana feeling exceedingly confused by her reaction to Captain Stanton. She had little time for reflection, however, because she found herself being addressed by Captain Stanton himself, who had been walking up at the front of the group, but fell back so that he was beside them.

"Miss Darcy, Miss Bennet, I am told I should apply to you as the enthusiasts of music in the family," he said. "Pray tell me what I may look forward to in the course of the season – it has been these five years since I have been in London, and I cannot tell you how I long to hear any worthy performance."

"We are planning to hear Haydn's Farewell Symphony at Hanover Square in about a fortnight," Marry said. "And Dibdin not long after that."

"Ah, Haydn – he is not so much a favourite of mine as Beethoven or Bach, but I would certainly like to hear him performed again," he said. "May I ask whom your favourite composers are, ladies?"

"I prefer Mozart above all others," Mary said. "However I try to incorporate much variety in my practise."

"Excellent, yes, we must none of us become too set in our ways," he said. "And you, Miss Darcy?"

"I enjoy playing Clementi and Field," Georgiana said. "And Scarlatti is a particular favourite of mine."

"Scarlatti? He sounds vaguely familiar, but I cannot say I have ever heard his work. You must excuse me, Miss Darcy – I fear I have been so long at sea, I am utterly lost as to what music is most fashionable in town."

"Scarlatti is rather more out of fashion, than in," Georgiana said, blushing. "His sonatas were written for harpsichord, but they play well on the pianoforte, I find."

"I honour you for translating them to your instrument, Miss Darcy." Looking to Mrs. Annesley, he said: "And you madam, whom do you prefer?"

"I have an enjoyment of music, but not the love of these ladies," Mrs. Annesley said. "I fear I cannot name a favourite."

"What of the opera? Is there also anything there I might look forward to?"

"We are to attend the opera with a friend of ours, the Viscountess Tonbridge, but we have not yet fixed on a performance," Mary said.

"Viscountess Tonbridge!" he said. "You are acquainted with the lady?"

"Yes," Mary said, "we have known her these five months."

"She is an old friend of my family," he said. "I must call on her – is she well?"

"Tolerably well," Mary said. "She is somewhat affected by gout, but otherwise in good health."

"Ah, yes, I had that from my uncle in his last letter. I hope it will pass."

Georgiana longed to mention the viscountess's musical evenings; such a lover of music as him would surely have much enjoyment in coming to listen, but the invitation was not hers to make. She contented herself in knowing that if he was so well-acquainted with the lady, the invitation would soon enough be given by the viscountess herself.

They walked on, although generally silent, once they had exhausted the topic of other composers and pieces they most wished to hear. After a while, Mary and Mrs. Annesley, neither of them very good walkers, began to fall behind, and Captain Stanton offered them each an arm, which they accepted gratefully. Georgiana, who spent many summers in long walks across the grounds of Pemberley with her brother, had no such need, and yet she felt a strange twinge of envy in seeing them, wishing it to be her hand on one of his arms.

Had she known what Captain Stanton was thinking, she might not have been so envious. Georgiana had a fine, tall figure, and he watched her carefully as she made her way through the slush in front of them with a strong, unencumbered gait. He had been five years in the close quarters of a frigate; he had no interest in women of delicate constitution. At this point, he was intrigued, he admired her, nothing more, yet he began to wonder how he might become better acquainted with the Darcy family.

Georgiana returned home in a state of agitation. She had never been so discomfited by a man's company before; she had not realised this was how she should react when presented with someone so handsome. She certainly had not reacted this way when she had met Lord Alfred, and he was not at all unattractive.

The thought of Lord Alfred made her flush. He might make her an offer at any time, and here she was, undeniably distracted by a naval captain! She felt guilty, she thought of how comfortable she had always been in Lord Alfred's presence, how she always enjoyed his company. And yet – if she could be so attracted to Captain Stanton, did it mean that her heart was not even so committed as she had thought?

They had been engaged to dine with the Fitzwilliams, but their coachman was concerned the slushy streets would refreeze, making them quite treacherous for the carriage, and so the family had a night in. This was a relief to Georgiana; she knew her aunt had invited Lord Alfred, and she was not quite ready to be in company with him again. Instead, she was able to sit with the family for a while, and then retire early, claiming fatigue.

Georgiana spent the next day alternating between thinking of Lord Alfred, and thinking of Captain Stanton, and finding no relief from her confusion. She practiced the pianoforte by way of distraction, thinking she might dismiss Captain Stanton for never having heard Scarlatti, but in truth many aficionados of music of their generation might not have heard Scarlatti; she only knew him for being her mother's favourite.

It was scheduled to be one of the evenings for the musical club, but their attendance was in doubt until just before dinner, when the coachman inspected the streets and found them to be passable. Georgiana went with no expectation of Captain Stanton's being there; he might be invited to future musical evenings, perhaps, but he should not be there tonight.

He *was* there, however; he was there wearing breeches and an evening coat, and tuning a very battered cello, Lady Tonbridge standing beside him. Both of them smiled a greeting at Georgiana, Mary, Elizabeth, and Mrs. Annesley, and they all made their way over to say their good evenings.

"Ladies, I am pleased to see you all again so soon," he said. "I trust I see you all well?"

As they were nodding in agreement, Georgiana could not help but say: "I did not realise you played, sir!"

"I am but passable," he said. "I do enjoy it, though. I had capital lieutenants on my ship, which left me with rather more leisure time than you might expect, and playing was my favourite way to fill it, as well as my only way to hear any music at sea, however ill-played it might be."

"I take it the ladies have somehow become acquainted with you, Captain Stanton?" asked Lady Tonbridge.

"Yes, we met while I was walking in the park with Captain Ramsey."

"Captain Ramsey, yes, of course," she said, with a knowing look to Elizabeth, and then continued, motioning toward Captain Stanton. "My friend here called on me this morning, and I insisted he attend tonight."

"I begged her to allow me to wait until I had at least purchased an instrument fit for polite society," he said. "She would not have it, however."

"You ladies know how long I have been attempting to recruit a cellist," she said. "We shall have some proper quartets, now. When does Lord Anglesey come to town? We must invite him to come listen; I know he loves a good quartet."

"I do not expect him here for at least another fortnight, but I am sure he would be delighted to attend. Just do not tell him I am one of the four, or he will never believe it to be a good quartet."

They all laughed at this, and, seeing that more of the club had arrived, went to take seats. As he knew few others in the room, it was natural that Captain Stanton should sit beside them, and he took the seat beside Georgiana. She had no concerned recollections of Mr. Davis, however, she found she wanted him to sit beside her, although she feared they would have very little conversation, between her nervousness and his reserve.

"Tell me, Miss Darcy, am I by any chance to hear your Scarlatti tonight?" he asked her, after some time.

"I am afraid not," she replied. "I did not think to bring it; indeed I did not think you would be here."

"Yes, of course. Might I apply to you to play it at a future meeting? I find any composer I have not heard, and even any new piece intriguing. I spent a small fortune on sheet music this morning; I cannot resist new music, and I have quite a lot to become acquainted with since I have returned to town."

They were interrupted, then, by the viscountess announcing the new addition to their group. There were fewer of them by far than in a usual evening; some had clearly still not thought the streets passable. However, Mr. Talbot and Mr. Wilmington, who played violin, and Mr. Barnham, who played viola, were all in attendance, and every bit as delighted as the viscountess to welcome a cello player into the group. All exchanged bows, and it was agreed that they should attempt something to begin the night.

There followed some discussion among them as they attempted to find a piece all knew reasonably well; finally, they settled on Handel's Eight Pieces. After a few stops and starts, as each player got a sense of the other's timing, they settled in, and it was delightful. It had been some time since Georgiana had heard a quartet, and these four, although not professionals, were all passionate about playing, and rather good. Captain Stanton, for all his modesty, played very well, and positively shone on the Sarabande. They were all roundly applauded when they finished, and encouraged to play something else. They would not have it, however; there were enough others present, particularly several young ladies, that should have a chance to perform. They did, however, fix on a few pieces that all should acquire, if not in possession of them already, and practise for future performances.

The viscountess then called on volunteers, as she always did, and Mary was, as usual, one of the earlier players to exhibit. She was working on a new piece, one she found quite difficult, but apart from stumbling a bit in the trickiest passage, she played very well. She was commended by all for the attempt, and invited to play it again when she had mastered it, which they had no doubt she would.

"Very well done, Miss Bennet," Captain Stanton said, to Mary's great delight. She had no romantic interest at all in a naval captain; someone who made war for a living was not compatible with her moral standards. However, she enjoyed a compliment on her accomplishments from anyone who should choose to give it.

Georgiana was never one to volunteer, but she was called on by the viscountess to be the last to perform before refreshments were served. She made her way to the front of the room with her heart beating wildly, wishing she had not chosen an Italian song to perform tonight, one that included singing. Mr. Palmer said she had a fine singing voice, but she could never bring herself to believe him, and she had only recently, and after much soothing of her nerves by the others in the group, begun to sing in front of them.

She tried to remind herself that this was the same group she had become so comfortable with, but it was impossible to forget the presence of Captain Stanton. Fortunately, once she took a deep breath and forced herself to begin, she quickly enough became focused on the music and could ignore her audience, enjoying the flow of the song before finally trilling to a crescendo to conclude. It had long been apparent to the group, although they were none of them the sort to talk of such things – and she would never have believed them if they did – that Georgiana was their superior pianoforte player, and quite a good singer as well. She had all the advantages of years of master instruction, but she also had put in hours upon hours of practise, all to build on her own natural talent and love of music.

To only one in the audience was all of this a new revelation on the day, but as Captain Stanton listened and watched her, he was most certainly affected. As someone who also possessed a deep love of music, he might have appreciated the performance with his eyes closed. But that it was performed by a pretty young lady certainly added much to his enjoyment of it, and when she was finished he applauded with as much enthusiasm as anyone in the room.

The footmen began setting out refreshments after a respectable pause, and all in the room began making their way to the two tables that held tea, coffee, little cakes and sweetmeats. Georgiana walked over to one of the tables and made her selections, accepting compliments for her own performance, and complimenting the other players. She did truly love this group, and knew she should not be half so confident a performer were it not for all of them.

"Miss Darcy, your playing was wonderful," Captain Stanton said, suddenly beside her. "And you did not mention you sang so beautifully."

Georgiana started, and nearly spilled her tea. "Oh, I do not sing *that* well. I was very nearly out of my range."

"It did not sound so to me."

"I assure you, I was," she said. "You, however, I must chastise for saying you were only a passable cellist. Your playing was splendid!"

"Perhaps we may call a truce, then, and admit we are both of us a bit modest," he said. "I will accept your compliments on my playing, if you will accept my compliments on your singing."

"Very well, I accept your truce," Georgiana said. "Do you mind if I ask how it is that you came to play the cello?"

"I do not at all, Miss Darcy. It was a project of my uncle's: I have two brothers, and a cousin, and one summer while we were all staying at his estate, he purchased instruments for us, and sent for a master to teach us to play. He sought to grow his own quartet, you see."

"That was a fine idea on his part."

"Indeed it was, although things did not come out as he might have wished. Everyone else soon enough gave up playing – they all had the diversions of land to distract them. So instead of a quartet, all he has to show for it now is a cellist."

Georgiana smiled at the conclusion of the story, and after a period of silence during which she desperately searched her mind for a new topic that they might discuss, but thought of nothing, he bowed and stepped away from her.

Their conversation did not go unnoticed; Elizabeth and Mrs. Annesley watched them from across the room, and each was about to comment on their observations, when the viscountess approached them.

"You need not worry about Captain Stanton, Mrs. Darcy," the viscountess said. "I assure you, I have known him since he was a boy, and he is every bit a gentleman. Although I must note his attention did seem far more welcome to Miss Darcy than that of Mr. Davis."

"Indeed, it did," Elizabeth said.

"Was she not near an understanding with Lord Alfred Mallory?"

"We thought so, but he has yet to offer for her," Elizabeth said.

"Hmm, well sometimes these things take longer than one might expect. If things do happen to tend *this* way, however, you need not worry about fortune. He has won more than enough in the war," the viscountess said proudly.

"May I ask how you are acquainted with him?" Mrs. Annesley asked. "I believe you said you have known him since he was a boy?"

"Yes, certainly. His uncle is the Earl of Anglesey, and the earl's family and mine have been well-acquainted for many generations," the viscountess said. "He was often at his uncle's house in town when he was not at sea."

"You said you knew him when he was a boy – how old was he when he went to sea?" Elizabeth asked.

"Oh, I reckon around eight or nine. His father was the previous earl's third son, and Captain Stanton was himself a second son. He had to make his own way in the world, poor child. Lord knows why he chose the navy, but it seems to have suited him."

CHAPTER 17

The day following the musical club, Elizabeth and Darcy, realising it had been some time since they had seen the Gardiners, determined they would call on them in the morning, and invited all to join them. Catherine, hoping that Captain Ramsey would call, said she should prefer to stay home, and pleaded with Georgiana to stay as well. Georgiana acquiesced, and tried not to tell herself it was because she hoped Captain Ramsey would indeed call, and bring his friend.

Mrs. Annesley said she would stay, Mary chose to go with them, and so Mrs. Annesley, Catherine, and Georgiana were in the drawing room when Captain Ramsey – and indeed, Captain Stanton – were announced. Captain Ramsey did of course sit near Kitty, and Captain Stanton took a place between Georgiana and Mrs. Annesley, asking how they had been since he had seen them at Lady Tonbridge's. They were quite well, they said, and inquired after his health, which also was good. There followed the usual discussion of the weather, and Captain Stanton commented it had been some time since he had known a London winter.

"I believe you mentioned previously it had been some five years since you had been in London," Georgiana said, waiting until he nodded his confirmation before she continued. "Might I ask where you were serving during that time?"

"Certainly. I have been in the West Indies and then North American stations, primarily."

"And have you been able to return to England at all?"

"No, this is the first time I have been on mother soil in all that time. We were always able to refit and resupply away from home, in Jamaica, Bermuda, or Halifax, until recently. We were battered about by a privateer and then a storm in quick succession, and sent back to Portsmouth for repairs. Now that the American war is over as well, we have no hope of returning to sea."

"What is the name of your ship?"

"She was the Caroline, a thirty-eight gun frigate, and a lovelier sailer I never saw. But now she is to be laid up in ordinary," he said, sadly, looking to her to see if she comprehended what he said. "I should not complain, of course; I was quite lucky to have her for so long. In that amount of time, every man jack on the ship learns his duty as well as ever he can; I should not have shied away from any fight with such a crew."

"What has happened to all of them now?"

"Paid off and gone ashore, some of them back to the positions they held before they were pressed, but most to nothing except whatever of their prize money they managed to save. The merchant navy shall have their pick of sailors, now."

"It must be so difficult for you, after living and fighting with them for so long."

"Yes, it is," he nodded soberly. "My lieutenants turned on shore on half pay, my midshipmen with no hope of promotion. I had hoped we should have some sort of major action, so that my first lieutenant might at least be promoted, but we were not so lucky. Once I thought we might have an American frigate, but it was not meant to be; she ducked into port before we had our chance at her – rather cowardly for an American, unfortunately. I could only assume the ship was somehow damaged, and not ready for battle, but oh, how we all wanted that fight."

Seeing that Georgiana looked nearly as grave as he did, he attempted a smile. "I must not dwell on such things, however. There are certainly many benefits to the peace, and being onshore. As you have seen, I am already overindulging in my love of music."

"Oh, I do not think it is possible to overindulge in music!"

"That is a sentiment I would not disagree with, Miss Darcy."

The gentlemen stayed another quarter-hour, and two separate conversations merged into one as the captains talked of what they had been doing in town since they had arrived. They rose to take their leave far too soon, it seemed to both Catherine and Georgiana.

Georgiana, remembering that Elizabeth had left an open invitation to Captain Ramsey to join them for dinner sometime when the weather was better, named a day she knew the family had no plans, and, although in an embarrassed tone, managed to ask if the date might work for both of them to join them in a family dinner. The date was suitable, the captains were all graciousness at the invitation, and they took their leave.

Catherine was all amazement. "Georgiana, you did *not* just invite them to *dinner*?"

"I believe I did," Georgiana said, a bit shocked at her own actions. It was what Elizabeth would have done in her place, had she been there, and her brother had been encouraging her to act as more of a hostess, before his marriage made this less necessary. But still, it was so very unlike her to think to do such a thing, and then to actually follow through!

She was interrupted in these thoughts by an embrace from Kitty which very nearly knocked the breath out of her. Kitty thanked her exuberantly, and only later did she seem to realise that Georgiana might not have been acting entirely in Catherine's interest.

"Now that I consider it," she said, looking up from a watercolour she was working on, "you and Captain Stanton seem to get on quite well. And he was at the musical club, was he not?"

Georgiana replied that he was.

"Georgiana, I never thought you had it in you! You must hope that you never go to a ball with the both of them there, because if you dance twice with Lord Alfred, and twice with Captain Stanton, you shall hardly have any other dances left! And who shall you *waltz* with?"

"I – did not expect to like Captain Stanton's company so much as I do," Georgiana admitted, blushing furiously. "I do not know what to do!"

"You see each of them in company as much as ever you can, without showing either of them preference, until you are sure which of them you do prefer," Mrs. Annesley said, her voice filled with level sense. "You are quite a lucky young lady, to have two such suitors to choose from. Viscountess Tonbridge indicated that Captain Stanton is a man of both fortune and family; either he or Lord Alfred would be a good match."

This put an end to Georgiana's outward debate, but she was not so sure Mrs. Annesley was right. Some ladies might enjoy having two such men to choose from, but all Georgiana could think of was making the wrong choice, of imagining herself to be in love with one of them, when truly she was not.

In turmoil over such thoughts, she retired early again after they returned from dinner at the Hursts's. Elizabeth, who had been positively shocked, as had Darcy, over the news (eagerly supplied by Kitty) that the two gentlemen from the navy had called, and Georgiana had invited them to dinner, went to check on her.

Georgiana had changed into her nightgown and dressing gown, but was sitting in her room, reading, when Elizabeth knocked and then entered.

"We are all in a bit of shock over your dinner invitation," she said.

"Oh, Elizabeth, I am so sorry! I did not mean to overreach your role," Georgiana said, looking quite upset.

"Never worry about that," Elizabeth said. "You are a lady of the household and you should always feel welcome to make a dinner invitation such as that. Indeed, I would have done the same thing if I had been here, so I am glad that you did."

"But you said everyone was shocked!"

"The shock was not that it was inappropriate, only that it was quite out of character for you," Elizabeth said. "Most everyone concluded that it was a kindness to Kitty. But then Kitty and Mrs. Annesley filled me in on your conversation, earlier."

Georgiana felt a wave of embarrassment pass through her. She made no reply, but moved over so that Elizabeth might sit beside her.

"Captain Stanton is very handsome, is he not?"

"Yes, I believe he is one of the handsomest men I have ever met," Georgiana admitted. "I might have forgotten him easily enough, if that were his only good quality; but he also has such a great love of music, and he is – I just find him so very interesting. Every time I am in company with him I want to know more about him."

"Then we shall have to find you more opportunities to get to know him."

"But what of Lord Alfred? I feel so guilty for being interested in another man when he has shown me such attention over the last few months. And I do truly enjoy his company!"

"Captain Stanton is new to you – it is natural that until you spend more time in company with him, you should be more intrigued by him. At some point, when the acquaintance is less new, you will be able to be more objective about which of them you prefer."

"What if Lord Alfred makes me an offer of marriage before I reach that point, though?"

"You need not give him an answer right away; as I said before, if he truly loves you, he will wait."

"Even if he knows I have another suitor?"

"I do not expect the two of them to have many common acquaintances, aside from Lady Tonbridge. It is possible he will never know, but even if he does, it is no matter, if there is no understanding between the two of you. Your only duty will be to ensure you show neither of them too much preference until you have made a decision."

"That is what Mrs. Annesley said."

"She has been through this process more times than any of us; her advice is very sound."

"Yes," Georgiana said. "However, sometimes I think the previous ladies she was companion to were very different from me."

"If you mean they were not nearly so intelligent nor so accomplished, I will certainly agree with you on that," Elizabeth said, hugging her sister.

After Sarah had helped Elizabeth change, she made her way to her husband's bed. Although she did not share the particulars of her conversation with Georgiana, she did let him know that Captain Stanton had been one of the motivators behind Georgiana's dinner invitation.

"A naval captain?" he asked. "I never should have thought her interested in a naval captain."

"You have met the man. He is very much a gentleman, and I have it from Lady Tonbridge that his uncle is the Earl of Anglesey, and he has done well in prize money."

"*Well* is relative. He would have to capture quite a lot of ships to be Georgiana's equal in fortune."

"Lord Alfred is not her equal in fortune, and you had no objections to him."

"I did not say I had any objections. I do not know enough about the man to know whether to object to him or not. Captain Ramsey as well – we know even less about him, and he and Kitty seem to be forming a rapid attachment."

"I could apply to the viscountess for more information – has she never mentioned Captain Stanton before in conversation with you?"

"She might have. I know she is well-acquainted with Lord Anglesey, but there are so many sons and brothers in that family it is difficult to keep count of them all," he said. "My acquaintance with her comes through her husband's side of the family; my father and Lord Tonbridge were good friends."

"Well, she seems quite willing to speak of him," Elizabeth said. "He had barely conversed with Georgiana and she was singing his praises to Mrs. Annesley and myself."

"Speak to her then, if you may," he said. "And I will ask around with some of the admirals who are members at White's – opinions of those less close to the captains will be more disinterested."

CHAPTER 18

A few days later, Darcy and Charles Bingley having dined at White's that evening, Elizabeth went to his bedchamber hoping he had some intelligence to share with her. Her hopes were met; he was rather more drunk than she had ever known him to be, and she soon found out that the cause was the large quantity of brandy he and Charles had drank with the three admirals who had been in attendance that night.

"They were all of them quite happy to talk, after a few toasts to the navy," he said, making a visible effort to control his deportment as he spoke, and still smelling a bit of the coffee and cigars he and Charles must have consumed to try to rectify the brandy.

"And what did they say about our captains?"

"Ramsey's family is from trade," he said. "They own a successful shop in Salisbury, but he is a third son, so with no hopes of inheriting the shop, he went into the navy. He has done fairly well with little help in promoting his interests, and he is said to have about fourteen thousand pounds in prize money."

"It would be a good match for Kitty," Elizabeth said. "With her dowry, they would nearly clear a thousand pounds a year. And I must admit, although he is always in quite good humour, he is a far more sensible man than I should have thought Kitty would attach herself to, a year ago."

"Yes, that was my thought, as well. And even if he does not return to sea, he would also earn half-pay for the rest of his life."

"Then it is even better than I had thought – he could certainly support a carriage. What of Stanton?"

Darcy paused for so long Elizabeth began to fear the man was some sort of secret rogue. The pause, however, was because although the two men might be equal in rank in the navy, they were not so in the eyes of society, and his brain was a bit too muddled to ensure he would impart such information well.

"As we knew from the viscountess, he is the nephew of the Earl of Anglesey. His father was a third son of the previous earl, and thus chose to become a rector. Stanton was the second son of the rector, and despite no military background in the family, fixed on the navy as his profession. Lady Tonbridge was also correct, that he had earned a fortune during the war: he has earned more than sixty thousand pounds."

"Sixty thousand pounds! All in capturing other ships?"

"Much of it was prize money, although there is also something known as freight – carrying goods in one's ship for a profit – which they assume contributed to his fortune, for it is commonly done. He is known to be one of the navy's more successful young frigate captains, in the way of fortune, at least. He has not been without help, either – his uncle has used his influence to ensure that Stanton was always promoted early, and had fortunate ships and assignments. One of the admirals also assured me that Stanton is quite a man for king and country, as well; he would be even richer, had he not burned two prizes rather than taking them up after capturing them, so that he might chase after an American frigate."

"I take it he was not successful?" Elizabeth asked, for certainly the capture of another American frigate would have been widely celebrated in the papers, as the Shannon's victory and others following had been.

"No, it would seem not. However, it does not diminish the fact that he would be a suitable match for Georgiana. Ideally, he might be closer to the succession in the earldom, but perhaps it is overly critical of me to note that. He would certainly bring more fortune to a match than Lord Alfred."

"So you would approve of the match, if Georgiana's preference is for him?"

"Oh no, I am far from approving the match. I shall have to have quite a few talks with the gentleman before any such thing. However, I am open to *considering* an approval of the match," Darcy said. "All of this may be needless, anyway. Perhaps the presence of another suitor will convince Lord Alfred to spread a little more canvas and make his offer."

"Fitzwilliam Darcy, did you just say *spread a little more canvas*?"

"Good God, I did. I must never drink with the admirals again."

"Oh no, I encourage you to do so frequently," Elizabeth laughed. "I find it quite diverting."

"If you want a diversion, Elizabeth, I will show you a true diversion," he said – and then he did.

CHAPTER 19

When the ladies arrived at the next musical evening, they found Captain Stanton had come early once again, and was talking with the viscountess. The battered cello was gone, and in its place was a very fine-looking new cello, which they all complimented him on after they had exchanged greetings.

"I fear it is made for a much better player than I," he said, "but I felt the temptation of a sailor ashore to spend more of his prize money, and this seemed the most noble thing to spend it on."

"It is indeed a most noble instrument," Georgiana said. She wanted to note that he was in violation of their truce, to once again be so modest about his playing, but it would be too embarrassing to do so with the others around her.

Soon enough, however, they all saw – or feigned to see – acquaintances come into the room they wanted to greet, so that Georgiana and Captain Stanton were left alone. Shyly, she held up the sheets of music in her hands, so that he might see what she had brought to play.

"Scarlatti! You have brought one of his pieces – delightful – I am all anticipation to hear it."

"I hope you will like it," she said, colouring deeply, for he had entirely been the reason for her choice. "I think there is something very beautiful about his music on the pianoforte; my brother took me to a concert of his, once, and although it was very well-played, I find there is not so much emotion in a harpsichord."

"I would agree with you there, Miss Darcy. I do enjoy a good baroque piece, but there the harpsichord supplements. It does not stand alone so well as a pianoforte."

"Yes, that is exactly what I mean."

"This should be quite a delightful evening," he said. "The other gentlemen and I have fixed on a Bach quartet to play tonight – it was my suggestion of the pieces we were all to learn."

"Oh, lovely – I know I did not mention him as a favourite of mine, but I do quite enjoy his work. I look forward to hearing your quartet."

Hear it Georgiana did soon enough, because after Captain Stanton had been introduced to the members of the musical club who had been unable to make the previous meeting, he and the other string players were encouraged to begin the night with their quartet. As soon as they began playing, Georgiana could sense Captain Stanton's discomfort with his new cello; he was hesitant, his tone was not nearly what it had been during the last evening he had played. It also became clear to her that he must enjoy Bach because the cello parts were so integral to the music, and quite challenging. On this night, however, they were past his capabilities, and she felt for him.

He made his apologies as soon as they had suffered through the first movement, and was given comforting remarks by many in the room. Those in attendance, however, were soundly split as to their estimation of his skill; those who had heard him the previous evening thought him to be a capable player whose new instrument had got the better of him, while those who had not heard him play before thought perhaps the viscountess was getting a bit desperate in her attempt to recruit a cellist.

Georgiana's own exhibition went much better. As she was not singing, she went to the front of the room with a great deal more confidence, and she found herself more sympathetic to Captain Stanton than intimidated by his presence, on this night. There were complexities in the Scarlatti piece that had challenged her skills as a player, but she had already mastered them, so she was able to infuse real joy into her playing. As always, she was roundly applauded as she returned to her seat.

Captain Stanton had sat with the other members of the quartet on this evening, rather than beside Georgiana. He did, however, make his way over to her soon after they broke for refreshments.

"Well, Miss Darcy, I find I am in agreement with you on your Scarlatti," he said. "I have not heard it on a harpsichord, but I cannot imagine how it should sound better than you played it on the pianoforte. And so difficult – I hope you will not deny your skill in playing, as you did in singing, when you have performed as you did."

"I thank you," Georgiana said, blushing deeply. "There was one passage I felt like I was attempting for weeks – it took forever to figure out the fingering. Even my instructor, Mr. Palmer, was completely vexed by it."

"You have certainly mastered it by now – your playing shall be the highlight of my evening," he said. "It will distract me from the infamy of having butchered one of my favourite composers, and in front of such an audience, no less."

"You did not seem so comfortable with your new cello as you had been with your old, if you do not mind my saying so."

"I do not mind at all – you are both correct, and tactful. I should have put in much more practise with the new instrument before attempting to bring it to this group. My old battered piece has suffered through much abuse and sea air, but it has also been my constant companion for many years."

"I know what you mean," Georgiana said. "My brother bought a new pianoforte for me last year, and it was magnificent – a much better sound than my old one – but it still took me months to feel comfortable with the keys."

"I hope it shall not be so long for me, or Lady Tonbridge will begin to rethink her invitation."

"I do not think she will; this group is very kind regarding mistakes, if they are made by someone endeavouring to become a better player."

"I am glad to hear that, Miss Darcy. It does make me slightly more at ease here."

After spending much of the refreshment break with Captain Stanton during the musical evening, for this time they did not seem to suffer for topics, Georgiana was to look forward to his company again the next day, as it was the date she had invited the captains to come to dinner.

There had been little opportunity for a close comparison between Lord Alfred and Captain Stanton thus far in her acquaintance with Captain Stanton, as she had seen very little of Lord Alfred over the past week or so. He called, however, the morning of the dinner, and apologised for not doing so earlier; first there had been the poor weather, and then with so many acquaintances returned to town, his days had been filled.

He begged her to fill him in on the viscountess's ball, and all else that had occurred since she had seen him last. She did note that the family had made two new acquaintances in Captains Ramsey and Stanton, but hoped she was able to divert Lord Alfred's thoughts from any special connection to herself by noting that Captain Ramsey called frequently for Catherine.

Soon enough they were conversing just as they always had, although Georgiana felt a bit disconnected from the conversation. His pleasing presence only increased her turmoil, especially when he rose to take his leave and said how much he had missed her company, how happy he was to see her looking well.

The captains both arrived quite punctually for dinner, and Georgiana noticed that while Captain Ramsey still showed an obvious affection for Catherine, they both endeavoured to converse with the whole family, allowing Captain Ramsey to carry far more of the conversation than his brother officer. The family all found the captains to be some of the most enjoyable company they had dined with – well-mannered, but with an honesty and a visible cheer in simply being back in mother England. They entertained all during dinner with tales of their time together as lieutenants on the Foudroyant, including the small action they had fought against the French while on that ship.

As they spoke, Georgiana could not help but feel more of that sense she had tried to explain to Elizabeth – that these were interesting men who had done things so outside her sphere of understanding, who had been to places she had only read about in books, if that. She had never travelled outside of England, and to hear of such exotic places in such detail made her want to go abroad for the first time.

The gentlemen lingered for some time over port, during which all of the ladies assumed some manner of questioning between Mr. Darcy and their guests was taking place. When they finally returned to the drawing room, Captain Stanton asked if Miss Bennet and Miss Darcy might be willing to play something for the group, if they were not too tired from exhibiting the previous night. Mary spoke for both of them in saying they of course were not; they practised at least an hour each day, and so both she and Georgiana played a few pieces.

Captain Ramsey, sensing Catherine to feel somewhat left out during the exhibitions, begged she would show them some of the work in her sketchbook. Catherine demurred; usually outgoing, she was sensitive about her drawing, and even moreso her watercolours, upon which she had only recently embarked. Although Mr. Shaw said she progressed nicely, she had not been doing it for so long that she felt any confidence in her abilities.

She was soundly coaxed, however, and finally showed them all a few pages, which surprised even her own family. Kitty's aesthetic sense, applied with much silliness to desiring the prettiest dresses and chasing the most attractive officers in Meryton during her younger days, was now used for much better purpose. Her work was very good already, and when they all considered she had not been doing this for much time at all, they were quite impressed, although none were quite so effusive in praise as Captain Ramsey.

The gentlemen took their leave at the appropriate hour, and the entire family – although perhaps Kitty and Georgiana more deeply – were sorry to see them go. It had been one of those easy, lively dinners that are so little valued in high society, and yet so very enjoyable to those who are fortunate enough to experience them.

CHAPTER 20

Elizabeth had thought that with few common acquaintances, there would be little chance of Lord Alfred and Captain Stanton meeting. She did not account for them calling at the same time, however, and this indeed was what they did the day after the captains had dined with the Darcys.

Captain Stanton arrived first, followed by Captain Ramsey, both of them speaking of their delight in the previous evening. They talked of lighter topics for a while, but having little new to speak of, they again prevailed upon Mary and Georgiana to play the pianoforte. When Georgiana completed her song, she turned back toward the group and was startled to see Lord Alfred standing in the doorway, applauding vigorously.

"Miss Darcy, you are the great proficient of the world," he said. "I could never tire of hearing you play."

"Lord Alfred! I did not realise you were here."

"I arrived in the midst of your song," he said. "I begged Mr. Miller not to announce me so that you might finish."

He strode across the room and offered her his hand, leading her to a place where they might sit beside each other. Georgiana was not certain how much the viscountess had told Captain Stanton about Lord Alfred, but even if the viscountess had not indicated Lord Alfred was a suitor to her, Georgiana was doing quite well enough of that on her own. She felt her face flush at the attentions he gave her, which were even more particular than usual, and could hardly look up at the rest of the room.

"Miss Darcy, would you do me the honour of introducing me to your friends?" he asked, finally requiring her to raise her eyes.

"Yes, of course. These are Captain Andrew Ramsey and Captain Matthew Stanton, of the Royal Navy. Captains, this is Lord Alfred Mallory."

"The navy! Indeed! You gentlemen must tell me of your battles," Lord

Alfred said. "There is nothing I like more than a great sea-story."

He was obliged, primarily by Captain Ramsey, who was of his usual jovial humour, but could not even match Lord Alfred's high spirits. Lord Alfred was constantly asking questions about what position the ships had been in, or what happened next, as Captain Ramsey again described their action against the French on the Foudroyant. Captain Stanton offered an occasional detail, when prompted, but mostly remained quiet, his face impassive. Georgiana had not wished to have an opportunity to compare the two gentlemen, but here it was, and there was hardly a comparison to be made. Captain Stanton was more handsome, certainly, but Lord Alfred had been everything amiable since he had arrived, and had been most gallant in his manners toward her.

They paused after the captains's time on the Foudroyant, as refreshments came out, and Lord Alfred insisted Georgiana stay seated; he would bring her whatever she wished to have. When he had returned with her selections, and then gone back to the table for his own, he sat back down beside her and said, softly, "I hope you are in health today, Miss Darcy. You certainly look very well."

"I am very well, thank you," she said, feeling her cheeks burning again.

When they were all seated again, Lord Alfred applied to Captain Ramsey to hear more, and the captain shared a few tales of his own smaller skirmishes, once he had been blessed with his own command, before motioning to Captain Stanton and saying:

"I am not the one to provide the best stories of naval action, however. This gentleman has had the good fortune to command one of the best frigates in the fleet. He has captured far more ships than I, so many that I am fairly certain he has lost count of just how many prizes he has taken."

"Then I must apply to you for your share of the tales," Lord Alfred said, to Captain Stanton. "One of the best frigates in the fleet! Surely you must have had your share of French frigates."

"My command was in the West Indies and North American stations," Captain Stanton said, stiffly. "I have not had the fortune to fight another frigate. I must beg your pardon and wait to share my stories another time, for I need to take my leave now."

"Well then, another time," Lord Alfred said. "I shall look forward to it. I am very pleased to make your acquaintance."

"Likewise, sir," Captain Stanton said, rising and bowing to the room. "Good day to you all."

Captain Ramsey took his leave a little while later, but Lord Alfred stayed longer, and continued to pay Georgiana every attention. After he had finally taken his leave, Elizabeth leaned over to murmur in her husband's ear: "Perhaps Lord Alfred is spreading a little more canvas."

Georgiana spent the rest of the morning thinking about the two gentlemen, and feeling a surge of affection for Lord Alfred. There was something very nice about feeling that her attention was wanted by him, of the way he had taken up her hand to lead her from the pianoforte, and she began to think that perhaps her attraction to Captain Stanton had been a fleeting thing brought on by his features and his love of music. It had been foolish to allow herself to be so overwhelmed by a handsome face; it had been a lapse into the childish judgement that had very nearly caused her to elope with George Wickham.

Still, though, he had been even more quiet today than at any other time during their acquaintance. She wondered if perhaps he was discomfited by new company, as she sometimes was, and knew her brother to be. Perhaps she should have done more, to try to draw him in to the conversation. Perhaps she could have changed the topic to music, which she had yet to see him unwilling to converse on.

These were things she would need to become better at, as a hostess, Georgiana thought. This was followed by the startling realisation that she had been thinking of herself as a hostess, as a mistress of an established household – perhaps Lord Alfred's household.

"Does this greater attention mean he will make an offer soon?" she thought. "Does this mean I should accept?" Still, she did not have an answer.

CHAPTER 21

Georgiana ate her breakfast the next day with the singular thought that perhaps that morning, or the following morning, or the morning following that, Lord Alfred might call and make her an offer of marriage. The thought made her tremble, but she did not dread it as she had Mr. Davis's proposal.

The family were only just making their way to the drawing room when Mr. Miller announced Colonel Fitzwilliam. They were all shocked that he should call so early, and at first could not tell if he was simply keeping military hours, or if he had some news to impart at this hour. Once they were all seated in the drawing room, however, it was clear he had news to impart:

"I am sorry to call so early, but I have had some intelligence which I assumed would be of the greatest import to the family: Viscount Burnley has been killed in a duel."

Shock, amazement. For a while, none of them was able to speak.

"Edward, you are quite certain of this?" Darcy asked, finally.

"Yes, a man in my unit acted as second for the other party. They met at sunrise this morning – Viscount Burnley died on the site. Young fools duelling with pistols instead of swords."

To all of the confusion Georgiana had been feeling of late was added this: with his elder brother dead, Lord Alfred would now be Viscount Burnley; Lord Alfred would now inherit the dukedom. She sat there, listening as Colonel Fitzwilliam related such details of the duel as he knew, quite overwhelmed with the news. It was shocking, to be sure, but the more she thought of it, the more she knew it was less shocking that Lord Alfred's brother should die this way. Among the elder brother's crowd, huge gambling debts, all-night drunken routs, and even duels were fairly commonplace. He had lived a life of dissipation, rather than showing any interest in the estate he was to inherit, and now his more worthy younger brother would inherit it in his place. What she could not decide was whether this made her any more likely to accept Lord Alfred's hand in marriage, should he offer it. It could not be denied that there was a certain abstract appeal in the idea of being a duchess, and that he would inherit such a vast estate, but Georgiana could not see it as being more important than his other qualities.

Colonel Fitzwilliam sat with them awhile, and then took his leave, saying he would return if he learned any more details of the event. The family quickly determined they should stay home for the day; Lord Alfred – nay, Viscount Burnley – would certainly need to return to the family estate at a time like this, and they did not intend to be out when he came to take his leave. They waited all morning, but their next caller was merely Lady Catherine de Bourgh, who bustled in and said what they all had been considering, but did not think it appropriate to voice:

"Georgiana is to be a duchess!" she said. "Congratulations, my niece, on choosing the right son. I had intended you for the dead fool, but you saw better than I, and now you shall have your reward. Well played, Georgiana, very well played. Your mother would be so proud if she were here to see it – a duchess."

"Aunt, you forget that Lord Alfred has not made me an offer," Georgiana said, quite embarrassed. "Nothing is guaranteed; everything has changed. And I spent time with Lord Alfred because I enjoyed his company, not because I had any notion that something like this should occur."

"Oh, but surely he will ask for your hand now. He wanted only fortune, and he shall now have one of the largest estates in England to offer you. Certainly there will be the period of mourning to contend with, but we should still have you installed as Viscountess Burnley by the end of the year."

Lady Catherine's visit continued on in this vein for much too long, until Darcy finally noted that she might better hear more intelligence that would be of use to the family if she would return to her own home and be available to callers. And so Lady Catherine left, and the family continued to wait. They waited until just before dinner, when a short letter was delivered, addressed to Mr. Darcy:

"As you and your family may be aware by now, today has been a day of great sadness for my family. My brother Stephen, Viscount Burnley, has been killed whilst duelling. I cannot account for the manner of his death, but still, it remains; he was my brother, and his death was a great shock to me, as it will be a shock to my parents.

"I had wished to take leave of your family before heading north, but I have determined it best that I escort my brother's body to the family estate immediately. I should only arrive a day behind my express to them, so that my parents might be able to see their remaining son, and we might bury him in the family cemetery, as I know they will want.

"Please know that I would much prefer to call on you all in more normal circumstances, and remain in town enjoying the pleasant company I have found in homes such as your own, without the tragic circumstances that occurred this morning. I leave with the greatest wishes for the health and happiness of your family.

"ALFRED MALLORY"

The letter was first read silently by Darcy, who then read it aloud, and allowed it to be passed around, so that each of them might read it and determine the nuances in such a short note. It ended in Georgiana's hands, and she found herself thinking that if she was so very important to him as she had seemed yesterday, he still could have found time to call, even just for a few minutes, before leaving for the north. Then she chastised herself for such selfish thoughts – he had just lost his brother, he must race the news to the north, his greatest longing must be to reach his parents and be ensconced in the family unit as a time such as this.

The letter had distracted them all so that it had passed the time when they usually went up to change for dinner, and upon realising this, the family all left the drawing room. Georgiana, however, found herself pulled aside by her brother as the others made their way upstairs.

"I hope you will remember our conversation, in light of this news," Darcy said. "I do have to rescind my saying I hoped you would not marry the heir to that dukedom, but it remains that I wish to see you marry for love, Georgiana. You will feel a great deal of pressure from your aunt Catherine now to accept him, if he makes you an offer. You must not let that influence your decision."

"I will try, Fitzwilliam. It will be impossible to think of him without thinking of how his expectations have changed, though."

"It is natural that you would think of that, and, indeed, if the fact that you would be a duchess and mistress of that great estate makes him more favourable to *you*, then you are making your choice for the right reasons. Just do not allow yourself to think that you must oblige your family and marry him."

"Thank you, I will keep what you say in mind," Georgiana said, feeling relieved. She knew there were some families where, in the same situation, she would have been required to marry Lord Alfred if he offered for her, and she was very glad hers was not one of them.

Georgiana retired early that evening, and the rest of the family followed soon after her – they were all still quite startled by the news, and yet there was only so long they could sit and discuss it in the drawing room. Darcy was reading when Elizabeth went into his bedchamber, but he put the book down when she got into bed, and she took this as an invitation to speak on the news of the day, as they had not yet had an opportunity to discuss it in private.

"I still cannot believe it – what a horrible waste of life," she said.

"The waste came far earlier than his death," Darcy said. "That young man had everything he could ask for in life, and absolutely no sense of duty. I hate to say it, but it is better for their estate that he died. It is not just the family – all of the servants and the tenants, all that depend on who will succeed the duke as master, will be much better off now that Lord Alfred is the heir."

Elizabeth was not so blatant as Lady Catherine; she did not wish to point out that Georgiana might also be among those better off, now that Lord Alfred was to inherit the estate and the title, although she expected Darcy was thinking the same thing as she.

"Have you ever been out, Darcy?" she asked, both to fill the silence and because she was truly curious.

"I have not. I seconded Edward once, when we were in school – he always did have a more martial side to him. They fought with swords, at least, and to first blood – they went for about a quarter-hour, Edward got in a good cut, and it was over. Thank God, for I would have had to answer to Lady Ellen if anything happened to him."

"My mother was terrified my father would fight Wickham, when he and Lydia ran off together. I could never see him doing it – it would be so far from his nature."

"I wanted to call Wickham out, after Ramsgate, although it would have given him far more consequence than he deserved," Darcy said, anger passing over his countenance for a moment. "Edward convinced me not to. If it had got out that we had been fighting, people would have been curious as to why. And he thought Wickham would go for pistols, and attempt to kill me. I could not do that to Georgiana – not after everything else she had been through."

"You could not do that to me, either."

"I did not even know you then."

"No, and you never would have, and that is the most horrible thing I can imagine."

"I seem to recall a rather significant period of time when you would not have minded."

"Well, thank heaven we are well past that," she said, leaning over to kiss him. "I would mind very much now."

CHAPTER 22

The day after the news of Stephen Mallory's death, Georgiana could not stop thinking of Lord Alfred; she wondered what he was going through, how far he had to travel before reaching his family home, how his parents must react upon reading the news. Her brother had written a longer response to Lord Alfred's note, expressing the condolences of the family and indicating that they would miss his company, and sent it off immediately, but they could not expect a reply for some time. All they might expect from Lord Alfred for many months might be a few letters; having lost a son and heir, the family could be expected to be in mourning for at least half a twelvemonth, and so Georgiana was unlikely to see him before autumn, if not next year's season.

Only when she realised they were to attend the Haydn concert in the evening did she return her thoughts to Captain Stanton, for she knew he would be in attendance. Although she had recognised the possibility of his only being a childish infatuation for her, the thought of seeing him again still gave her a little thrill of anticipation, and she resolved to be very careful. Certainly, Lord Alfred's departure would give her that which she had originally wished for – time to get to know the captain without the potential of a proposal from Lord Alfred looming over her. Yet with Lord Alfred gone from town, she would have no more opportunities to compare the two gentlemen.

The entire family was to go to the concert, and Elizabeth found herself staring wearily at the dress Sarah had chosen for her, and not knowing why. She did not have the dedication for the amount of pianoforte practise her sisters put in, but she still had an enjoyment of music; indeed, she had continued to attend Lady Tonbridge's musical evenings long after Mr. Davis had ceased to be a threat.

No, it was the prospect of another night in heavy company, of introductions to people who would judge her, and possibly shun her, another night of constantly trying to ensure she was comporting herself as Mrs. Darcy should. This, she thought, was the cause of her weariness, as it was on so many other evenings, although on this particular evening she had the knowledge that her courses had started again that morning – quite painfully – to further depress her thoughts.

"Shall I select another dress, ma'am?" Sarah asked.

"What – oh, no, Sarah. It is fine. I was thinking of something else. Please, continue."

"Yes, ma'am."

"Sarah, are your family in Ireland from the city, or the country?" Elizabeth asked, as Sarah helped her out of her day dress.

"They are from the country, ma'am. A small farm outside of Galway."

"Do you miss the countryside?"

"Sometimes I do," Sarah said. "Not that I do not appreciate London, ma'am, or the opportunities you've given me here."

"Of course, but it is not the same as what you have been used to all your life."

"That is very much what I mean, my lady."

The realisation had been gradually gaining on Elizabeth, that she felt stifled here in town. She had come to understand why her father did not like it. For all the diversions London held, she missed the close, friendly society of Hertfordshire, she missed long walks, great rambling gardens, even merely fresh air.

After avoiding Pemberley for so long, she came to realise it was where she most wanted to be, as she could not return to Hertfordshire except to visit. She developed a deeper fondness for the walks she remembered, for the stream, and the gardens, and yet she knew they would not likely go there until the summer. Even with Lord Alfred gone, there was still Captain Stanton, and she and Darcy agreed that Georgiana should have a chance to remain in town and become better acquainted with him, as well as participating in all the season had to offer. There was no guarantee either of the gentlemen would ever make her an offer of marriage, or that if they did, she would accept them, and so Georgiana should continue to increase her acquaintance, particularly with single gentlemen of her rank in society. It was irritating to admit it, but Lady Catherine was correct in this regard.

As well, there was Captain Ramsey, and the thought of him did bring a true smile to her face. He and Kitty showed a clear preference for each other; there seemed to be no misunderstanding at all between them, and his calls had been increasingly frequent. She and Darcy had both written Longbourn about him; they had even invited her father to come to town and observe the captain's courtship if he so chose, but her father did not so choose. So long as the man had Elizabeth's and Darcy's good opinions, it saved him the trouble of having to go out of his way to form his own opinion. Her mother's response was more troubling – her two elder daughters's marriages had apparently raised her sights higher than Captain Ramsey's fortune, and she wished Kitty would try for a man with at least three thousand a year. Fortunately, however, Catherine showed no inclination to listen to her mother's advice when she had found a good-looking, very amiable man who wore a uniform and had more than enough fortune to keep her in pin money for the rest of her life.

So they must stay in town, and as long as they stayed in town, their social engagements would not cease, and Elizabeth knew this was even more difficult for Darcy than for her. She remembered her vow to have the family remove to Pemberley, and realised now that she would not be able to make it happen. Mrs. Annesley was a fine companion, but being left as chaperone for not one but two ladies receiving suitors, plus a third single lady, was too much for any one person. Elizabeth doubted that another Mr. Davis would come along, but his disastrous proposal had made it clear that they could not leave the single ladies without sufficient support during the season. Perhaps, though, she could suggest to Darcy that he spend a week or two at Pemberley; although he received regular correspondence from his steward, certainly he would wish to look in on the estate before summer, and it would give him the break from company she suspected he needed even more than she.

Elizabeth thanked Sarah and offered her a weak smile, and then headed down for what was to be a quick dinner before the carriage ride to Hanover Square. There were some acquaintances there she was happy to see, among them Lord and Lady Brandon, and Lady Tonbridge, escorted by Captain Stanton. There was, of course, also Lady Catherine, who regularly attended concerts here, so that she could fully maintain her reputation as a lover of music.

They made their way around, exchanging greetings with their acquaintances and making a few introductions. Georgiana and Captain Stanton shared a brief discussion about the night's programme, but their attention was quickly diverted when the viscountess asked how their family was holding up on the news about Viscount Burnley.

"We were only a little acquainted with Viscount Burnley," Elizabeth said. "The younger brother, Lord Alfred, is a closer friend of our family. He wrote to us to take his leave. We all feel what a tremendous tragedy it was for them."

At the mention of Lord Alfred's name, Georgiana coloured deeply, and dropped her gaze. Elizabeth watched Captain Stanton carefully for a reaction, but he only looked as serious as he usually did, except when talking about music and the navy. He stood up a bit straighter, it seemed, but was silent.

"He *wrote* to take his leave, hmm?" the viscountess asked.

"Yes, he was in a great hurry to reach his family."

"Of course. News such as that travels a great deal faster than good news," the viscountess said. "On a brighter note, us meeting here allows me to tell you all of my next ball."

They were all amazement that she should hold a ball again so soon, but she said she loved nothing quite like hosting a ball, even if she could not dance so much as she had in her younger days, and her previous ball had only served to remind her of such enjoyments. She named the date, and said invitations should be forthcoming. No one was happier than Catherine at the news, for if Captain Ramsey had been invited to the previous ball, there was no reason to assume he should not be invited to this one. Georgiana suffered more mixed emotions; she had no doubt Captain Stanton would be there, and she might have her first opportunity to dance with him. Yet it seemed strange that she would be dancing with him, while Lord Alfred was in mourning.

Soon enough, it was time for all of them to take their seats for the concert. Despite her reservations about going out for the evening, Elizabeth did find herself enjoying it very much. Certainly it was preferable to the stilted conversation and card games that had comprised many of their other evenings, or even worse, the at-homes, and at times, Elizabeth could even remember when London had been novel to her, when every shop she visited with her aunt was cause for excitement, when concerts and the theatre seemed the most diverting thing possible.

During the intermission, the family found themselves intercepted by Lady Catherine, and by the disappointed looks on Georgiana's and even Mary's faces, Elizabeth could tell they would have much preferred to discuss the concert with the viscountess and Captain Stanton. However, Lady Catherine was not to let them go, and so Georgiana and Mary were forced to share their observations on pacing and tone with her, instead. Lady Catherine looked at them blankly for a moment, stated broadly that she had of course loved it, there was no greater lover of music than she, and then she turned to her favourite topic of late: how Georgiana was to be a duchess.

"That woman is insufferable," Darcy whispered to Elizabeth, as they made their way back to their seats, and she was glad he had said it, for she could not very well open such a topic; Lady Catherine was not *her* blood relation.

"You should look to her as a source of amusement," Elizabeth whispered back. "For example, during that conversation, I was imagining my mother saying every thing she said. I assure you, not a sentence would have been out of place."

The muscles of his arm tensed under her hand, but he managed to suppress most of his mirth.

"I suppose I should not criticise her so much," he said. "If Georgiana does become a duchess, we will have her to thank; she introduced them."

"And we shall never hear the end of it. She will require our gratitude until the end of her days."

The remainder of the concert passed pleasantly; they found themselves waiting with the viscountess and Captain Stanton for that lady's carriage, and so Georgiana and Mary were able to discuss the concert with those they had most wished to.

Back at home, in the comfort of her husband's bed, Elizabeth noted that it had been quite a pleasant evening.

"Yes, we must find a way to include a greater proportion of concerts in our evening entertainments," he said. "I infinitely prefer them to cards and at-homes."

"I was thinking exactly the same thing, earlier."

"And balls. Concerts are much preferable to balls. All of the music, none of the dancing."

"I cannot agree with you there, Darcy."

"You are allowed to sit out a dance, madam. I am not."

"Poor Mr. Darcy," she said, slipping her hand across his chest. "There are enough men back from the war now, perhaps I shall let you sit out a dance or two."

CHAPTER 23

Georgiana had thought she would not see Captain Stanton again until the next musical evening, but he called with Captain Ramsey the day after the concert, and, as they soon learned, this was because he had an invitation to issue:

"I spoke with an acquaintance at the concert, and learned that there is to be a concert at one of the lesser-known halls Wednesday next, with a programme that includes Scarlatti," he said. "I did not want to raise the topic last night until I had a chance to inquire about seats; they are still available, and if you are all not otherwise engaged, I hope you will join me. I know Scarlatti is a favourite of yours, Miss Darcy."

"Oh, we are to dine with the Gardiners Wednesday," Elizabeth said, then paused, considering. "They are family; I do not think they would mind if the young ladies went to the concert instead. Mrs. Annesley can attend them there."

Georgiana and Mary were all excitement at the scheme; Catherine was not so sure whether she would prefer the concert or dinner with her aunt and uncle, until she understood that Captain Ramsey was to attend the concert as well, and then she was very much for the concert.

They did not see Captain Stanton again until the next musical evening. He had brought his new cello again, and was speaking with the viscountess and a man older than he, but about the same height, and what appeared to be some family resemblance. He and the viscountess saw them, and beckoned Georgiana and her family to come over to them.

"My uncle has asked if he may be introduced to you and your family, Mrs. Darcy," Captain Stanton said.

"Of course, we would be very pleased to make his acquaintance," Elizabeth told him.

"My uncle, the Earl of Anglesey," he said. "Uncle, the ladies are Mrs.

Darcy, Miss Darcy, Miss Bennet, and Mrs. Annesley."

The earl said he was pleased to make their acquaintance, and soon showed himself to be of the same staid but good manners as Captain Stanton. He was only recently in town, and had already had quite a happy evening, dining with his old friend and long-absent nephew, and now he had the promise of music as a further delight.

This evening also saw the return of Lady Julia Barton to town, and once they had all taken seats, she, like Mary, was one of the first volunteers to exhibit. Lady Julia was not much older than Georgiana, but a much more confident performer; she played the harp with an easy elegance, and this evening she had chosen a piece that sounded lovely, although Georgiana knew from her own experience on the instrument that it was not very difficult. Mary returned to Mozart, although it was a new piece for her to exhibit, and she played as well as she had ever played. Georgiana applauded eagerly for her friend, and whispered her congratulations, as well, when Mary returned to her seat.

The quartet, after the previous week's less-successful performance, was called upon by the viscountess to play as the last act before refreshments were served. This time, they were to play Haydn, and Georgiana felt a great anxiety for Captain Stanton, to once again attempt work with such complexity in the cello part. He did acquit himself much better than the last time, although his performance was not to the level of his first time with the group. He still seemed uncomfortable with his new cello, but that he had practised enough on this piece that his part at least did not distract from the whole.

The viscountess did not call on Georgiana to exhibit before refreshments, but Georgiana did not mind at all. She had chosen another singing piece, and if she did not exhibit tonight, it would give her another week to practise. When they broke for refreshments, therefore, she happily congratulated those who had exhibited already. What she would have liked was an opportunity to compliment Captain Stanton on his progress with the new instrument, but she found that he and the earl seemed deep in conversation with Lady Julia. On watching them for a while, she also saw that Lady Julia seemed to have an admiration for the captain, and Georgiana was surprised that this observation caused a sudden jealousy to well up inside her.

After the usual time, they all began to make their way back to their seats, and Georgiana noticed Captain Stanton murmur something to the viscountess as he passed her. She could not tell what it was, nor the lady's response. When they were all seated, however, the viscountess noted that Miss Darcy had not yet played tonight, asking if she should like to exhibit, and Georgiana could not help but wonder if she had been the topic of the brief exchange.

Georgiana was as satisfied with her performance as anyone of her modest character could be, and when the carriages were called, she found herself and Mary being congratulated by both Captain Stanton and his uncle. Lord Anglesey declared himself to have thoroughly enjoyed the evening – such a quality of music from amateurs indicated how much everyone in the group loved to play. They were all enthusiasm in seconding his observation, and the group waited companionably together.

"Captain Stanton, do you find yourself growing more comfortable with your new cello?" Georgiana asked, during a lull in the conversation.

"Sadly no, Miss Darcy. I find we do not get on very well."

"It did not seem so to me – you sounded much improved."

"Miss Darcy is too kind to note that last week I massacred Bach as much as ever he could be massacred, and therefore anything would have been an improvement this week," he said to his uncle.

"I listened to him when he was first learning the cello," the earl smiled. "I hope it was not such a massacre as that."

"Only slightly," Captain Stanton said. "I refrained from outright screeching."

The earl's carriage arrived first, and, with parting compliments again to Mary and Georgiana, both he and the captain got in. Georgiana assumed that with the earl now in town, Captain Stanton would shift from his current lodgings to stay in the earl's house, for certainly an earl would have a town house. The general agreement in the carriage was that they liked the uncle's company almost as much as the nephew's, and would not at all mind furthering the acquaintance, if the earl so chose.

The earl did so choose to further the acquaintance, and called with Captain Stanton the day before the concert; he was to attend as well, and he invited the young ladies to have an early dinner at his house beforehand, so that they might all travel to the concert together. Elizabeth and Darcy saw nothing wrong with the scheme; the Gardiners had already released the young ladies from their later dinner engagement, and so they went thither at the appointed time.

The earl, they learned, was a widower with no daughters, and the ladies found his house lacked the comforts a female might have installed, although it was well-furnished. Captain Stanton had indeed left his inn and taken up lodgings there, and Captain Ramsey had been invited by the earl to do the same, so they did at least have the reassurance of familiar company already there when they arrived.

Also dining with the party, although not going to the concert, was the earl's eldest son, who went by Lord Stanton – the family having no additional titles – and was engaged to be married to Miss Lucy Darlington, who would be returning to town in a fortnight for the wedding. Lord

Stanton proved to be a most unremarkable man; he was neither particularly intelligent, nor particularly stupid, neither particularly kind, nor particularly ill-tempered. It soon became clear to all of the ladies why the earl should so frequently seek out the company of his nephew, with such an unexceptional son. Yet Georgiana could not help but think of Stephen Mallory, and how certainly an heir such as this was preferable – no one need have any fear of Lord Stanton being killed in a duel or throwing away the family fortune at the gaming tables. And yet the earl was an interesting enough man himself. Georgiana wondered what the mother had been like, to have raised such an average son, and what Miss Lucy Darlington was like, to be marrying him.

These were not the most polite thoughts to be thinking at a dinner party with new acquaintances, and so Georgiana refocused her concentration on the conversation, which had turned to the navy, the party having little else in the way of common topics.

"We are likely to be on shore for some time now, if not permanently," Captain Ramsey was saying, with Catherine, seated beside him, attending very closely.

"Indeed, we have spent so much on this war that Parliament will be forced to retrench for a while," said the earl. "I expect eventually many of you will be called back into service, however. We have too many trade interests to leave them unprotected."

"I think we will see our frigates in heavier use," Captain Stanton said. "The line of battle ships perhaps not as much – they are best at just that, a line of battle, and we are not likely to see any more of those with Napoleon in exile."

"He just wants to see his poor Caroline brought back into service. He is so smitten with that ship you might think she was a lady," the earl said, and Georgiana blushed in spite of herself. "A lovely looking ship, though, I will grant you. I ran him down to Portsmouth when he took possession as captain, and while I will admit I have a landlubber's eye, she had the prettiest paint job, and every gun gleaming."

"That would be Lieutenant Campbell's doing," Captain Stanton said. "My first lieutenant – he is an excellent seaman, but he also has quite a penchant for ensuring the ship looks her best."

"How does he get on, with the peace?" the earl asked.

"I had a letter from him a few days ago. He is living with his family, although he is looking to set up his own establishment, and purchase a cottage, or something of the sort. A lieutenant's half-pay is hardly enough for a man to live on alone, but he has been very careful with his prize money."

The conversation continued on in this way through the course of dinner, uninteresting to Mary and Mrs. Annesley, but not so for Catherine and Georgiana, who always enjoyed hearing more about the captains's former shipmates and the voyages they had taken, before they all took to the carriages.

In Cheapside, Elizabeth and Darcy were only just arriving at the Gardiners's house. It was nearly the same size as the Darcys's town house, but always seemed smaller when the young Gardiners were about. They were in the drawing room with their parents when Elizabeth and Darcy arrived, the younger ones playing about the floor, while Susan, the eldest, sat with her parents, drinking milk with a little tea.

When they had all said their greetings, Elizabeth made her way to sit next to Susan, so that she might inquire after her niece, not at first noticing that her husband had not followed her. When she looked up, she found him kneeling on the floor, speaking with the boys. This was not an unusual sight; he was often attentive to the Gardiner children, although he got on better with the boys than the girls, which was to be expected. It was quite unusual, though, to see him playing at toy soldiers in his dinner clothes, but there he was, doing just that, and telling the overawed boys of his cousin, who was a real soldier in the regulars.

Of all the scenes Elizabeth might have thought she would ever see Mr. Darcy in before they were married, this was certainly not one of them; this was a sight of himself that he only occasionally offered, and only when they were around close family. And of all the scenes that could pain Elizabeth, this was the worst. It would be a rare eldest son indeed who did not wish for children; heirs must be had, so that estates and titles could be passed on. Both she and Darcy, however, genuinely loved children, and at this moment Elizabeth felt the full ache of not having conceived a child of their own. They had not yet been married a year; she felt there was still hope, and yet she was glad when Anne Gardiner, who had been playing with her doll at the edge of the room, and was feeling left out, made her way over to Elizabeth so that her aunt could pull her up onto her lap. Little Anne's presence was a comfort and a distraction for Elizabeth, and both were desperately needed.

Eventually, the nurse was summoned, and the children left their presence; Susan with a very proper little curtsey, Anne with a cute bob of her own. The adults then made their way into the dining room, there to avail themselves of the delicacies Mr. Gardiner was always acquiring through his business. They meandered through a range of topics, and had been speaking of Parliament, when the Corn Bill came up, as it very well would in any conversation about legislation.

"God-willing, it shall pass soon, and give us all some peace," Darcy said, unthinkingly. Among those he usually conversed with – the gentlemen at White's, the men of great estates – this would have been a wholly supported statement, one that would be toasted by his companions, and indeed it was likely this was not the first time he had made it. His host was not such a man, however; Mr. Gardiner's wealth came from far different sources.

"I am afraid I cannot agree with you," Mr. Gardiner said. "I do not do a great deal of business in grains, so it has little direct impact on myself, but I can never support the dampening of free trade, and the Corn Bill is most certainly that."

This statement necessarily cast a pall over the dinner table; Elizabeth felt deeply the discomfort of seeing two people she cared about fall on two different sides of such a critical issue.

"I apologise, I did not mean to – " Darcy began to speak, but could not seem to determine how to continue his statement.

"Of course, I understand the impact to all of our estates, and our dear niece and nephew," Mr. Gardiner said, picking up the conversation and nodding to Darcy. "The real villain in all of this is Bonaparte – without the war, we should have none of this business. It is a most unfortunate situation for us all."

"Indeed," said Mrs. Gardiner. "I still feel compelled to drink to his confusion, even with him in exile. Perhaps we may toast the peace, instead."

They all did so, and felt the relaxation that must come from passing through an awkward situation amongst people who were generally so fond of each other's society. There was still a certain tension among them when they had finished, and Elizabeth and her aunt made their way into the drawing room.

Elizabeth expected that the gentlemen would make their way thither as soon as was possible, but instead they remained in the dining room for some time. When they finally came into the room, it was with expressions that indicated mutual goodwill, and Elizabeth expected that some manner of apology had passed from her husband to her uncle. She felt a deep sense of relief that all was well between their families, for she could not bear the thought of discord between those so dear to her.

The concert room, off Newman Street, was much smaller and looked more worn than Hanover Square, and looking about the crowd, Georgiana could see that it was a mix of fashionable people and others who were here strictly for their interest in the music, and that it tended more toward the latter.

Georgiana was most anticipating the Scarlatti, and she could not help but think most kindly of Captain Stanton for seeking to invite her, upon hearing of a concert where one of her favourites formed part of the programme. She was very pleased to find that she enjoyed all she heard in the beginning of the concert, and just as pleased when Captain Stanton applied for her verdict during the intermission.

"Oh, it has been delightful," she said, smiling. "Some of the pieces have been quite innovative interpretations, and the Bach piece was exquisite."

"Ah yes, he sounds quite different when performed by someone with greater proficiency," he said.

"Captain, I believe you are very close to breaking our truce."

"I am not sure our truce should apply while I continue to do battle with my new instrument." He smiled, but she could also sense his frustration, and felt for him.

"Come, let us focus on more positive things," he said, offering her his arm so they could return to their seats; she accepted it with a little thrill of happiness, in spite of herself. "We still have much more music to go on the night, and I am curious to see how you will like it."

Georgiana had enjoyed everything in the concert thus far, but she was most anticipating Scarlatti, and these pieces began shortly after the intermission, on harpsichord, giving Georgiana an opportunity to once again compare them to how they sounded on the pianoforte. Scarlatti always reminded her of her mother, and she was most affected by hearing them as her mother would have played them, but it was not until – most shockingly – a guitar player and percussionist came out, to close with Scarlatti's Fandango, that she was truly enchanted. It seemed at once a reinvention of the piece, and wholly natural, at the same time elegant and exotic, unlike any other piece she had heard. It spoke of Spain, of Southern America, of the ports the captains had told them about. She sat, transfixed, and completely unaware that Captain Stanton was also watching her, delighted by her reaction. After she had joined everyone in the room in rousing applause for the players, she turned to him and said:

"It has been a long time since I have enjoyed a piece so much as that – I am so grateful to you for finding a concert where Scarlatti was played at all, much less so inventively."

"I am glad you enjoyed it," he said. "Although I suspect Captain Ramsey, who has spent more time stationed near Spain than I, will tell you it is not so much invention as it is playing the piece like a natural fandango."

"If that is the case, I wish I had heard a true fandango before now," Georgiana said. "I so wish the musical club could hear such a thing."

"There we may find some difficulty, unless we can convince Lady Tonbridge to recruit guitar and castanet players."

"Yes, it would not be nearly the same without them," she said, taking his arm again. "We shall have to begin convincing her, then."

CHAPTER 24

Georgiana awoke the next morning with the thought that perhaps they should not have to recruit a guitar player. After all, it was a string instrument, and so perhaps her harp might serve as an adequate substitute. Perhaps, it might even be an interesting balance between the harpsichord the piece had been intended for, and the guitar that had so struck her imagination at the concert.

Although they had sent for the instrument from Pemberley, she still played it but rarely; the pianoforte was by far her preference. It took her some time simply to warm up her fingers and recall what it was like to play with some level of fluency. Then she tried to remember the key guitar parts, and began plucking them out as best she could remember.

"What on earth are you playing, Georgiana?" her brother asked, entering the drawing room with Elizabeth.

"It is Scarlatti's Fandango, is it not?" Mary asked. "We heard it last night."

"Yes, it is. Or rather, I am trying to make it so. The part was played on a guitar, but I think I may be able to make it work on the harp," she said, then realised she might be able to recruit Mary to help. "Mary, I should so like to play this for everyone in the musical club. If I can make the guitar part work, would you be willing to try the castanets?"

"Castanets?" said Darcy. "Should I apply to a troupe of gipsies to come teach her to play?"

"Brother, it really is a lovely piece. Once we have practised enough, we shall perform it, and then you will see."

Mary, meanwhile, had been considering how much more accomplished she would be considered with the addition of something so exotic as castanets to her skills, and decided they certainly would be interesting, if nothing else. As well, it would be fun to work on something new with

Georgiana.

"I would be willing to learn the castanets," Mary said.

"Thank you, Mary! Brother, may we send for the sheet music for Scarlatti's Fandango, and a pair of castanets?"

Darcy groaned, but called Mr. Miller into the drawing room.

"Mr. Miller, I am told we must send for Scarlatti's Fandango, and a pair of castanets," Darcy said. "Wherever you will find castanets, I do not know."

"Leave it to me, sir. Scarlatti's Fandango and castanets, very well," Mr. Miller replied.

Both the music and the castanets were procured that very day, and Georgiana and Mary continued to experiment the day following, Georgiana with translating the music to harp, and Mary with her entirely new instruments, which she found to be not so difficult. By the time Captains Stanton and Ramsey came to call on them, the pads of Georgiana's fingers had turned pink and sore, but she was very desirous of showing Captain Stanton their progress.

"Might Mary and I play a piece for you?" she asked. "I think you may be surprised."

"We are all for a surprise," Captain Stanton said, and Captain Ramsey agreed.

They were surprised enough when Georgiana took to the harp – although they knew she played, neither had ever heard her do so. They started into the song, and Captain Stanton laughed as soon as he realised what they were at.

"You have found a way to play the Fandango – I am delighted, ladies."

"I find I am filled with reminders of Spain these last few days," Captain Ramsey said. "If you play just a bit more I will show you how the Spanish ladies dance."

This was not a request that could be resisted, and so they continued on, and the captain rose and began clapping his hands together. They all laughed to see a man attempting to dance like a delicate lady, and once Catherine had a sense of the dance, she stood with him and made a far better imitation of a Spanish lady, and they danced together quite gleefully.

Mrs. Annesley certainly had seen nothing like this in any of the other houses she had worked for, but she also saw no harm in it – there was quite a lot of clapping, but Kitty and Captain Ramsey were farther apart than they would have been dancing a reel. Elizabeth and Darcy, meanwhile, who had opted to hide in the study while Mary learned the castanets, could only listen and wonder what on earth was going on.

"Perhaps I should go out and see what is happening," Darcy said.

"Mrs. Annesley is there; they should be fine," Elizabeth replied.

"Are you quite certain? It sounds a regular Bartholomew Fair in there.

Next it will be tambourines and jugglers."

"Now there are some fine accomplishments to add to Caroline Bingley's list," Elizabeth said, smiling archly. "An accomplished lady must be able to play the pianoforte, harp, and tambourine (and let us not forget Mary's castanets); she must sing and dance; speak all of the modern languages; draw and paint; and juggle. And there must be a *certain air* in the way she juggles. None of your lacklustre juggling will do, if she is to be called truly accomplished."

Darcy looked at her for a moment with the sternest, most incredulous expression he could muster, but Elizabeth could see the corners of his mouth twitching before he finally could not help it anymore, and burst out laughing.

"Come, let us go call on Miss Bingley now, so that we may tell her how we have amended her list," she said. "There will have to be masters hired on all over town. Indeed there will likely be quite a shortage as all the young ladies learn their juggling."

"Let us go see Cook, is more like it, to see what she has slipped into all of your breakfasts, to make this entire house go mad," Darcy said, and this time it was Elizabeth's turn to laugh most heartily.

CHAPTER 25

It had been cold for the past few days, but the weather on Saturday was quite mild, so much so that Darcy asked over breakfast if Elizabeth and Georgiana had any interest in going to Hyde Park, Elizabeth with him in the phaeton, Georgiana on Grace. Georgiana was all enthusiasm at the idea, and Elizabeth saw great appeal in anything involving fresh air and some amount of open space, even if it was only Hyde Park.

The phaeton and Grace were brought around, as well as a groom on horseback, in case Georgiana should need any assistance. They found the park quite full when they arrived; clearly they had not been the only people to have this idea, and Darcy commented that perhaps they should have put a little more time into planning, and gone to Richmond.

"I think you would like it, Elizabeth – it is one of the few places where one can find uncrowded open space around town these days."

"Open space does appeal to me right now," she said, motioning to the line of phaetons trotting along in front of them, and the riders cantering along on either side.

"I must admit to missing Pemberley more and more these days," he said. "I have never been away for such an extended period of time before, and I did not realise myself so susceptible to homesickness. I almost forget what it is like to own one's own land, and – "

Elizabeth waited, but he did not finish his thought. "What is it, my dear?"

"I had a letter from my steward this morning," he said. "I do not know how much longer we can continue to discuss the Corn Bill over correspondence. The price of wheat is not going to wait for Parliament to act, and I would much prefer to be able to talk to Richardson in person. I do not see us removing there anytime soon, so I suppose I shall have to summon him here, although I do not like to have both of us absent from the estate at the same time."

Elizabeth had been waiting for an opportunity to release him from town, and here it was. It had the added benefit of perhaps easing his mind on the Corn Bill, which she knew would continue to wear on him until it was clear whether it would pass or not.

"Why do you not go to Pemberley instead? We can manage without you for a week or two. I am sure you would prefer to look in on the estate before the summer."

The idea clearly appealed to him; his countenance brightened, and he said: "Are you quite certain? It would be very good to go, just for a little while. I could sit down with Richardson and settle our contingency plans, and I do not want my tenants to think I've become an absentee landlord."

"Go, Darcy. Mrs. Annesley and I will be here, and we have plenty of friends in town. I will miss you, but we will be fine without you for a little while."

They fixed on him leaving Tuesday or Wednesday next, dependent on the weather, and then Elizabeth settled back into the phaeton to enjoy the ride as much as she could. He could not relax, driving a team of horses with the park as crowded as it was, but Elizabeth was free to watch Georgiana, whom she had never seen ride before. The girl's tall stature made her and Grace stand out among the other ladies as she rode, several horse lengths ahead of the phaeton in a small gap in the crowd of riders. Elizabeth watched as Georgiana was signalled by an acquaintance up ahead, and saw that it was Captain Stanton.

"Well that was quite fortuitous timing," she said.

"What do you mean?"

Elizabeth pointed them out; they had moved off to the side of the path, among the trees, and were talking. Darcy attempted to steer the phaeton there, but there were too many riders in the way, and he had to circle back around in order to join them.

They all exchanged greetings and the usual civilities, and Georgiana filled them in that Captain Stanton, had, like them, seen the break in weather and determined it would be a good day for a ride; he had borrowed one of his uncle's horses and come out to the park.

"I imagine it has been some time since you have ridden," Elizabeth said.

"Indeed, I am fairly certain he gave me his most gentle mount, and I still find I am quite out of practise," he said. "I have been giving some consideration to purchasing my own horse, now that the peace is here."

"Charles Bingley and I were considering going to Tattersalls on Monday," Darcy told him. "No particular reason; Charles and I just enjoy seeing good horses. Should you like to come with us, and perhaps give us a true purpose?"

"I would be honoured. I certainly would benefit from having two better judges of horseflesh with me," Captain Stanton said.

"I am sure you are much more used to judging ships than horses," Elizabeth said, pleased that Darcy had extended the invitation, although not sure that it would be the most enjoyable day for poor Captain Stanton. Aside from any manner of interrogation he would undergo, Charles and her husband could talk about horses for hours on end, if so indulged, which was why they were encouraged to go to Tattersalls periodically, to keep such conversation where it belonged.

"You are very correct there, Mrs. Darcy. Although I will note that Grace and your pair on the phaeton seem to be very fine animals."

Georgiana could not help but think of Lord Alfred and Gambit at this moment. She wondered if he had taken the horse with him to the North; solitary rides would be considered acceptable while in mourning, and he would have few other opportunities to be out of doors. Did he go for long rides around the estate and survey the grounds that were to be his some day?

The party all agreed to continue on through the park, allowing Georgiana and Captain Stanton to ride together, ahead of the phaeton. She was pleased to discover that he had again been modest in his assessment of his riding skills; he rode well, particularly for one who had not been on horseback much in the last five years, although certainly he was not such a good rider as Lord Alfred.

There should of course be no doubt that the gentleman also noted the skill of the lady as they rode along. She sat Grace beautifully at the canter and even the trot, and although the horse was restive from lack of exercise and required a firm hand, Georgiana had no difficulty controlling her and conversing as they went along. The Fandango was again their topic of discussion, both were all excitement in discussing when Georgiana and Mary might be ready to play it for the musical club.

CHAPTER 26

They had not seen Lady Catherine for some time, as she had made a trip back to Rosings, but she was there at St. George's on Sunday, striding up the aisle and taking a seat beside her brother, with only time for a few words to Lord Brandon before the service began.

Thus they all said their greetings to her after church was completed, but then the family group split into two – Elizabeth, Darcy, and the Fitzwilliams had not seen each other for a little while, and lingered behind at their seats, while Lady Catherine, Mrs. Annesley, and the young ladies made their way down the aisle and out to wait for the carriages.

"I have heard a most outrageous rumour!" Lady Catherine exclaimed, storming out of the church doors. "Viscount Burnley is to be married to some nobody, a Miss Foster. I had it from Lady Denham, and she knows all of the ladies in the country with a portion of ten thousand pounds or more, which this Miss Foster certainly does not have."

They were all of them shocked, but only Georgiana felt a rush of the strangest feeling. She could not understand how he could come to be engaged while in mourning, how he could come to be engaged when he had shown her such attention, such partiality, and she felt her eyes filling with tears.

"If it is a rumour, then it is only that," Mrs. Annesley said, firmly. "There is nothing this town loves more than a rumoured engagement, and a great many of those I have heard did not turn out to be true. The elder brother's death drew a certain amount of unfortunate attention to the family. I would not be surprised if the rumour stems from that."

"Lady Denham is an excellent source," Lady Catherine said. "She is not one of your rumour-mongers, prattling on with idle gossip."

"I understand," Mrs. Annesley said. "However, he is in mourning; it would be terrible form to become engaged at such a time. I find it difficult to believe after what we have observed of the gentleman that he would behave in such an infamous manner."

"Regardless, Georgiana, I shall take you to Almack's again Wednesday next," Lady Catherine said. "You must be introduced to more company so that we are prepared if the rumour is true. It will not take long for you to gain other suitors."

Georgiana sighed at the thought of returning to Almack's, although she knew she should go. She was readying herself to respond with some goodly amount of gratitude and enthusiasm, when Kitty instead spoke:

"Georgiana already has another suitor – Captain Stanton, of the Royal Navy."

"Captain Stanton, of the navy?" Lady Catherine sniffed. "I do not consider some nobody of the navy to be a suitor for Georgiana. The navy is good for nothing but puffing up men of inferior birth, so that they think they stand higher in society than they should."

"Aunt, he is the nephew of the Earl of Anglesey," Georgiana said. "He is not a nobody."

"And even if he was, I would beg you not to criticise the navy," Kitty said, standing up straighter and speaking more firmly than any of them had ever heard from her. "Were it not for the Trafalgar victory, the French would have invaded. All of the land and wealth that you enjoy in your position in society would have been gone. You had best think about that before you say anything against our sailors."

"Why, I – " Lady Catherine visibly quivered, so angry was she. "I will not say I have never been thus spoken to, as your impertinent elder sister has come before you in that regard. However, I will hear no more of this. Georgiana will join me Wednesday next at Almack's, and I have nothing to say to the rest of you."

Without taking any further leave, Lady Catherine strode off to her waiting carriage, just as the rest of the family walked outside.

"What in the world was that about?" Darcy asked.

He, Elizabeth, and the Fitzwilliams were apprised of Lady Catherine's news, her critique of the navy, and Kitty's subsequent set-down, which seemed to amuse them all, although none could say so aloud. They returned to Lord Alfred's rumoured engagement once in the carriage, all attempting to soothe Georgiana, who was visibly disturbed.

Darcy firmly agreed with Mrs. Annesley's assessment that it was most likely a rumour, nothing more, and that it was most unrealistic that the young man should enter into an engagement while in mourning. Elizabeth had hardly been in town long enough to have a sense of how many rumoured engagements came to be true, but she did not think such a thing to be in Lord Alfred's character.

This assessment by her brother and sister provided some comfort to

Georgiana, although she found she could not turn her mind away from the thought of Lord Alfred, engaged, throughout the remainder of the day.

CHAPTER 27

The ladies saw nothing of Captain Stanton on Monday morning; Mr. Darcy took the carriage to the Hursts's home to pick up Charles Bingley, and they were then to make their way to the earl's house for the captain, and thence to Tattersall's. The ladies all stayed home, and had the pleasure of both Lady Ellen and Jane as callers during the course of the morning.

Lady Ellen stayed a half-hour, and wished to know how her niece was getting on in the new Viscount Burnley's absence; she gave no credence to the rumours of his engagement. Elizabeth was heartened to find that although Lady Ellen seemed pleased at the potential for Georgiana to be elevated in rank and marry into more fortune than would previously have been expected, Lady Ellen's greater pleasure was in feeling it to be a great match in personality for Georgiana. Having seen them in company many times, and watched how Lord Alfred had drawn her shy niece out, she would have been happy to see them marry even if he was not to inherit the dukedom. She was aware of Captain Stanton, but had only just been introduced to him at the Haydn concert, and was surprised to learn that Elizabeth considered him to be a suitor.

When Mr. Miller showed Jane in, Elizabeth felt the usual stab of envy that came at the sight of her sister. Jane's pregnancy was just beginning to show, and beyond the more notable physical symptoms, Jane had a happiness to her countenance that was beyond her usual serenity, as she talked about planning for the child. Charles had begun looking for a suitable party to take over the lease at Netherfield; they hoped to be free of the burden of living so close to Longbourn, and settled into an estate of their own well before it was time for Jane to begin her confinement. Jane mentioned that they planned to look near Derbyshire, and Elizabeth was mostly enthusiastic about this – if she should not have a child of her own, at least she could be a good aunt to Jane's son or daughter. Her only hesitation was that it would be a regular reminder for Elizabeth and her husband of what they did not have, but this was not enough for her to express any concerns about the idea, and she offered the use of Pemberley as a place to stay while the couple were searching for their new home.

After Jane left, the mail arrived, and among it was a letter addressed as being from Viscount Burnley, which they were all eager to know the contents of, to see if it contained any reference to Miss Foster. However, the letter was addressed to Mr. Darcy, and while Elizabeth had opened his mail during his previous absence, and would once he again went to Pemberley, she did not feel right to do so while he was still in residence. The letter, therefore, sat in the tray in the entrance-hall, until Mr. Darcy himself returned.

They were also curious about how the morning with Captain Stanton had gone, and it was this event they learned of first. Captain Stanton had purchased a lovely black filly, Phoebe, who was of an excellent disposition and thoroughly approved of by both Mr. Darcy and Mr. Bingley. They were not to have his company until the evening, however, although he had asked the gentlemen to communicate that he was looking forward to seeing them at the viscountess's house. He had brought saddle and bridle with him in the carriage, should a suitable purchase appear, and as it had, was to ride Phoebe directly back to his uncle's house.

This did mean that the letter could be read more immediately, however, and once the outing to Tattersall's had been thoroughly reported, the letter's existence was brought to Mr. Darcy's attention, and he read it to them. It contained no reference to an engagement, or Miss Foster; Viscount Burnley was soothed by their family's words of condolence, his family had been terribly shocked at the news and now passed many quiet hours in the mourning of Stephen Mallory, and Alfred Mallory did indeed take many solitary rides about the family estate on Gambit. He hoped their family were in health and that all was well with them. It was generally concluded by all that he had written as much as they could hope he would write, and yet it was not at all a satisfactory letter.

Elizabeth found herself thinking of what a disadvantage Viscount Burnley now stood in, with regards to Georgiana, and sympathising with the young man. He must lead a quiet life for now, he had no news to impart, no stories of interest, and even if he did, it would not have been appropriate for him to share any such things while mourning. He could not write to Georgiana directly, and during his absence, Georgiana would continue to spend time in company with Captain Stanton. She only hoped that, as she had told her sister, once the newness of Captain Stanton wore off, Georgiana would be able to look at them both objectively, and, if Viscount Burnley was her choice, that she would be able to wait for him. But then, it was impossible to entirely ignore the possibility that he was truly engaged, and had no further interest in Georgiana at all.

Captain Stanton had again arrived at the viscountess's before them, although his uncle was not in attendance on this evening. He was tuning what looked to be his old cello, somewhat improved in appearance and far better in sound than anything they had heard from him in the last two sessions; he dashed off little snippets of Bach in very good form as he warmed up. Georgiana noticed the change in instrument immediately, and commented on it after they had exchanged greetings.

"Ah yes, Miss Darcy, I will not say that I have given up on the new instrument, but I determined that I missed my old cello too much," he said. "I took her in for a thorough refit and we shall see if perhaps it is the best of both worlds."

"It sounds very well to me," Georgiana said, smiling gently.

Elizabeth observed them carefully, as she always did. They seemed to have a certain amount of comfort in each other's presence, but they were still both of them very reserved. Georgiana's shyness had improved much since Elizabeth had known her – with a great deal of the credit due to Viscount Burnley – but she was still quieter than other young ladies her age. Captain Stanton's reserve seemed mostly to come from his being very serious at heart, but the overall effect was that they seemed to be two people who always wanted to speak more than they did.

Elizabeth herself inquired after his new horse, and he informed them that she had been fine in the ride to his uncle's house, but she had been somewhat stressed by the noise and crowds of the auction, and so he had left her home this evening to rest. His uncle needing the carriage, and it being a nice night, he had come on foot, as he had on his first two such evenings.

Elizabeth and Mrs. Annesley went to take their usual seats in the back of the room, so Elizabeth only observed the animated discussion between Georgiana, Captain Stanton, and some of the other members of the club, as well as Mary, who was motioned over by Georgiana to join them, after Georgiana could be seen making strange gestures with her hands, which Elizabeth realized must have been pantomiming playing the castanets. When the playing began, Elizabeth was pleased to see that Captain Stanton greatly redeemed his previous few performances, and on this evening the quartet received rousing applause from the entire room.

Mary's and Georgiana's performances were also very well done, so that it looked to be a very satisfactory evening, up until they stood, waiting for their carriage. They waited and waited, watching all of the other carriages depart, and still the carriage did not come. Finally, their groom came to the door, and said that one horse was showing lameness; and the cause could not be determined.

There followed a discussion of how they should get home. They could send a groom back for another horse, and the viscountess offered to have her own carriage prepared. Elizabeth, however, was eager to get home to see Darcy, who had planned to depart for Pemberley in the morning, and she declared that they should need no such trouble made for them. It was a fine evening, and a short distance; they should easily be able to walk with the groom, while their coachman waited with the horses.

Captain Stanton, who had been standing with them while they waited, agreed that this was a solid plan, with one change – that he attend them home instead of the groom. It was hardly out of his way, and he could send someone for his cello in the morning. The groom was a small young man, not much older than twenty, if that, and although Elizabeth had no concerns about the walk, she agreed readily to Captain Stanton's accompanying them instead, mainly for its benefit to Georgiana.

They set off pleasantly, still recounting the performances of the night, and particularly complimenting Captain Stanton on his improvement. It was not until they turned down Audley Street, which was not so well-lit as the previous street, that an event happened so quickly that Elizabeth was only able to piece it together a few seconds after the action had taken place.

A young boy, darting out from the mews, ran straight into Georgiana, knocking her down as he snatched her reticule and made to run away. He might have done so, but Captain Stanton brought him down by knocking the boy sharply in the knees with his walking stick. The boy fell, Captain Stanton kicked him so that he flipped over, and then the captain pressed the end of his walking stick into the boy's throat, and this was the position they were in when the rest of the party realised what had happened.

"Miss Darcy, are you hurt?" Captain Stanton called out, and Elizabeth only just registered the pained expression on his face as she swooped down beside Georgiana, asking her the same question.

Georgiana, for her part, was more stunned than anything. She had been walking along, and then she had been on the ground, and like Elizabeth, it took her a while to comprehend how this had come to happen.

"No, I believe I am fine," she said, only after she spoke beginning to realise that there was a dull ache in her wrist that was beginning to get worse; when the boy had grabbed her reticule, its ribbons had caught around her wrist before he had finally managed to pull it off, and then she had landed on it as she fell. Thus weakened, it had bent most painfully under her weight.

Elizabeth and Mrs. Annesley, kneeling beside her, expressed relief, while Mary busied herself with picking up the sheets of Georgiana's music, which had scattered as she fell. Captain Stanton removed his walking stick and leaned over to pick the boy up by his very tattered shirt, holding him there. The boy wriggled and attempted to escape, but the captain held him fast.

"What shall I do with him, then?"

"Please let him go," Georgiana said. "He has done me no permanent harm, but they will cut off his hand for it."

"They would do more than cut off his hand," Captain Stanton said, pulling the boy up higher so that he was standing on his tiptoes. "He likely would hang, for robbing and assaulting a lady."

"Please do let him go, then – I could not bear to know that a boy was hanged for this. He is too young to know any better."

"Georgiana, he has likely made his living this way for some years," Elizabeth told her, gently.

"Still, he is too young to hang for something like this," Georgiana said, nearly in tears. "Look at how thin he is – he must be desperately hungry."

"If I still had a ship, I would take him on board and see if he was capable of earning a living in an honest way. However, I do not, so I will let him go, as Miss Darcy requests." Captain Stanton said. Then, directing his comments to the boy: "You will do best to remember that you live, and with all your limbs no less, because this lady was exceedingly generous to you. If you must make a living by thievery, will you promise never to do so by attacking a lady again?"

His eyes wide with fear, the boy nodded vigorously, and Captain Stanton all but threw him down the street. The boy stumbled, rose, and set off at a lame, lumbering sort of run. Then the attention of the entire party turned to Georgiana, as Elizabeth and Mrs. Annesley helped her to her feet. Mrs. Annesley touched her wrist as she did so, and Georgiana let out a little yelp of pain.

"You are injured," Captain Stanton said, his voice both concerned and angry, his countenance showing that he would readily chase the boy back down if any of them so asked.

"It is only my wrist," Georgiana said, explaining how it had come to be hurt.

"Are you able to bend it?" he asked, making a few motions with his hand about his neck, before she realised he was removing his cravat.

"It hurts, but yes, I am," Georgiana said.

"It is most likely not broken, then, but you should have it looked over by a surgeon," he said, tying the two ends of the cravat's fabric together in a neat little knot, and then indicating that he would slip the loop of fabric over her head. It was a strangely intimate gesture; it left Georgiana feeling flushed and embarrassed, particularly when she noticed that his open shirt now revealed a quite inappropriate glimpse of his chest. She half wished it was he instead of Elizabeth and Mrs. Annesley who arranged it into a sling for her arm, and yet she realised she would be completely overwhelmed if he were to stand so close and touch her arm in that way.

"Please do take my arm, Miss Darcy," Captain Stanton said, handing her reticule to Elizabeth and moving around to her good arm and offering his, which she accepted with the slightest of tremblings. "You have had quite the ordeal this evening."

"It was not so bad," she said, as they all began walking again. "I hardly even knew what was happening."

She did not tell him how grateful she was that he had been walking with them; if he had not calmly taken the situation in hand and stopped the boy, she might have been far more frightened. Nor did he tell her how greatly he admired her fortitude; such an event would have put most young ladies into hysterics, and yet she was walking along calmly beside him, although her grip on his arm was heavier than he had ever known it to be. They walked along silently for some time, before he spoke again.

"I cannot help but keep thinking of that boy," he said. "I wonder if any of my own ship's boys have turned to making their living in such a way, or even some of the older hands. They all have earned plenty of money from our prizes, but a great many seamen are parted with their prize money after a short run on shore. They are shortsighted; they do not think about what will happen if they cannot get another ship when the money runs out."

"You care a great deal for your men," she said.

"I do – I had responsibility for them for five years' time, and I find it is not an easy thing to give up."

They were interrupted at this point by Georgiana's brother, who was striding up Audley Street with a servant behind him, holding a lantern and looking very concerned. The concern ebbed when he saw them, and then redoubled when he saw Georgiana's arm.

"What on earth has happened?" he cried. He was informed of the lame horse, the boy and his attack on Georgiana, and in turn he told them of how he had grown increasingly concerned at home when the usual hour for their return had passed, and then another half-hour after that. He had organised all of the male servants into small search parties, and they had gone out into the streets along any route the group might have taken home.

Darcy's face showed a certain anguished concern that all in the party took as a feeling of inability to protect his sister, and for a moment it looked as if he would pull Georgiana off of Captain Stanton's arm and escort her home himself. He recollected himself, though; although Georgiana had assured him there was nothing wrong with her aside from the pain in her wrist, she looked very tired and eager to go home. They resumed walking, therefore, after he had despatched the servant to go find the others and tell them the ladies had been found, and to have a surgeon sent for. Elizabeth took up his arm, leaned close and whispered that he should relax; Georgiana was fine, they all were fine.

They came into the house amidst the returning servants, and entered into a period of confusion where Catherine and the female servants, as worried as Darcy had been, must all be informed of what had happened. Eventually, Mrs. Wright and Elizabeth restored some amount of order, and they all attended Georgiana upstairs, to wait for the surgeon. The surgeon came, and repeated Captain Stanton's diagnosis that Georgiana's wrist was most likely not broken, but recommended that it be immobilised as a precaution. It was bandaged, and she was given a small dose of laudanum for the pain, which also sent her promptly to sleep.

Throughout all of this, Captain Stanton remained waiting in the entrance-hall, quite forgotten by everyone as they watched the surgeon upstairs. Eventually, Darcy remembered his presence, and asked Mr. Miller to show the gentleman to his study, if he had not departed, and to offer him some refreshment. He had not departed, and Darcy joined him there after another quarter-hour, noted that Captain Stanton was not drinking anything, and poured both of them a generous brandy.

Captain Stanton accepted his, but took only the slightest of sips, then asked: "How is Miss Darcy?"

"She is as well as can be expected. The surgeon does not think her wrist is broken."

Captain Stanton nodded, looking relieved, and said: "I am very sorry, Mr. Darcy. If I should have suspected anything of the sort that happened tonight would ever happen in Mayfair, I would have insisted we find some other way for the ladies to get home."

"Let your mind rest easy on that regard," said Darcy, who already knew from his wife that the idea to walk home had been her own. "I have never known such a thing to happen, either, though I intend to make enquiries tomorrow. If this is not an isolated incident, my neighbours and I may need to invest in some sort of private security force. It is unacceptable that such a thing should happen here, even once."

"Should a security force become necessary, might I suggest that it be manned with unemployed seamen or soldiers? I myself could provide you with a score of applicants easily."

"Let us hope it does not come to that," Darcy said, struggling with the thought of sailors wandering around Mayfair, then thinking of them perhaps uniformed in some sort of livery not of the naval line – something more refined – and becoming somewhat easier with the idea. "I did want to ask why you let the boy go. Mrs. Darcy indicated that Miss Darcy asked that he be released. Was this your reason for letting the criminal run off?"

"It was one of my reasons, yes," Captain Stanton said. "However, I had others. I understand Miss Darcy is only recently out in society, and for her name to be attached to such an attack, even though it is all innocence on her side, I thought would give her a level of notoriety that your family would not find desirable. More simply, attempting to restrain the boy while also walking the ladies home would have been a distraction, and I felt it a higher priority to ensure I was ready to see to their safety, should anything else occur."

Darcy nodded, mollified by both arguments. He knew Georgiana to have a deeply sentimental heart, and he had feared that by letting go of the boy, Captain Stanton showed a weakness to be swayed by his sister's sentiment. That he had considered other ramifications of the decision in such a moment spoke well of his character, and it occurred to Darcy that of course Captain Stanton was used to making such decisions. The man had a gentleman's manners, and it was easy to forget that he had commanded a frigate full of men, that he had led them into battle and captured a great many ships.

"Please do not think me ungrateful," Darcy said. "Indeed I am remiss in not thanking you immediately for doing such a service for my family. I merely wish to have the fullest understanding of what happened, as I was not there myself."

"I understand completely, Mr. Darcy. If I had a sister, I am sure I would have shared your alarm in finding such a thing had happened to her, without my being there."

"Well then, I hope you will allow me to raise a glass to you in gratitude," Darcy said, and did. Captain Stanton mimicked him, and drank more deeply this time.

It was late by the time Darcy went to his bedchamber, but Elizabeth was there, awake and attempting to read a book.

"How is she?" he asked.

"Sleeping peacefully," Elizabeth said. "I think she has been the least affected out of all of us by this."

"You may well be right," he said, climbing into bed and kissing her. "I cannot tell you how worried I was that something had happened to one of you – all of you, even."

"I know," she whispered, returning his kiss.

"I will write to Richardson tomorrow and inform him I will not be coming to Pemberley," he said. "I can hardly leave at a time like this."

"You need not cancel your trip," she said. "Georgiana's wrist will heal whether you are here or not, and we will need to stay in while she rests. Do you want to sit in with a group of ladies for several days when you could be back at Pemberley?"

"I need to make enquiries around the neighbourhood as to whether this is an isolated incident. If it is not, we will need to look at what is to be done about security."

"Then delay for a day. Leave Wednesday."

"Perhaps I will."

"How late did Captain Stanton stay? I wished to thank him, but I did not want to leave Georgiana."

"He left just before I came upstairs," Darcy said. "And I did thank him. I fear, though, that this incident will elevate him in Georgiana's eyes."

"Is there anything wrong with that? I think him quite a good match for her."

"My preference is for Viscount Burnley. I am sure these marriage rumours are nonsense, and he shall return when he is out of mourning to make his offer."

"Oh, because he is to inherit a dukedom now, so he must be the preferred choice."

"No, because he shows clear preference, and affection for her," he said. "I have no objection to Captain Stanton in any of his particulars; I quite like his company, actually. But he is indifferent to Georgiana."

"How can you possibly say that? He is always seeking her out in company," Elizabeth said, indignation rising in her voice.

"They both love music – I have no doubt he enjoys conversing on that topic with her. But he shows not the slightest bit of affection. When he calls, it is always with Captain Ramsey. It may very well be that he converses with Georgiana so that his friend may enjoy more of Kitty's undivided attention."

"He is reserved – so is she! I need not remind you that you thought the same thing about my sister – that she was indifferent to Charles, and anyone who sees them now can see they are very much in love," Elizabeth said, fully upset now. "And you did not see the look on his face when he saw she had been knocked down. He was very concerned."

"As well he should have been, when one of the ladies he was escorting was attacked."

"Oh, do you blame him for this event, now? Need I remind you that it was *my* idea to make the walk?"

"You need not," he said, his temper finally gone. "You also think it perfectly acceptable for a single lady to go on a solitary three-mile walk through the countryside, so I would have assumed the idea to be yours, even if you had not told me so."

There were few things he could have said that would have hurt Elizabeth quite so much as this statement. She already felt a tremendous amount of guilt that the walk had been her idea, and this statement drew out many of the insecurities she had developed since coming to town. It questioned her judgement; it questioned her propriety. She felt the keenest disappointment in him for having said it, and in herself for letting it affect her. Propriety had never been a concern of hers before marrying, and yet now she felt herself constantly judged on it. Her eyes welled with tears, and she rose from the bed before he could see them.

"I am going to my own chamber," she said. "If we keep on this way we'll wake Georgiana."

"Elizabeth – Elizabeth!"

If he had anything else to say, she did not hear it. She was in his dressing room and then her own, closing the door and leaning back against it as her tears came in earnest.

CHAPTER 28

Sarah seemed to sense that her mistress was even more tired and listless than usual in the morning. After informing her that Hughes had already dressed Georgiana and the young lady was feeling well, she kept up a steady, cheerful chatter about the weather and other meaningless topics that Elizabeth did find to be a little soothing.

They were both startled by the knock on the door leading to the hallway, which Sarah answered. Elizabeth could hear Darcy's voice, asking if he might have a moment with Mrs. Darcy, when she was dressed. Sarah looked back at Elizabeth with an expression of concern, and Elizabeth nodded her assent. She was not looking forward to the conversation with him, but she thought it right to have it over before breakfast; she had no desire to pretend that all was well for the benefit of the rest of the household, without their at least having spoke.

Sarah completed her hair. Elizabeth sat down at her desk chair, then decided she would rather remain standing, and she was thus when he came in, looking as exhausted as she felt.

"Elizabeth, I am so sorry," he said, striding across the room and taking up her hands with such a fervency she thought for a moment he was going to kneel in front of her. "I cannot say that I would have had the same idea in such a situation, but I truly did not see any fault in it, and I told Captain Stanton the same thing. It is no excuse, but I had just been through one of the more terrifying times of my life, and I let my anger get the better of me."

"You hurt me," she said, already crying again in spite of herself. "I spend most of every day trying to do everything proper, everything Mrs. Darcy would be expected to do, and you called it all into question."

"No one finds you improper in your role, least of all me," he said. "Lady Ellen has told me several times how impressed she has been by your transition."

"Lady Ellen said that?" Elizabeth felt the slightest twinge of hope and assurance, to be praised by such a source.

"Yes, she did. But I worry about you, Elizabeth. Before we came to London, you had a spirit and an independence to you that was one of the things I most loved about you – it is what caused you to walk three miles by yourself to visit a sister who was ill, and while I cannot say I condoned it, I certainly admired you for having done so. Now I fear your role here has taken your spirit – I fear you are not happy."

These words were so true they caused a renewal of her tears so strong that for some time she could not speak.

"Do you regret marrying me, Elizabeth?" he asked, his countenance so pained that it was clear he feared her answer would be yes.

"No, of course not – please do not *ever* have any doubts about that. But I have grown very weary of town, and society – I miss the country so."

"Then why do you not come with me to Pemberley?"

"We cannot both be absent with three single ladies in the household. Mrs. Annesley is wonderful, but that is too much to ask of her."

"Should you like to go to Longbourn, then, at some point?"

Just the mention of it brought such a wave of sudden homesickness that Elizabeth could at first only nod in response, and then note that Mary might be desirous of returning home, and perhaps she could attend her there. He promised her an immediate outing to Richmond, as well; the weather looked fine, and there was no reason why they could not go that very day, after he made a few quick calls around the neighbourhood – just the two of them, in the phaeton.

"Thank you," she said softly. "That does sound like just the thing I need, right now."

"Then you must tell me what you need more often, and I must think to ask you, if you do not," he said.

She responded simply by seeking his embrace, feeling greatly relieved, and soothed, to stand there and be held tight for a little while, to feel him kiss her forehead. After such a night, there was no greater peace than this.

The delay in Mr. Darcy's departure to Pemberley and the sudden Richmond scheme were explained at breakfast as being for Elizabeth's health; she was not feeling well, and in need of fresh air. She did not look well at all to anyone at the table, and Georgiana assured them she was feeling quite fine aside from the lingering pain in her wrist, encouraging them to go. Catherine told them that she, Mary, and Mrs. Annesley should have no trouble coming up with diversions for Georgiana, who would not be able to play the pianoforte or the harp, or even attempt any needlework so long as her wrist was still in pain.

Darcy made a few quick calls to his closest Curzon Street neighbours, and dashed off notes to a few others elsewhere in Mayfair, asking discreetly if they had heard of any crimes within the neighbourhood. This took little more than an hour and a half, and allowed Mrs. Wright to have the kitchen pack them some cold meats, pastries and other delicacies by way of a picnic, so that by the time Darcy's correspondence was completed, the food was ready, and the phaeton waiting outside.

Darcy helped Elizabeth up into the phaeton, and took up the ribbons, looking back and nodding at the groom who was to ride behind them on horseback, and saying: "Today I want you to be just Elizabeth, my Elizabeth – not Mrs. Darcy."

"I will do my best," said Elizabeth, already feeling much better, and certain she would be even more so when they had left the thick air of the city behind.

In the house, Catherine and the other ladies had very little to do to entertain Georgiana, for soon after Mary had played a few of her friend's favourite songs on the pianoforte, Captains Stanton and Ramsey arrived. The latter expressed his concern, having heard of the previous night's events from his friend, while the former was relieved to learn Georgiana was feeling better.

"I fear this will have to delay everyone's hearing the Fandango," Georgiana said. "Perhaps I should give it over to Lady Julia, to play."

"Absolutely not – we will wait until you are better," Captain Stanton said. "It was your idea, and you must play it, whenever you are well enough to do so."

"Do you think you will at least be able to dance at Lady Tonbridge's ball?" Captain Ramsey asked, with a private smile to Catherine, who had already promised him the first set, the supper set, and the waltz. "If so I must ask you for a dance."

"I had not thought of it," Georgiana said. "It does feel better today, so I hope it should be well enough by Thursday. It might still be bruised, but my gloves will cover it."

"Might I engage you for the second dance, then? Miss Catherine has already promised me the first."

"Yes, thank you, I would like that very much," Georgiana said, wanting to look at Captain Stanton, but unable to, for she wished deeply he would ask her for the first dance.

"If you are unengaged for the first set, I would appreciate it if you would oblige me, Miss Darcy," Captain Stanton said.

"Oh, do dance the supper set with her as well," said Catherine. "Then we all might sit together at supper."

"Very well then – Miss Darcy, might I dance the first set *and* the supper set with you?"

"Yes, I would like that very much."

He then asked Catherine if he might also dance with her, and both captains applied to Mary for her hand in a set. They spoke for some time about their excitement for the ball, until they had exhausted the topic.

"We do have a new invitation to make to you and the rest of your family," Captain Ramsey said. "A friend of ours, Captain Shaw, of the Daphne sloop, came in last week up the Thames – he is to take a few government men to France at the end of the month. He has offered us the use of his cutter, and so we wish to know if your family would like to go sailing up the river."

"Sailing! I have never been sailing!" Catherine said, in a tone that clearly indicated her enthusiasm for the scheme.

"Nor have I," Georgiana said, looking over to Mrs. Annesley to see if she indicated any issues with the idea. Mrs. Annesley gave her a slight nod and said she also had never been sailing, and thought it would be quite an interesting diversion. Mary was less enthusiastic, but still agreed to go, and the group fixed upon Saturday as the day they should plan for, although Mr. and Mrs. Darcy should of course be consulted before then. The captains took their leave, and the viscountess's ball was nearly forgotten in excitement over the sailing outing.

Elizabeth was enchanted by Richmond. She had certainly seen more extensive grounds and more beautiful vistas, even so little travelled as she was, but to encounter them after so long in town was a revelation. They saw a few riders and another phaeton as they entered the grounds, but it was quite peaceful, and a balm to her soul.

Generally, she preferred walking above all else, if she had a choice in how she was to enjoy the countryside. As they took up one of the paths here, however, she realised she had never been out with such a skilled whip before – for skilled her husband most certainly was – and there was a new sort of enjoyment to this, to covering the park at such a rapid pace, but with the crisp air in her face. There being so much less traffic than at Hyde Park, Darcy did not need to focus all of his attention on the horses, and so they were able to comment on all they saw as they rode along: the herd of grazing deer, the stark bare trees, the vast open fields, and the gentleman accompanying a lady who wore the most ridiculous red riding habit with a green hat, which they both agreed made the lady look rather like a strawberry from their vantage.

They made a whole circuit of the park before cutting down one of the lanes that led to the lake, where the groom took up the horses and led them to the water to drink, while Darcy and Elizabeth walked some way down the shore so they might spread out their blanket and picnic in some privacy.

"We must come here much more often," Elizabeth said, once they had laid out the contents of the basket. "At least once a week."

"I would be for this plan," Darcy said, looking closely at her. Although she still appeared tired, there was a light in her eyes and a freshness to her complexion that had been increasingly absent over the past few months. "You do seem much improved."

"I feel much improved," she said, smilingly. "Perhaps all I needed was a little fresh air. I will be quite jealous of you when you go to Pemberley."

"I have been thinking that I should not go. I hate to leave you so soon after – after everything."

"Darcy, you told me that I must tell you of what I needed, but you must admit that this is what *you* need," she said. "I know how important it is for you to look in on the estate, and how concerned you have been over the Corn Bill."

"There is nothing more important than your well-being, Elizabeth. Even now, you will not stop putting everyone else ahead of yourself. I must go because it is what I need; you must stay because Georgiana and Kitty are receiving suitors."

Elizabeth took some time to order her thoughts, for she was not quite certain how to explain what she wished to explain. "Darcy, I do not know that you can understand how impossible it seemed two years ago that Jane and I should both marry for love, and also be able to live comfortably, much less well. We may not have fretted about it so vocally as our mama, but I assure you, each of us sisters felt it, although perhaps Jane most of all, as the eldest. It is too late for Lydia, but if I am in a position to help Kitty and Georgiana do the same, it is my due. It is what I owe them as a married sister."

"I cannot say that I understand, without having been in your situation, although I may sympathise, and I do," he said. "But you must not neglect yourself at their expense – they would not want it, either. Jane, perhaps, could assist with Kitty and Mary, and attend them to some events."

Jane would be planning for her own family, and should not be exerting herself frequently, Elizabeth thought, but would not say. She was not yet ready to open that topic today, not when she was feeling so much improved, and knew it could not help but upset her, so she only said:

"Perhaps she may assist more, but I do assure you, my well-being is much better than it was yesterday. Go on the morrow as you had planned, stay for a little while, and then to make up for it you may take me here *very* frequently when you return."

"You are quite certain?"

She assured him she was, and then they fully availed themselves of the picnic. For once, Elizabeth found herself fully relaxed, and quite hungry, although the kitchen had prepared far more food than the two of them could ever eat. She could not stop eating for long before he was suggesting she try one of the tarts, or some other kickshaw, and although she was by now familiar with almost all of Cook's work, she still appreciated how attentive he was.

They offered the quite-substantial remains of their picnic to the groom, and took a little walk further down the lake while he ate. Elizabeth sensed Darcy would stay as long as she wished to, and so finally she drew herself even closer to his arm, and said that she was ready to return if he was.

They made the ride back in streets thickening with carriage traffic as evening came on. Over dinner at Curzon Street, they were acquainted all in a rush with the sailing scheme, which was readily approved by both Elizabeth and Darcy. Although Darcy would still be at Pemberley on Saturday, he saw no issues with the outing so long as Elizabeth and Mrs. Annesley went. Elizabeth herself was quite excited by the idea of sailing – it was something new, perhaps the marine equivalent of their ride through the park, and it gave her something to look forward to until her husband should return, and they could have another outing to Richmond.

CHAPTER 29

Elizabeth found herself being wakened most reluctantly, far too early in the morning. She waved her arm languidly at her awakener for some time before remembering that it was her husband, rousing her at her own request, and then groaned, opening her eyes. He was already dressed for travelling, and smiling at her fondly in the candlelight and what faint grey of the morning was coming through the windows.

"I hope whenever we all remove to Pemberley, you do not expect us to leave at such an hour," she said, sleepily. "I am glad to see you off, but I must admit I did not have a notion of your leaving *this* early.

"I have no such expectations, and anyway, I expect we shall overnight at Longbourn then, so we may leave at a leisurely pace," he said. "However, I am hoping to arrive by tomorrow noon, so that Richardson and I may start our tour of the farms. I wish to see the state of the farms before we discuss contingencies, although we are still well off of the spring planting."

"How long will it take you, to do your tour of the farms?"

"Three to four days, I expect. After so long away, I wish to give every tenant as much time as he needs to discuss any concerns with me, although it sounds as though all has been well during our absence."

"Please give my greetings to them, and to all of the staff, and let them know I am looking forward to when I may finally meet them all."

"I shall. I expect I will be met with more disappointment and curiosity, particularly from the staff," he said. "I think they begin to feel slighted by our extended absence; I know Mrs. Wright and Mrs. Reynolds correspond frequently, so I expect not a dinner has gone off without Mrs. Reynolds being informed of what a success it was."

Elizabeth smiled at the thought of Mrs. Wright's writing to crow to Pemberley's housekeeper. Mrs. Wright certainly seemed to be enjoying having the family in residence for such an extended period of time; she got a certain light in her eyes whenever Elizabeth informed her they were having guests to dine, and had made her way about the house with a triumphant look for a full week after Georgiana's coming-out ball.

"I hope they do not feel *too* slighted. I am sure there will come a time when we are there more often than we are anywhere else."

"I certainly hope so. I will explain to Mrs. Reynolds that we stay for the benefit of your sisters; she is very fond of Georgiana, so I am sure the notion of this being for Georgiana's sake shall make her more supportive, and the rest of the staff will follow."

"That is a fine plan," Elizabeth said. "Now, I have been tarrying you far too long. You should go."

"You are quite certain that you are good with my absence? I may still cancel the trip."

"I would not say I am *good* with your absence, but I am fine to bear it," Elizabeth said. "I am feeling much refreshed today, even with waking at this horrid hour. We only have Lady Tonbridge's ball, our sailing outing, and a few other minor engagements – it should be a fine week. But you must write to me; that is my requirement. Nothing but a letter so fine as your last shall do."

"Very well, then, I shall write to you," he said, leaning down to kiss her good-bye before he slipped out of the room.

Elizabeth smiled against her pillow long after he had gone, unable to go back to sleep despite a certain aching tiredness brought on from having woke so early. As miserable as she had been, two nights ago, she felt the good that had come out of it – a new openness between them, and the realisation that he was right, she should be more thoughtful about her own needs.

It troubled her to think about the one thing they had not yet been open about – it would be her topic to raise, when the time came, but once again she pushed it from her mind.

The time leading up to Lady Tonbridge's ball passed as pleasantly as it could for Georgiana, given that she was still unable to practise either of her instruments. Her wrist did feel increasingly better, and by the time she woke the morning of the ball, she felt certain that she would be able to dance. Her wrist might still hurt a bit, but it should be bearable. Georgiana flushed as she thought of her partner for the first dance; she had spent quite a bit of time in company with Captain Stanton, but now finally would come her first opportunity to dance with him.

Georgiana's only cause for concern came after Hughes helped her into her dress, and they attempted to put on her gloves. She had thought her glove might go over the wrap on her wrist, which Hughes had been faithfully applying every morning on the surgeon's instructions, but it did not. She could hardly go to the ball without gloves, particularly with her wrist wrapped, and so she asked Hughes to remove the wrap, once again exposing a wrist that had turned very ugly colours in its bruising, and was still swollen. Georgiana's glove did fit without the wrap, but she found her wrist hurt a little more in its absence.

She was determined to enjoy herself, however, and spent the short carriage ride there in a state of increasing anticipation. The viscountess was as cheerful as ever, and many of their acquaintances from the musical club were there, greeting the family as they made their way in. Georgiana could not attend their conversations as she would have liked to, however; she was too distracted, looking out for Captain Stanton. She finally saw him enter along with Captain Ramsey, both of them dressed fashionably, but not flashy. Georgiana knew Kitty would be disappointed that they were not in uniform, but for her own part Georgiana did not mind; she thought Captain Stanton looked very well this evening.

The captains made their way over to the family, exchanged greetings, and inquired as to the absence of Mr. Darcy. His having gone to Pemberley was explained, and Georgiana and Elizabeth were applied to for their description of Derbyshire and the estate, so that the time leading up to the first set went quickly.

When the viscountess called for the dance to begin, Captain Stanton offered Georgiana his arm to escort her to the floor, and said, softly: "Miss Darcy, do let me know if your wrist hurts at all during the course of the set, and we may step out."

"I will, thank you."

Georgiana need not have worried at all about her wrist while she was dancing with him, however. Any time the dance caused his hand to touch hers on that side, he gave her just the slightest of touches, and it became clear that he was doing so deliberately, as his contact with her other hand was more natural. He was a good dancer, though perhaps not so good as Lord Alfred, and fairly quiet through the course of the dance, although she found it to be a comfortable sort of quiet. One of them would occasionally remark on something, and they would exchange a few comments, and then return to silence. She felt no urgency to be talking while it was silent, she simply enjoyed the dance.

Captain Ramsey was not quite so careful with her wrist, and far more talkative, so that what little time Georgiana had for reflection during their set was spent in thinking what a good match he was for Kitty. She danced the next few sets with gentlemen from the musical club, glad to not have any partners she did not know, and common topics for conversation. Her poor wrist, however, continued to take the abuse of hand after hand catching hers, and she was very glad when the viscountess announced the supper set, and she was returned to the gentle touches of Captain Stanton.

"How is your wrist holding up?" he asked her, a bit into the dance.

"It hurts a little," she admitted.

"Do you wish to stop?"

"Oh no, it is nothing I cannot bear. And you are very careful," she noted, in a tone of some embarrassment.

They had begun the set next to Captain Ramsey and Catherine, so that they might all go into supper together, and they all conversed like old friends throughout the meal. Sitting with two people so convivial as Catherine and Captain Ramsey ensured that they never lacked for a subject, and the only difficulty for Georgiana was that she must take care to only request servings of food she could eat with one hand. If anyone at the table who was unacquainted with her injury noticed she was doing so, however, they did not say anything.

They saw Lady Julia as Captain Stanton was escorting Georgiana back to the ballroom, and went over to greet her. Lady Julia had embraced the trend for diaphanous ball gowns, if her current dress was any indication, and Georgiana did not at all like the look she gave Captain Stanton as he approached.

"Captain Stanton, Miss Darcy, it is so good to see you," she said. "How are you enjoying the ball so far?"

"It has been lovely," Georgiana said.

"Lady Tonbridge always puts on quite the event," Lady Julia said. "Oh, there is Mr. Albury! You must wait here while I introduce you to him. He is not quite my type, but he absolutely doats on ladies with musical talent."

The latter was said in an aside to Georgiana, but still loud enough that Captain Stanton could hear, and Georgiana stood beside him in helpless mortification as they waited for Lady Julia to return.

"Mr. Joseph Albury, this is Miss Georgiana Darcy, and Captain Matthew Stanton," said Lady Julia, returning to them accompanied by a very plain but kindly looking young man. "They are in the musical club with me."

"Oh, indeed?" Mr. Albury asked. "Might I ask what you play?"

"I play the cello," Captain Stanton said. "And Miss Darcy plays both the pianoforte and the harp."

"Miss Darcy – I did not realise you also played the harp!" Lady Julia exclaimed.

"I must admit I much prefer the pianoforte, although there is a piece I have been working on for the harp that I quite love," Georgiana said, pleased to be rewarded with a small private smile from Captain Stanton. "Besides, you play so well we have no need of additional harp performances."

This was true; Georgiana readily admitted to herself that Lady Julia was the superior player to her, although found it a bit disappointing that the lady did not take any risks, as many of the other players in the club did. She preferred pieces she seemed to have utmost confidence in playing, and then exhibited them very well.

"I am sure you are being modest, and even if you are not, to play the harp as well when you are so skilled on the pianoforte is quite impressive," said Lady Julia.

"Indeed, I find it exceedingly impressive," Mr. Albury said. "I should very much like to hear you play sometime, however, for now I wonder if I might have your hand in a dance."

Georgiana was not engaged for the next set, and told him he could. This, of course, left Captain Stanton to ask Lady Julia for her hand in that set, which Georgiana realised was likely the lady's purpose for the entire exchange.

Mr. Albury proved to be a fine enough dancer, but it was during his set and the others following that Georgiana found her wrist getting increasingly worse. The constant contact on her hand from the other dancers brought increasing pain, and she could feel it swelling against the confines of her glove. She knew she should begin refusing requests to dance, she knew she should sit out the rest of the ball, and yet she could not bring herself to do so. Captain Stanton had not asked for her hand in the waltz, but she longed for him to do so, and she was unwilling to give up the opportunity.

Georgiana felt a great deal of relief, therefore, when the viscountess announced the waltz, and she determined that if Captain Stanton did not ask her for the dance, she would refuse anyone else who did. She stood in fear that Mr. Albury or some other gentleman would make his way over to their party, or that Captain Stanton would not. Captain Stanton did come over, however, with Captain Ramsey, who made the formalities of asking for Catherine's hand and being given permission by Elizabeth, although they had all known the dance to be long-promised.

"Miss Darcy, would you do me the honour?" Captain Stanton asked, then, looking to Elizabeth. "With your permission, of course, Mrs. Darcy."

"Yes, I would like that very much," Georgiana said, waiting for Elizabeth to nod before she gave him her hand and allowed him to lead her to the floor.

Georgiana managed the Marche well enough; indeed, she felt more aware of Captain Stanton's hands, one placed upon her shoulder, the other delicately grasping her hand, than she felt the pain in her wrist. The trouble began for her as soon as they had transitioned to the Pirouette. To hold her hand above her head, grasping his, required her to bend her wrist and keep it bent in a way that she had not done all night, and it was already throbbing. She might have continued with the dance anyway, but her eyes welled with tears of pain, and in a dance where their eyes were to be on each other constantly, a far less observant man than he would have noticed immediately. His hand tightened around her waist, pulling her slightly closer, and her breath caught in her throat.

"You are unwell," he said.

"It is my wrist," she admitted. "I cannot keep it bent like this."

"Come," he said, simply, and escorted her from the floor; his hand on the small of her back and her memory of how close he had held her the only pleasant thing about the entire situation.

Elizabeth, Mary, and Mrs. Annesley met with them immediately, encouraging her to sit, Mrs. Annesley fanning her as though she had taken faint. Captain Stanton disappeared for a while and then returned with both a glass of wine and an ice. He placed the wine glass in her good hand, and then asked the ladies to remove her glove. Her wrist only looked a little worse than it had when Hughes had unwrapped it earlier, but they all still looked horrified at the sight of it.

Captain Stanton then instructed them to hold the ice against her wrist, and after the initial shock of cold, Georgiana sighed heavily at the relief it brought. They opened her fan and placed it in her lap so that she might sit with the ice against her wrist without it being seen by others at the ball, and then they all sat around her, looking concerned. There were more concerned parties to come, as well, once the waltz was over – Catherine and Captain Ramsey had noticed them leave the dance, as had the viscountess, Lady Julia, and Mr. Albury, and they all came over after it was done with expressions of worry and hopes that she should soon be recovered. Georgiana received their concerns as gracefully as she could, but she felt only embarrassment and frustration.

CHAPTER 30

Georgiana's wrist was much improved in the morning, but Elizabeth and Mrs. Annesley still agreed that the surgeon should be summoned to examine her. He arrived, looked at her wrist, chastised her as much as a man of his position could for abusing it so, and said that it should be fully rested for a few days. He left the family with instructions to produce a sling similar to the one Captain Stanton had made, and to ensure that she wore it.

Fabric for the sling was located by Mrs. Annesley, who tied it together and placed it sternly in the correct position, but did give Georgiana a gentle pat on the shoulder when she was done. Georgiana was encouraged by all to rest, and this she did, waking from a shallow sleep to go down to the drawing room. There she was informed that the captains had called, that they had stayed nearly an hour, and that they had left with sincerest wishes to see her returned to health.

Georgiana, not desiring to be around company, made her excuses and went to the conservatory, so that she could fully settle into the despondency that wanted only a lack of distractions to overwhelm her. She could not help but think back to the ball with regret and disappointment, and continuing mortification at being seen by everyone not acquainted with her injury as one of those young ladies who fainted away at the slightest thing. And even to those who were, it was such a little thing to be overcome by. What must Captain Stanton think of her? To have fought in battles, he must have seen a great many wounds, and yet she could not even make it through a waltz with so little as a sprained wrist.

He had certainly been all kindness and attention, though. That she remembered pleasantly, and when she finally allowed her mind to turn to the way he had held her, just before escorting her from the floor, she still found the thought of it made her breath quicken. These thoughts were interrupted when Catherine came into the room. She was carrying her sketchpad; she did not seem to have come with any intent to interrupt, and indeed, immediately said:

"Oh, there you are! I am sorry – I did not mean to disturb you. I will go out to the garden."

"No, please stay," Georgiana said. "I do not mind a little company."

Catherine sat and sketched in silence for a while, but she was of too sociable a temperament to stay so for long.

"Mr. Albury called," Catherine said. "He expressed his concern that you were unwell. I hope we were right to not come and get you."

"Indeed, you were," Georgiana said. "I am ready for *your* company, not for a new acquaintance I do not have any particular interest in."

"Oh, good – Georgiana, I hope you do not mind my saying so, but I was sorry to see you have to sit out the waltz. I was so hoping Captain Stanton would ask you, and pleased to see he did, but then we saw you had to leave. It must have been so disappointing."

"I am not sure which was worse – the disappointment or the embarrassment," Georgiana admitted, her throat tight with emotion at her friend's concern and her own remembrance of the event. "I so wanted to dance that dance."

"You will have other opportunities – I doubt that is the last time he will ask you to waltz," Catherine said. "He looked very worried about you."

"He is a gentleman; of course he would be concerned."

"That is one explanation."

"How were your dances with Captain Ramsey?" asked Georgiana, unwilling to allow herself to speculate on any other possible explanations, or how she would have felt about them.

"Quite lovely," Catherine said, her countenance brightening immediately. "Although – he was very interested in my opinion of Bath. He is thinking of settling there, with the peace. I think – I think he meant to know if I should be interested in settling there, too."

"Do you think he means to make you an offer of marriage?"

"Oh, do not make me answer that question! I so hope he will, but I do not mean to risk my luck."

"Would you be interested in settling in Bath?"

"I do not know. He says it has a great number of diversions, plenty of assemblies and opportunities to go to the theatre, and I have always wanted to try the mineral baths. I would want to visit it, though, and then make up my opinion. Have you ever been?"

"I have not, but I certainly would visit you if you do settle there," Georgiana said, smiling. She was glad Catherine had come into the conservatory; Kitty's prospects were a far more positive place for her thoughts to dwell than focusing on her own situation following the ball.

The requirement that Georgiana wear the sling meant that she could not participate in the shopping outing Elizabeth and Jane had planned for later in the morning, to purchase new dresses for Jane's growing figure. Georgiana encouraged them all to go without her, however; and in the end she was able to convince all but Mrs. Annesley, who, in deference to her original purpose of employment, would stay behind with Georgiana.

Elizabeth, Mary, and Catherine, therefore, rode with Jane in the Bingleys's carriage to one of their favoured clusters of shops. Elizabeth had fortunately found that as visible evidence of Jane's pregnancy increased, she was no longer wracked with the same level of jealousy as she had been before. She had attuned herself to the idea of Jane having a child when she, perhaps, would not, and she found herself able to attend to Jane's descriptions of the delights and difficulties of being with child with genuine happiness and sympathy.

They spent much of their time at the modiste in seeing Jane fitted for new dresses, but Elizabeth discovered several bolts of muslin she thought her youngest sister should like, and showed them to her sisters, asking if they approved of them for Lydia. Rarely did a letter go by from Lydia when she did not ask for money or some manner of advancement for her husband, although she was fortunately still an indifferent correspondent, so the requests were not frequent. Elizabeth, however, preferred to send things she knew her sister would need. She feared that any money that was sent might merely end up on a gaming table in front of Mr. Wickham, and if she sent fine fabric, at least it could be turned into new dresses, which she knew Lydia would appreciate.

The fabric was approved of for Lydia, and Kitty presented a fan she thought her younger sister would also like, which Elizabeth readily added to their purchases. Mary had little interest in any shopping, but sat companionably with Jane while she was measured, and Elizabeth, who did not turn her mind to Lydia quite as often as she perhaps should have, now felt her sister's absence. Yet she also saw the impossibility of Lydia being here with them – she would have been darting around the store, all giggling and silliness, drawing Kitty to follow her and making Mary more severe in censure. With some time away from Lydia and their mother, her unmarried sisters had improved substantially, and Elizabeth only hoped such improvements should last when they returned to Longbourn. Kitty, at least, would not return for some time – so long as Captain Ramsey continued to court her, there was no doubt of her staying in town.

When they returned home, it was clear Georgiana was agitated, and as soon as it was polite to do so, she informed them that there had been another letter from Viscount Burnley. Elizabeth was immediately concerned, but also hopeful – it was too soon after his last letter for him to have written them casually, but perhaps he was refuting the rumours of his engagement. When they had all settled in the drawing room, she opened the letter, and first silently read:

"It is my understanding that reports of a nature I had much rather keep private have now escaped this county, and from thence I can only imagine it will be a little time before they make their way to London, if they have not done so already. Although I should much rather impart the truth behind such reports at a more appropriate time, my respect and esteem for you and your family is such that I wished to do so immediately.

"I am engaged to be married to Miss Amelia Foster. She is an old friend of the family – her family's home neighbours our own, and they are close enough acquaintances to have called to pay their respects at such a time. Miss Foster and I came to an agreement and had been of hopes that we might keep the engagement concealed until the appropriate time, but the news spread regardless.

"I know it would be impossible for your family to wish me joy at such a time, when we are all still mourning my brother. I hope you will understand, however, that this has made such a time more bittersweet than it has any right to be.

"Please accept my continuing wishes for the health and happiness of your family.

"Your devoted servant,

"VISCOUNT BURNLEY"

Elizabeth wished deeply that her husband was here; although he might be equally upset by it, he would at least be able to consider reading the letter aloud without his eyes filling with tears of concern for their sister. Then she reflected that the letter should not be read aloud immediately, that its contents should be given, gently, to Georgiana before the rest of them.

"I apologise," she said. "There is some news here that I would wish to impart to Georgiana first. Georgiana, perhaps we could go to your chamber?"

They made their way up the stairs silently, although Elizabeth knew Georgiana must have sensed that the news was not good. They stepped into Georgiana's room, and Elizabeth encouraged her to sit, before confessing the letter's contents.

"He confirms his engagement to Miss Foster," she said, softly, handing over the letter. "I do not understand how such a thing could have happened, when he devoted so much time to you."

Georgiana took the letter, and spent some time studying it. Her eyes filled with tears, but she seemed otherwise in control of her emotions.

"I believe I understand what happened," she said. "He has been in love with Miss Foster all this time, although he could not afford to marry her as a second son – assuming what Lady Catherine said about her dowry is true. Once he gained inheritance of the dukedom and the family estate, such a barrier was gone."

Elizabeth considered Georgiana's theory, which did make a great deal of sense. He had indicated Miss Foster to be an old friend of the family, which meant they must have spent much time in company, enough time, perhaps, for a love to form. So he had gone to London knowing he could not encourage such an attachment, and there had been Georgiana, and her thirty thousand pounds. Then his brother had died, and he had distanced himself from their family immediately – not even calling to take his leave from a young lady he had paid very dedicated attentions to over the last few months. Perhaps he had thought that with the distance, and his family in mourning, any expectations of him would be lessened.

Elizabeth was distracted from her thoughts by Georgiana's first sob, as the poor girl broke down finally, and she sat down beside her sister and embraced her.

"He was only after my fortune, too," Georgiana said. "And I thought him so interested in me. I was so foolish. How will I ever know if any man truly loves me?"

Georgiana could only be referencing Mr. Wickham, and Elizabeth felt the sting of having brought Wickham into the family.

"He at least did not make you an offer of marriage, that you might have felt compelled to accept," Elizabeth said. "Perhaps he was too much of a gentleman to make an offer while he felt his heart bound to another."

"Or perhaps he felt his brother would do something stupid eventually, and he would gain the inheritance, and I was just his back-up plan if that did not happen."

"Oh, Georgiana, it makes me sad to hear you sound so bitter."

"I do not mean to. But twice now I have been fooled into believing that a man had affection for me, when his real interest was in my dowry."

"I know," Elizabeth said, hugging her closer. "But there is perhaps one thing that you should consider as positive to come out of this event. He has used you ill, and he has damaged your trust, but what I have not heard you say is that he has broken your heart."

"No," Georgiana said, looking startled. "No, he has not."

Only after Elizabeth had left to acquaint the rest of the household of the news could Georgiana turn her full attention to her sister's statement that Lord Alfred had not broken her heart. Elizabeth was right – she had felt betrayal, most of all, upon hearing the news in the letter, but at no point had she felt jealousy over this Miss Foster, that she should be the one marrying Lord Alfred. At no point had she despaired over never receiving his attentions again.

Once she had affirmed such a conclusion, she turned her mind to why this was, and from there it was only a little while before she arrived at the truth: Lord Alfred could not break her heart, because she was in love with Captain Stanton. It hit her with the same overwhelming shock that his holding her close had; it rushed up past her and she understood that she had been in this state for some time, but had not allowed herself to admit it. It was not a childish infatuation with a new, handsome acquaintance; her affections were far deeper than what she had ever felt for Mr. Wickham, or even Lord Alfred.

She spent some time merely sitting there, adjusting to her realisation: she was in love; she was in love with Captain Stanton. Such thoughts were eventually followed, however, with the consideration that little would come of it unless he was also in love with her, and she had no notion of whether he was. He often sought her conversation, but he was not nearly so particular in his attentions as Lord Alfred had been. She had not been so, either, however, she was forced to admit. Perhaps he was as cautious with his heart as she was with hers, and now that she had realised her own love, she would have to take care to indicate it to him. The thought of this filled her with terror; she had no idea how to go about anything resembling a flirtation.

She went down to dinner occupied with these thoughts, and was unprepared for such expressions of concern and sympathy as her family gave her. They felt sorry for her; they all agreed Lord Alfred had behaved outrageously, to have so obviously courted her and then immediately become engaged to another – while in mourning, no less. Georgiana listened to them with lingering unease, reminded again of how deceived she had been. Even if she was able to indicate where her heart lay, to Captain Stanton, how was she to ensure that he would not deceive her, as well? Everything about him indicated that he was a most upstanding gentleman, that he was not a man who would do such a thing, but she would have said the same thing about Lord Alfred, before all this had happened.

Elizabeth, after breaking the news of Lord Alfred's engagement to Georgiana, had informed Mary, Catherine, and Mrs. Annesley, and then written two letters. The first was an express to her husband, informing him of the news. She had told him she did not see any reason for him to curtail his time at Pemberley, as Georgiana was taking the news fairly well, but she had thought he would want to know. The second was a note to Colonel Fitzwilliam, to be delivered to the Fitzwilliams's town house by servant. As Georgiana's other guardian, she thought it right that he be informed, as well, and she also hoped that perhaps as a second son himself, he might be able to provide Georgiana with some perspective. She had invited him to dinner, or perhaps tea, if by chance he was free for either. He had penned back a note expressing his concern and telling her that he was engaged to dine with a colleague at White's shortly, but would see if he could come by for tea later.

He did come, and was announced by Mr. Miller, to the surprise of everyone else in the household. Elizabeth poured him a dish of tea, and quietly thanked him for having come as she handed it to him.

"I was very sorry to hear of your disappointing news today, Georgiana," he said. "Particularly when combined with your injury. This must have been a very trying week for you."

"No, it has not been my greatest week," she admitted. "I cannot believe I was so deceived."

"We were all deceived by him, Georgiana," Elizabeth reminded her.

"Indeed, my mother seemed certain he would make an offer soon," Colonel Fitzwilliam said. "Perhaps he would have, if his brother had not been killed."

"And I might have accepted him," Georgiana said. "I might have married a man who was only pretending to care for me."

"I would not say that," Colonel Fitzwilliam said. "I do believe he enjoyed your company, and that he did have some affection for you, although it must not have been so deep as what he felt for Miss Foster. We younger sons are not able to marry whomever we choose."

"But you cannot deny that he would have had no interest in me, without my fortune."

"No, that I cannot deny. But I do think you could have been very happy together. I think you could have had a very good marriage." Colonel Fitzwilliam said. He saw no need to tell her that it was possible in such a marriage that some of Georgiana's money would be used to set up Miss Foster as Alfred Mallory's mistress somewhere.

"Perhaps you are right." Georgiana thought it would be unkind to state that she hoped for something more in marriage; she hoped for love, not simply affection combined with a need for thirty thousand pounds. She hoped for what Edward would have to be exceedingly lucky to achieve himself, to find and fall in love with a lady whose fortune was compatible with his situation. She let the subject flag, therefore, and eventually the group moved on to other, more pleasant topics.

CHAPTER 31

Georgiana made it immediately clear during breakfast on Saturday that she would not hear of staying home from the sailing outing. Everyone involved was aware of her injury; she would wear her sling as directed, but she could not possibly bear to miss it. They all agreed she should not, and thought she certainly deserved something to cheer her spirits after the events of the week.

Mrs. Annesley cleverly sewed one of her shawls to the sling, so that it would not be visible to casual eyes, and, wearing them both over her pelisse, she got into the carriage with the rest of the party. Any diversion that got her out of the house after staying in the previous day would have been refreshing, but her anticipation for this particular event was so great that she found her stomach churning as they made the drive down to the river. She must find a way to indicate her feelings to Captain Stanton, and as they travelled, she fixed upon a plan – she would observe Catherine in her interactions with Captain Ramsey, for although Catherine was by no means a flirt, she certainly had made her affections clear enough, and there must be things that Georgiana could learn by watching her more closely.

The carriage left them quayside, where both captains were standing, together with another colleague of theirs, a pleasant-looking man of average height, wearing a slightly different uniform jacket than those of Captains Stanton and Ramsey, which Catherine quietly explained as due to his being a Commander, and lower in rank than the other men, who were Post Captains, although all were given the title of Captain in address. They approached, and asked if they could be introduced.

"This is Captain Shaw, who has been so good as to lend us the use of his cutter," Captain Ramsey said. "Captain Shaw, this is Mrs. Darcy, Miss Darcy, Miss Bennet, Miss Catherine Bennet, and Mrs. Annesley."

"I am pleased to make your acquaintance, ladies," Captain Shaw said.

"We cannot thank you too much for your kindness," Elizabeth said. "None of us have been sailing, and we are very much looking forward to it."

"It is nothing," Captain Shaw said. "I can certainly spare it for the day. I wish I was able to go with you – you have a fine breeze and should have quite a nice trip. However, I cannot complain about missing a day of leisure, when so many of my colleagues are on shore and I am still fully employed. I must leave you now, but I hope you will enjoy your outing."

They all said goodbye, indicating their gratitude, and then Captains Stanton and Ramsey told them they should go up the quay, to a boat with two masts. It was not nearly so large as many of the other ships they saw out on the river, but still more than large enough to hold them all comfortably. It was well below the side of the quay, so that they should all have to step down into it, and Captain Ramsey did so first, the boat rocking slightly as he did so.

"You will all have to mind your step carefully," he said. "Do we have any volunteers to go first?"

"I will!" Catherine said, walking over to the edge of the quay.

Captain Stanton was standing there, to assist her down, but before he could so much as take her arm, Catherine had jumped down into Captain Ramsey's arms, the boat rocking violently as she did so, but neither of them very concerned about its doing so. Georgiana watched Catherine give him a broad smile, watched the way Kitty held his eyes as she did so, and the way her hands lingered on his arms until Captain Ramsey asked her to sit on the other end of the boat, to help stabilise it.

Elizabeth, Mary, and Mrs. Annesley were all far more careful in their descent, requiring Captain Stanton to take their arms and assist them down to Captain Ramsey. Georgiana waited so that she could be the last, trying to work up the nerve to mimic at least some of Catherine's actions. When she finally walked up to Captain Stanton, though, she felt the import of the moment so deeply that she could hardly meet his eyes.

"How is your wrist, Miss Darcy?" he asked.

"I have been required to wear a sling until it is better," she said, moving her shawl slightly with her good hand so that he might see how it had been concealed.

"Ah, very clever," he said. "And I am so glad you have been able to join us."

"I am too. I would not have missed this for anything."

"Now, let us make sure you get into the boat safely," he said, then, to Captain Ramsey: "Be sure to mind her wrist."

Georgiana had expected him to take her arm, as he had all the others except Catherine, she had thought perhaps she might be able to attempt some sort of lingering touch as Catherine had done to Captain Ramsey.

169

Instead, however, she found his hands on her waist, picking her up entirely and then lowering her down into the boat, where Captain Ramsey helped her settle. She told herself it had been the most expedient, the safest way to do things, and yet she still required a few moments to regain her breath, so unexpected and so delightful his touch had been.

Captain Ramsey indicated where she should sit, an open bench just behind Elizabeth, as Captain Stanton stepped down into the boat. The captains then entered into a period of busyness, sometimes thinking to explain what they were doing to the ladies, but more focused on ensuring they raised a sail up on one of the masts and then got the boat untied from the quay. Captain Stanton stepped to the rear of the boat, then, and put his hand on a long wooden handle he explained to be the tiller, which he would use to steer. Captain Ramsey, in the middle of the boat, gave them a tremendous push off of the quay; Captain Stanton tightened some of the ropes on the sail, and it caught the wind, sending them into motion.

For Georgiana, all other thoughts – even those of Captain Stanton – were quite driven from her mind in those first few magic minutes under sail. The boat glided along the river with an effortlessness that was like nothing she had ever felt. In a carriage, even riding Grace, there was always a feeling that work was going into movement, but here there was nothing except the breeze on her face and the slight sound of water moving under the boat.

The river was crowded with other boats, and it was clear Captain Stanton needed all of his concentration to mind the tiller and the sail. After Captain Ramsey had raised the other sail from the mast in the front of the boat, however, he set about teaching them what was happening.

"Can you feel which direction the wind is coming from?" he asked, holding up a hand in the wind and indicating they should do the same.

"That way!" Catherine said, with a look of intense concentration on her face, pointing up the river.

"Yes, exactly, from the west," Captain Ramsey said, smiling at her. "But we mean to go west, which is a problem because the boat cannot sail straight into the wind. We would go nowhere – we might even be blown backwards!"

The expression on his face was so animated they all laughed, and then he continued: "We are able to sail at angles to the wind, however, so what we are going to do is make our way back and forth across the river, but also make some progress up the river at the same time. This way when we have to return home, we will have an easier time of it – we can let the wind push us. So have no worry about our not being able to return back here."

"Ready to tack, sir?" Captain Stanton asked, in a voice far louder than they were accustomed to hearing from him, and delaying any further explanation.

"Ready, sir," Captain Ramsey said.

"Helm's a-lee," Captain Stanton called out, pushing the tiller and causing the boat to turn sharply. At the same time he did this, they both adjusted the sails so that they were angled differently when the boat completed its turn, and they were gliding across the river, further down from the quay where they had begun.

"We call it a *tack* when we turn the front of the boat through the oncoming wind," Captain Ramsey said. "When we keep tacking up into the direction of the wind, as we are now, we call that *beating up*."

His explanations continued on in this same manner as they continued to weave their way up the river, and Georgiana noticed that whenever he would be silent for any length of time, Catherine was always asking him a question about what this part of the boat or that was, or asking what he was doing with the sails. Eventually, Kitty even asked if she might help, and Captain Ramsey enlisted her to pull on one of the ropes – sheets, he called them – when they tacked in one direction, and to loosen it when they tacked in the other. Catherine did her new duty with the keenest attention and constant smiles to Captain Ramsey; it was clear to anyone in the boat that she was as delighted as any young lady could possibly be, and that Captain Ramsey formed a large part of her delight.

Georgiana watched them for a while, then turned her attention to Captain Stanton at the back of the boat. The traffic on the river had begun to lighten, where they were, but he still focused very intently on all that was happening around him, and Georgiana did not wish to distract him by saying anything. Eventually, though, he looked up and caught that her attention was on him, and offered her a smile, which she returned fully, feeling that it was a little thing, but at least a small step in beginning to show her affection.

They made their way along the river far enough that the city began to thin out on either side, and they saw more people out for pleasure sails, as they were. They had also left the busy quays behind, and Captain Stanton steered the boat directly toward the shore, where he and Captain Ramsey jumped out, to pull the boat up onto the grass. They were all then invited to get out and stretch their legs a bit, and take some refreshments. Captain Stanton pulled a large basket and two blankets from the boat, and made up a little picnic for them, while Captain Ramsey saw that the boat was tied to a tree some way up the bank.

Georgiana found the sensation of walking on dry land to be strange after sitting in the boat for so long. She had become a little accustomed to the feel of the water underneath her, and now it was strangely gone. All the ladies agreed that it was all very handsomely done; it was quite peaceful here, by the water, and they had been growing a bit hungry. Georgiana sat down with Elizabeth and Mrs. Annesley, ensuring there was ample space beside her, and then doing her best to look up at Captain Stanton and invite him with her eyes to sit beside her. Whether she was successful or whether he simply wanted to do so of his own accord she could not tell, but he did sit beside her, offering them all wine and such delicacies as the basket had to offer. There was quite a lot of food, and all of it very good; Georgiana assumed it to have been prepared by the Earl of Anglesey's kitchen.

"So how do you find you like sailing, Miss Darcy?" he asked her, when they had all settled into eating.

"Oh, I quite love it!" she said, overcome with enthusiasm and not thinking for the moment about any means of showing affection. "I must admit, I had always wondered how you are able to sail wherever you are needed, regardless of the direction of the wind. Now that Captain Ramsey has explained how we kept tacking to get here, I feel I understand."

"Ah, you do understand! The difference is that in a large square-rigged ship, it is a much larger undertaking to tack," he said, taking three Naples biscuits and placing them on his plate to act as sails, in order to further his explanation. "You see, if the wind is coming in this direction, we must swing the front of the ship all the way through the oncoming wind, so that we might catch the wind again, here. If the ship is not going fast enough, it will get stuck where there is no wind to propel it, and then it is very difficult to get it moving again. We call that missing stays. So if the conditions are not optimal, we may wear ship instead, coming around like this in a wider turn. It takes longer, but it is safer."

"If one commands a crack frigate like the Caroline, same crew for five years straight, trained as well as ever they can be trained, however, tacking is not quite so substantial an undertaking as Captain Stanton makes it out to be," Captain Ramsey said loudly, from his seat beside Catherine on the other blanket. "I am surprised he even remembers what it means to miss stays."

They all laughed, to hear Captain Ramsey tease his friend, and Captain Stanton took it good-heartedly. Georgiana, determined to show her interest by asking questions if she could, asked him what Captain Ramsey meant by a *crack frigate*.

"It is a term we use for a ship that can execute all of the things it needs to execute quickly, and well," Captain Stanton said, in a tone of some embarrassment. "Taking in or letting out the sails quickly, tacking without ever missing stays, and, most importantly in my opinion, being able to fire three broadsides in less than five minutes."

"And the Caroline could do all of these things?"

"Yes, but as Captain Ramsey notes, I had quite a lot of time to train them to do so. Many captains are not so fortunate to have the same ship for so long as I did."

"Yes, sir, but you are also very modest in all things I have known you to do," Georgiana said, colouring deeply, but determined to continue. "So I must assume at least *some* praise is due in your quarter for your accomplishments."

"I cannot deny that I have been successful," he said. "However much of my success has come from being in the right place at the right time. My station in the American war put my ship in the path of one rich merchant ship after another, so that all we needed to do was be able to chase them down."

"And that you were able to do," Georgiana stated.

"Yes, we were. But it is rather like if you or I were determined to chase after a great fat chicken," he said. "It might run about for a bit, but eventually, we should catch it. What I always longed for was a fight that was at least equal."

"You have mentioned the American frigate that you chased – that it got into port."

"Yes, it is my greatest regret, that we could not catch it in time. There is wealth, certainly, in your merchant ships, and we did catch the occasional heavy privateer, but the only distinction is in taking on a ship of war, of at least your own strength in guns, and the American frigates generally have more than ours. They built them large and heavy, you see, because they were just starting their navy and had no preconceived notions of how many guns a frigate should have. We are only just catching up."

"Still, there must certainly be some honour in the ships you captured."

"No, I cannot deny that. They lined my own pockets, and those of my crew, and England could certainly use such riches to help fight the war against Bonaparte. But it is not the same as an equal fight – I would have given a great deal for an equal fight."

Georgiana did not attempt any consoling remarks at this statement; she knew that with the war over he would not have any chance at an equal fight, that the crack frigate HMS Caroline was in ordinary somewhere in Portsmouth and that Captain Stanton might never go to sea in her again. She let a little time pass, therefore, occupying herself with her food, and then finally asking him to explain more about how their trip back should be different, with regards to the wind.

"I think you will find it very different," he said. "On our way here we were sailing in what we call a close reach, but as we return, the wind will be behind us, pushing us, in what we call a broad reach, or perhaps we shall even get to running, where the wind is blowing directly at our stern. We shall also have the benefit of the tide, which will be pushing us back home."

"Captain Ramsey did say it would be easier to return."

"Yes, much easier," Captain Stanton said. "What a parcel of fools we should look, were we to strand you ladies somewhere short of our destination."

The captains did not at all strand the ladies short of their destination. Captain Ramsey took the tiller on their return, and their return path was much straighter – there was none of the zigging and zagging across the river. Captain Ramsey did still need to mind the other boats on the river, although they were fewer, the sides of the Thames turning into a forest of masts as they made their way down the river, the working boats tied up as evening approached. They all found the return trip colder, with the wind blowing behind them, but Captain Stanton readily provided blankets for all to drape around themselves, so that they should not be bothered by a cold that threatened to cut through even the thickest of pelisses.

Georgiana, who had found herself a place in the middle of the boat right next to Captain Stanton, when the ladies had all re-embarked for the return trip, asked in a tone not nearly so decisive as Kitty's (although she still did ask) if she might help him with something, and he gave her a sheet that she might let in and out as he told her. There was not nearly so much adjustment needed as when they had been tacking up the river, but occasionally Captain Stanton did call for adjustment, and Georgiana would take it up or let it out in her one good hand, quietly helped by Mrs. Annesley whenever she struggled.

The changing tide meant that the boat was nearly even with the quay when they returned, and so there were not the same difficulties of getting in and out of the boat as there had been when they departed. Still, both captains were very attentive in ensuring the boat was tied up properly, and that they each had as much assistance as was needed in stepping from the boat to the quay. Captain Stanton took particular care in attending Georgiana, taking a firm hold on her good arm as she stepped out of the boat. In return, she managed to catch his elbow with her good hand, and softly say a thank you for his assistance.

They all agreed during the carriage ride home that it had been a most enjoyable day, that it was a diversion unlike any other they had ever undertaken, and they should readily agree to do it again, if they were so invited. Georgiana, however, could only think of how she was making progress – however slight – in showing her affections to Captain Stanton, and she retired to rest before dinner with the greatest satisfaction in such thoughts.

CHAPTER 32

Sunday came, with a quiet morning at church, and word from Lord Brandon that he thought the Corn Bill near passage; he expected it should go to committee in the Commons as soon as the morrow. This relieved Elizabeth, and she thought it unfortunate that her husband was from home, and farther from this news than he would have been if he had stayed in town. Still, she knew it would reach him soon enough, and it might mean a quicker return for him, as he would no longer have so much to discuss with Richardson.

She thought tenderly of the letter he had written her, every bit as fine as that of his last absence, just as he had promised, and wondered what he might be doing now. It was likely he had not yet finished visiting all of the tenants, and she thought of him riding the roads she remembered from her visit there. Something he had said to her, on that sleepy morning of his departure, rose again to her mind, of how he would allow the tenants as much time as they desired, to discuss any concerns with him. Her mouth quirked in a little smile as she was reminded of how she had once thought him so proud, so above his company, this husband of hers who must now be sitting down at the worn dining tables of every single one of his tenants, for so long as they chose to speak to him.

They stayed inside Monday, wishing to keep Georgiana company, and Mrs. Annesley and Catherine would stay behind with her in the evening, for her wrist was still not well enough to play. Even if it had been, Georgiana was certain she would be very out of practise when she was finally able to take up her instruments again. Elizabeth and Mary were making their way out the front door to the carriage when they heard the sound of a horse's hooves coming up fast at them. Elizabeth looked up, and was entirely shocked to see that it was Captain Stanton. He pulled the horse – Elizabeth assumed it to be Phoebe – up to a hard stop just before their carriage, and said:

"Do not go tonight. There is rioting and looting in the West End and there is no telling how far it will spread. Have your man take the carriage back around and then get everyone into the house. Ramsey is gathering up some men, and he will be here soon."

"Rioting? Why should there be rioting?" Elizabeth asked, feeling suddenly as if she was in some sort of strange, confused dream, and wishing very much that Darcy was there.

"The Corn Bill – the people protest what it will do to the cost of bread," Captain Stanton said. "My uncle's house is nearer to them. We heard the noise and I rode down to see what was happening."

"Is your uncle safe?"

"Yes, he is fine, although the house is too close to the action for my comfort. He has gone to Lady Tonbridge's home to weather the storm," Captain Stanton said. "Is Mr. Darcy still from home?"

Elizabeth nodded. She was not one usually given to fear, but she felt it now. This was a situation unlike any she had ever faced, or ever would have expected to – their very home, and safety, threatened by this unseen mob. She was not certain it was one Darcy had ever faced, either, but she very much wished for his presence here now, so that they might at least brave the situation together.

"Captain Ramsey will stay the night, then, until we are sure it is safe," he said.

"That is far beyond considerate," Elizabeth said. "We will have a bed prepared for him immediately."

"I hope things are not so bad that he may have use of it," Captain Stanton said, grimly. "It may be a very long night. He should be here soon – keep your doors locked until he arrives. I must leave you now. Please give the rest of your family my best wishes."

He cantered off at this, and Elizabeth ordered the carriage sent back around, then rushed back into the house with Mary. Georgiana and Catherine had seen Captain Stanton ride up from the drawing room window, and greeted their return with confusion. Elizabeth acquainted both them and Mr. Miller with the news of the riots; Mr. Miller left them and returned with some of the male servants, all of them armed with pistols and taking up stations at the front door and windows, after tightly shuttering the latter.

"We have plans for this sort of event, my lady," he told Elizabeth. "You need not worry."

Yet worry Elizabeth did, and after she had requested Mrs. Wright have a room made up for Captain Ramsey, she joined the other ladies in the drawing room, where they all sat, silent and tense. Mrs. Annesley had spent the most time in town of any of them, and she could never remember anything the likes of this happening. There was occasional unrest, but never such a widespread threat to the homes of the genteel.

Perhaps a half-hour later, there came a knock at the door, and Mr. Miller opened it in his usual manner, but flanked by a footman and a groom, each of them carrying a pistol. Elizabeth rushed up to stand behind them and was relieved to see it was Captain Ramsey, and he was not alone. Behind him stood perhaps a dozen men – clearly seamen, large burly men, most with their hair braided in long pigtails, and each of them carrying an axe or a spear in his hand.

"Greetings, Mrs. Darcy," Captain Ramsey said, looking more serious than usual, although not overly worried. "Are your family all well?"

"We are startled by the news of the rioting, but otherwise fine."

"I am glad to hear it. You need not worry about a thing now. Each of these men served under Captain Stanton or myself – they are all trustworthy, and it would be quite a mob that attempts to get past them."

Mr. Miller looked a bit vexed by this statement, as though it was an attack on his staff's ability to defend the house. Yet, Elizabeth thought, even he must admit that a group of seamen who looked every bit like they had known battle and would not mind another tonight was a far greater deterrent to any attack on the house than its liveried servants, wielding their pistols with varying degrees of awkwardness.

Elizabeth asked if Captain Ramsey would introduce the men to her, and as he did, each bobbed his head stiffly in greeting. Captain Ramsey said he should like to have the men stand in front of the house in shifts, six men on, six off, through the night, ready to call the other shift out at the least sign of the rioting reaching Curzon Street. They would camp in the entrance-hall, if she approved; they did not wish to disturb the rest of the house.

Elizabeth did approve – although these men were certainly not of the sort she would ordinarily have in the house, if they carried the approval of the captains, that was more than sufficient for her. She asked Mr. Miller to see to moving chairs and bedding into the hall as the men not taking the first shift came in, looking quite uncomfortably at their surroundings and gingerly taking seats in the chairs when the footmen carried them in. Elizabeth asked Captain Ramsey if he would come into the drawing room and sit with them. This he did, and the rest of the ladies were informed of the presence of the men and the state of the riotous crowd, which was growing and moving on from Bedford Square, where they believed the first damage had been done. Mrs. Wright came in, and stood at the edge of the room, waiting quietly until a lull in the conversation, and then she made her way to Elizabeth's side.

"Shall I see to some refreshments for the captain and his men, Mrs. Darcy?"

"Yes, please do. Coffee, tea and port and some light food here in the drawing room," Elizabeth said. "I must admit I have no idea what to feed the men."

"Never you worry, ma'am. My brother is a quartermaster on the Superb," Mrs. Wright said. "I know the naval stomach. Bread, cold beef, cheese, and the remains of the pudding from dinner would go over very well, together with a few bottles of wine from the very front of the cellar. Perhaps we might mull some of the wine, for the men outside – it is quite cold tonight."

"Very well, Mrs. Wright, please make it so, and let them know they shall have as much food as they like. They do look like men accustomed to eating rather a lot."

Mrs. Wright smiled, nodded, and left the room. Elizabeth returned her attention to the conversation, which moved from one nervous, meaningless topic to another. They were all still tense, although much less so now, and Kitty, though looking mildly worried, seemed more pleased that Captain Ramsey was there than anything else.

Only now could Elizabeth really turn her mind to the fact that he *was* here, that both he and Captain Stanton had put in quite a lot of effort to see to their safety – had really treated them as though they were family. Perhaps it did mean that one or both of them wished to become part of the family; or perhaps they were merely being gentlemen, knowing Mr. Darcy had been away from home, and wishing to ensure the safety of a house full of ladies.

Elizabeth could not help but think of the rest of their family and acquaintances. The Bingleys and Hursts came to mind first. She wished Jane was there with her so that she could be certain her sister was safe, but knew Mr. Bingley and Mr. Hurst to both be accomplished shots when hunting, in addition to whatever defence their servants would be able to mount. The Gardiners would be far from the rioting, in Cheapside, and certainly Colonel Fitzwilliam would be seeing to the safety of his family, and perhaps that of Lady Catherine as well. Elizabeth stifled a smile at the thought of Lady Catherine, on her own doorstep, demanding with nothing more than force of will that the mob leave her house alone, and then sobered. She might not like the lady's manners at all, but she did not wish to see her come to any harm.

Their first disruption on the night came with loud voices outside the house. Captain Ramsey rose and left the drawing room, Elizabeth following him into the hall, where the men had risen from their chairs and their meal, and were making their way out the door.

"Let 'im through, Tom, ye damned swab, ee's one man off 'orseback an' ee ain't on the riot. An' ee's wearin' an army uniform."

Colonel Fitzwilliam came in following this, looking somewhat rumpled but mostly amused.

"I came to see if your house was adequately defended," he said. "I see it is in fact the best-defended house in all Mayfair."

The seamen in the off shift followed him into the entrance-hall, some of them looking sheepish, all of them retaking their seats as delicately as men of fifteen stone and more could.

"Captains Ramsey and Stanton have been so kind as to see to some men for our defence," Elizabeth said. "Are your family safe? And Lady Catherine?"

"They are fine – some of my former soldiers are on guard, much the same as your setup here. Lady Catherine is staying with us, much to my mother's delight."

Elizabeth laughed. "I am glad to hear she is safe."

"Only because my mother possesses infinite patience."

"That she does," Elizabeth said. "Will you come into the drawing room and take some refreshment?"

"No, I beg your pardon – I should be off. I came only to see that your family was safe, and now that I see that is certainly the case – " with a respectful nod to Captain Ramsey " – I should get back to the house. Please do introduce me to your friend before I take my leave, though."

"Oh, I am sorry," Elizabeth said. Captain Ramsey had become such a fixture at Curzon Street that it was easy to forget that he had not yet been introduced to all of their family, although Edward did know of him, and his courtship of Catherine. "This is Captain Andrew Ramsey, of the Royal Navy; Captain Ramsey, Colonel Edward Fitzwilliam of His Majesty's 33rd."

"I cannot thank you enough for seeing to the safety of Mrs. Darcy and her sisters," Edward said, shaking Captain Ramsey's hand. "I must admit to being quite worried for them, and concerned at not being able to make my way here any earlier."

Captain Ramsey said all that was proper, and Colonel Fitzwilliam made his bow and left. Elizabeth took advantage of his departure to ask Captain Ramsey if she might have a private word with him, before they returned to the drawing room, and they made their way down the hallway, stepping into the dining room.

"I do of course wish to pay your men for their efforts," she said. "I am not sure what would be appropriate, however. What would you say to ten shillings per man?"

"That is very nearly a half-month's pay," Captain Ramsey said.

"Then let it be a guinea per man, and let them know they shall receive the same for every night they return while the rioting continues."

"There are some among them who were quite happy simply to be fed well," Captain Ramsey said. "They will be very appreciative of your generosity."

"We are very appreciative of their protection, so this perhaps makes us more equal," Elizabeth said. "Let me go see to the money."

Within one of the drawers of the desk in Darcy's study was a little strongbox containing a few hundred pounds in case ready money was ever needed within the house; he had shared its existence with Elizabeth before his first departure to Pemberley. She went to the study and pulled it out now, removing the necessary coins and then returning to the dining room to give them to Captain Ramsey so that he might share them out.

They both returned to the drawing room once the men had been paid, and sat there for only a little while before Elizabeth suggested they should all go attempt to sleep. Everyone rose reluctantly and left the room, Kitty most reluctant of all. Captain Ramsey refused the bedroom that had been prepared for him, although he thanked Elizabeth for the family's kindness; he preferred to stay in the hallway with his men, should anything happen.

The second disturbance on the night came well after Sarah had helped Elizabeth change, and Elizabeth found herself lying in her own bed, wishing once again that her husband was here, if just to give her enough comfort that she might sleep, and instead faced with a bed that felt most empty. The sound of people – loud, angry people – on the street outside reached the room, and Elizabeth rushed to the window. There was a small crowd of perhaps thirty or forty people making its way down Curzon Street, accompanied by the occasional crash – they must have been throwing things through the upper windows. There were not enough people for this to be the full crowd of the riot, merely some offshoot that had found their street. Elizabeth watched as they drew closer to their house, and disappeared from view – they were below her, now, right in front of the house.

"Bugger off, ye whoreson swains – this 'ere 'ouse is defended!" one of the seamen called out below, and the crowd scattered off away from their house, some of the people walking quite quickly, others outright running. Elizabeth took a deep breath, her heart racing, and watched as the crowd continued on down the street. She returned to her bed, but it was some time before she finally fell into a tense, shallow sleep.

Out of everyone at the breakfast table, Captain Ramsey appeared the least exhausted, although by all indications he had slept on a blanket in the entrance-hall. He greeted them all cheerfully, expressed appreciation for Mrs. Wright's seeing to a substantial breakfast for his men, and asked how they had slept. This question was met with middling lies as they all attempted to assure him that they had not been disturbed, and said they had slept well. Kitty made much the same indications as the rest, although her reasoning was different; she had been distracted by his presence in the house, and had even contemplated coming down in her dressing gown when the crowd had come down the street, but the thought of all the other men in the hallway had deterred her.

Captain Stanton was announced while they were still at breakfast, and was invited to join them in the meal, although he had already eaten at the viscountess's. His reason for calling was simply to ensure they had passed the night safely, and to inform them that his uncle and the viscountess were also safe, although the earl's house had not been so fortunate – it had suffered several shattered windows. Compared to houses at the centre of the riot, however, which had been entered by the crowds and utterly torn apart, this was not so severe.

He stayed with them until they had all finished eating, drinking a few cups of coffee but not accepting any food, and taking his leave when the meal was over. Most of the family made their way to the drawing room, but Elizabeth would see Captain Stanton out, and Georgiana saw no reason why she might not follow them. He noticed she did so, and slowed his pace so that he might inquire about her wrist.

"It is much better, thank you," she told him. "I think I might attempt the pianoforte sometime in the next few days and see how it does."

"I am very glad to hear it, Miss Darcy," he said, hesitating. "I hope you were not too worried by the events last night."

"No – we were all a little tense, certainly, but I felt quite safe," she said, gathering her courage to reach out and touch his arm. "I do not know how to thank you and Captain Ramsey for your care for our family last night."

"It is nothing, Miss Darcy. Surely you must know that – that we care deeply for your family's welfare."

Georgiana could not help but think that he had meant to say something else, but could not, and by now they had reached the area where the seamen were standing, and Captain Stanton stopped in front of one of them.

"John Taylor, how do you do?"

"Very well, sir, very well. Spending a night half-on, half-off in a town house, wi' good food an' wine may be the easiest livin' I earned yet," the man said. "Sure beats reefin' topsails on a dirty night."

"That it does," said Captain Stanton. "Although I hope you would go to sea again, if the opportunity arose. And I do hope you shall return here this evening."

"I would surely go to sea again, was you the captain, an' I surely will return this evenin' and as many evenin's as I am needed," John Taylor said, looking cautiously over in Elizabeth's direction. "The lady has been very generous-like with the pay an' I mean to put a little aside. Things has been lean, of late."

"I am very glad we found you, then," Captain Stanton said. "And I do hope you will put a little aside. Good day to you, Taylor."

There were several other men who had served under him, and he spoke to each before he would leave. Georgiana watched him carefully, observing that with these men, his reserve seemed to come across as more of a quiet authority; it was clear each of them respected and esteemed him, and that he cared deeply for their welfare.

Now that the mob had dissipated in the daylight, the streets were deemed passable enough for Elizabeth to send a servant with a note over to the Hursts's town house, asking how they had passed the night. He returned an hour later with Jane's response that they were all fine, although they had been worried, both for themselves, and particularly for the Darcys, with Mr. Darcy away, and so Elizabeth's note had been most soothing to Jane. Elizabeth received a similar note from the Gardiners, who had worried about their nieces, and sent back a quick response, as well as penning an express for Darcy.

The riots continued on for two more nights, although the crowd never again reached Curzon Street. Indeed, the only eventful thing that happened was Mr. Darcy's return on the final evening. By now, the seamen had worked out who should be allowed to approach the door and who should not, and a well-dressed, albeit dusty, gentleman who had arrived in a very fine-looking carriage was surely to be allowed passage. Darcy came in the front door, therefore, looking confused and concerned, and rushing toward Elizabeth to embrace her there in the entrance-hall. He held her so tightly she felt all the force of his worry; it must have been great, for him to hold her so in front of an audience.

"I came as soon as the news of the riots reached me," he said, releasing her. "Are you all well?"

Elizabeth calculated when that would have been, and realised he must have travelled without stopping; he certainly looked exhausted. She had been so shocked by his appearance and then so comforted by his embrace that it was only now that she realised the risk he had taken in arriving at this hour – the papers had been filled with stories of the damage, and among them mentions of the few carriages foolish enough to be out on the streets having been attacked by the crowds, and surely his would have been identified as belonging to a man of fortune, and thusly accosted. The image came to Elizabeth, quite unbidden, of the carriage doors being pulled open, or the whole thing being tipped over, and her husband pulled out into the mob and beaten, and she shuddered a little at the thought of what might happen next.

"Captain Ramsey, do you think a few of your men could see the carriage safely around to the mews?" Elizabeth asked. Captain Ramsey nodded, and instructed one of the men inside to make it so. Elizabeth then turned to her husband: "We are fine – you must have just missed my express. Captain Stanton came and told us of the riots on Monday, and Captain Ramsey has been staying here every night. He brought the men you see outside and in the hall here. There was a little crowd that came down the street Monday night, but the men chased them off, and there has been nothing since."

"I cannot thank you heartily enough, then, for seeing to my family's safety," Darcy said, turning to Captain Ramsey and shaking his hand. "Would you be so good as to introduce me to your men?"

The introductions were made, and then they all retired to the drawing room, where he ate and drank as greedily as a gentleman could do in company from the tray Mrs. Wright brought in, and listened to them all recount the events of the last few days in further detail. After a little while, though, he began visibly drooping, as though the anxiety that had fuelled him in his journey here had left him, but not been replaced by anything else, and Elizabeth suggested they retire.

Elizabeth was all impatience as Sarah helped her out of her dress, and Sarah sensed this, working quickly, with none of her usual small talk. Elizabeth knocked on Darcy's dressing room door before entering – Sarah had worked so quickly there was a possibility she had outpaced Mr. Mason. He called out to her to come through, though, and upon entering the bedroom she found herself enveloped in another embrace, even tighter than he had held her in the hall. She found herself torn between the comfort of finally having him here with them, and anger at the risk he had taken to do so, and at first she let comfort win.

"My God, Elizabeth, I have never felt so helpless in my life as I did in that carriage," he said. "To know that something might have happened to you, to Georgiana, nearly two days ago and there was nothing I might do. And for you to have to face such an event on your own, even if you were safe."

"We were not on our own. Captain Stanton was here before we even knew anything was happening, and then Captain Ramsey after him. Edward came to check on us as well. I daresay even poor Mr. Miller and the servants would have put up a defence if needed," she said. "But *you* very nearly got yourself torn apart by the mob. What could you have been thinking, coming into town at such an hour, with a riot on? Did you not find out through the papers? Did you not see they were attacking carriages?"

He was quite taken aback by her outburst, and it took him some time to speak. "I did not find out through the papers – our neighbour, Mr. Sinclair, has a son who is an attorney in town. He happened to be near Bedford Square when the rioting broke out, and got an express off to his father late Monday. I had called on Sinclair; he knew me to be the only one at Pemberley while the rest of the family stayed in town, so he sent a servant over with the news as soon as he had it."

"Do you have any notion at all of the risk you took? You were in far more danger than any of the rest of us."

"I do travel with a brace of pistols, Elizabeth, and I should rather take such a risk than tarry a night outside town, with no idea of whether you and our sisters were harmed or not."

"What is a brace of pistols against a mob?" she cried. "I cannot stop thinking of you being pulled from that carriage and being beaten – possibly killed. Every time I have a moment to think, that is what I see."

"Elizabeth – " he reached out his hand to clasp her own " – I understand fully what you mean; it is what I faced the entire drive here, thinking of this house being attacked, and you here with no defence. All that I care about most in this world is in this house, and I had no notion of your safety."

"It is not the same! You willingly put yourself in harm's way!" Here Elizabeth gave in to the tears that had been long coming. "What happens to all of us, if something happens to you? And not just Georgiana and I – what of all of the servants, the tenants?"

Elizabeth thought, but could not bring herself to say, that everything was currently without an heir – just the thought of it made her cry far more strongly.

Darcy gave her a deeply sympathetic look before enveloping her in another embrace. "I promise you will be well provided for, should anything happen to me. I know you grew up worrying about what should happen to you and your mother and sisters on the death of your father, but you need never worry about it again. Whenever you like, we may sit in my study and go over the plans for what should happen, on my death. You will always live well, from now on."

"I never had any doubt of that," she said, looking up at him, with a face wet with tears. "But we *should* grow old together. I am two-and-twenty years old – would you see me widowed and without your love for the remainder of my life?"

"I would not," he said, pulling her even closer. "I am sorry, Elizabeth. I cannot say I would not do it again, but I promise you I will think more carefully the next time anything like this happens, although I pray there will never be anything like this again."

Elizabeth cried against his shoulder, still upset, but all of her anger spent. After some time, she felt him wiping the tears from her face, caressing her cheek, and finally kissing her with such an intensity she trembled.

"You see, you cannot deprive me of that," she said, attempting to tease, although a little sob gave her away, and she returned his kiss, hoping that he would feel all of her worry, and soothe it away.

Things moved quickly after that, as they should between a gentleman and a lady who have been deprived of each other's company in most difficult circumstances. She felt his attention torn between kissing her, removing her dressing gown, and pushing her back towards the bed, and found her own similarly divided until she felt the bed beneath her and felt his very familiar and very pleasant weight on top of her. It had been far too long for this.

Some time later, she laid beside him, bereft of even her nightgown and breathing heavily, but feeling sated and much easier in her mind than she had been since he arrived home. She drew closer to him; she loved the feel of his bare skin against her own, warmer somehow than wearing her nightgown, particularly after so many nights of her own empty bed. He seemed terribly exhausted, now, but no nearer sleep than she was.

"I must think of a way to thank Captain Ramsey," he said, absently.

"My hope is that he wishes you to thank him by giving your blessing for him to marry Kitty."

"Mine as well, but still, something must be done beyond that," he said. "He loves a good port; I shall see what Miller has set aside down in the cellar and send him a case. The men – I assume they are being paid?"

"One guinea each per night – Captain Ramsey thought it perhaps overly generous, but I wished them to know our gratitude, and some of them looked quite down at the heels."

"If they made you feel safe, they would have been a bargain at twice that," he murmured.

"Well, then I suppose we have set the standard for riot protection wages," she said. When he did not respond, she looked closely and saw that he was already asleep, and she could not help but kiss his cheek gently, before rising to blow out the candles that remained burning in his bedchamber.

CHAPTER 33

Thursday's newspapers indicated there had been more rioting over Wednesday night, and so it was decided over breakfast – a bit more delicately than in previous mornings, with Mr. Darcy returned to the house – that Captain Ramsey and his men should return again that evening. They were there already when Colonel Fitzwilliam arrived, on horseback, but still causing concern among all in the household.

He was questioned heavily after entering the drawing room and expressing his relief at having received Elizabeth's note earlier in the day, indicating that Darcy had returned safely to the house. He informed them that the Fitzwilliams and Lady Catherine were all still well, and that he had heard no sounds of rioting, so perhaps it had finally run its course.

"Do not tell us you have come for a social call," Darcy said.

"No, I have come with entirely different news," the colonel said. "This news is not so far spread, although I expect it will move rapidly. Napoleon Bonaparte has escaped from exile. He is understood to be moving towards Paris, and all expectations are that he will raise an army. I wished to let Mr. Darcy know in case you had any investments that you should back out of before the news becomes more widely known, and I thought your friends in the navy would wish to know as soon as possible."

The news was so shocking to Georgiana that she could not at first comprehend what it should mean, and she sat, silent and stunned, as the others reacted with every expression of surprise.

"You are quite certain of this news?" Darcy asked. "I do have a little invested that I should like to move if the peace will end. I will do so first thing tomorrow."

"Yes, I am," Colonel Fitzwilliam said. "I was asked to begin recalling my men immediately. We shall have to raise an army to match his, and transport them all back to the continent. A man like Napoleon does not escape in order to negotiate. There will be another war."

Another war, Georgiana realised, meant that Captain Stanton and the Caroline would go to sea, that they should have another chance at the distinction he so longed for. Such thoughts were vindicating to her, until she realised that in going to sea again, Captain Stanton would be very nearly lost to her. After all, he had been gone from England for five years in the course of his previous command.

"Might I let the men know of the news?" Captain Ramsey said, and when Colonel Fitzwilliam nodded in the affirmative, he excused himself to go out to the entrance-hall.

Georgiana looked over at Kitty as he left, and saw her friend looked every bit as stunned as Georgiana felt. The sounds of muffled conversation reached them from the hallway, and someone cried out, "we'll thump 'em again, those frogs, we will!" Then Captain Ramsey re-entered, and, quite purposefully took a seat beside Kitty, which did seem to mollify her a little.

They had little of substance to say about a theoretical war, but it was all they could speak of until Elizabeth, sensing Catherine and Georgiana to be agitated, suggested the ladies retire for the night. Colonel Fitzwilliam refused Elizabeth's offer of having a room made up for him, but said he might drink another glass of port with the gentlemen before leaving, if they were so inclined, which they were.

Georgiana went up silently with the other ladies, and it was only after Hughes had undressed her and she had climbed into bed that she fully allowed herself to think about what another war might mean for her and Captain Stanton. If he would be gone for another five years, or anything like, could she wait for him? There was nothing decided between them, no love confessed, and Georgiana would have to do her best to make things progress to that point in whatever time they had left before he went to sea. In five years, would she be like Caroline Bingley, desperate for an offer from any suitable man who came along? Such thoughts occupied her late into the night, until she finally drifted off to sleep.

Georgiana still woke in time to break her fast with the rest of the family, and was surprised to learn that Captain Ramsey was not with them that morning. He had left very early, telling Mr. Miller to inform them that he must call on the Admiralty immediately, and if they gave him any expectation of his having a command in the coming war, he would have some business he needed to attend to immediately, out of town. They were not to expect him back that evening, therefore, but could consult with Captain Stanton as to whether the men should return; Captain Stanton would arrange it, if they desired the protection for another night.

Catherine entered the room, her eyes red, so that it was clear she had already had this news. She sniffled and made no attempt to eat anything, and Georgiana felt for her. She could not understand why Captain Ramsey might not have waited a little longer to take his leave of Kitty, particularly since he had nearly become a fixture in the house over the last few days. It seemed strange that he should be absent, and in such a way, after giving no indication the evening before that he might leave them.

Over the last few days, Captain Stanton had always called early, while they were still at breakfast, to see that they had passed the night safely. Today, however, he called much later, when they had made their way to the drawing room to wait. He strode in, wearing his uniform, looking even taller than usual, and he stood before them, quickly pulling his hat from his head.

"Good morning," he said. "I must apologise for my absence this morning, although all indications are that the rioting ceased last night, aside from a few bands of ruffians, determined to do a last little bit of damage. I wished to call at the Admiralty as soon as I heard the news of Napoleon's escape had become public."

"Do you have any sense of the certainty of war?" Darcy asked. "When my cousin, Colonel Fitzwilliam, delivered the news last night, he seemed convinced there was no other path."

"War is not yet declared, but preparations are underway," Captain Stanton said, taking a seat beside Georgiana. "I am to return tomorrow to learn what ship I shall be assigned."

"Will you not have the Caroline?" Georgiana asked, feeling a rising panic in her throat that it was certain he would go to sea again.

"I hope so, but there are no guarantees," he said. "They are currently determining which ships can be most quickly readied for sea."

"Is – is Captain Ramsey also to be assigned a ship?" Catherine asked.

"Yes, although like myself, he does not yet know which one," Captain Stanton said. "And I must apologise for not telling you before – he makes his regrets for not taking better leave of your family. I believe he gave some indication that he might need to leave town to get some of his affairs in order before going to sea, and he was indeed required to do so."

Captain Stanton had delivered his message in a tone of utmost kindness, but Kitty still appeared ready to cry. Georgiana felt deeply for her – certainly Captain Ramsey could have found at least a few minutes to take his leave of Kitty before leaving town. She remembered Lord Alfred's rapid departure on the death of his brother, and looked at her friend with even more concern.

"What is involved in preparing a ship for war?" Georgiana asked, both because she was genuinely interested, and she thought it might serve as a distraction for Catherine.

"Quite a lot, and everyone will be attempting to do it all at once," he said. "We must ensure that the ship has ample food and water, as well as all of her supplies – extra sails, cordage, spars, gunpowder and shot. Everything that might be needed for a long voyage, or to begin blockade duty – how I hope we will not be on blockade duty, although I suppose I have been lucky enough in my assignments so far that it is probably my time. There is no tedium quite like blockade duty, sailing back and forth and waiting to see if the French will come out of port."

"What of your crew?" Georgiana asked. "Do you think many of them will return?"

"Most of them I expect will re-enlist – we did quite well in prize money last time, and I feel she was a happy ship. I will have posters drawn up, to attempt to recruit as many men as I can, although you would be amazed at how your seaman manages to find out through word of mouth when a ship he wants to join is preparing for sea. I have hopes I will not have need of the press gang, although many ships will – there are too many of us preparing for sea all at once. Some men will certainly have to be pressed into service."

"Will Lieutenant Campbell still be serving with you?"

"I requested that he be assigned to me, and sent an express to him – his family lives in the west, beyond Plymouth. My other officers, as well, I expect will re-join. I do not have any expectations that I will have a ship smaller than the Caroline, so they will all be needed."

Elizabeth had quietly sent for refreshments after Captain Stanton's arrival, and they came out now. Captain Stanton's morning had been quite busy; he noted that he had barely broken his fast, and was very much obliged to Mrs. Darcy for thinking of him. They all made some selections from the table to assure him that he was not the only one eating, and then returned to their seats.

Georgiana's wrist had by now improved so much that she had no difficulty using it to eat and drink, but she gave it no thought, and was surprised to find herself addressed by Captain Stanton:

"Your wrist appears to be much better, Miss Darcy. I hope we might see you back at the pianoforte soon enough."

"Thank you, it is feeling much better – I might attempt it later today."

"I should very much like to hear you play, but I will not press you," he said. "I know what it is to be uncomfortable with an instrument."

"Yes, I fear how I will sound after going so long without practise."

"I expect you will still play better than any other lady of my acquaintance," he murmured, so that Mary should not overhear him.

The directness of his compliment startled her, and she blushed deeply, unable to meet his eyes. She chastised herself: here had been an opportunity, but she had not been prepared; she had not had the courage to act on it. He stayed only a little longer, all of their conversation tinged with bittersweetness that he would be gone soon, and Georgiana wishing for another chance to attempt to make her heart known.

Such an opportunity did not arise, however, and as he rose to take his leave, she had the mortification of Mr. Miller entering the room to announce Mr. Albury, who had determined the unrest was sufficiently over to resume social calls. There was no possibility of avoiding it; Georgiana must greet him, as he had most certainly called for her. She looked at Captain Stanton with desperation as he gave Mr. Albury a bow, and clarified that he had just been leaving.

"I am afraid we are not the greatest of company right now," Georgiana said to Mr. Albury. "I am not sure if you are aware, but Napoleon has escaped, and we are likely to go to war again. It is news that affects not only our cousin, who is a colonel in the regulars, but also some very close friends of the family who are in the navy."

She summoned all the courage she possessed to look Captain Stanton in the eyes after she said this; he returned her gaze, and gave her the slightest of nods, but she could not tell what he meant by it, and then he was gone, and she was forced to listen to Mr. Albury's exclamations over the news, as he had not yet heard it.

Mr. Albury, after having settled into the news of war beginning again, proceeded on to other topics, which Georgiana attempted to attend to as best she could. He then asked if it would be too much to desire her to play something on the pianoforte, as he had heard such great things from Lady Julia about her skills. Georgiana demurred – if she was not ready to test her wrist in front of Captain Stanton, she certainly was not ready to play in front of someone unfamiliar – and, when he persisted, asking her for just one song, she claimed a headache, and said she should probably retire to the conservatory, where the air was better. Mr. Albury was perceptive enough to take the point that a lady who was always ill when he called likely did not wish to further their acquaintance, and he took his leave as she went up the stairs.

Georgiana had been hoping Catherine would join her; she sensed her friend would want to talk after the events of the morning, and she had barely sat down before Catherine entered, saying: "Are you truly feeling ill? If so I will leave."

"No, it was simply an excuse for my wrist, and because I found myself running out of patience to stay in Mr. Albury's company, which is a shame, because he is a perfectly well-mannered gentleman. His only failing is that he is not Captain Stanton," Georgiana said, blushing, but still glad that she was able to admit so to someone else.

"So he *is* your choice," Catherine said. "I wondered that you were not so upset over Viscount Burnley's being engaged, but then I thought perhaps it was because Captain Stanton held your affections."

"He does," Georgiana said. "I only hope I have not realised it too late."

"Oh, but he must be committed to you," Catherine said. "He might not show it in the same way as other men, but he made it a point to be here today. Unlike Captain Ramsey."

At this, poor Kitty finally broke down in tears, and Georgiana moved to embrace her.

"He must have had a very good reason for not being able to take proper leave," Georgiana said. "I am sure nothing but what was very important would have kept him from coming to see you. No one doubts that he is devoted to you."

"I never would have doubted it myself, until today," Kitty sobbed. "Did he not know what such a snub would do to me?"

Georgiana felt herself growing closer to tears. To see Kitty so disappointed, and to know that her own prospects would likely have to wait was more than she felt she could bear, and finally she did break down. Both ladies sat there for some time, silently embracing as they wept, in lower spirits than either of them had ever before felt.

Mr. Darcy had taken advantage of the breaking up of the party in the drawing room to go to his study, and as he had done so, had given Elizabeth a look that indicated she should join him there at some point during the course of the day. Elizabeth had for some time been desiring an opportunity to criticise Captain Ramsey, and she could only do so to her husband, so when Mrs. Annesley took up her needlework and Mary began her pianoforte practise, she went to the study.

"I cannot believe Captain Ramsey!" she said, as soon as she had closed the door behind her. "To have paid Kitty such attention, and then to run off without taking his leave of her! It reminds me too much of Lord Alfred – it disappoints me so. Arranging his affairs out of town – I do not know what should have been so important or where he could have gone that precluded him from seeing her, even for a few minutes. He was already in the house – he only need have waited a little longer!"

"He could have gone to Longbourn," Darcy said.

"Poor Kitty will be so – what did you just say?"

"The affairs he had to settle could have been at Longbourn," Darcy said, checking his watch. "Indeed, I expect he is probably there by now."

"At Longbourn?"

"Yes, at Longbourn. After you all retired last night, and Colonel Fitzwilliam departed, Captain Ramsey asked if I would be willing to write him a letter of introduction to your father. He wishes to propose to Catherine, but would not do so without your father's consent. I would have told you last night, but you were already asleep when I came up."

Elizabeth stared at him in astonishment, and indicated he should go on.

"He laid out his plan for marriage," Darcy said. "He does expect they would have more than a thousand pounds a year, but even so, he wished to settle in Bath. He thought there they might partake in the sort of diversions they both enjoy at comparably little expense – they may not even have need of a carriage there, although they would easily have the means to afford one. They would also be close to his family in Salisbury. There was not one element of his plan that I could find fault in – it speaks of great sense and frugality, but also an understanding of what will make his wife happy.

"Of course, he does not expect that they will be able to be married before he must go to sea, but he wished to at least have the engagement settled so that Catherine might look forward to his return knowing they are to be married. I told him I wholeheartedly approved of the match and would both introduce him and recommend it in my letter, which I did. I understand he was to call on the Admiralty and then take a hired carriage to your parents's house."

"Oh! I regret everything I have said about him – I should not have let poor behaviour by one gentleman colour my opinion of another," Elizabeth said, with the deepest thrill of happiness for Catherine. "But why did you not say anything? Why did Captain Stanton not say anything?"

"I was sworn to secrecy," Darcy said. "I expect Captain Stanton was as well. Captain Ramsey wished for nothing to be said until he had secured the consent of your father."

"I hope he did not have any doubt of my father's giving his consent," Elizabeth said. A thousand pounds a year was not perhaps what she or Jane had, but it was quite respectable. Indeed, two years ago, if Elizabeth had thought that any of them should be married with a thousand pounds a year, she would have been thrilled. "My mother – oh, how I wish you had not sent him off to face my mother alone!"

"He has captured enemy ships, Elizabeth. Certainly he can face your mother."

"They are two very different things, Darcy, and you know it. He is completely unprepared – he has never met her."

"Not *completely* unprepared. I did give him some idea of what to expect," Darcy said. "I considered attempting to find a way to have you accompany him, but I did not know how I could explain your absence without ruining the confidentiality he requested."

Elizabeth decided not to give the topic of Mrs. Bennet any further worry. If Captain Ramsey had determined to go to Longbourn immediately after receiving news of war, he certainly could not be too frightened off by such a mother-in-law, particularly if he would be settled in Bath, which was not *too* easy a distance from Longbourn.

"Oh, I am so happy for Kitty!" she said. "She will have a difficult night, I am sure, but am I right in hoping that he should be here tomorrow to pay his addresses?"

"Yes, barring any difficulties in his journey. He had planned to call at Longbourn for some time, if his suit was successful, to become better acquainted with your parents, but then begin his return journey home, so that he should arrive sometime in the night. I expect we will see him here tomorrow at his first opportunity."

They were both correct. Catherine passed the most difficult night of her life, crying into her pillow for most of it, unable to sleep until she finally drifted off in exhaustion. She slept late, and had no desire to break her fast or join the rest of the family, until Georgiana knocked urgently on her door and indicated that Captain Ramsey was returned to town, and had just arrived to call on them.

Sarah, Hughes and several of the other maids saw to it that Catherine was dressed and her hair attended to in an impossibly short amount of time, so that Kitty made her way down the stairs somewhat stunned and disoriented. She entered the drawing room, and there he was, all of his usual smiles and goodwill.

"Ah, Miss Catherine, there you are!" he said, with a particular smile for her.

"I apologise," she said, with a look of mild accusation towards him. "I slept ill last night."

"Are you unwell?" he asked, all of the lightness gone from his countenance. "I hope you are not unwell – I had hoped to request a private audience with you this morning, but I will wait, of course, if you are ill."

Catherine's limited life experience had taught her that there was only one reason for a gentleman to request a private audience with a single lady. She felt faint, she felt tears threaten, and finally she landed on such a feeling of ecstasy that she could barely say: "No, I am able to have such a conversation."

At this, the rest of the family melted away from the drawing room, some with little murmured reasons of something they must check on, others simply getting up and leaving, so that quickly enough, it was just Catherine and Captain Ramsey sitting there. He rose, he walked over to her and kneeled in front of her, taking up her hand in his.

"Miss Catherine, first let me apologise for not taking proper leave yesterday," he said. "Were it possible for me to be in two places at the same time, I would have, but I wished to speak to your father immediately. I went to Longbourn yesterday to call on your parents, and I am most happy to tell you that your father has given his consent for your hand in marriage."

Kitty could not help herself; she emitted a little sob of happiness at his words, but then smiled at him so that he might continue.

"I know that we will not be able to marry for some time, but I hoped to secure your hand before war begins again," he said. "I do not know how long I shall be at sea, but when I return I wish us to be married, and that we may have our honeymoon in Bath. If you find it to your liking, I think it would be a good place for us to settle. With our combined fortunes and my half-pay, from the navy, we would have a little over a thousand pounds a year, and it will go far in Bath – there are any number of assemblies and opportunities for theatre there, and at less expense than we would find here in London.

"I find I have gone about this all out of order, however. I should first have said that ever since we were acquainted I have admired you greatly, that I have been so impressed by your progress in drawing and painting, and that – "

"Oh, you do not need to say any more!" Kitty cried. "There is nothing I would like more than to be your wife – you do not need to convince me."

He laughed heartily at this, and Catherine joined him, laughing and crying at the same time, and completely overcome when he lifted her hand and kissed it.

"Miss Catherine, I must note that there is a chance I will be knocked on the head during this war, and that I will not return," he said. "But if that is how things are to happen, I did not want you to be in any doubt of how much I love you."

"Oh, I love you too," Kitty said. "I cannot believe this is happening!"

He took up both of her hands in his and assured her repeatedly that it was, until eventually the couple were ready to re-open the drawing room to the rest of the household. The news of their engagement was shared, to the surprise and delight of all except Elizabeth and Darcy, who did their best to appear as surprised as everyone else, while they all congratulated the couple on their engagement.

Of all of them, only Georgiana could not quite find it in herself to be fully wholehearted in her congratulations. She was happy for Catherine, and yet she could not help but think about how they had been two sad young ladies yesterday, and now Catherine had no reason for sadness – her temporary heartbreak was over, and now all her wishes had been fulfilled. As soon as she had met Captain Ramsey, Catherine had known what she wanted, she had clearly shown her preference, and now she had the benefit of being absolutely certain of Captain Ramsey's affections. She would enter into the war engaged, knowing she held his heart.

Georgiana could not help but wonder how things might have been different if she had been similarly upfront with Captain Stanton, if she had known her own heart sooner. And yet she knew, even as she thought it, that they were both very different people than Kitty and Captain Ramsey – more quiet, more serious, more reserved – and she could not be certain that even if she had begun much earlier to show her preference, that she might have been the recipient of a similar proposal. The others were so animated that it was not an issue, that Georgiana should sit, outwardly pleasant but somewhat listless, until Captain Stanton was announced.

He came into the room, and was immediately acquainted by Captain Ramsey of the engagement. Captain Stanton said all that was enthusiastic and proper, and yet the overall look of his countenance was of disappointment. Once the initial rush of the news had passed, he said that he had called at the Admiralty, and began to better explain the reason for his unhappiness.

"I am to have the Jupiter, of fifty guns," he said. "She was only just finished in her build as peace was declared, so she is a little more ready for war than most other ships."

"I do not understand," Georgiana said. "Fifty guns is twelve more than what the Caroline had. Is this not a better ship?"

"I understand how it would seem that way," Captain Stanton said, gazing at Georgiana with what kindness he could muster. "However, our fifty-gun ships – we call them fourth-rates – are most unfortunate ships. They have two decks, and cannot match up against a frigate, which would be smaller, with any honour. Yet they are not large enough to fight any of the larger ships – say your standard seventy-four gun ship of the line – successfully. They are in a strange middle ground."

"Oh, I am so sorry," Georgiana said. "I had been hoping you would have the Caroline again."

"So had I, Miss Darcy," he said. "However, I must accept my lot, and attempt to recruit nearly a hundred more men to man her."

"He is still better off than I," said Captain Ramsey. "I am to have the Andromeda, a mere twenty-eight gun frigate, which was about to be sold out of the service, and so was in a better state of readiness than most of our ships. Now, instead, we will be relaying messages and poking around on blockade duty, for that is about all a twenty-eight gun frigate is good for. If my friend's fifty-gun ship has too many guns, we certainly have too few."

Most of the family still did not entirely understand how twenty-eight and fifty guns were not a good number for a ship to have, but thirty-eight and seventy-four were, but they still commiserated with the captains, and discussed the course the naval portion of the war was likely to take. It was as yet unknown how much of the French fleet was mobilised, or even how much of it would be willing to fight for Napoleon, versus the captains who would align with the royalist cause. At this point, the Admiralty was quietly preparing all ships that could be readied for sea, and details in strategy and tactics would be worked out later.

They talked with a sense that very soon they would all no longer be in company, but none of them realised how short a time it was they had left, until Elizabeth noted the lateness of the hour, and invited them to stay to dinner. Captain Ramsey readily accepted, with such expressions of happiness as would be expected of a man invited to dine with the lady who had just accepted his offer of marriage, but Captain Stanton could not stay. His uncle was holding a farewell dinner for him, and it could not be delayed, as he and Captain Ramsey would be taking the earl's carriage down to Portsmouth first thing on the morrow.

They were all shocked; they had not understood the suddenness of naval time, but now it became clear to them with what urgency Captain Ramsey had gone to Longbourn. Kitty was the only one who wept, to only spend part of a day in the company of her betrothed, but she did at least have the satisfaction of their engagement to console her. Georgiana, however, felt a strange, paralysing fear come over her – soon, Captain Stanton would leave to prepare for his dinner, and then she might not see him again for years. She fell mute; she could not attend to any of the conversation for fear that the next hour might determine her fate, and there was so very little she could do.

After another half-hour, Captain Stanton did rise, and said: "I regret I must take my leave of you all now. Miss Bennet, Captain Ramsey, please allow me to repeat my deepest congratulations – there are few things more pleasing than to know two dear friends shall be married."

They each thanked him, and then he continued: "Mrs. Darcy, I wonder if I might write to you. I would like to continue to hear news of your family while at sea."

"Of course," said Elizabeth. "We would certainly enjoy hearing anecdotes of your naval life."

"You may count on it," Captain Stanton said, bowing. "Mr. Darcy, Miss Darcy, Miss Bennet, Mrs. Annesley, my best wishes for your continued health and happiness."

He turned and left the drawing room, and Georgiana trembled. To hope for her happiness, when she knew there could be no happiness with things so unsettled! She looked over at Elizabeth, who was gazing at her with an expression of such sadness that Georgiana felt her throat tighten with tears. She could not leave things in such a way! She could not!

It did not matter what her family thought – it did not matter what propriety dictated – she must have a private farewell with him. Georgiana stood up and rushed from the drawing-room, out into the entrance-hall, and he was still there, standing in the doorway with Mr. Miller, who was about to open the door for him.

"Captain Stanton!" she cried. He looked up sharply, he took a step towards her, and Georgiana realised that now she held his attention, but she had no idea what to say. She walked up to him, attempting to order her thoughts. "I know you wished for honour. I hope that you may have it, somehow, even with such a ship. But I also hope you will return safely."

She blushed deeply; he held her gaze, but for some time did not say anything.

"It means a great deal to me that you say that, Miss Darcy," he said. "I assure you that I have every intention of returning safely; after all, I must still hear you play that Fandango."

Georgiana mustered a faint smile at this, although there were tears in her eyes. "Yes, you must – I will hold you to it."

"Goodbye, Miss Darcy," he held out his hand. "I will miss your company more than I can say."

Georgiana gave him her hand, and he held it tightly; she returned his grasp, and took what comfort from the gesture she could.

"Goodbye, Captain Stanton," she said.

He released her hand, and, as Mr. Miller had quietly moved down to the other end of the hallway, opened the door himself and closed it behind him. Only when he was gone did Georgiana allow herself to cry openly.

It was much later in the evening before Elizabeth was able to go to her husband's bedchamber. Captain Ramsey had stayed very late, and they could not blame him for wishing to do so, not when he and Kitty had no idea of when they might next see each other, although at least now that they were engaged, they would be allowed to correspond privately.

Elizabeth sighed as she took her place in bed. She wished she could be wholeheartedly happy for her sister, and indeed she was as happy for Kitty as she could possibly be. She could not help but keep thinking of poor Georgiana, however. After abruptly leaving them to say her own good-bye to Captain Stanton – a move Elizabeth approved of, although she was not sure her husband would – Georgiana had retired to her room. Elizabeth had given her a little time alone, and then gone to her there. It had not taken much prompting for Georgiana to admit to the whole of her affections, to realising that Alfred Mallory's engagement mattered little to her heart, because she was in love with Captain Stanton.

Their more private parting had given Georgiana some cause for hope, but she was still filled with regrets that she had not known her heart soon enough, that she had not been able to show her preference. There had been little Elizabeth could say in consolation, only that at least they should hear from him when he wrote to their family, and that at some point he would return home, and then certainly they could renew their acquaintance.

Georgiana had managed to rally her spirits enough to come to dinner, looking sapped, but managing a great deal of enthusiasm for Kitty and Captain Ramsey. If she was quiet and introspective over tea, they all understood, and had done their best to keep the conversation away from Captain Stanton, although they could hardly avoid the war.

"Well, Mrs. Darcy, I certainly hope you have no cause for complaint against Captain Ramsey now," Darcy said, as she settled under the covers beside him.

"No, I certainly do not. It has come about as handsomely as I could ever have hoped for Kitty." she said. "It is regrettable that he must go to sea so immediately, but then, I believe that also expedited his proposal. Who knows how long he would have waited, without the war to prompt him."

"I do not think he would have waited too much longer," Darcy said. "He clearly had put much thought into his plan for the marriage. I think perhaps he was waiting for an opportunity to become acquainted with your father in more natural manner."

"He might have waited quite awhile, then. I do not believe my father had any intention of coming to town to meet him."

"I think eventually we could have managed a house party at Pemberley, or something of the sort, so that they might meet. Or perhaps we could have found some reason for him to escort you and Mary back to Longbourn."

"Darcy! Even my mother would be proud of such plots! I wondered why you kept bringing up the possibility of my going to Longbourn."

"Believe me, now that it is done, I will put all plotting out of my mind."

They were silent for some time, and then he said: "How is Georgiana? I wish that I could speak to her of such things, but I found long ago that they are not the province of a brother."

"She is not well," Elizabeth admitted. "I know you were worried about what the news of Viscount Burnley's engagement would do to her. But in some ways, after she got past the deception, it was to her benefit. She came to realise that she loved Captain Stanton. It is just unfortunate that she did not have any time to act on it."

"She certainly seemed to act on it as he took his leave."

"You would not criticise her for that, would you?"

"No," he said. "I cannot say it was entirely proper, but it was done among family, and if she does love him, I cannot fault her motivation. Indeed, if it gave her any amount of comfort, I am glad that she did it."

"I believe it did," Elizabeth said. "It at least gave her some cause for hope."

"I do not like to bring up our argument over the merits of Viscount Burnley versus Captain Stanton," Darcy said. "Particularly as history has proven me to have been quite incorrect in my choice. But I have been meditating on this for some time, and there is one merit to Captain Stanton that neither of us considered perhaps as much as we should have."

"What is that?"

"He has his own fortune – more than enough that the two of them could live quite well, even if Georgiana had nothing of her own. The attention he shows her – even if it is with very little display of affection – is on her merits alone, not because of her fortune. Perhaps it took the incident with Viscount Burnley for me to appreciate that fully."

"And I will admit that although I preferred Captain Stanton, I never thought Viscount Burnley to be such a poor suitor as he turned out to be. I am so very glad that they were not in any way entangled. If he had offered for Georgiana, and she had accepted, they might have spent their entire marriage in love with other people."

Elizabeth shuddered slightly at the thought of it; despite how weary she had grown of this life in town, she was still very much in love with her husband. The thought of town, however, made her realise that they had very little reason to stay, now, with both captains going down to Portsmouth.

"Darcy – do you think we might return Kitty and Mary to Longbourn, and then remove to Pemberley?" she asked. "I realise we will have to stay through Caroline's wedding, but after that there is no longer any reason for us to stay in town. Indeed, Jane and Charles might be willing to go there with us, so that they might look for an estate in the area. They have several parties interested in Netherfield – it cannot be long now before one makes an offer to take over the lease."

"I have been considering exactly the same thing," he said, a smile spreading across his face. "I see no reason for us to stay in town any longer than we must. If we stay, there will be no peace for Georgiana – once society resumes fully, I do not doubt Lady Catherine will attempt to take her to Almack's again, and all of our other engagements will continue. At Pemberley, we might all have some peace."

Elizabeth felt her spirits lighten at the thought of leaving town, and drew closer to him. "Tell me about Pemberley."

"You have been there yourself, Elizabeth."

"It is not the same – I have been there as a guest, to view the public rooms and the grounds, not as anything approaching one of the family."

"You had been invited to be so, well before your visit."

"Yes, and I cannot say that I did not think of how I might have been mistress of such an estate, upon seeing it. But you know such things have little true influence on me."

"Indeed I do."

"So tell me about Pemberley. Tell me of your Pemberley."

"I hardly know where to start," he said. "I have spoke of the library, and must admit it to be by far my favourite room in the house. There is, though, a room beyond it that I do not believe I have mentioned – one of the bookcases is actually a door, leading to a private sitting room, and as much as I adore the library, I fully understand what would have motivated my ancestors to create such a space – it is small and musty, despite all Mrs. Reynolds's efforts to air it – truly a refuge within a refuge, if you will."

"Oh, I must see it," Elizabeth said. "I am wild to see the library, but I must admit the idea of a secret space beyond intrigues me greatly. Longbourn is such a straightforward house; it has none of those secret spaces, and it is not so large that any place of substance could be overlooked. I must admit I enjoy gothic novels simply for the discovery of these hidden rooms and passages – to think of a house so large and so old that it has rooms undiscovered!"

"I cannot claim so many spaces in Pemberley, although parts of it are old enough that perhaps there may be a few that have escaped notice in this century, and perhaps you may be the one to uncover them."

"I shall greatly enjoy searching for them, then," Elizabeth said. "But what of the grounds? You have said nothing of the grounds."

"You have seen the highlights of those, at least, although I expect an accomplished walker such as you will quickly develop your own favourites. I suppose it is all dependent on whether you prefer hills, forest, field, or stream, in your scenery."

"I enjoy them all," Elizabeth said. "I shall hardly be able to choose."

"You will not need to, given your favour for frequent walks. I will say, though, that nature has obliged you in your desire for secret spaces perhaps better than the house itself. There are some hidden spaces in the grounds that are even more delightful than anything I believe the house can muster."

"And will you promise to show me all of them, and kiss me in every single one?" she asked.

"I will show you them all, and there are some in which I may give you more than a kiss," he said, stroking her arm with that particular lightness of touch which she could hardly bear, and yet adored.

CHAPTER 34

Elizabeth did not wish to remove to Pemberley without first discussing the plan with Georgiana, and she found the young woman alone in the conservatory after breakfast. Georgiana looked up from her seat with a tired face, one lacking all of its usual good humour, and Elizabeth felt deeply for her.

"Darcy and I have been discussing the possibility of removing to Pemberley in a fortnight or so, after Miss Bingley's wedding," Elizabeth said, sitting beside her. "I wanted to check and see what you thought of such a scheme – if you wish to stay for the full season, we will certainly do so."

"I have no desire to stay for the rest of the season," Georgiana said. "To be honest, the thought of meeting any more suitors makes me weary."

"We had thought that might be the case. I will also admit to being weary of society – I have a great desire to return to the countryside."

"Oh yes," Georgiana brightened slightly. "There are so many places on the Pemberley grounds I would like to show you. It will be beautiful as spring begins."

"Then it is settled – we will make our preparations to leave town. You may have to suffer another visit or two to Almack's with your aunt in that time, unfortunately."

"I do not mind it so much," Georgiana said. "Everyone there dances well and has good conversation. I only hope that Lady Catherine does not expect a match will come out of it."

"Not in a few visits, I hope. We shall have you out of here before she can attempt any serious matchmaking."

"Thank you," Georgiana smiled. "Elizabeth – I wish – I wish to wait for Captain Stanton to return, regardless of how long it takes. I know it may be years, though, and I know that must put a burden on you and Fitzwilliam."

"Nonsense," Elizabeth said, embracing her. "You may stay with us as long as you wish, and you will never be a burden. Do not ever think that."

Elizabeth could not help but wonder if time would lessen the strength of Georgiana's affection; if Captain Stanton was gone long enough, perhaps Georgiana might meet with someone else, and fall in love again. She could not suggest such a thing to her sister now, however.

"I had thought we should call on the Bingleys and Gardiners today – I have missed them so, and we have much news to tell them," Elizabeth said. "Would you like to go with us, or would you prefer to stay here?"

"I shall go," said Georgiana. "I enjoy their company so, and it would be nice to have a diversion."

When the family arrived at the Hursts's town house, they were pleased to learn that they did not need to call separately on the Gardiners, as the Gardiners were already there, and the Hursts were out. All were pleased at the timing, but such pleasure was nothing to the reaction when they were all seated, and Elizabeth made the announcement:

"I have some news to share of the greatest kind – Kitty and Captain Ramsey are engaged to be married."

"Oh, Kitty! It is indeed the greatest news!" Jane was still not so heavy that she could not rush across the room to embrace her sister, although her aunt Gardiner reached Kitty first.

Kitty blushed and accepted the congratulations of all, and when Mr. Bingley asked her if the couple had set a date, responded: "No, we cannot. He has received his orders to make HMS Andromeda ready for sea – it is a twenty-eight gun frigate – and he has left for Portsmouth this morning. He wished to secure our engagement before he went to sea."

"Well, how very romantic," said Caroline Bingley, contemptuously. "This is the captain with the family who owns a shop?"

"I think it is *very* romantic," said Jane, who assumed Caroline to be jealous that this news had distracted them all from discussing her upcoming nuptials. "Captain Ramsey is quite an attractive, amiable man, and he has won a nice fortune in the war. He is an excellent match for Kitty."

Elizabeth caught her husband's eye, and gave him a slight, sly smile. To point out Captain Ramsey as attractive, considering Caroline's own match, was the closest Jane would ever come to a barb at her sister-in-law, although it was likely too subtle for Caroline to feel.

"We also wished to let you all know that we will be leaving town a little after Caroline's wedding," Elizabeth said. "We will be stopping at Longbourn so that Mary and Kitty may return home, and then on to Pemberley. We do hope that you will all visit us – Jane and Charles, perhaps you might stay there while you look for your new home."

"That would be capital!" Charles exclaimed. "We do wish to find a place well before Jane begins her confinement, and I believe I can manage the transition in the Netherfield lease by correspondence."

"Then it is settled. Aunt, uncle, I do hope you might find time to visit as well."

"Oh, we certainly will," Mrs. Gardiner said. "I would never turn down an opportunity to see Pemberley again, and to visit with my old friends in Lambton. It would be a most perfect trip."

"Yes, I will look for an opportunity when I might leave my business for a few weeks," Mr. Gardiner said.

"You must avail yourself of the stream while you are there," Darcy said. "We shall warn Cook to prepare her full repertoire for trout."

"I should like that above all things," said Mr. Gardiner, who had been hoping opportunities for angling would form part of their stay, and was very pleased to have this confirmed already.

"Sir Sedgewick and I will be honeymooning in Brighton, and then on to Hilcote – that is the name of his estate, you know, in Warwickshire," Caroline said. "So I do not think we shall be able to visit this year, but perhaps another time. Once I am settled in as mistress of Hilcote, we may have you to visit instead."

"That sounds delightful, although perhaps we should wait a while, before visiting," Elizabeth said. "I expect you will wish to do some redecorating, as the new mistress of Hilcote, and we would not want to intrude before you have things as you like them."

"Oh yes, of course," Caroline said. "I have not been there, as yet, but Sir Sedgewick has promised me a more than ample budget, for decoration. He says I may change whatever I wish, which is for the best – you cannot trust a bachelor to decoration."

Elizabeth opened her mouth to note that Mr. Darcy had done just fine, decided that would not be the best thing to point out, to Caroline, and finally said, "I am sure it will keep you quite busy, but we will look forward to seeing it when it is complete."

The group returned to talk of Kitty's engagement, and the joys of visiting Pemberley, for at least an hour more, and for Elizabeth, the time passed most pleasantly but for one exception. Georgiana was largely silent, although she seemed to be attending to the conversation. She answered questions when asked, and she smiled when it seemed appropriate, but there was clearly a listlessness to her that worried Elizabeth.

CHAPTER 35

Georgiana did attempt the pianoforte, and found she could play without pain, but upon hearing her, Elizabeth and Mrs. Annesley insisted the surgeon be called in again, to ensure she was truly ready to resume. The surgeon blessed her returning to her pianoforte practise, although starting with only a half-hour per day. Even this little amount was a relief to her – she had missed practising, and she found it was one of the few things that distracted her from thinking about Captain Stanton. For thinking about Captain Stanton was something she could not help but do throughout each day. She wondered constantly what he was doing – if he was preparing his ship for sea, or if he was at sea already – and she could not help but wonder if he ever thought about her.

Georgiana was not yet confident enough in her return to the pianoforte to attend the next musical evening, and so she learned of the viscountess's latest invitation when Elizabeth and Mary returned home. Upon learning that they were preparing to leave town, she had determined to make good on her promise to have them to the opera in her box before it was too late, and they were all to go see Handel's Orlando the day following Caroline Bingley's wedding. This stirred Georgiana's spirits somewhat; she loved the opera, and she had missed Lady Tonbridge's company.

In the days leading up to the wedding, Georgiana busied herself with increasingly longer practises on the pianoforte, and with helping Elizabeth prepare for the trip to Pemberley. They had all grown so settled into the house on Curzon Street that there was much to attend to – determining which dresses, books, and even horses should be sent back to the estate, and ensuring the staff had all they needed to close the house upon their leaving, so that those servants who worked wherever the family was in residence could then make their way to Pemberley. As well, there were shopping trips, as this would be their last opportunity to easily purchase that which Lambton's little shops could not provide.

There came a day, however, where Elizabeth was too distressed to participate in any of the preparations. She was in the study when Mr. Miller knocked and delivered the day's post for Mr. and Mrs. Darcy, among it only one letter for Elizabeth, from her father. She opened it cautiously, for her father was still an indifferent correspondent, although he had been making an effort to write more often, with so much of his family gone from home. It was equally possible that it would contain news of significance, or simply a few pleasantries before Mr. Bennet descended into a description of what books he was reading and only rose from it to ask if Kitty and Mary were behaving themselves.

It was news of significance, however. Lydia had dashed off a letter to Longbourn, to inform her parents that Ensign Wickham's regiment had begun its movement south, towards Ramsgate, so that they could embark on the transport ships that would be sortied there, and make their way to the continent. Lydia, lacking any deep connexions in Newcastle, had deemed it best to follow her "dear Wickham" over to the continent, for she did not wish to be parted from him.

"Oh, Lydia, what are you doing?" Elizabeth gasped, as she read the letter.

Darcy looked up in concern as she spoke, and his concern doubled when he saw the distress in her countenance. "What is the matter?" he asked.

"Wickham's regiment is making its way to the continent," she said, in a most agitated voice. "Lydia has followed him there, and it is too late to attempt to intercept her now. She has little money and no connexions on the continent, and yet she goes willingly into a war zone to follow after that man."

"Good God, I would rather she had shown up on our doorstep unannounced," Darcy said. "She is younger than Georgiana; I cannot imagine a girl of her age in such a place."

"I wish I would have made it clearer to her that she was welcome here, even if her husband was not," Elizabeth said, very near to weeping. "I know it was necessary to distance her – believe me, I should never wish to put Georgiana through the pain of encountering him again – but I wish she would have known that she had more family support. I wish she would not have thought that the most drastic action was the one she should take."

Darcy deposited a very little glass of brandy in front of her, and she choked and spluttered through her first sip of it before finding the rest a small comfort.

"Why did she not go to Longbourn, though?" he asked, refilling her glass with more, this time. "Surely she must have felt welcome there."

"I do not know. Lydia has always been a bit of a wild romantic –

perhaps she did consider Longbourn and this house as possibilities, and still decided she should go to the continent. Somehow, her love for Wickham still seems unabated, even after all this time married to him."

"In some ways, perhaps that is for the best. I would hate to see someone so young as her having regrets over her choice of marriage, even if we think it a poor match."

"I suppose you are right, although right now I must say I wish she was having those regrets and had come to us, instead of following him. I never expected to go into this war wondering for *her* safety."

"Edward is preparing for his own unit's crossing through Ramsgate," Darcy said. "We may ask him to inquire about her, if ever he can, and send her back to us if he does hear of her. I do not know that there is anything else we can do, at this point."

Caroline Bingley's wedding was quite well-done, they all had to admit. Caroline would have the ceremony nowhere but in St. George's, and had outfitted herself in the very latest fashion. Elizabeth was a bit surprised to note, as Charles Bingley walked his sister down the aisle, that Caroline looked completely and utterly happy. They had all imagined Caroline's marriage to Sir Sedgewick to be a compromise, and perhaps it was, but it was clear Caroline had embraced it fully. The ceremony was quick – St. George's kept up a regular flow of marriages among the ton during the season – and as the rector spoke, Elizabeth found her attention drifting.

She could not help but look at her sisters, seated down the pew from her. Mary, of course, was attending most closely to everything the rector said. Kitty had the most dreamy, faraway expression on her face, and Elizabeth assumed her to be imagining her own wedding, with Captain Ramsey. If Elizabeth was right, Kitty would be conjuring a wedding involving a great many men in naval uniform, Captain Ramsey looking the finest of all of them, Kitty herself meeting him at the altar in the finest dress of the latest fashion, and a quite a lot of swords and pomp. She had the contented look of a woman in love, and engaged to the man she loved, which was quite a contrast to Georgiana's expression, similarly faraway, but unmistakably sad. Elizabeth wished to embrace the poor girl and tell her all would be well in the end, for Elizabeth still felt that there was a true affection between Georgiana and Captain Stanton, although neither had done much to show it, but she was too far away from her sister to even do anything so comforting as pat her hand.

The wedding breakfast, at least, proved to be most well-done, and Elizabeth hoped it was a suitable distraction for her sister. It was held at the Hursts's, and featured the finest dishes Mr. Hurst's French cook could supply. Mr. Hurst, in addition to providing a meal of undeniable quality, also proved to be a better host for such a large group than expected. He described every dish in great detail, and encouraged everyone at the table to try those he thought they would favour, as well as keeping up a steady stream of toasts for the newly wed couple. Mr. Hurst might have toasted a bit too much; by the end of the meal he was clearly drunk, but now his wife Louisa took over, ensuring tea as well as port were served to the gentlemen as they remained in the dining room, and leading the ladies off to the drawing room.

They all remained in the drawing room for only a little while after the gentlemen returned. Caroline and her new husband were eager to be off, and once they had left, there were only so many pleasantries that might be exchanged between Sir Sedgewick's family and acquaintances, and Caroline's side of the family. They all called for their carriages, and as the Darcys and Bingleys waited together, Elizabeth could not help but notice a certain new lightness in the countenances of both Charles and Jane.

CHAPTER 36

Georgiana found herself in a state of anticipation during the carriage ride to the Theatre Royal. None of her relations had ever seen fit to keep a regular box for the opera, although her brother or her uncle would engage one periodically if there was a performance they were particularly interested in. So while Georgiana had been to the opera many times before, it was never so frequently as she would have liked, and she knew on this evening it would be a very welcome distraction.

The viscountess had already arrived, and was mingling with the thin crowd – those in the ton who were merely there to be seen would arrive fashionably late. As soon as she saw Georgiana, she rushed over and took up her young friend's hands.

"Miss Darcy, I am relieved to see you out in society again," she said. "I had been worried for your health. Indeed, you do not quite look fully recovered."

"Thank you, Lady Tonbridge, I am still a little tired," Georgiana said, wondering if her malaise appeared as some lingering illness to others. "It is very good to see you, though. I have missed your company."

"I have missed yours as well, my dear, especially as it comes along with the departure of so many of my military friends from town. It is cruelly unfair that we should go to war when I thought I would have their company for the whole season."

The viscountess turned her attention to Kitty, then, looking at her with a frank smile. "Miss Catherine Bennet, do allow me to congratulate you on your engagement. You must let me claim my little piece of credit for introducing you to Captain Ramsey."

"You should claim more credit than that," Kitty said. "We would never have met if not for your ball."

"Well, then, if you insist, I will take more of the credit," the viscountess said, taking up Kitty's arm and indicating they should all follow the two of them.

Lady Tonbridge's box was located close to the stage, an excellent location for those most interested in hearing the performance, and also a place to be clearly seen by all in attendance. It was also already populated, to Georgiana's surprise, by the Earl of Anglesey.

"Lord Anglesey, it is good to see you again," she said, dropping into a curtsey as he rose to bow to everyone entering the box.

"And you, Miss Darcy," he said. "I understand from Lady Tonbridge that you return to your family estate soon, so I am glad I have the opportunity for your company once more before you leave London."

He stepped away from her, so that he could greet the others as they entered the box, but then returned.

"I do not suppose you have had news of my nephew since he returned to Portsmouth," he said.

"No. Do you – do you know how he does?"

"He is very nearly ready for sea. I had a short little letter from him only yesterday. He is still thirty men short of his full complement, but he hopes with another few days, more of his old shipmates will make their way to the Jupiter."

"When will he go to sea?"

"I expect it will not be long before the Admiralty officially announces the remobilisation of the fleet – he should go to sea as soon as he may after that. He already has his orders – he is to patrol the French coast, and supplement the blockade, if needed."

"I hope he may spend more of his time in patrolling; I know he did not wish to be on blockade duty."

"Indeed, no sailor does. It is perhaps a little consolation to make up for his being assigned the unfortunate Jupiter. You must believe I raised hell with every contact I had in the Admiralty when I learned of his assignment, but it was too late. It is all chaos, when it comes to ship assignments – they attempted to determine what ships could be made ready for sea most quickly, and then assigned them as captains came in to report. Matthew is at least fortunate that he was in London when news of Bonaparte's escape came about; I expect there are some captains from the farther counties who will be given ships that will take some time to be ready for sea."

"Do you know if the Caroline has been assigned to anyone else?"

"You sound precisely like him, Miss Darcy, so worried about the fate of that ship," the earl said. "And no, from what I understand, the Caroline is to remain laid up in ordinary."

Georgiana wished to know every last thing the earl knew about Captain Stanton, every detail that had been in his letter, every conversation Lord Anglesey had undertaken with his contacts at the Admiralty, but she could not think of how to ask for such details. She could not ask anything else now, anyway, as a sudden hush from the crowd indicated that the performance was about to begin, and everyone in the box began to settle into seats.

Orlando was new to Georgiana, but she found it to be everything she would have expected of Handel, beautiful and powerful. If she might have had a choice given her current situation, she would not have chosen a work where love was so central to the storyline, but every time thoughts about love encroached on her enjoyment of the music, she forced them away and required herself to simply listen.

The intermission came quickly, and Georgiana, having been transfixed by the last song, was slow to rise from her seat. Everyone else in the box was making their exit, so that Georgiana was the only one to overhear several ladies conversing in the box beside her:

"Did you see they finally announced Viscount Burnley's engagement in the papers?"

"I did! Not that they needed to announce it; all of town knows already. Positively scandalous. I wonder if he – well, it would be impolite to speak of it."

"Oh, he has been in love with Amelia Foster for years. I am quite certain this was no accident on his part, although they could have done a better job of keeping it secret. I have seen them in company together – completely besotted."

"Was he not courting the Darcy girl, though?"

Georgiana felt her cheeks flush at the mention of herself, but could not bring herself to leave the box.

"Mrs. Burke had it on good authority from Miss Bingley – oh, I am sorry, she is Lady Harrison now. You know she just married Sir Sedgewick Harrison."

"Yes, of course. How good of her to take him off the marriage market."

There followed some amount of tittering, before the conversation continued.

"Anyway, Lady Harrison said that Viscount Burnley was quite particular in his attentions to Miss Darcy. I suppose he was courting her thirty thousand pounds. Poor thing, she shall have to begin again."

"Well, poor she is not, with thirty thousand pounds."

"True, and Lady Harrison says she lacks for no accomplishments; her skill on the pianoforte is particularly exceptional. She should have no trouble finding someone else – perhaps she shall manage a first son this time."

"I heard there was a naval captain courting her."

"No, that was Mrs. Darcy's sister, Miss Catherine Bennet. Her announcement was in the papers a little while back. Captain Andrew Ramsey – never heard of him, but then, I had never heard of the Bennets before Mr. Darcy married one."

It was mortifying for Georgiana to think of herself being spoken of in this way by others in town, although the praise for her accomplishments she could not help but find a little pleasing, and she did think a little better of Caroline for having spoken of her thus. Fear that she might overhear something that would further disturb her spirits had by now overcome Georgiana's curiosity, and she rose from her seat to make her way out of the box. She was surprised to find her brother waiting just beyond the curtain for her, instead of Mrs. Annesley.

"Fitzwilliam! I am sorry, I did not mean to make you wait."

"We thought you might need a little time," he said, looking at her with an expression of concern. "Are you unwell?"

"I am as well as I can be," she said, and forced herself to give him a faint smile, before taking up his arm so they could go find the others.

Part Two
April, 1815

CHAPTER 1

It had begun to seem to Elizabeth that Pemberley's grounds offered limitless beauty, that every trail she tried would offer up something new and delightful to the eye. Even in a fortnight of daily walks, she had yet to run out of recommendations from Darcy and Georgiana. Sometimes, the three of them walked together, sometimes she went out with one or the other, but this morning brother and sister were out riding. Thus, Elizabeth was walking with Sarah, for she knew she could no longer walk alone without raising the concern of the staff, as well as her husband, but she hated the thought of being followed by a servant. This was her compromise, and she found it to be quite a pleasant one; Sarah was a strong walker like herself, and enjoyed discovering Pemberley's grounds as much as Elizabeth did. As well, she was quiet when Elizabeth was silent, but conversed readily whenever Elizabeth raised a topic.

Elizabeth was enjoying their present silence; she felt herself still adjusting from the pace of town, and quiet time such as this was still something she savoured. In a few days, the Bingleys would join them, and there would be greater demands on her a hostess, but for now she still had the simplicity of days spent walking, reading, and listening to Georgiana's practise on the pianoforte.

Elizabeth smiled; hostess was no longer a role she feared, even at Pemberley. Her concerns about beginning again with another, larger staff at the great estate had been unfounded. Certainly, there were more names to learn, and Elizabeth was still not entirely sure she had even viewed all of the rooms in the house, but she had no difficulties in giving orders with an authority she had not even realised she had developed at Curzon Street.

Mrs. Reynolds, rather than being reluctant to relinquish her command over the house, had been quite happy to see a Mrs. Darcy returned to Pemberley, and had initially been so deferential to her new mistress that Elizabeth had to take her aside and request she act with something closer to the level of autonomy she had grown accustomed to over the years. This had pleased Mrs. Reynolds, and although Elizabeth still did not have the same level of comfort in working with Pemberley's housekeeper as she did with Mrs. Wright, she felt it should come in time. She spent less time with Mr. Parker, the butler, but found he was a master of all his duties, yet with every respect for her that she would have expected.

Elizabeth did find herself missing Kitty and Mary; she had grown accustomed to having them about her in London, and without Kitty's lively presence to help keep conversation moving, and fewer guests for dinner, their evenings were certainly much quieter. They had stayed one night at Longbourn only; as much as Elizabeth missed her father and mother, she could not subject Darcy and Georgiana to any more time around Mrs. Bennet while she was still in the throes of happiness at having one more daughter engaged to be married, occasionally interspersed with fits of nerves regarding poor Lydia, whom they had yet to receive another letter from. Still, Jane would be here soon enough, and Mr. Bennet had even threatened to overlook his dislike of travel long enough to make the trip to Pemberley at some point during the summer.

Checking her watch, Elizabeth observed they should make their turn for the house. They were to begin making their calls around the neighbourhood after noon, and she did not wish to keep Darcy waiting; the calls were primarily for Elizabeth's benefit, so that she might meet all of the primary families in the area, as well as the tenants of the estate. Elizabeth and Sarah made their way back along the stream, passing a copse of trees so that the house was in full view, and with it, Darcy and Georgiana, entering the field that sided the stream. They waved to her, and Elizabeth felt a twinge of jealousy; a few falls when she was learning had put an end to any desire of hers to become a horsewoman, yet if she had known she would marry into a family so passionate about riding, she might have been more persistent. They saw her, they waved, and set across the field at a full gallop to meet her and Sarah.

They began with the tenants first, taking the landau in the opposite direction of Lambton. Elizabeth clutched one of the many baskets she'd had the staff make up, each filled with a bolt of linen, soap, candles, dried fruits and salt cod. Darcy had looked at the items she had chosen and noted the baskets as quite well done – everything very useful, but a touch above what the tenants of the smaller farms might afford themselves. Only after Elizabeth met them might she have a better idea of each family's individual needs – whose children were outgrowing their clothes, what families might require new stockings or blankets before the winter.

This process was not entirely new to Elizabeth; she and Jane had sometimes accompanied her father and mother on their calls to the tenants of Longbourn. However, when the landau pulled to a stop in front of the first tenant cottage, Elizabeth came to see that things were quite different here. The cottage was in perfect repair, as was the dress of the woman sweeping the stone walk leading up to the front door. Stout and ruddy-faced, she dropped into a deep curtsey when she saw the landau. Darcy helped Elizabeth down from the landau, and then led her through the cottage's front gate.

"Mrs. Miller, please allow me to introduce my wife, Mrs. Elizabeth Darcy," he said. "Mrs. Darcy, this is Mrs. Agnes Miller."

"It is very nice to meet you, Mrs. Miller," Elizabeth said, dropping into a slight curtsey.

"Please ta make your acquaintance, Mrs. Darcy. Do please come in. Yes please, right in here."

Mrs. Miller leaned the broom against the house and bustled in the front door. The Darcys followed, into a home that was simple, but as well kept up as its exterior. A young boy of about five or six was inside, and seemed startled to see them.

"This here is Tom," Mrs. Miller said. "Tom, go find yer father and tell him ta come in right quick, the Darcys are come ta visit."

The boy scampered off, and in the awkward silence that followed, Elizabeth remembered her basket.

"This is for your family, Mrs. Miller," she said.

"Well, now, thank ye kindly, Mrs. Darcy," Mrs. Miller said, taking the basket. "Ay, you've been so generous to us, just like your husband."

"You are welcome," Elizabeth said. "How are your family, are they well?"

"Yes, ma'am, all very well. You'd not be knowin' this, but we lost our little Sarah these two years past. Now it's just Tom and Mr. Miller and me."

"I am very sorry to hear that, Mrs. Miller."

"Ay, well, time is a great healer, and Lord-willing we'll have another," Mrs. Miller said, looking down so that Elizabeth came to see that some of her stoutness came from being with child.

"Oh, bless you," Elizabeth flushed, but managed a smile for the woman.

Tom and his father came in then, both of them breathing heavily, and Elizabeth assumed they had run in from the fields.

"Now there you are, Tom Miller," Mrs. Miller said. "The Darcys are honourin' us with a visit, and this is the new Mrs. Darcy – Mrs. Elizabeth Darcy."

The elder Tom bowed to her, and Elizabeth curtsied to him.

"Beg parmn for my bein' away, Mrs. Darcy, Mr. Darcy," Mr. Miller said.

"I'm preparin' the fields – we're only a day or so from sowin', by my estimatin'."

"Very good," Darcy said. "Richardson says your winter wheat field comes on well. Shall you plant oats again, in your other corn field?"

"Yessir. 'Tis rotated round to the field nearest the house this year, which I'm particular glad of, with Mrs. Miller wearin' her apron high 'afore the harvest."

"Ah, yes, you must let us know if there is anything we can do to assist you and Mrs. Miller, as she draws closer," Darcy said, and the Millers nodded in response. "And I should be glad to purchase the same of oats from you, as I did last year. My grooms were very pleased with your crop."

"Thank ye, Mr. Darcy, we're much appreciative. Mr. Richardson says he'll be round to talk about what may go good in the little side fields for this year. Onions and peas, again, I 'spect, but he says my crops grown so good last year, he may try us on cucumbers. Just a very little patch, in case they don' take."

"We have rarely had good fortune with cucumbers," Darcy said. "However, you've done so well with this land, I think you could do it. Mr. Smith had a nice little crop last year."

"He did, did he? I'll talk to Smith, then, too, Mr. Darcy. I thank ye kindly for lettin' me know."

"Very well, Mr. Miller."

They took their leave soon enough; they had a great many tenants to visit that day. When they regained the road toward the next farm, Elizabeth asked:

"Are all the cottages so well-kept?"

"Almost all of them, yes," Darcy said. "Those that do not keep up their homes risk losing their tenancy. I have no shortage of applicants for the farms – the land here is quite fertile, and the terms of the lease are more lenient than most estates offer."

Elizabeth recalled Mrs. Reynolds's description of her now-husband as the best landlord, and felt she was better beginning to understand why. With lenient terms on the lease, the families could live better than most of their station, keep up their homes and purchase clothing and necessities when needed. "And to think he does all this, and still is able to clear ten thousand pounds a year!" she thought.

To him, she said: "That is very generous of you."

"I cannot claim the credit for such generosity," Darcy said. "My father and his father before him put it into practise; I merely continue the family legacy. It ultimately benefits the estate, to have a stable tenancy on all of the farms."

Elizabeth felt a surge of affection for him. To think that he had taken on all of this at such a young age, and had possessed the wisdom to continue on with traditions which were successful. Many other young men in his place – those like Stephen Mallory – would have been determined to draw as much money from the estate as possible, even if this showed to be foolish in the long run. They would have cared not for the Corn Bill, and kept their rents high, even if it put their tenants in danger of starving.

"Who implemented the crop rotations?" she asked.

"That was my father, although Mr. Richardson and I have taken on firmer control of what is grown. Nearly all of them use Townshend's four-field rotation – even the smaller farms, such as Miller's – and then supplement with some smaller fields for vegetables," Darcy said. "Richardson studies the agricultural reports obsessively – it is a rare occasion that he suggests a crop that does not do well, and I have some more daring farmers like Smith who enjoy the challenge of something new. You will meet him tomorrow, unless we make exceptional time today."

The landau passed a field already ploughed, the earth churned up so that its richness was evident, and Elizabeth settled back into her seat.

They returned with only a little time to rest before dinner, and despite the apparent cleanliness of all of the cottages, Elizabeth could not help but feel dusty and exhausted when she came into the house. She did not return to her apartment, however; she made her way immediately to the room that most delighted her in the house – the library.

The lure of this room was impossible to ignore. The stillness, the delicious smell her husband had described to her so many letters ago, the soaring ceilings and the bookshelves with their ladders on long brass railings all combined to make it a place which could not help but stir the soul of a lover of books. To all of this was added most comfortable seating – large, worn chairs – and a series of tall windows, letting in the spring sunlight. None of these things, however, were Elizabeth's object in coming here. Instead, she sought one of the bookshelves on the wall opposite the windows, feeling under the fourth shelf from the bottom for the little latch. The latch clicked under her hand, she pushed the shelf forward, and revealed the secret room.

It was, as promised, musty and old. The furniture could not be less than a century old, the wallpaper seemed just this side of mouldering, and Elizabeth had to carry in a candle so that she could have any light at all. And yet she loved it. She could not help but recall her eagerness to see this room, and her husband's eagerness to show it to her, as well as the library itself, the highlight of his showing her around the main rooms of the estate.

They had been married one year and one month, now, and Elizabeth had made her decision. This room, this very private place, was where she would tell him what he likely already realised, that she was barren. That she, the daughter of a woman who had produced five healthy girls, one after the other, should not even be able to conceive one child.

She had come into her marriage confident that she would have no such difficulties, and now was ashamed to understand that she had no notion of what would happen to Pemberley after her husband's death, with her failure to have a son. She did not even know if it was entailed, and never did Elizabeth sympathise with her mother so much as she did now. Frances Bennet must have felt similarly confident that she would be blessed with sons, although at least Elizabeth's mother had always possessed causes for hope – every one of her pregnancies had been a chance for a son.

Elizabeth had always felt she possessed ample courage, but broaching this topic with her husband she had no courage for. It seemed to her that admitting it aloud should make it more real, that it would send her irretrievably on the path to a life without children. Admitting it to him, her husband who would happily play on the floor with the Gardiner boys in his dinner clothes, seemed the most difficult thing she should ever have to do, and she considered discussing it with Jane, first, when her sister arrived.

"I knew you would be in here," Darcy said, startling her so that she very nearly dropped her candle.

"This secret room shall not work very well if you always know I will be in here."

"I disagree. I believe there are few things better than the thought of a secret room in my house where I know I may find my wife," he said, taking the few steps necessary to kiss her.

Elizabeth set her candle down on a quite historic table, so that she might better return the kiss, and found herself filled with a longing to sink back into some dusty piece of furniture and have yet another attempt at making a baby. Oh, but the impropriety of it, and herself just installed as the new mistress of the house!

"I think perhaps we should save this for tonight," she said, breathing heavily.

"The door does have a lock," he said, closing the opposite side of the bookshelf behind him, and sliding an ornate old dead-bolt into place. "And the staff only clean here when the family are all known to be away. The secret room would not work very well if everyone could just be walking in at any time."

"Everyone except the master of the house."

"Well, there are certain benefits to being master of the house."

Elizabeth abandoned her meagre protests and let him kiss her all the way back to an ancient chaise, let herself sit there and feel his hand on her ankle, pulling her skirts up. There was something that made her whole being flutter at this, this delicious, dangerous thing that smacked in the face of all propriety, something that drove her earlier thoughts of what she must do in this room almost entirely away. She would tell him; she had to tell him. But not on this day.

CHAPTER 2

The introductory visits continued on for three more days, so that Elizabeth had met not only all of the tenants, but also the rector, Mr. Clark, and the more notable families in Lambton and on the neighbouring estates. Such was the size of Pemberley's lands that it dominated their quarter of the county, and it was clear to Elizabeth that the Darcys were and had been for a very long time the first family of the area.

Here, unlike in town, Elizabeth did not feel herself judged by all she met; she was treated exceedingly well simply because she was Mrs. Darcy, and none she met could afford to shun her. Still, most people she met had good manners and seemed truly kind, and she found she particularly enjoyed the company of the Watsons, in Lambton, who were old acquaintances of her aunt Gardiner, and the Sinclair's, of Berwick Hall. Elizabeth assumed both families would return her call shortly, and decided she should ask them and some of the others to dinner, for now that the Darcys were returned to Pemberley, they would be expected to maintain a certain flow of social engagements at the great house, although fortunately they need not be at the pace Elizabeth had grown used to in town.

She had only one family expected for dinner this evening, but they were people most dear to her heart: the Bingleys. Jane had written from London and indicated today as their most likely date of arrival, so long as nothing delayed their travel. All was ready; Elizabeth had asked Mrs. Reynolds for a recommendation as to the best apartment for them to use during what might be an extended stay, and a lovely little suite of rooms toward the back of the house had been readied by the staff.

Elizabeth would be delighted to see Charles, but she had not lived in the same house as Jane since their marriages, and the thought of once again being able to share daily confidences with her sister left her walking through Pemberley's halls with a pleased countenance. The only thing that caused it to fade was the sound of Georgiana once again practising furiously in the music room. Since their return to the house, the young lady's practises had grown longer and more intense, and Elizabeth wondered if she was trying to distract herself from thoughts of Captain Stanton by playing for hours on end.

Elizabeth wished she could think of something that might bring Georgiana relief, but the wound, if it could be called that, was still too new. A letter from him might, perhaps, help in at least establishing his present situation; it might be gleaned for evidence of his affection. There had been nothing, however, although Elizabeth knew from Kitty's latest letter that Captain Ramsey had already written her a brief note on the day the Andromeda had departed Portsmouth, and promised more once he had been at sea for some time. She knew they had not the same right to expect correspondence from Captain Stanton, but still, he had asked particularly if he might write to them.

Not wanting to disturb Georgiana, Elizabeth decided to go to the saloon, so that she might read one of the volumes she had borrowed from the Pemberley library, and would be able to hear immediately if the Bingleys arrived. One of the strangest aspects of taking up residence at Pemberley had been adjusting to the size of the place. At Longbourn and Curzon Street, she had always had a general sense of where everyone in the house was; here, she often found herself asking the nearest servant where she might find Mr. Darcy or Miss Darcy. There were several sitting rooms in addition to the large yellow drawing-room and smaller blue drawing-room, each connecting to its equivalently sized dining room. All of these rooms were dwarfed by the immense ballroom, and the portrait gallery on the floor immediately above it, and added to all of this was a vast quantity of bedchambers. Darcy had told her that the house could entertain up to two hundred without great difficulty, and sleep at least fifty, although it had been some time since it had done so, and more staff would be needed to see to the comfort of that number. Startled by the notion of entertaining so many, she had assured him she had no such plans any time soon, although the idea of a large summer house party with all of their family and friends gathered there did appeal to her.

She read quietly until the faint sound of carriage wheels outside reached her, and then she sprang up, ready to run to the door until she remembered herself and walked outside at a more appropriate pace. Jane was grown large enough now that she required more assistance getting out of the carriage, although not quite the level of vigilance that Charles applied as he eased her down. Elizabeth rushed forward and carefully embraced her sister as they exchanged greetings, and it was only when she stepped back that she realised there had been a third with them in the carriage.

"Papa!" she exclaimed, rushing over to embrace him as well. "We did not expect you, but this is a most delightful surprise."

"You have left me with no entertainment, Lizzy. Despite your mother's best efforts, she cannot turn your sisters back into the silly creatures that left us. Mary spends all her days practising the pianoforte, but she actually sounds quite good, and none of us can pull Kitty's nose out of the Navy List," he said, looking up at the house. "I came here looking for something else to divert myself, but now that I am arrived, I see there will be no space for me, your home is so small. Jane and Charles, I shall require the use of your carriage to return home."

"We shall certainly find quarters for you, papa," Elizabeth said, laughing. "I assume you would prefer a place near the library."

"Oh no, Lizzy, you might just put me up in the library. A cot will do very nicely. I have heard great things from Charles, and I can assure you I do not intend to leave it, once I am there."

At some point during her father's teazing, Darcy had made his way out to the drive, and was greeting the Bingleys. His greeting with her father was more reserved, Elizabeth noticed, but much of the reserve was on her father's side. Perhaps it made sense that it should be so; Elizabeth realised that Darcy had, without any effort to do so, become in essence the patriarch of their larger family, by force of both fortune and consequence. There would be little done where his approval was not sought – Captain Ramsey had come to him first, to discuss his plans to propose to Kitty, and certainly the Bingleys would not purchase an estate without applying to him for his thoughts.

Elizabeth loved her father dearly, but she also knew his flaws, and she wondered if he was perhaps relieved that Darcy was taking on a role that he himself had never really sought. With all but one daughter married or engaged, he might ensconce himself in the Pemberley library and avoid responsibility indefinitely. She thought back to Darcy's active management of his tenants's crops, and wondered how much more Longbourn might take in, if her father were to institute similar measures. Darcy would never suggest them, though, without his advice being especially solicited, and Elizabeth harboured no hope that her father would do so in his elder years, or that Mr. Collins would make a more effective estate manager. Longbourn might be beginning its decline; it might even be in the midst of it.

Mrs. Reynolds met Elizabeth as they were making their way back inside the house, and said: "Ma'am, I noticed there is an additional gentleman in the party. Do you wish us to have a room made up for him?"

"Yes, Mrs. Reynolds, he is my father, Mr. Bennet; he has decided to surprise us. If you could have something made up for him near the library, I am sure he would appreciate it very much."

"Near the library – yes, I have just the apartment," Mrs. Reynolds said.

"I will see to it. In the meantime I'll have Henry show Mr. Bennet to a temporary chamber where he might freshen up after his travels."

"Thank you, Mrs. Reynolds, that would be lovely."

The travellers all disappeared, Darcy with them, and Elizabeth found herself returning to the sitting room to pick up her book again, unexpectedly alone. Jane was back down soon enough, however, changed for dinner and with the happiest countenance.

"Oh, Lizzy, Pemberley is the most amazing place! I am so delighted for you, to be mistress of such a house – and the grounds look beautiful. If Charles and I are able to find an estate half so wonderful, I will be quite content."

"I am certain you will find something wonderful," Elizabeth said. "I only hope it is close, so that I might see my nephew or niece as often as possible."

"I do hope for something close, as well. The countryside is so beautiful here – my aunt was quite right when she talked of all the merits of Derbyshire," Jane said. "I am a little worried that we will not find a place before I must begin my confinement, though. Charles's father always intended to purchase an estate, but he never quite managed to, and now that I hear all of Charles's requirements for the perfect home, I fear we shall never find a place that matches all of them."

"Well, you need not worry if you do not find anything before it is time for the child," Elizabeth said. "You are perfectly welcome to stay here through the birth and beyond if you need to."

"Lizzy, that is so generous of you."

"It is nothing of the sort – I want my Jane near me for as long as possible, and if you have the child here, I shall not even have to travel when it is time," Elizabeth said, steeling herself for what she had determined to do. "And it would be nice to have a child about, for a little while, since – since it does not seem that I will have one myself."

"Oh, Lizzy," Jane said, her expression instantly changing to one of sadness, as she picked up her sister's hands. "I know you have not spoken of it, but have you suffered a miscarriage?"

"No, in a way I almost wish I had," Elizabeth said. "It might at least demonstrate that I was in some way able to carry a child. No, Jane, I seem to be barren."

"Have you seen a physician?"

"I have not." Elizabeth blushed at the thought of having such a conversation with a man, even one of the physical line. "I do not see what he could tell me that would help. I should have been with child long before now, and yet I am not."

"There is still hope, Lizzy – you have only just been married a year."

"A year should have been more than enough time," Elizabeth said, her eyes moist as she looked about the room. "No, it seems the truth is that I will leave all you see around you without an heir."

"Lizzy, I am so sorry, but I beg you will not give up hope."

They could not very well turn to a more cheerful topic, after such a conversation, and so Jane made a selection out of the sewing basket, and Elizabeth, after her spirits had settled a little, decided to do the same. They were interrupted after a while by Mr. Bennet, who, as it turned out, had news that very much cheered Elizabeth.

"Jane, have you told Elizabeth of our other news?"

"Oh, papa, I forgot! I seem to be doing more of that these days," Jane said, too kind after her recent conversation with Elizabeth to note that she suspected this to be another symptom of her pregnancy.

"What news?" Elizabeth asked.

"Well, Lizzy, you might have wondered how I could come here, when your mother's poor nerves were still suffering over Lydia's actions," he said. "We have had a letter from her, however. She is in Brussels; she has taken up a room with several other soldiers's wives who have need to economise – food and lodging are quite expensive there, now, with such an influx of people. While they cannot be said to be living well, she is at least safe, and she promises to go no closer to what is expected to be the war front."

"Oh, thank goodness," Elizabeth said. "Do you think there is any chance she may be compelled to return? She might stay here, or at Longbourn."

"I do not," Mr. Bennet said. "You must never expect your youngest sister to do the rational thing, Lizzy. It is not in her nature."

CHAPTER 3

The party at Pemberley quickly fell into a routine: Jane and Charles would leave in the morning to look at an estate or two, sometimes accompanied by Mr. Bennet, although more often than not that gentleman preferred to shut himself in the library for the course of the day. Darcy continued to convene with Richardson on estate business, studying all that he had missed during his absence, and only making his way to wherever they had gathered after hours spent poring over the books or riding Pemberley's lands. Georgiana, meanwhile, if she did not accompany her brother on these rides, rose late and spent much of her time practising the pianoforte. Elizabeth thus found herself with emptier mornings than she had expected, although they all dined and spent their evenings together.

Admitting that she was likely barren to her sister had proven both liberating and depressing to Elizabeth. As she had expected, there was a certain realness to it that came only in admitting it to another, yet also a certain relief, that it was no longer a secret thought. It had been nearly easy, though, to share it with Jane, with whom she had shared so many secrets over the course of her life. Elizabeth knew she would have to speak to Darcy of it, but she also knew it would be a far more difficult conversation, one she would gain no relief from, to tell him that the future of the estate he cared so deeply for must remain in uncertainty, that the children she knew he longed for would never come.

After some deliberation, she decided to take Jane's advice and see a physician, first; it was possible there was some physic she could take that would aid in conceiving a baby, or something else that might be done. Elizabeth shared this change of mind with Jane, who would need to begin seeing the local physician, Dr. Alderman, and the sisters determined that Elizabeth could quietly apply to him for advice following Jane's first appointment.

As for her husband, she only asked him one night if he thought one of the grooms might be able to teach her to ride; she was willing to give horses another try.

"Nonsense," he said, looking quite pleased that she had suggested it. "My father and I taught Georgiana; I will teach you myself."

Thus the next morning he had an ancient-looking pony saddled and led into one of the paddocks next to the stables. Elizabeth met him there wearing a yet-unused riding habit, and feeling very ridiculous.

"Are you quite certain that pony can hold me?" she asked, looking dubiously at the side saddle strapped to its back.

"Buttercup is quite sturdy, I assure you," Darcy said. "And you are very slight anyway; I do not believe you weigh too much more than Georgiana did when she learned on him."

The advantage of the pony, at least, was that he was closer to the ground, so that Darcy barely had to lift her up into the saddle. It had been a very long time since Elizabeth had attempted to ride a horse; the saddle felt strange to her, and it took her some time to even just arrange her legs in what she thought to be the correct place. Darcy helped her with further adjustments, and then remained standing there, one hand on her hip and the other on the pony's reins.

"Are you quite situated?" he asked. "Grip with your legs, but you should also lean back a little more, to compensate for most of your weight being on this side of him."

Elizabeth leaned back, and then said she was as situated as she thought she could be. He took up the reins in his own hand, and began leading her around the perimeter of the paddock. The pony was moving, certainly, but at a sedate walk, and it was so very different from when one of the Longbourn grooms had attempted to teach her how to ride, by placing her in the saddle, giving her barely a moment to settle, and then tapping her father's horse with his whip so that the startled animal moved immediately into a fast trot, that Elizabeth felt her nerves settle.

"Are you comfortable, Elizabeth?" he asked.

"Yes, very," she said, smiling down at him.

"Very good," he said. "We will make a few laps and then perhaps try a trot."

Through the course of the next week, they would go out to the paddock every day so that Elizabeth could practise. She graduated from a trot to a canter, the pony safely tethered to a longe line held by Darcy, standing in the middle of the paddock. Elizabeth felt her confidence, as well as her love for her husband, growing, if it were possible. He was exceedingly patient, and did not seem to mind at all when a spring rain soaked the paddock, resulting in his boots and breeches becoming quite spattered with mud.

Once Darcy felt she had mastered her balance in the saddle, he began to teach her how to hold the reins, steering Buttercup, and then, finally, how to hold the whip in her right hand, and use it to command the pony, with both of her legs on the other side. She took up the whip, and had no difficulty putting Buttercup through his paces: his jittery little trot and then smoother canter, along the rail of the paddock, with no assistance at all from her husband.

"Very well done, Elizabeth," Darcy said. "You are well on your way to becoming a horsewoman. Let me have Kestrel saddled and then we may take a little ride along the grounds."

Elizabeth felt nervous at the idea of taking Buttercup outside of the confines of the paddock, yet also thrilled with the idea of going on even the shortest of rides across Pemberley's grounds with her husband. Kestrel was duly saddled, and Darcy given a leg up into his saddle, and it became immediately clear to Elizabeth the extreme difference between their two mounts. They left the paddock, and Kestrel danced under Darcy's hand until they reached the open field.

"Please do excuse me for a moment, Elizabeth," Darcy said, and he let the horse move into a powerful canter and then finally a full-out gallop across the field. For Elizabeth, who had been working quite hard to get to the point where she felt comfortable controlling a sedate pony such as Buttercup, it was the clearest possible indicator of how very far her husband's skill exceeded her own. Kestrel tore along the open space, and Darcy barely moved on the horse's back as they swept across the field – it was easily the fastest she had ever seen a horse move, and she might have been concerned at the pace if anything in horse or rider showed the situation to be the slightest bit amiss. They did not, however; they seemed to be a well-paired team at the top of their skill, enjoying every aspect of the fresh air and spongy April turf.

They had galloped ahead some ways before Elizabeth realised that she was alone with Buttercup, and not at all concerned, and she urged the pony into a trot to follow them with the slightest little flick of her whip. It would have been some time before she caught up with them, but Darcy turned Kestrel back toward them, and returned at a pretty little canter, sitting tall and clearly in control of the horse as they approached.

Kestrel seemed to have energy without bounds, but he accepted walking along beside Buttercup, with the occasional trot in open spaces, once his initial desire to run had worn off. Elizabeth could not deny how nice it was to be up on horseback, alongside her husband, covering far more of Pemberley's grounds than they ever would have on foot.

They made their way to the woods, along one of the bridle paths; somewhere distant Elizabeth could hear the stream trickling along its way to the front of the house, but the dominant sound was the clipping and clopping of the horses's hooves as they made their way along. Elizabeth breathed deeply and turned with a contented smile toward her husband, which turned wry as she looked up at him, already taller than she, even without their comically mismatched mounts.

"We must look completely ridiculous, riding together," she said. "Was that why you chose the path through the woods?"

"I cannot say that was my motivation," he said, laughing. "But yes, over time we shall graduate you to taller mounts, and eventually find you a horse of your own. If you are comfortable cantering along for the rest of the path, I may show you my real reason for coming this way more quickly."

Elizabeth did feel comfortable, and rode alongside him in eager anticipation, Darcy holding Kestrel at a trot, else he would easily have outpaced Buttercup's stout little legs. They came to a point in the woods where an old stone wall bordered one side of the path, in a state of crumble, and then finally a little clearing. Elizabeth gasped when she saw the clearing, for ahead of her was a most romantic ruin, too real and too far gone to be a folly.

"Oh, I love it!" she exclaimed, bringing Buttercup down to a walk as they approached the corner of what once had been a large stone building. "Whatever was it?"

"It was the original house, at Pemberley," he said. "From what I understand of the family records, it was meant to be kept up as a dower house, but fell into disrepair during the Civil War. It has been left to ruin since then."

"We must come here again, with someone to hold the horses," she said. "I should so enjoy exploring it more closely."

"We certainly may. Edward and I passed many hours of our youth here; I daresay you will find some of our childhood toys strewn about," he said, concern crossing his face at his mention of Colonel Fitzwilliam.

"The papers said his regiment made the crossing successfully – I am sure in Lady Ellen's next letter she will have some better idea of how he does," Elizabeth said, hoping to reassure him. War had, for her, always been such a disconnected thing from her life, with little more than the militia's quartering at Meryton to affect her. Now, she knew so many whose lives she feared for – including her own, foolish sister – and she understood fully the constant wear Darcy and the Fitzwilliams must have undergone, in the last war.

"He never has time to write much," Darcy said. "Wellesley always keeps his men busy, both with military duties and society, if there is any to be had. But you are right, he will write to Lady Ellen, at least. He would never have her angry at him, if he can help it."

"I did not think Lady Ellen was capable of being angry."

"Oh, but that is the thing of it. She never *shows* she is angry, which makes it all the worse," he said. "When we would get into trouble as boys, our fathers would just take us round to the stable to be disciplined, but Lady Ellen would sit us down over milk and tea and say, 'Now boys, I am very *disappointed* in you.' It was the worst punishment imaginable."

Elizabeth laughed at the thought of it, her husband and Colonel Fitzwilliam, being quietly chastised over tea by Lady Ellen. She would do the same for her nephew or niece, she thought; she would attempt to be that elegant aunt whose disappointment was far worse than anything their father could dole out. Which – knowing Charles Bingley's temperament – was not likely to be much punishment at all.

CHAPTER 4

It was Sarah who first noticed Elizabeth was pregnant.

"Shall I prepare the blue riding habit for you to wear after you break your fast, ma'am?" she asked one morning, well before Jane's planned appointment with Dr. Alderman.

"Yes, please do. It looks as though we have a clear morning, so I see no reason why Mr. Darcy and I will not go out today."

"Indeed, ma'am, and you must get your riding in before the baby is too far along."

"We still have some time before Jane will begin her confinement, although you are right, I will want to provide her company once it begins."

"Oh, but I did not mean Mrs. Bingley's baby – I meant your own bairn."

"My *bairn*?" asked Elizabeth. "Sarah, whatever do you mean by that?"

"My lady, I do apologise – I should not have said anything. It is surely not in my place to say anything."

For some time, Elizabeth and Sarah had shared a very comfortable relationship – Sarah was never one to overstep her bounds, and yet now she looked positively frightened for her job.

"Never mind that, Sarah – I do not understand what you mean."

"Mrs. Darcy, I was the oldest of eleven brothers and sisters, and I can see you have all the signs – your stays don't lace up quite so tight as they used to, and you sleep later, but you still seem so tired – and I beg my pardon for saying so, but you often look ill in the mornings."

Elizabeth had been feeling a little ill in her stomach every morning, including this one, but she had attributed it to Pemberley's cook using different spices than their cook back at Curzon Street, and she had been experimenting with skipping this dish or that during dinner, to see if she might discover which had offended her stomach. She had not thought there could be any other cause, and she turned and embraced a very surprised

Sarah.

"You truly do think I am with child?"

"Yes ma'am. I'm no physician, but I did see my mamma have many of her babies," Sarah said. "You should have confirmation soon enough, if you miss your courses."

"I do not understand, though. Why now, after I have been married more than a year?"

"On the farm, sometimes we had good years, and sometimes we had lean years," Sarah said. "My mamma never was with child in the lean years. She used to say her body knew when it was time to have a bairn, and when it was not. Forgive me for saying, ma'am, but London is not the healthiest place, and then you were so busy all the time you was there. Perhaps your body did not think it a healthy enough time for having a baby."

Elizabeth's legs were shaking; she sat down heavily, thinking on what Sarah had said. Could the thick air of the city and the stress of the season have been what prevented her from growing pregnant? After all, Jane had been at Netherfield for nearly half a year before she and Charles had come to town, and chaperoning Caroline was not the same as three very young ladies. And Darcy was right, she had grown very slight – she found much of the food in town too rich for her taste, and at many events had found her stomach tense, so that if she ate at all, it was sparingly. She had felt her weight returning to that which was more natural, now that they were at Pemberley, but would never have thought that some of it was caused by the beginnings of a child.

"Sarah, you have given me cause for hope when I thought all hope might be lost. Please speak not a word of this to anyone – I want to wait until I am certain. I could not bear to give false hope."

"Of course not, ma'am."

Elizabeth realised she was weeping, although with the deepest relief and happiness; she certainly could not go down to breakfast like this, and anyway, she had no appetite for it.

"Will you tell them I am feeling ill – a headache, perhaps – and will not be down to breakfast today?"

"Very well, ma'am."

Once her spirits had settled, Elizabeth found herself seized with a certain restlessness, and she realised she would have preferred to be in company, where conversation could serve as a distraction. Only time would confirm whether she was with child, and time seemed to pass most slowly in her bedchamber.

The quality of the room could not be faulted. Elizabeth had been impressed by the size of her bedchamber at Curzon Street, but this one was easily twice its size, so large that if the furniture had not been carefully arranged, it should have been an awkward space. This arrangement, she knew, had been Georgiana's doing; her sister had also seen to the placement of a few more comfortable chairs from elsewhere in the house, for in addition to being outdated, the furniture was otherwise ostentatious, and uncomfortable. Elizabeth had been invited to redecorate this room, as well, by her husband, and thought it likely that this should be the first place where she would attempt such a thing.

The rest of the master's and mistress's apartment was much better-done. She and Darcy each had an impossibly large dressing room – even with all of the dresses from her wedding trousseau and the ones she had purchased since, Elizabeth thought her wardrobes could hold four times the number of dresses she currently possessed. There was even a small, private sitting room, between their two dressing rooms, and Elizabeth would have much preferred to pass her time there, rather than lying in bed.

As it turned out, however, Elizabeth could not claim illness without several concerned parties coming to her bedchamber, so that she had at least some manner of distraction. Darcy was first, knocking and entering slowly, so that Elizabeth had plenty of time to tuck the book she had taken to reading below her bedcovers.

"I was sorry to hear of your headache, my dear," he said, looking at her with such concern that Elizabeth very nearly confessed to him that she did not have a headache at all, and what she hoped she did instead have. "What may we bring you for relief? Jane asked that we have the kitchen send up some willow bark tea. Is there anything else you would like?"

"That is good of her to think of it – willow bark tea often brings me relief. It is not a very bad headache; I believe I shall be better in a few hours. Thank you for checking on me, though."

"Of course," he said, leaning over to gently kiss her cheek.

There came a disruption, then; from outside the bedchamber, Elizabeth could hear Sarah say very loudly that she should take the tea in and attend to her mistress, followed by some manner of porcelain rattling. Sarah then entered, looking a little flustered and out of breath, carrying a tray with the tea.

"You are very devoted to Mrs. Darcy, Miss Kelly," Darcy said to her. "I appreciate it very much, and am glad to see how well-deserved was your promotion."

"I thank you kindly, sir," Sarah said, making a curtsey and then setting down the tea on a distant table.

"Will you not bring the tea over?" Darcy asked. "I should like for Mrs. Darcy to gain its benefits as soon as possible."

"I beg your pardon, Mr. Darcy, but it is much too hot to be drank right now," Sarah said, her voice very tense, and Elizabeth thought she must be intimidated by the presence of Darcy, with whom Sarah rarely had reason to interact. "I shall bring it over when it is ready."

"Very well, then," Darcy said. "I will leave you to drink your tea and get some rest, Mrs. Darcy. You will have Miss Kelly tell us if there is anything else that can be provided to make you more comfortable?"

"I will. Thank you, Mr. Darcy."

As soon as he had left the room, Sarah gasped and put her hand to her chest, looking exceedingly relieved, and breathing even more heavily.

"I ran all the way here, my lady. Mrs. Reynolds said they were sending up willow bark tea to you."

"Yes – I have used it many times to bring relief, for a headache. I do not have one now, but I supposed I should drink it anyway, to keep with everyone thinking I was thus afflicted."

"I beg you will not drink it, ma'am. It may just be a silly superstition, but nobody in our neighbourhood would let a woman with child drink willow bark tea after Mrs. O'Malley's baby. She had the megrims, while she was in the family way, and she drank willow bark tea so very often, the first time she was with child. Her baby – oh I cannot speak of it, but it was terrible," Sarah said, shuddering. "Please make my mind easier and do not drink it."

"If you think I should not drink it, I will not drink it," Elizabeth said. "You clearly have more experience with babies than I, and I would not risk this child – if it is indeed a child – for anything."

"Oh, thank you, my lady," Sarah said, looking most relieved. She waited until the tea had cooled a little, dumped it into a vase of flowers, then made her exit with the tray.

Elizabeth was glad that Jane did not come to check on her; she was not certain she could keep the secret from her sister, after having confessed her concerns of being barren, and in addition to that larger omission, she would certainly have to lie outright about having taken the tea.

Georgiana did, however, come in very hesitantly, asking as her brother had if there was anything else that might be brought for her. Elizabeth assured her there was not; with a little more rest, she should be better.

"I am so sorry, I should have let you rest!" Georgiana exclaimed, when given this excuse. "I will leave you now."

"No, do not worry, stay a little while," Elizabeth said, for in truth, Georgiana looked like the one who should be claiming illness, as she had to some degree ever since Captain Stanton's departure. "I will sleep in a little while, but it has been some time since we have had a chance to really talk, and I wonder how you are feeling."

After some time, Georgiana spoke, with tears in her eyes. "I miss him. I miss him more than I can say. It is not as though I saw him frequently, but now that I am deprived of all contact, I am always thinking of things I would like to tell him; I am wishing for just a few minutes in his company. And I worry for his safety, constantly."

"Oh, Georgiana, I know it is not easy to wait," Elizabeth said. "But wait for him, and if he truly is constant, he will return to you."

"But I have no notion of whether he is constant, whether he has any reason to be constant. I have no notion of whether he loves me."

"I find it very difficult to believe that he would pay so much attention to you if he did not love you. And if he loves you, he will not need a reason."

Elizabeth could not bring herself to mention another possibility – that Captain Stanton did love her, but he would not return. There were certainly any number of men who had set off for the war who would not see England again – they would die on the continent, or on the oceans surrounding it, and there was every chance that one of their acquaintances would be among them.

Elizabeth was more than ready for her feigned illness to be over, and she came down to dinner as usual, telling everyone that she was feeling much better. She had less enthusiasm for breakfast the following day, but did attend, requiring herself to eat a little so as not to cause her family any further concern. Darcy asked if she felt up to riding, and she told him she did; perhaps just a short ride today, but it would be nice to get out on horseback. They went out, therefore, Darcy on Kestrel and Elizabeth on Buttercup, making their way through one of the trails in the woods.

"We should wait until you are fully recovered," Darcy said. "But I have been thinking it is time for you to graduate beyond Buttercup, to Georgiana's old cob, Spartan. He will be a bit more of a challenge for you, but he is still quite manageable."

Elizabeth felt fear clutch at her stomach – she trusted old Buttercup thoroughly, but she was not willing to trust what might be her unborn child to a new mount.

"I do not feel ready yet," she said, tensely. "I should like to stay with Buttercup for a while."

He looked at her strangely, and said, "Elizabeth, do you mind my asking, was there something that happened when you were younger that makes you distrust horses so?"

"My father's groom was not so patient a teacher as you are," she said. "I fell quite a few times, and the last time the horse's hooves were so near to my head I could feel all the ·force they would have brought had they stepped on me."

"Oh, my dear, I am sorry you had to suffer such an experience," he said. "The groom started you on a full-sized horse?"

"We did not have the – variety of mounts – you keep here at Pemberley."

"Of course," he said. "I admit we likely would not, either, if not for Georgiana. She cannot bear to see them go, and it is not as though we cannot afford to keep them. And then I thought perhaps my – my niece or nephew might use them to learn. Or, as it turns out, my wife."

He finished his statement with a smile, but Elizabeth felt certain he had meant to say "son or daughter," rather than "niece or nephew," and it took all of her determination not to tell him of Sarah's suspicions immediately. After so long, to raise his hopes and then have to dash them pained her just to think about it, and she dared not think about how devastating it would be for her. She had spent so long wishing for merely hope, but now that she had it, she knew it would not be enough.

CHAPTER 5

A few days later, Elizabeth and Georgiana were spending the morning in the music room, waiting for Jane, Charles, and her father to return from yet another estate visit, and Darcy from a ride with Richardson around some of the tenant farms, when Mrs. Reynolds came in.

"Forgive me, my lady, but there's a letter come from London for you, under cover from Mr. Miller," she said. "The most prodigious thick letter I've seen in some time. I thought you might want it immediately."

"Yes, thank you, Mrs. Reynolds."

Mrs. Reynolds looked every bit as curious about the letter as Elizabeth was, but she dutifully retreated from the room. Elizabeth opened the seal and read Mr. Miller's brief note of explanation, that the letter had arrived by servant from the Earl of Anglesey's house, and he was thus forwarding it on to Pemberley. She shared this with Georgiana, who was immediately all attention at the mention of the earl, and moved to sit right beside Elizabeth as she removed the next layer of the letter, a brief covering letter from the earl, and then the next, a piece of oiled silk, so that she finally reached the letter beneath and they both saw what they each had suspected, that it was from Captain Stanton.

Georgiana exhaled audibly, and Elizabeth felt her relief. He had written; he had written rather a lot, by the looks of the letter. Elizabeth opened it, saw that he had a neat, firm hand, and held out the letter so that they might both read at the same time:

"HMS Jupiter

"March 29, 1815

"Dear Mrs. Darcy,

"I hope whenever this letter finds you, that it finds all your family in good health, particularly Miss Darcy, whom I hope has by now made a full recovery from her injury. We are now two days out of Portsmouth, and what a great relief it is to be at sea again after several weeks spent fighting with my fellow captains for men and supplies, with far too many of us trying to make ready for sea at the same time. We were obliged to wait an extra few days for want of enough wood for casks, for the great ships of the line take precedence in their victualling. There are an even greater number of the lesser ships like ourselves than the higher-rated ships, and there will be many uses for us. Some will go out to support the troop ships, or carry troops themselves, and still others to blockade duty, or to harry the coast, which is the Jupiter's role.

"We were thus obliged to wait for them, but the delay did at least allow me to take on my full complement of men – there are three hundred and sixty-three of us living within these wooden walls, and all of us volunteers, I am glad to say. Among them are a few familiar faces to you – some of the men who stayed with you during the riots. I am fortunate to have so many men returning from the Caroline, and a great many of my new volunteers are experienced seamen. Still, they are not all used to working together, and last night when we exercised the great guns for the first time, they were not nearly so quick as I would have liked – we will never beat the French at three broadsides in nearly eight and a half minutes. We will practise every evening that we are able – shall I tell you what goes into working the great guns?

"First, we must clear for action, which means making a clean sweep fore and aft – everything that may be removed is taken down into the hold, including the bulkheads to my cabins, and everything inside. Then you can look up and down the full length of the ship, and see nothing but the guns and their crews, waiting. In order to fire, each gun must be cleaned, filled with powder and a wad of cloth, those items rammed in, and then the shot placed inside, along with more cloth. Then the men heave the gun forward – we call this running it out – place more powder in the touch hole, and finally it is ready to be fired, by pulling a cord attached to the gunlock. In most ships we do not fire all of the guns at once – it is very rough on a ship's timbers, although the Jupiter is young enough she could bear it if needed. So each gun fires off in succession, aiming to hit whatever target we have been able to put together with scrap wood and the like. It is uncommonly loud, and the gun kicks back with tremendous force, so the men must be careful to stay out of its way. As soon as the gun has fired, its crew must prepare it again, all the while our ship's boys – we call them powder monkeys – running up and down the stairs from the magazine to the guns. The magazine is where we keep all of the powder – it is lined with lead and we take great care to ensure it is protected, for there is enough gunpowder inside to turn this ship to little but splinters, if it ever were to ignite.

"March 30, 1815

"Now that I reflect, perhaps the firing of guns is not the most interesting topic to write of, to a lady, so do allow me to attempt to find something else. We are making our way along the coast, now, and there are few things I enjoy more than the sight of the coast of England. Beachy Head is perhaps the most dramatic, but all along, you see the usual rolling hills of our country fall off into great cliffs of white chalk, and far below them shingle beaches, with the surf rolling in. Every once in a while, there will be a little cottage or even a village visible on the top of these cliffs, and I cannot help but wonder at the audacity of those who would build on the edge of such a drop. Perhaps some of them are the men who work the little fishing boats we pass. Most of them turn and sail away, although they are English – they fear I shall stop them, and press them into the navy. Once they see I have no such need, however, they return to their previous tack, and a few have been so brazen as to cheer us, while others have been happy enough to sell us their catch.

"We will depart such sights shortly, though, as we are to patrol the channel between Calais and Lorient. It is a fortunate assignment for what many might call an unfortunate ship – we certainly have more freedom to act than those on blockade duty, or involved in transporting the troops. We are under general orders to harass the enemy in any way we might, and I hope we come upon a French ship soon, so that we may do so in the best way possible.

"I must say that the ship has been a pleasant surprise, thus far – faster than I had expected, dry and weatherly. Out on deck, if you were to look up, you would see a cloud of canvas (I shall not bore you with the details of each sail), and over the side, a fine wave of foam along the side of the ship, for we are making an easy eight knots. I do not expect such sweet sailing to continue – not on the channel, and not with the barometer dropping – but for now it is as fine a day at sea as I could ask for.

"April 4, 1815

"The barometer never lies – it did come on to blow, a usual channel storm. The ship came through it well, with hardly a foot of water in the well even at the worst of it, for you see, even the most weatherly ship makes a bit of water as she is working. The men, too, did all I could have asked of them, and indeed, a little storm early on may help tie them together as more of a singular crew. There are so many old Carolines and friends of Carolines aboard that it has been a bit awkward for the others, and I must be very careful not to be too familiar with those I have sailed with for so many years, so that the newcomers do not feel unwelcome.

"April 5, 1815

"We are back to our usual morning routine, today. The men have been piped up from below decks, carrying their hammocks so that they may be placed in the hammock netting along the sides of the ship – there they give the crew extra protection against splinters, if we should go into battle. They are scrubbing the decks with their holystones, for we have a great care for cleanliness in the navy, and soon enough they will be flogged dry, and I then may properly make an appearance on deck.

"For now it is breakfast, which I share with one of my midshipmen, Mr. Ashton, a boy of thirteen years of age, who eats as voraciously as a boy of that age should. He is the third son of Baron Ashton, a friend of my uncle's, and has the makings of a promising young officer – this is his first time at sea, but his father saw him to a most extensive education in the mathematics, so that he is far ahead of the others in navigation. I try to have each of my midshipmen – I have only four, on this cruise – in for breakfast or dinner in the cabin, so that they may all remember something resembling manners, and all of my officers, save the officer of the watch, shall dine here this evening.

"We do eat better here on board than you might expect, at least at the beginning of a cruise, while we still have livestock on board, fish readily caught and purchased, and even fresh bread. Many of my officers and I have brought our own private stores, well beyond what the navy supplies, spending a bit of our prize money from our days on the Caroline. I will not deceive you, though, back on the Caroline there were times when we were out so long all of us were down to salt beef or pork, steeped and boiled, same as the men, and a few times we were precious short of water, and hoping deeply for rain.

"April 6, 1815

"You may have noted I have hardly mentioned the enemy, and the reason for this is quite simple – we have yet to see any French ships of substance. We chased a little fore-and-aft rigged smuggler yesterday – only a bit larger than the cutter we all went sailing in – but she was too nimble for a ship of this size to catch, and it was too late, by the time we got the boats lowered. I am not sure how much of the French fleet is even out – it may well be that our preventative blockade is keeping them in. I shall get a better sense of the situation when we reach Brest.

"So we stay close to the French shore and hope we might see someone to fight. The shore batteries are manned, at least, and there are few things the crew likes better than to have a go at trying to hit them, which gives us the dual purpose of practising our gunnery and at least providing some harassment to the French. I am pleased to say we destroyed one quite thoroughly yesterday.

"April 8, 1815

"This morning our lookout spotted a sail on the horizon, which turned out to be the Squirrel sloop, bound for Greenwich, and Captain Allen has been so good as to offer to carry in our mail. I shall send this to my uncle, who will see it reaches your home. I hope your family are all well, and wish you to know that while I have great joy in being back at sea, I do miss the society of my friends in London most terribly. I should love to hear how you all do, if you have time to write – my uncle knows the ways of naval mail, and has offered to send on anything sent under cover to him.

"Your most devoted servant,

"MATTHEW STANTON"

"I must admit I did not understand why he had not yet written," Elizabeth said. "I suppose he had been writing, all along, but I did not appreciate what it would take to get a letter to us."

"I wish he had not thought we would have no interest in some of the things he wrote of," Georgiana said. "I would want to know of all of it."

"I cannot say most ladies would, Georgiana, although surely this letter is meant for you, even if he could not say so. I believe your brother will want to know of its contents when he returns, and then we may turn it over to your possession."

"Might I read it again, now?"

"Of course."

Elizabeth quietly slipped out of the room as Georgiana reread the letter, feeling soothed for the first time in a very long while. He had written nearly every day, except during the storm, and if Elizabeth was right and the letter was intended for her – although it could not be addressed so – it meant he had thought of her on each of those days. Perhaps more importantly, though, it meant that as of the eighth of April, all had been well with him. That was a fortnight ago, but it was better than many weeks of not knowing at all how he did.

News of the letter spread beyond Mr. Darcy, so that the entire house party longed to hear it read. Evening diversions were not so easy to come by in the countryside, particularly since none of them was very enthusiastic about cards, so a long and interesting letter was not an item that could be held back. Elizabeth read it over tea, after Georgiana had entertained them with a few songs on the pianoforte, and it was the topic of discussion for the rest of the evening until they all retired.

Elizabeth quietly slipped it into Georgiana's hand as they made their way up the stairs, and no more was said of it until she settled into her husband's bed.

"I believe there were more words in that letter than I have heard that man speak in the entire course of our acquaintance," Darcy said.

"Do not be so severe on him, Darcy."

"I was not being severe – it was merely an observation, and I certainly would not be severe on anything that gave Georgiana so much relief as this letter seems to have done. Perhaps he is better able to express himself in writing than in speech."

"He would not be the first man of my acquaintance who was so," said

Elizabeth, with a pointed look at him.

"Oh, so now you will be severe on me." He smiled to show her he was teasing, as well, and then surprised her by leaning over to kiss her deeply.

"What was that for?"

"That was for the return of my spirited Elizabeth," he said. "It seems Pemberley has been good to you."

"I suppose it has," she said, although she knew the more significant reason for her lightness of spirit was her continued illness every morning. By now it had progressed to actual physical sickness, the evidence of which Sarah had been spiriting away and disposing of without the other maids knowing of it, Elizabeth knew not how. Once again she longed to tell Darcy, and once again she willed herself to wait until she was certain. She expected her courses soon, and if she missed them, she would take that as her confirmation, and then share with him the happiest of secrets.

Elizabeth and Georgiana were in agreement that the letter must be replied to immediately, and they spent the next morning at Elizabeth's writing desk, Elizabeth scribing a letter whose greater parts were all suggested by Georgiana. There was a description of their house party – the Bingleys he was a little acquainted with, but not Mr. Bennet, and of the house itself, and of spring as it emerged on Pemberley's grounds.

"Oh, it is no use!" Georgiana exclaimed, reading over what Elizabeth had written. "You write so well, Elizabeth, but the subject matter is not nearly so exciting as what he has to write about."

"It will be to him," Elizabeth said. "Just as we know little of the life aboard his ship, he knows little of the life on our estate. And I suspect that he will be interested in knowing about anything that involves you. Remember that he thought we would be bored by his account, and yet you longed for more detail."

"Perhaps you are right," said Georgiana, doubtfully.

"I might, though, suggest that we tell him of your pianoforte practise – that, certainly, is a topic that he would be very interested in. Pray tell, what are you working on right now? Let us write of that next."

The letter, eventually, was written, and although it did not match Captain Stanton's in length, they both felt it was at least a creditable response. Elizabeth wrapped it in the same piece of oiled silk, and wrote a cover note to the earl, thanking him for forwarding on the letter, inquiring after his health, and informing him briefly of how the family did.

Georgiana left to go begin her practise, but Elizabeth was not alone for long, as Jane joined her in the sitting room.

"You are back early," Elizabeth said.

"This last place was not at all to our liking," Jane said. "We are left with Clareborne Manor, which has the most delightful grounds, but requires a great deal of repair on the house, and Kellmore Abbey – I love the house there, but the estate has been mismanaged for so long it would take many years to bring it back in line."

"If neither of them feels right, Jane, you should continue to stay here as long as you wish, and continue your search."

"Lizzy, I fear if we do not purchase something soon, we never will. We have seen all the available estates within fifty miles of here."

"I would love to see you settled closer, but you could always expand your search."

"That is what Charles said. Before that, though, I wonder if you and Fitzwilliam might come with us to view Clareborne Manor and Kellmore Abbey. We would so value your advice."

"My advice on such matters is hardly worth the breath I use to speak it, but I am sure Darcy will be happy to lend his."

"Do not say such things, Lizzy. You manage one of the largest houses in all the county."

"I manage a house with a housekeeper who has been on the staff since my husband was a child, and has been well-run for many generations. It is hardly the effort you make it out to be."

"Oh!" Jane exclaimed. "The baby – she has just started kicking these last few days, and she caught me quite good there."

"She?"

Jane blushed. "I have always assumed the baby was a girl. After all, our mother had five girls."

"Do you think such things run in families?"

"They seem to, at least in my acquaintance."

Elizabeth could not help but think of Captain Stanton, and how overcrowded his family seemed to be with sons, when her own parents would have been beyond happiness to have just one, and thought there might be something to Jane's theory.

"I suppose you might be right," Elizabeth said. "There seem to be some families who are filled with one sex or the other, and Charles does have two sisters."

"At least I am fortunate – Charles does not care what the sex is, so long as the baby is healthy, and since we are yet to even purchase the estate, we do not have to worry about an entail."

Elizabeth felt a cold chill run through her at the word *entail*. She had not considered that she might have inherited a tendency to bear girls, and she still had no notion of Pemberley's status, so far as entail went.

Clareborne Manor and Kellmore Abbey were within fifteen miles of each other, so that both could be seen in one day, and on the following day the Darcys and Bingleys set out, again in the landau.

It took better than two hours to reach Clareborne Manor, but it was a pleasant drive, and much of the countryside was unfamiliar to Elizabeth – she came to realise that Jane and Charles must have seen far more of Derbyshire than she had. There were some farms and smaller estates, but also areas of great wildness, and she thought she might propose an expedition merely for expedition's sake sometime in the future, perhaps when her aunt and uncle came to visit.

Clareborne Manor was first, a great stone structure, grown shabby, poorly situated on low ground in a little hollow between open field and forest. The housekeeper let them in, but they saw no evidence of any other staff, and as soon as they made their way into the entrance-hall, Elizabeth saw that Jane's assessment of it needing a great deal of repair on the house was generous. They could not enter a room without finding some deficiency, and there were places where water had got in and stood in little pools on the floor. It would not be a comfortable or even a dry house for some time, and Elizabeth could not fathom living here with a new baby.

She was relieved when, after looking over the estate books for some time, Darcy suggested they have a little drive around the grounds, and here the estate was quite beautiful, somewhat like Pemberley in its mixture of rolling hills and forest. They drove out a little further, to view some of the tenant farms, and although it was clear they were not kept up to the same standard as those of Pemberley's tenants, the land was fertile, and would provide a good return.

It was, as Jane had indicated, the opposite of Kellmore Abbey, where many of the farms were vacant, or at least seemed to be, and the estate's grounds were mediocre at best. Here, it seemed all the money had gone into the house, which was indeed spectacular, an old rambling gothic building in perfect repair. Here she and Jane made their way from room to room, exploring, while their husbands spent nearly an hour looking at the books.

By the time they made their way back to the landau, Elizabeth, who had eaten very little at breakfast, was quite hungry and feared they would be late for dinner. Her concerns were somewhat allayed when Darcy got the landau moving at a cracking pace; this was his best carriage team, and the horses had wanted only a little rest while the couples had been inside.

"Well, Darcy, what do you think?" Charles asked, as they raised the main road back to Pemberley, looking very much like an eager terrier. "Which do you prefer? Or neither?"

"I will give you my answer if you choose, but you may not like it."

"Do not be silly, Darcy, we have been friends far too long for me to think you would mince your words."

"Go with the land," Darcy said. "Kellmore Abbey may take years to recover from its present neglect. I had never seen it before, but I know it quite well – I have several tenants who have come to Pemberley from there.

I can send Richardson to examine the soil, but I am fairly certain he will say it is completely sapped, at least for the farms that are still being worked. How an estate can go without crop rotation in the modern era is beyond my comprehension."

"You said go with the land," Charles said. "Does that mean you are for Clareborne Manor?"

"I am, but here is where you may not like what I have to say. The house – I would recommend tearing it down and beginning again, in a better location, and with a better style."

"Tear it down? You cannot be serious."

"I am completely serious," Darcy said, with such a dour expression Elizabeth very nearly laughed. Indeed she might have, if Charles did not look so disappointed.

"Charles, you must admit that house is hardly the place to raise a newborn baby in," Elizabeth said.

"It is better than a pile of stone, which is what you both seem to recommend."

"Nonsense, Charles," Darcy said. "Pemberley is close enough that you might ride over every day, to check on the progress and see to your tenants. If you like, keep the old house standing at first, for there are any number of locations where a new house might be situated better. But do not make Jane and the baby take up residence there. You are both welcome at Pemberley for as long as you need."

"You really think this is the best course of action?"

"The purchase price is a bargain," Darcy said. "Even with the expense of building a new house, you will be doing quite well. You might start with a core house, and then add on wings in later years, as they are needed. And you may build exactly to your taste, which is something few gentlemen have the luxury of doing."

"Oh, now you will tell me that Pemberley is not quite to your taste," Charles said.

"There are some things I might change, were I to build it from the ground up."

"Dear husband," Elizabeth said, turning to touch his shoulder. "You might stop talking now, for none except you in this carriage can be brought to believe Pemberley has any flaws."

CHAPTER 6

They went riding the next day, Elizabeth and Darcy, Elizabeth still on old Buttercup, and in the happiest of moods, which owed partly to their destination. They had opted to return to the old house on this morning, followed at a distance by a groom on horseback, who would watch their horses while they explored the ruins.

Elizabeth considered as she cantered through the woods that now, just when she was beginning to enjoy horseback riding, she would have to face giving it up, for certainly she would reach a point soon enough where she did not feel comfortable riding even Buttercup. The sight of the ruins was not novel this time, when they reached the clearing, but she still delighted in it, as she did the way her husband assisted her down from Buttercup's saddle with his hands firmly on her hips.

For the groom, watching the horses seemed to consist of tying his own mount and Buttercup to a nearby tree branch, and then walking Kestrel in restless circles. They left him thus, and made their way to the uneven stone wall that had once been the front of the house, mottled with weather.

In most places, the walls were still taller than Elizabeth, and once they had gone through what had been the front door, she could see that the rear of the house was more intact than the front – rising up nearly two storeys in places, with its old window openings largely choked with vines and tree branches, only allowing in a little sunlight here or there. There were little hints in places to indicate where rooms might have been, but the most wonderful feature was a large stone staircase, still largely intact, curving up just beyond the entrance into nowhere.

"It is stunning," Elizabeth breathed. "You shall have to check more than the secret room in the library now, if you find I have gone missing."

"I shall check the stables, then, to see if Buttercup is also missing, so I will at least know where to begin my search."

Elizabeth had for so long been acting as Mrs. Darcy that she was a bit surprised at how easily she slipped back into the young girl who had devoured gothic novels, taking up his arm and leading them in a walk along the outer walls. The floor had long since gone to grass and weeds, but it seemed they had been trimmed recently, and she wondered if Darcy had sent one of the junior gardeners here on the task, anticipating their visit. She could not help but look down periodically, scanning the ground for the toys of her husband and his cousin, but she did not see anything there which caught her eye.

"Is it strange to think of your ancestors living here, once?" she asked him.

"Indeed it is," he said. "They were the D'Arcys, with an apostrophe, for most of their time in this house. They changed it to Darcy at some time after the Plantagenet dynasty fell. I understand there was a desire to sound less French."

Elizabeth considered what he had said, and what it meant for what she was now only a few days away from being fully sure was the child in her womb. If she should have only girls, it would be beyond breaking an entail, it would be the end of – as Lady Catherine had called it – an honourable and ancient line that had come down through Darcy's father. She only asked him about the entail, however.

"Darcy, is Pemberley entailed?"

He stopped walking and looked at her, his countenance thoughtful, "That is a very strange question for a walk through ruins on a country morning, Elizabeth."

"I did not think it *that* strange, when we were speaking of your ancestors. And you did not answer my question."

"It is not entailed; it never has been. It saved my family quite a lot of worry when my mother failed to produce the usual *heir and a spare*, although I suppose my parents were even more careful of my welfare than they might otherwise have been – at least while they were alive."

"Were there any children – between you and Georgiana?"

"Three stillborn, and rather a lot of miscarriages," Darcy said, looking pained. "Or so I understood from my father later. I did not truly understand what was happening at the time."

"I do not even know if my mother had any miscarriages. I must assume she did, or she might have had even more children, but it was never made known to us."

He looked at her carefully again, and said: "You did not answer my question, either."

"I do not remember you asking one."

"Oh come, Elizabeth, I wished to know why you would be asking about whether the estate was entailed."

"Because I have not produced even the slightest hint of an heir, is that right?" Elizabeth had not meant to sound challenging, and yet that had been her tone; and she tried to soften her countenance. She had not meant to begin this discussion now, and yet she had, most poorly, and she had only the comfort of knowing that it should likely have the happiest of outcomes.

"Because *we* have not produced an heir," he said. "It is not your responsibility alone."

Elizabeth had only once before seen him look so devastated, when she had first refused his offer of marriage, and she felt her own eyes overflow with tears, to think this had been such a hurtful topic for him, as well, and she had never had the courage to broach it with him.

"I am sorry, Elizabeth, I did not mean to make you cry. I think we may have a happy marriage, even if we are not blessed with children," he said, taking up her hand and grasping it tightly.

"You mistake the reason for my tears," she said. "I am nearly at five weeks without my courses. Sarah says I have the other symptoms – she is the eldest of eleven. I asked about the entail because Jane believes we are more likely to have girls, on account of our mother having nothing but."

Darcy was usually a man of quick comprehension, but it took him some time to absorb this news, and when he finally did, he pulled her into the tightest of embraces, kissing any part of her available to him – her hair, her cheek, her neck, her lips – before finally asking: "Why did you not tell me as soon as you suspected it?"

"I could not bear to raise your hopes and then be wrong."

"I would rather you raised them, but I will leave that for now," he said. "Why now, after so long? You have not – miscarried – have you? Please say you would have told me, if you had gone through such a thing. It pains me more than I can say to think of you having felt you needed to bear it alone."

"I have not – of course I would have told you if I had lost a child," Elizabeth said. "There was nothing of the sort. After a while, I feared I was barren."

"And I must tell you I feared the opposite." Even now, while they spoke of such a difficult topic, he would not release her from his grasp, and Elizabeth felt so comforted she might have told him anything, but she had no secrets left to share.

"Sarah had a theory, that the climate of London was not conducive to conceiving a child," Elizabeth said.

"Is Sarah also a secret physician?"

"No," Elizabeth laughed. "But I can think of no better explanation."

"Elizabeth – we must never again fear speaking of this to each other. It seems a shameful topic, but I cannot tell you what a burden I feel has been lifted from me, and it is not just the possibility of a child."

"I completely agree, my dear," she said, taking up his face in her hands and then kissing him, feeling most infinitely relieved.

"Tell me, was this the cause of some of your malaise in town?"

"It was, although if Sarah's theory is correct, it seems the two were intertwined."

"Well, we need never spend that much time in town again, and you must not worry at all about Pemberley leaving our immediate family," he said. "If the child is a girl, she may still inherit the estate if we do not have any sons, and even if, God forbid, the child should not survive, the succession is left in my hands. Currently, Georgiana or her heirs would inherit, should anything happen to myself – that was the wish of our father."

Elizabeth sighed, "Poor Georgiana. I hope beyond all things that the child is healthy, but the thought of how far she is from marriage, much less heirs, saddens me deeply. I may have grown weary of town, but, as I think back, I do not regret the time we spent there – it was the least we could do for Georgiana and Kitty. It was their due."

"Yes, but in the future we might rely on Mrs. Annesley more. At some point Kitty will even be married, and I expect she would enjoy staying with Georgiana in town, particularly if Captain Ramsey is at sea, and then we may spend more of our time at Pemberley," he said. "For Elizabeth, I must tell you, I can hardly stand the thought of spending any more time apart from you, after what happened with the riots."

"I cannot say I am willing to be parted from you, either, my dear. You and I and our little one must stay together," she said.

One of the traditions Elizabeth had begun, following her early attempts to learn to ride, was a bath following her outings. This languid time in the warm water would always have been restorative for those muscles she had never really used before, but with her pregnancy had come additional soreness in most unexpected places, and she now saw it as a necessity. The bath could do nothing about the lingering tenderness of her lips, but as that had been the result of her husband's learning of her pregnancy, she was perfectly happy to retain that reminder of his own happiness.

Sarah saw to everything perfectly, from the water brought up warm from the kitchen to the lavender oil that was added to it. Elizabeth trusted Sarah with a fairly liberal allowance, to purchase things seeing to her lady's needs, and as she sank down into the water and inhaled deeply, she felt most confident that it was being well-spent.

This was a time where she allowed herself to relax, and her thoughts to wander, and she revelled again at being back in the country, at being at Pemberley. Mrs. Reynolds could see to things for days on end, if needed, and Elizabeth could seek society only as often as she herself wished it. She had every luxury at her disposal, from her ever-growing set of dresses and jewellery to the days she spent in leisurely walks or rides across the most beautiful of grounds. She lived in a handsome and comfortable estate – her own chamber's furniture notwithstanding – and had easy access to a most incredible library.

"And now, finally," she could not help but think, "I have earned all that I have been given. I have justified myself by becoming with child, and soon enough if all goes as I pray it will, I shall have something far more precious than any luxury that can be provided, even with ten thousand pounds a year."

Yet she could not help but think that there had been nothing in Darcy's demeanour, in telling him she thought herself to be with child, which had indicated she needed to justify herself. He had not laid the responsibility on her; he had been every bit the kind and wonderful man she had known she married.

"You are very beautiful when you are deep in thought," came the low voice that could only be her husband's, from the doorway behind her.

Elizabeth started so that some of the bath water splashed out onto the floor. She could have no grounds for understanding what propriety was in her current situation, but she was fairly certain that this was not it, and she felt herself grow most overheated.

"Am I to understand that you have taken a position as my lady's maid?" she asked, thinking teasing to be her best course of action. "For I can think of no other reason for your presence here, and I believe Sarah may have objections at your usurping her role."

"Perhaps I shall take her role as lady's maid, so that she may continue as your secret physician," he said.

"Do not tease on her account. It might have been weeks more before I realised I was with child, were it not for how observant she was."

"And how secretive," he said. "I thought something was odd in her behaviour, the morning of your headache, but I could not figure why."

"That was the morning we realised I was pregnant. I was too emotional to go down to breakfast, and could only think to claim a headache. Sarah had concerns over my drinking the willow bark tea," Elizabeth rested her hands protectively over her belly. "It might only be an Irish superstition, but I would rather be safe than sorry."

"I would rather you did, as well," he said, slipping his hand into the water to place it on her stomach alongside hers. "Here is the next master of Pemberley."

"Darcy," she warned urgently. "Do not forget that all of my children may well be girls."

"Do not worry so, Elizabeth. If it is a girl, and she takes after her mother, I have no doubt of her capacity to be master of Pemberley."

Elizabeth blushed at the notion, and then felt fully the most pleasant danger of his hand's present location, such a short distance to those most sensitive places in her being, a danger that was confirmed presently. She caught fully the amorous expression on his face, and knew he would not be content with merely leaving her dressing room having touched her stomach.

"Darcy, the deed is already done, successfully – this is merely overkill."

"I find I am rather more in favour of overkill than I was previously," he said, kissing her.

"Sarah will be returning soon – we cannot."

"I told her you were not to be disturbed, and would ring the bell when you had additional need of her services."

"Darcy! You did not! Whatever will she think of us?"

"You did say Sarah is the eldest of eleven, did you not?"

"I did."

"And she attends you in your chambers every morning, with the bed still made up?"

"Well, yes."

"Then I expect she has some idea of what we are about, regardless of our particular actions today. Thankfully, I also have a goodly degree of confidence in her ability to keep a secret."

Later, when they had finished, and laid in a slightly damp mass of limbs in Elizabeth's bed, he kissed her temple lightly, and said, "I understand why you did not, but I do wish you had told me, as soon as you suspected you were with child, so that Sarah had no need for secrets."

"You would rather hope, and have those hopes lost?"

"I would rather experience all that you do. If you hope, I want to share that hope. If your hopes are lost, I want to know – I want for us to comfort each other. If we must encounter darker times, we should do so together," he said. "I do not mean to reproach you for it though, my dear. Either of us could have spoke of it, and neither of us did. I thought I had learned that lesson, and yet I still could not apply it to our not having produced a child."

"What do you mean, that you thought you had learned that lesson?"

"You remember the day we first talked of the Corn Bill?"

"Yes, I do," she said, thinking back to that time in his study.

"I had been growing increasingly worried over the cost of grains, and what it would mean for the estate, in the weeks before we spoke. I cannot tell you what a relief it was to talk of it with you."

"I never noticed you were worried, until that day."

"Some have called me *reserved*," he said, smiling faintly. "I suppose I am rather good at hiding my concern."

Elizabeth could not help but feel both soothed and ashamed by his words. For so long she had lived with the worry, for so long she had assumed that everyone – including him – was judging her for her inability to conceive an heir. She had carried around that weight, and with one conversation with him, it would have been lessened. Certainly, it would not have been the same to speak of it when the possibility was strong that she *was* barren, but still, even that sad future would have been easier had they faced it together.

It perhaps should not have been surprising, given the amount of difficulty with which they had come together as a couple, that they should still not quite get things right in the beginning of their marriage, that they should both avoid a topic that, if raised, might instantly have brought them each a great deal of comfort. She found herself crying again, overwhelmed by both relief and regret, and enveloped in an even tighter embrace.

"I wish now that I would have spoken to you much earlier. I fear I have been trying so hard to be Mrs. Darcy – to produce an heir as I was supposed to – I forgot that it was not the same as being a good wife."

"Elizabeth, listen to me," he spoke firmly, cupping her chin in his hand. "Do not ever think you have failed in either regard, no matter what happens with this child. Do you have any notion of how happy you make me?"

If she did not, she had a good idea of it now, for he was staring at her with the most intent expression on his face. He did not require an answer to his question, however, for he continued speaking:

"As for this Mrs. Darcy nonsense, I wish you would forget it. Mrs. Darcy is *you*, my Elizabeth. You need not try to be her – you *are* her."

"But you cannot deny there are certain expectations of a Mrs. Darcy."

"You have met – nay, surpassed – all of my expectations," he said. "I should like to think my say in the matter is most important, given I am Mr. Darcy."

"I suppose so," she said, laughing softly.

"So if you must improve on Mrs. Darcy, let it be only that she shares all of her hopes and fears more freely, and if you will promise to do that, I shall do the same."

"I promise."

"As do I," he said, kissing her. Elizabeth was not sure she had ever known a sweeter kiss, in all the time they had been married.

Now that Darcy knew the news, Elizabeth could not bear to keep it from Jane and Georgiana, and a few days later, with Darcy, Bingley, and Mr. Bennet shut up in her husband's study, calculating the cost to build a new house at Clareborne, she asked them both if they might like to take a turn about the garden. Just a little walk, of course, for Jane did not like to go far anymore, but enough for some fresh air.

They came with her readily, and all three walked silently for a little while, staying to the gravel path, for the rest of the ground was still quite wet from an overnight storm.

"I have some news that I believe you both will like," Elizabeth said. "There is a good chance you are to be aunts – I believe I am with child."

"Oh, Elizabeth! I have been hoping to hear that for so long!" Georgiana exclaimed, stunning Elizabeth with the force of her embrace.

"Lizzy, that is the greatest news!" Jane exclaimed, and took her turn in hugging Elizabeth as well as her size would allow. "But I thought you said – "

Elizabeth gave Jane as sharp a look as she could ever give her older sister, reminding her of Georgiana's presence, for barrenness, and by extension the conceiving of babies, was hardly something they could discuss with an unmarried lady present, particularly one who was not so long out in society. She explained, as delicately as she could, the theory of the London climate and schedule.

"It makes great sense to me," Georgiana said. "You did grow thinner than you were when I first met you."

"I hardly noticed," Elizabeth said.

"Georgiana is right – I must admit I was a little startled when we first saw you in town," Jane said. "Oh, Lizzy, now I do hope we purchase Clareborne Manor – I should so like for our children to grow up together."

"And if you should have your baby at Pemberley, you will not require a pregnant woman to travel," Elizabeth laughed. "So it may be a comfort to us both."

CHAPTER 7

Elizabeth recognised that in some matter of months, she would no longer possess even the energy she did now, and she determined they must put Pemberley's large dining room to use at least once during the spring, and perhaps many times during the summer, if she could bring about the house party she desired. They had invited many of the established families in the area over for a family dinner on one night or another, but never all of them as a group.

She discussed these plans with her husband, first, in one of the few times when he and Charles were not ensconced in his study, poring over maps of Clareborne's lands, or their notes from the estate's books. He looked up when she entered, quite pleased to see her.

"You must never tell him, but how glad I am you are not Charles," he said. "He must have all of Clareborne's lands mapped to the foot in his mind, and yet still he cannot decide where he would build the house."

"Not everyone inherits an estate so well-placed as Pemberley, Darcy," she said. "Charles has the pressure of doing right by many generations, on an estate where the previous owners clearly did wrong."

"You are right," he said. "I am so used to his being indecisive, I forget that perhaps this is a topic that bears more careful consideration."

"Still, it must be noted that you are a good friend to him. I do not even know how many hours the two of you have spent holed up in this study discussing that estate, when you might have been focused on your own."

"My dear, have you been feeling neglected?"

"No, not at all. We still have our rides, although I am not sure how much longer I will want to continue them. And you are very attentive in the evenings," Elizabeth said, blushing furiously. There was no other way she could think to describe the notion that their activities in the marital bed had perhaps become even more intense now that she was quite certain she was with child. "I came to discuss our entertaining, here, which I never can seem to broach while we are otherwise occupied."

Darcy groaned. "I feared you would not go very long without some plan of entertainment, once we returned here."

"It is not substantial, my dear. I wish to have a large dinner, in a fortnight or so, for all of the major families in the area," she said. "And later in the summer, when the season is over, I should like to have a house party. Only close friends and family. I would like to have them all to visit before the baby is too far along."

"Those are very much my ideas of entertainment," he said. "Our local families, and our own friends and family. If we are lucky, we shall have no one new move into the neighbourhood, and you may continue on with such entertainments until the end of days."

"Darcy, you had better not be too hard on Charles in his indecision over this estate. If you lose his friendship, you may well end your own days as a hermit."

"I shall not," he said, giving her a very particular smile. "I shall have my wife and child with me, here, and therefore cannot be classed as a hermit."

"I believe your wife will be the judge of that."

Her plans thus shared, Elizabeth went calling with Jane and Georgiana, distributing her invitations and introducing Jane to those who might someday be her neighbours. Again, she was received with utmost respect and kindness, and her invitation was accepted immediately by all, even a few who already had fixed plans. The Watsons had been engaged to dine with the Fullers, but upon learning the latter family was also to receive an invitation, felt certain they could find a new date for the lesser event, and by the time they called on the Fullers, that family informed her their smaller dinner had been moved to another day.

The first difficulty in planning the dinner party came about slowly; Mrs. Reynolds and Mr. Parker spoke of it so delicately at first, she could not understand what seemed a certain reluctance on their part about the event. They did not say so directly, but eventually, she came to understand that they felt the house understaffed for such an event; the estate's income could support many more servants, but the current Mr. Darcy rarely had even so few as eight to dine, and he did not wish to employ servants who would be idle.

Once she understood the cause for their concern, Elizabeth gave them ready approval to hire on additional servants from the inn at Lambton for that evening, but the messenger to the inn returned with the news that no servants could be spared for at least a fortnight, for Pemberley's staffing necessarily influenced the inn's staffing as well. With a little over a week to go before the dinner, therefore, Elizabeth and Mr. Parker went calling on each of Pemberley's tenants who had boys of at least fourteen years of age. They explained the situation, and asked if the boys might like to come train as footmen for a week in the great house, and then to serve on the evening of the dinner. They would be paid for the entire week, as well as the dinner, and those who did well might be called upon to return for future dinners, and would have a character from Mr Parker.

Some of the families could not spare their children from farm work, but there were three large families who had more boys than they felt they could support in farming. The prospect of a week's pay, and such an easy entry into service – a letter of character from Pemberley's butler would carry heavy weight in Derbyshire or any of the neighbouring counties – was a blessing to them, and they thanked Elizabeth profusely.

Once the additional servants were in place, the only remaining difficulty came in the weather; the morning before the dinner saw a tremendous thunderstorm strike the county, and Elizabeth worried that the heavy rain might make the roads impassable. Darcy assured her that it would not; the roads in the county were in good repair and could readily take a rain such as this. The storm did, however, delay the post, so that the mail was delivered just as they were all taking to their chambers to dress. Among the letters was another thick bundle from the Earl of Anglesey, which Georgiana looked at in desperation, knowing that there could be no time to attend to it until the next day. Their guests would arrive soon, and the letter could hardly be read publicly in front of so many families, so it would have to wait until the next morning.

It had been some time since Pemberley had hosted an event so large, but when these families did begin to arrive, they did so in the old style, with the torches lit all the way down the drive, and the master and lady of the house waiting in the entrance-hall to greet them. The lady, they observed, was most elegantly dressed and wearing jewels that most found more tasteful than those the late Mrs. Darcy had worn, although some of the older ladies thought them underdone.

This entrance pleased the guests, but did not delight them quite so much as the servants who handed them glasses of champagne upon entering the yellow drawing room, for Mr. Parker had laid in a vast number of cases during the peace, and the fact that it was once again difficult to procure did make it seem to taste even better. Introductions were few, and generally between the dinner guests and the Bingleys and Mr. Bennet – the families had all been settled in this area for some time, and knew each other well.

There were some who did not like each other so well, but Elizabeth had this intelligence from her husband, and had arranged their entry into dinner carefully, so that when they all were seated, she had no concerns that any area of the table should be overtaken by cold silence. They were in the large dining room, and although it was still not filled, there were a good four-

and-twenty of them seated. All the dishes came out well; the new footmen looked very young indeed, and quite nervous, but they did not make any mistakes. And Darcy, who had always looked a bit pained in company in town, unless they were with only their closest acquaintances, seemed completely comfortable here at home, even with such a large group, conversing easily with those around him.

They would of course not say so to Elizabeth, but the general feeling among the families was of happiness in seeing entertainment returned to the great house. Certainly, Mr. Darcy, who had inherited the estate so terribly young, and then continued a bachelor for many years, could not be expected to entertain in the way the late Mr. and Mrs. Darcy did, when they both were alive. Yet they had all felt the infrequency of invitations to the house, and those always to dine in very small parties. The addition of a Mrs. Darcy – and her finally appearing in the neighbourhood, just when they had feared she was one of those ladies who loathed leaving town – appeared to mean that their society would increase, and they looked at her with fondness.

Georgiana was fortunate to be seated amongst people who had a great deal of conversation, so that she had to contribute but rarely. She could think of nothing but the letter and what it might contain. Its existence, at least, told her that at some point after April the eighth, he had been well, and that was some comfort, but not enough to settle her desire to know its contents.

With such a large party, dinner was a lengthy event – there were many who had not yet had a chance to toast the new Mrs. Darcy, and they took the opportunity. The gentlemen were long over their port, and when the whole party finally settled in the large drawing room, they were all still desirous of entertainment. Elizabeth saw that a few card tables were made up; the doors to the music room were opened, and Georgiana and several of the other ladies were compelled to play the pianoforte or the harp.

For several hours, they all sat, drinking tea, playing cards, and listening to the music, and when only a few of the most elderly guests had called for their carriages, and the rest showed no inclination to do so, Elizabeth leaned over and said quietly to Georgiana:

"Why do you not retire? You are still young, and recently out in society. Jane is going to as well – they will all understand."

Georgiana had indeed been growing tired for some time, and she knew she contributed little to the conversation, as distracted as she was. She saw Jane standing in the doorway, waiting, and rose to join her and take their leave.

It was only after Hughes helped her change that Georgiana saw the letter sitting on her bed. It had been opened – and by the looks of it, read – and Georgiana felt a deep surge of affection for Elizabeth. Somehow, in the course of hosting such a large dinner, her sister had managed to review the letter and see that it was placed in Georgiana's possession.

She unfolded it eagerly and saw that it was even longer than the first. Much like that letter, he spoke of naval life, describing each of his officers and their duties, and detailing their slow path along the French coast, as they searched for any ship they might fight, and continued to destroy any shore batteries they saw. He was experimenting with a different type of gun, called a carronade, which he described as shorter and more powerful than the longer guns, but less accurate. If successful, the carronades were to replace the smallest guns on the ship, and he was quite pleased by the progress of the crews manning them. This was followed by another apology, for writing of such topics to a lady, and Georgiana wished he did not feel the need to do so – this was clearly a topic he was enthusiastic about, and she would have been quite happy to read another page on it, if he had chosen to write it.

Georgiana saw that he had written at least a little every day – they had seen no more storms – and each day's entry included the news that they were yet to see any French men of war. This he explained finally on his entry of May the seventh, when his ship reached the Brest blockade and found that most of the French were still in port. Meeting up with the blockade meant they should receive mail, and one of his entries indicated he had just received Mrs. Darcy's letter, and he had greatly enjoyed hearing of their country life at Pemberley, and of Georgiana's progress on the pianoforte, particularly as it confirmed her wrist was fully better. He described in turn his cello practise, which was kept shorter than it had been on the Caroline, with a new crew and the ship so close to the French coast, so that he kept to old favourites whenever he was able to steal away a half-hour for practise.

Meeting up with the blockade also meant the company of his fellow captains, including Captain Ramsey, and he wrote of a lively dinner hosted by Captain Lord Downing aboard the Barham, of seventy-four guns. Captain Ramsey, it seemed, was the person who was to see the letter to English shores, and the letter concluded with both his and Captain Stanton's wishes for their family's health and happiness.

Georgiana finished the letter feeling something much closer to health and happiness; she sat there for some time on the edge of her bed, feeling a glow of relief and love.

The last of the guests left at two in the morning, but though Elizabeth was tired, she found she woke ill in the morning, and could not return to sleep, although even her husband managed to sleep late on this morning. She made her way down to the breakfast table, found no one else there, and thus made no attempt to eat anything, only drinking a little small beer before making her way around the primary rooms of the house. The servants had been busy; all was clean, and there was no sign of the disruption caused by having so many people to visit.

She thought she might pass a little quiet time in the library, before the others began to stir, and was surprised to find her father already there when she entered.

"Papa! I did not know anyone else was awake."

"When you reach my age, Lizzy, you will find that you wake early, regardless of when you retired, and if you did retire late, you must bear the punishment for the remainder of the day."

He had been reading, as he had for much of his time at Pemberley, but he marked his book with a worn little piece of ribbon, and Elizabeth took this as an invitation to take a seat near him.

"I hope we did not keep you up too late," she said.

"Not at all – it is perhaps not when I would have retired by choice, but I would not have missed the chance to see my daughter as such a hostess," he said. "Indeed, Lizzy, I would hardly have known you but that you still converse with your usual wit. You are every bit the mistress of a great house, now."

"Thank you, papa," Elizabeth said, colouring slightly at his praise. "I must admit there was a time when I was quite intimidated by the thought of being mistress of such an estate."

"One would not have known it, to see you these last few weeks, and particularly last night."

"Well, I did have quite a lot of practise in town," she said. "It was not always so easy, but here in the country I find I am quite comfortable in what is required of me. We may set the pace of society here."

"Now perhaps you may better understand why I do not like town. You and your sisters never could understand why we did not go more often."

"Yes, I do fully understand now. Various circumstances kept us there far longer than is normal, and I must admit that I grew quite weary of it all well before we left."

"If you do not mind my saying, Lizzy, you did look a little weary still, when I arrived here. Jane worried for you, and so did I, when I first saw you here."

"It was nothing that a little country air and quiet time did not cure," Elizabeth said, realising there would be no better time to tell her father that she was with child than now. "I do understand your concern, however. Indeed it seems the wear of the London season was such that I could not conceive, and only since we have returned to Pemberley have I found myself in the family way."

A slow smile spread across Mr. Bennet's face. "Lizzy, my dear, my deepest congratulations. And I must ask, would you mind terribly if I shared the news with your mother on my return to Longbourn? For soon enough I must return, and I will share with you now that the topic of you not yet having conceived an heir has been her greatest preoccupation – next to worrying about Lydia – for some time. She of course cannot speak of it in front of Mary and Kitty, but I am certain if you had stayed a day or two longer at Longbourn, she would have pulled you aside and informed you of how remiss you were in your duties as a wife."

Elizabeth blushed to think such a thing was a topic of conversation among her parents. She had never been her mother's favourite – Lydia was most like Mrs. Bennet in personality, while Jane had been thought to have the greatest chance of making an advantageous marriage – and Elizabeth had certainly become her least favourite in rejecting Mr. Collins's proposal of marriage, if she was not already such. Her mother had been all enthusiasm at Elizabeth's marrying a man of such consequence, and of ten thousand pounds a year, yet it seemed she had watched the marriage ready to find any point on which to criticise her daughter, and this was one of substance.

"Thank you, papa, of course you may tell her." she said, not wishing to call her mother's affection into question, for her father's affection for her had always been clear. "It is still early on, so we have not yet made it widely known."

"You do know that as soon as I tell her, it will be widely known in Hertfordshire, at least."

"I know, papa. We must endeavour to keep you here longer, then, so the news will not spread."

CHAPTER 8

In the end, Mr. Bennet did stay longer – more than a fortnight so – and his leaving was not precipitated by anything of his own doing. They were all in the saloon, passing the time through books and embroidery, when Mr. Parker brought in the papers.

Georgiana had for some time been studiously reading the Morning Post and the Naval Chronicle, the latter a subscription Darcy had begun in London and then doubled on their removal from town, one copy going to Longbourn and one to Pemberley. Therefore, they all took it as natural when she rose and eagerly took up the Morning Post, to see if there was any news on the naval portion of the war, and the gentlemen had no issue with her taking it first.

They were all startled, therefore, when she gasped, and cried out, "Oh, my God!" and looked as close to fainting as any of them had ever seen her. Mrs. Annesley moved most quickly, kneeling beside her with smelling salts, but Georgiana, although very pale, waved her off. She took a great deal of time to compose herself, before finally saying, in a wavering voice:

"Captain Stanton has captured the French ship Polonais, of seventy-four guns. It is a remarkable achievement, and he – " here, she emitted a strangled little sob " – he is to be made a baronet if he survives his wounds."

Georgiana fully collapsed into tears, and Elizabeth and Mrs. Annesley helped her rise, and led her back to her apartment. Mrs. Annesley left them once they had got Georgiana situated in bed, still clutching the newspaper. Elizabeth took it from her, and read the remainder of the article, such as it was. There was little in the way of detail, but it seemed HMS Jupiter had boarded and taken the Polonais off the French coast, near Lorient, and that both ships, much battered, had come limping into Plymouth, few more battered than the Jupiter's captain. He had sustained grave wounds to the arm, stomach, and leg, and was currently in hospital in Plymouth.

"Oh, Georgiana, at least he is alive," Elizabeth said, after she had related the later contents of the article to her sister. "As long as he is alive we may hope for his recovery."

"But what if he does not recover? I could not bear it." Here Georgiana broke down in another bout of crying, and Elizabeth embraced her for some time, until it seemed she had run out of tears, and wanted only to lie there quietly on the bed. Elizabeth left the room only long enough to ask one of the maids to bring a small dose of laudanum, and Georgiana, upon taking it, did seem much calmer. Eventually, she drifted into an exhausted sleep, and Elizabeth left the room, to find her husband waiting outside, exceedingly worried.

"How is she?"

"Not well. I think she understood that such a thing might happen, but did not believe that it truly would. I tried to encourage her to maintain hope – I do not know how she shall bear it if he dies."

"We must all pray he does not. Certainly the pain would be deepest for Georgiana, but I do not think there is any who knows him who is not affected by the news."

"No, indeed not," Elizabeth said, recognising the truth in what he said. She had until now been more concerned about Georgiana than Captain Stanton, but the thought of his dying struck her beyond its impact to her sister, and she embraced her husband in grave worry.

They could not go to Plymouth. For Plymouth, in such circumstances, could only be a place for family, and despite Georgiana's hopes, they were none of them family at this time. They stayed at Pemberley for four days, therefore, and on the first three days had only new editions of the Morning Post to bring them any news of how Captain Stanton did. There were more articles on the capture of the Polonais, but with little in the way of new details aside from noting that more than one hundred men had been killed on the Polonais, with something more than another hundred wounded, while only eighteen had been killed on the Jupiter. None contained an update on Captain Stanton's condition, however; they were mostly filled with enthusiasm for the navy, and confidence that the war should not last long, if more such displays of British might and bravery were to follow.

These three days were the most miserable of Georgiana's life. She had not really been happy for many weeks, afflicted with both heartache and worry, but her feelings during this time were far more raw and painful than she had ever known, even after Mr. Wickham had imposed on her. She could hardly eat, attempting to do so only when Elizabeth or Mrs. Annesley admonished her to try, and she remained in her chambers, alternately praying and weeping. She regretted deeply not making her love known to him before he had left town, that he might die without having known of it. Occasionally, she even found herself angry at him for putting his life in such danger – he had told her he intended to return safely, and then taken on a ship that he himself had said was too large to fight in the Jupiter – but her heart was too formed for tenderness to allow this to continue for long.

Relief came, finally, in an express from the Earl of Anglesey, who had gone out to Plymouth himself. He had found his nephew seriously injured, but not nearly so bad as the papers made him out to be, and he wished for Captain Stanton's friends to not be so worried for him as he feared they were currently. The arm wound was particularly concerning, but, he noted, it was only a limb, and therefore Captain Stanton would recover from it one way or the other. He hoped within a week or two that his nephew might be able to be moved to the earl's house in town, where he might complete his recovery in some level of comfort.

This brief note brought Georgiana a rush of relief more intense than any she had ever known, and she found herself breaking down again as she had so many times over the last few days, but this time with tears of relief. For the first time, she came to wonder what should happen next. He was returned to England; he was likely to be so for some time, while he recovered. She had been expecting his absence for years, and now she might have some opportunity to see him. Nay, she *must* find some opportunity; she must tell him of her affections, openly, if need be. It was the only thing she could do, after feeling so wretched at the thought of his dying.

Elizabeth and Darcy had been discussing the same thing in his study, and had determined that at least some of the family must return to town. If Captain Stanton was to go there, then Georgiana must have an opportunity to see him. Darcy proposed first that Mrs. Annesley attend her there, but they both knew this plan to be inadequate. There was no guarantee that the gentleman would not die from his wounds, or survive only to reject Georgiana, and they would not make her go through either event without being there to support her. They then needed to find a reason beyond Captain Stanton's being there – they were known to have removed to Pemberley, and it would seem quite odd were they to return to town suddenly for a man who had no understanding with their sister.

"I had been thinking we should have your portrait done, before the baby is much farther along," Darcy said. "We could of course have someone come here, but it would be much more easily done in town. It might be seen as a suitable reason, if you are willing to share the news of your being in the family way to at least our closer acquaintances."

"I must admit I do not see how it would add that much urgency," Elizabeth said. No one in her family had ever had a full portrait taken, only miniatures; Longbourn had nothing like Pemberley's gallery, with generation after generation hanging there for posterity.

"This is not a topic I ever would wish to turn my mind to, nor to have you do the same," he said, looking very disconcerted. "But it is best for a lady to have her portrait done *before* the birth of her first child."

Elizabeth flushed with the realisation of what he said, for of course there was a chance that the lady would not survive the birth. She knew it was a risk both she and Jane now faced, but he was right, there was little use in any of them turning their minds to it.

"I am sorry, Elizabeth," he said, taking her hand. "I did not mean to bring up something so upsetting. Your mother had five healthy children; I have every belief that you shall do the same."

"If I have five daughters, I will fully believe the fates are against we Bennet women, and I make no guarantees that I will not become as obsessed as my mother was with marrying them off."

"If that is the case, we shall just have to get to work befriending more families like the Stantons, which find themselves overcrowded with gentlemen."

"I would be more than satisfied just to see the current Miss Darcy married off to a Stanton. I do not have the capacity to worry about any future ones, before they are even born."

"Indeed, neither do I," Darcy said. "Perhaps you should also see a physician in town, now that I think of it. I know you were planning to see Dr. Alderman when he came for Jane, and I have every respect for him. But he is a country physician – he treats all conditions – and seeing someone who does specialise in birthing would be readily accepted by our acquaintances as a reason for our being in town."

"I suppose that would be prudent in any case."

There came a knock on the door, and Darcy said, "Do come in."

It was Georgiana, looking very resolute. "I wish to go to town," she said. "You do not need to attend me there; Mrs. Annesley has said she will go with me."

"Please be seated, Georgiana," Darcy said. "Elizabeth and I had just been discussing how we had a few things to attend to in town, now that she is with child. It would seem quite good timing to go soon, would it not, so that we might also see how our friend is recovering?"

Georgiana quickly comprehended what he meant, and could not help a broad smile spreading across her face. "Oh yes, thank you, Fitzwilliam! I agree it would be very good timing."

Before they made their departure for London, they had another letter from Plymouth, this one addressed in an unfamiliar and quite ill-written hand, so that it took Elizabeth a moment to realise it was from Captain Stanton himself. She opened it to find the handwriting inside even shakier, and understood he had written it with his left hand. The gentlemen were again in Darcy's study – Charles had an architect coming in a few days, and he wished to hear Darcy's and Mr. Bennet's thoughts again before they departed, for they were to convey Mr. Bennet to Longbourn on the way to London. All of the ladies were sitting in the music room – Georgiana had finished her practise some time ago, but they had felt no desire to stir – and so Elizabeth read the letter aloud:

"Dear Mrs. Darcy,

"I understand from my uncle that he has sent news to all of our friends regarding my condition, and so I hope it will not be a surprise to you that I am – while far from well – not anywhere near my death-bed. It seems a gravely wounded captain makes naval success far more dramatic, and so somewhere between the Admiralty and the papers, my health grew far worse than it truly is.

"I am well enough that they say I may be moved tomorrow, so I will travel in my uncle's coach to London, there to stay at his house until I am better. At least I need not worry about not being ready to return to sea before my ship – the poor Jupiter was cruelly knocked about. Eighteen of my men were killed, and a great many more wounded – I grieve for them, although I know it is a small number, for such an engagement.

"My uncle told me of your family's being at Pemberley for the spring and summer, so I believe I am to be deprived of your company while in town. I hope you will continue to write so that I may be assured of your family's health and happiness.

"Your devoted servant,

"MATTHEW STANTON"

It was a short letter, but so laboriously written Elizabeth could find no fault with it. She concealed the nature of the handwriting until Georgiana made to leave the room. Elizabeth followed her out, and said, "I will give you this, now, but before I do I must tell you it appears to have been written with his left hand."

"Oh no – do you think he has lost an arm, like Nelson?"

"Now that I think on it, his uncle did seem to indicate that his arm might be – might be amputated," Elizabeth said. "Would this make a difference to you, if he has lost an arm?"

"No, not at all! – except that I do not see how he would still be able to play the cello, and I grieve for him in that," Georgiana said. "But the thought of it certainly has no other influence on my affections."

CHAPTER 9

Their return to town could not be done comfortably without at least one night at an inn, and they could not very well return Mr. Bennet to Longbourn without spending another night there. No sooner had they stepped out of the carriage than Kitty had rushed up to embrace Georgiana, and after briefly greeting the rest of the party, Kitty was leading her friend off to the garden so they could walk and speak more privately.

Elizabeth, Darcy, Mrs. Annesley, Mary, and Mr. and Mrs. Bennet made their way into the drawing room, and once Mrs. Bennet had called for Hill to bring some refreshments to the poor, weary travellers, she sat down and immediately said:

"Well, this business with Captain Stanton is very vexing! What if the same happens to Captain Ramsey? What is poor Kitty to do then?"

"Mama, we are at war, and it is the risk of their careers. And I beg you would not speak of it around Georgiana; Captain Stanton was a suitor to her, before this war began, and this topic is very upsetting for her," Elizabeth said. She did not know if Kitty had expected an outburst like this, or simply wanted to comfort her friend, but either way, she found herself tremendously grateful that her sister had sequestered Georgiana away from the rest of the party.

"Their careers! I suppose Captain Ramsey could stand to earn more in prize money – I should like to see he and Kitty with at least three thousand a year. So I suppose it makes sense that he should have gone to war, although I hope he will not regret it, for Kitty's sake," Mrs. Bennet said. "But I understand Captain Stanton already *has* more than three thousand pounds a year. What more did he need? He should have left the Polonais to the other captains to be captured."

"Mrs. Bennet, I believe you are not fully comprehending how *war* works, nor how very large the oceans are," Mr. Bennet said, finally, for neither

Elizabeth nor Darcy could muster a response to their mother's statement.

"I do have some better news, mama," Elizabeth said, glancing over at her husband to see he was in agreement with her about distracting Mrs. Bennet with the only good news they had to share, at present. "I am in the family way."

Mrs. Bennet stared at her daughter for a few moments, so unexpected a turn was this news, before exclaiming: "Well, it is about time! All those months you spent frittering away in town and not producing an heir. You should have begun as early as possible, Lizzy! You never know how many daughters you shall have before you reach a son."

Elizabeth felt her face burn so hot she was certain she must be a bright shade of pink, and the expression on her husband's face – some combination of sympathy and embarrassment – was of no assistance.

"Where are those refreshments? Hill!" Mrs. Bennet eventually called out, into the silence that had overcome their party.

The refreshments were produced, and all but perhaps Mrs. Bennet were happy for the distraction that eating and drinking them brought. Into this came Kitty and Georgiana. The latter looked better than she had in the last few days, but still far more thin and wan than a girl her age should. This did not go unnoticed by Mrs. Bennet, who rose, and approached Georgiana. Elizabeth tensed at the thought of how her mother might act, but Mrs. Bennet merely put her arm around the young lady's shoulders and said, "Oh, you poor thing. Let me have Hill bring you a cup of warm milk. I always say there is nothing like warm milk, for comforting the soul."

It was a memory from childhood Elizabeth had very nearly forgotten, but with just the mention of it, she could very nearly taste the warm milk on her tongue, and feel the unequalled comfort of a mother's embrace. Georgiana, who had not known such comforts in a very long while, leaned into Mrs. Bennet and did seem at least a little consoled, and Elizabeth found herself smiling fondly at her mother, for the first time in a very long while.

By the time they reached Curzon Street, the papers were already filled with the news of "gallant Captain Stanton" having arrived in town. There being no mistress at the earl's residence, the ladies could not make a morning call there, but Darcy went, learned that Captain Stanton was upstairs resting, and stayed about half-an-hour with the earl.

This was the closest any of them came to Captain Stanton during their first three days in town. Georgiana was disappointed, but so long as he was still recovering, she knew that she could have no expectations of seeing him. Elizabeth had an appointment made with an accoucheur physician, and a portrait painter was found, so that she could begin sitting with him. Aside from this, they called only on Lord and Lady Brandon, the Gardiners, and Lady Tonbridge, and kept the knocker off of their door, wishing to wait quietly and keep their presence in town as little-known as possible. If they did not, the regular stream of social engagements would no doubt begin again, and Darcy was adamant that nothing should exhaust Elizabeth while she was with child.

It was on the third day when Captain Stanton's name began appearing in the gossip pages of all the papers, for he had been a guest of honour at a dinner given by the Duke of Clarence. He appeared again the next day, having dined with the Prince Regent himself, after the promised baronetcy had been bestowed on him. Upon reading that he had been out in society for not one, but two evenings, without coming to call on them, Georgiana began to fear that she was not so important to him as she had hoped to be.

He did call that day, however, well into the morning, all of them in the drawing room, rustling to attention when Mr. Miller announced: "Captain *Sir Matthew* Stanton, and Captain George Campbell, of the Royal Navy," for Mr. Miller had been reading the papers as thoroughly as the rest of them, and had a great abhorrence of announcing a guest improperly.

As soon as Georgiana saw him, she felt guilty at having wished he had called earlier. He had always been a tall, handsome, healthy-looking man, but now he looked pale and gaunt, and it took him some time just to make his way into the room, for he seemed to be using his walking stick for support rather more than was proper. Georgiana noted with relief that his arm was intact, although in a sling rather like the one she had worn, and only after she had observed all of this did she pay any notice to Captain Campbell, a slightly stout man of average height, wearing a uniform like Captain Shaw's and with only a jagged gash across his cheek, heavily stitched, preventing him from having a fully joyous countenance, so that Georgiana realised he must be Lieutenant Campbell, newly promoted.

"Would you do us the honour of introducing us to your friend?" Darcy asked, for although he had been announced, and they knew him from Captain Stanton's letters, none of them had met the man in society.

"Yes, of course," Captain Stanton said. "Captain Campbell, this is Mr. Darcy, Mrs. Darcy, Miss Darcy, and Mrs. Annesley."

"It is very nice to meet you," Captain Campbell said. "Although Captain Stanton has told me so much about your family, I feel I already know you all."

"I feel the same way," Georgiana said. "And I believe we are to congratulate you on your promotion?"

"You are too kind, Miss Darcy – yes, I was indeed promoted to Commander for the action against the Polonais."

"As well he should have been," Captain Stanton said. "He will not say so, but he brought home two ships that had battered each other about most completely, with three hundred angry Frenchmen in the hold of the

Polonais. It was as thorough a cause for promotion as ever I have seen."

"Oh!" Georgiana exclaimed, looking to him. "I do apologise – we also must congratulate you on your baronetcy."

"Never worry, Miss Darcy, I find I am still adjusting to the notion myself," he said. "And I in turn will apologise for not calling sooner. My time has not been my own – even today, I could hardly leave my uncle's house for all the callers. Every distant acquaintance of my own, and my uncle's, wishes to see me. Captain Campbell was so kind as to help me make my escape – I could not bear any more of it."

"Are you allowed enough time to recover?"

"Not so much as the physicians and my surgeon, Clerkwell, would like, but I assure you I feel better than I look," he said. "I would be remiss if I did not say you look very well, Miss Darcy. I hope you are all in health."

They assured him that they were, and could see that he was right – Georgiana did look very well. Despite his assurances, she still looked at him with a worried eye – they all did – but after months of despondency, much of the humour and lightness seemed to have returned instantly to her countenance, simply with his entrance.

"Might we beg you both to give us an account of the battle?" Darcy asked.

"Of course," Captain Stanton said. "It would have been a few days after my last letter to Mrs. Darcy. We had another storm, and it blew the blockading squadron off course, and disturbed our own course – it seems the Polonais slipped out of port at that time. We spotted her off the coast, near Lorient. We had the weather-gage, thankfully, so that it was our choice whether to fight her or not."

"What is the weather-gage?" asked Georgiana.

"My apologies, Miss Darcy, I should have explained it more thoroughly," he said. "Perhaps you will remember when we went sailing on the Thames, and had to keep tacking, to make our way up the river, because the wind was not blowing in the most favourable direction for us."

"Yes, I do remember," Georgiana said.

"Then you may also remember how easy it was for us to return back down the river, for the wind was very nearly behind us, pushing us forward," he said, waiting for Georgiana to nod her understanding. "Now, if you will, imagine that we were instead two ships, one moving down the river, the other moving up the river. The ship with the more favourable wind is said to have the weather-gage, for she may choose whether to fight the other ship, or decline the battle."

"Oh – I understand," Georgiana said.

"I thought you would," he said, smilingly. "So we were so fortunate as to have the weather-gage on the Polonais, and based on the way she was sailing, it seemed she had a very green crew. Even so, it was not an easy decision, to fight her – in addition to having far more guns than us, her largest guns take thirty-two pound shot, while ours are twenty-four pounders. On many a day, we would have run from a fight with her."

"What made you choose to fight, then?" Darcy asked.

"The seas were still rough, from the storm," Captain Stanton said. "In such circumstances, she could not manoeuvre and keep the gunports on her lower deck open, for fear they would flood the ship. The Jupiter is quite manoeuvrable for her size, so if we were able to make it a contest with a good deal of movement, things should be more even. You see, the largest guns are on the lower deck of a ship of the line – with both of our lower gunports closed, it would only be her eighteen-pounders against our twelve-pounders, and although that is hardly even, it is much better odds. My primary reason, though, was knowing our crew to be down to three broadsides in just under six minutes – as you may remember from my last letter, we got in quite a lot of practise, with great improvement. French gunnery has never been good, and I expected it to be much worse with a crew newly out of port, and war just beginning again."

"His assumption was correct, otherwise neither of us would be here to speak of it," Captain Campbell said, laughing.

"Yes, and she did maul us horribly as we came at her – even did get her lower gunports open for a little while, before she thought better of it," Captain Stanton said. "We were well within her range before she was within ours, so that all we could do was keep as many men below decks as possible, and lying down next to their guns, so that they would not be hit by the shot. We pressed on every sail we could, but still, I assure you, it was the longest sea mile of my life. We got in a few shots with our bow chasers, but only cut up a little of her rigging – her ropes."

"Oh, but we served her out once we were within range," Captain Campbell said. "She was barely five minutes to a broadside, and when we finally turned to give her ours, we gave her a full broadside, all our guns at once – you can only do that with a young ship, you know – and on the uproll, to see if we could dismast her. It shocked them most prodigiously, and her foremast did come down."

Georgiana had read both of Captain Stanton's letters through so many times they had grown thin at the creases, from folding and refolding, and she was glad for it now. She had an idea in her mind of how it looked, what they described, and although she was not sure whether it was accurate, at least it was something to base their account upon.

"Did you keep the carronades?" Georgiana asked.

For her question, she was rewarded with a very particular smile from Captain Stanton. "I did," he said, then, by way of explanation to the rest of the group: "I changed out our six-pounder long guns on deck for carronades of thirty-six pounds apiece. They are shorter, so the ship can still bear the weight, but not so accurate until you get within close range. Still, I was glad to have them when we did get in close."

"Indeed, your thirty-six pounder carronade is a true smasher," Captain Campbell said. "I am not so sure how we would have fared without them, although all of our gun crews were working hot and fast."

"All of the Jupiters did the ship proud, and the men at their sails did their duty every bit as much as the men at the guns," Captain Stanton said. "We were able, finally, to cut across her stern, and hit her terribly hard there – we shot away her rudder, so that she could not steer."

"I thought then we would have her, so long as all of us did our duty," Captain Campbell said. "We came about and hit her a few times with grape – bundles of smaller shot that break apart when fired – so to clear her decks a little more, for although by now we suspected her to be well below her full complement, she still had far more men than our Jupiter."

Georgiana paled a little as she comprehended what he had meant about the grape, and clearing the Polonais's decks; she had of course known that far more men on that ship had been killed than on the Jupiter, but she had not understood how it had happened, or how necessary it was so that Captain Stanton's ship could win.

Her brother was apparently thinking the same thing, for he said: "I think perhaps that might be sufficient detail on that portion of the engagement, with the ladies present."

"Of course," Captain Stanton said. "All you need know of that time is that we knew by now our gunnery was far superior to theirs, which grew even worse as the engagement went on, and with their rudder disabled, they could not manoeuvre. So we waited as long as possible before we ran the Jupiter across her bow and boarded her. From there it was all muskets and pistols, and of course hand-to-hand fighting."

"Our captain never said a word to anyone," Captain Campbell said, proudly, nodding to Captain Stanton, "but he had taken a piece of the Polonais's grape shot to the belly – for they were firing it at us, although not so promptly as we were firing it at them – even before he led us in the boarding."

"I hardly realised it myself," Captain Stanton said, looking a bit embarrassed. "In battle, one becomes so focused on the task at hand that only the most critical of injuries may raise themselves to the point of requiring attention."

"Aye," Captain Campbell said. "That was clear enough when we boarded, for our captain took a pistol shot to his leg, and still he charged on. Then one of the Frenchies took a wicked cut to his arm – our Amos Brown took care of the frog with – with – nay, that is a detail that I believe Mr. Darcy would wish we pass over. Our captain, he dropped his sword with the hit, but he picks it up with the other hand, and fights on. You must believe what a fire this put in the bellies of all our men – it was over not long after that."

Georgiana paled again, more deeply this time. She had known Captain Stanton for so long as a rather quiet gentleman that this more martial side of him had always been an abstract idea to her. Of course he had been wounded, but she had not understood it had been in brutal hand-to-hand fighting. He had in all likelihood killed men on the Polonais's decks, and had been very close to being killed himself. It changed him in her eyes, but not for the negative; she esteemed his bravery, she cherished that he could be so kind to her and still lead a group of men in such a fight.

"When a ship surrenders, she hauls down her colours – takes down her flag – and once she did so, we chased all the French sailors down into the hold, in case they should change their minds," Captain Stanton said. "Their captain was dead, as was their first lieutenant, and so their second lieutenant gave me his sword, as is the custom. After that, you will have to apply to Captain Campbell, for I do not remember the rest of it."

"You were awake a little while longer," Captain Campbell said. "But we were obliged to carry you back to the Jupiter, so old Clerkwell could go to work. Then we began repairs at a rather furious pace – we did not know what other French ships had got out of Brest and might stumble across us, and we certainly were in no shape to fight another ship of the line. Towards the end, what guns the Polonais could bring to bear she had pointed down, as far down as they could go, to try to hole us below the waterline – they meant to sink us – it was their only hope of escaping – and so we had nine feet of water in the hold at the worst of it, the pumps going all the way back to Plymouth.

"I took the Polonais, and Rigby, our second lieutenant, the Jupiter. They were still fitting out ships to go to war there in the harbour, and their crews smoked what had happened at once, for we had our own ensign flying above the French colours, as is tradition when a ship captures a prize, and they all stood along their rails to cheer us. I must admit that up until that point I felt mostly relief, but hearing that swelled my heart as much as anything ever has caused it to swell. I only wish Captain Stanton – I am sorry, Captain Sir Matthew Stanton – had been on deck to hear it."

"Captain Stanton will always be perfectly suitable to me. Indeed every time someone says *Captain Sir*, I look around to see who else they might be addressing, for I never expect it to be myself," said the object of Captain Campbell's correction.

"You would not tell us that you dislike being made a baronet," Darcy said. "If so, you may be the first man in the realm to have such sentiments."

"Not at all," Captain Stanton said. "I fully appreciate the honour, both for myself and my heirs, and of course for the navy, but I always will take more pride in being *Captain Stanton* than *Sir Matthew*, and I find when the two are combined, it creates more awkwardness than I would wish."

His voice was quite weary as he spoke, and it was clear to Georgiana that his strength was flagging; he had been animated enough, in recounting memories of the battle, but he was still very much the man who had not been awake for much of the trip between Lorient and Plymouth.

"Sir, you look tired," she said. "Is there any refreshment we might get you? Some coffee or tea?"

"Clerkwell has encouraged me to drink as much porter as I might, if indeed you would have any of that. He believes it rebuilds the blood, and it seems I have lost quite a lot of it."

Georgiana rose, to see if she could speak to Mr. Miller, but Elizabeth waved her off, and soon enough, one of the servants came in with a glass of porter, and one of Madeira, Captain Campbell's preference. The rest of them took a little tea, and the men of the navy did not stay long after they had finished their drinks, for Captain Stanton still looked very tired after drinking down his glass of porter.

Georgiana watched through the window as he left, helped carefully into the Earl of Anglesey's carriage by Captain Campbell. She felt herself restored to as much happiness as she had a right to presently: he had called, he had stayed far longer than any man in his state should have been expected to, and he had said she looked *very well*. This was still a very long way from any understanding between the two of them, and yet she felt at least she had a chance, now. He was alive, and they were both here in London, and she *would* attempt to capture his heart, now that she had been given this chance.

CHAPTER 10

Elizabeth had her appointment with Dr. Whittling the next morning, and after an examination far more close than she would have preferred anyone but her husband to be, he agreed thoroughly with her assessment that she was with child.

Elizabeth heard his pronouncement of such with a tremendous feeling of relief. She had been increasingly certain that she was – everything Sarah said, and the changes she could feel in her own body seemed to confirm it. Yet to hear it said by an expert in the field was quite another thing, and cause for the greatest happiness.

"Thank you, sir, I am so pleased to hear you confirm it. May I ask why it was so long in coming, after we were married?" she said. "My maid thought the climate of London might not be conducive to conceiving a child, and when I mentioned this theory to my family, they noted that I had been thinner than perhaps was healthy, while we were here. I must admit I did not notice it at the time."

"Your family may have been correct," he said, "although I would encourage you not to make your lady's maid also your midwife, unless she is somehow qualified in such things. There is also a chance that you did conceive, but could not carry the child. We are accustomed to thinking of miscarriage as a dramatic event, but there is increasing thought that it may happen very early in a pregnancy, if circumstances for carrying the child to term are not proper. In such a case, the miscarriage would appear to you as little more than your courses being a little irregular."

"I believe I had a few instances of that," Elizabeth said, her voice thick. "I did not realise it could be something of that sort."

"Do not worry yourself, Mrs. Darcy. If your womb was not capable of carrying a pregnancy to term, it did the best thing possible. However, I must ask why you are here in town now, if you believe this atmosphere so improper."

"There are a few things that have called us back here. Among them, of course, my husband and I wished I might see an accoucheur," she said, nodding to him. "We shall return to Pemberley soon enough."

"Very well," he said. "That is all I could ask of you, for in such a case what you believe to be healthy for the child is quite important. No one of your station stays during the summer, of course, but I would encourage you to leave in a fortnight or so, if not before. I shall write up notes, if you wish, for your country physician, on my recommendations for your care."

"Yes, if you please, I would very much appreciate that."

Dr. Whittling's practise had a little private sitting room, outside the room where he examined his patients, and waiting here was Darcy.

"All is well," Elizabeth told him. "Dr. Whittling confirms I am with child, and thus far it seems a healthy pregnancy."

"Thank God," he said, taking her up in an embrace, and then kissing her. They did not speak, for quite some time; Elizabeth could see how very happy he was, and knew her own happiness must have been equally clear to him.

"He is writing up some notes, for Dr. Alderman, on my care."

"Good – I would do anything in my power to keep you both healthy. Would it help to go to Bath, or the seaside?"

"My mother had five children in Hertfordshire, and Sarah's mother had eleven in Ireland," Elizabeth said, laughing. "I do not believe such measures are necessary. Although he did recommend we not linger in town much longer than a fortnight."

"I only hope things for Georgiana shall be resolved by then," he said, placing a little silk bag clinking with guineas on the waiting room's table – Dr. Whittling was a gentleman, and as such would never ask for payment.

"I cannot say they will be fully resolved, but unless he rejects her before then, they should be in such a place where Mrs. Annesley might attend her; he certainly does not seem at risk of dying, now. And Georgiana does seem more determined to act."

The objects of Elizabeth's and Darcy's conversation were, at the same time, conversing themselves, for Captain Stanton had called again at Curzon Street. Captain Campbell was not with him today, and Mrs. Annesley had that rare talent in a companion, of making herself central to a conversation when this was necessary, and fading well into the background when this was instead important. She sat, utterly focused on her embroidery, in a corner of the room, so that Georgiana and Captain Stanton were able to converse entirely by themselves.

Georgiana noted that he looked a little better; he seemed to be walking more freely, although the colour still had not returned to his face. He told her he was indeed feeling better, and that he had come in part to deliver an invitation – his uncle was holding a dinner in his honour in three days' time, and he hoped the Darcys would be able to attend.

"Yes, we should be able to," Georgiana said. "I can answer for our having no fixed engagements. We have been making very few since we are only to be in town for a limited time."

"Yes, your brother shared your reason for being in town with my uncle, when he called," Captain Stanton said. "Please give your sister my congratulations – I did not mention it yesterday, for I was not certain how widely known she wished it to be."

"Thank you, I will tell her. We are trying to be discreet with the news, for now – only family and close friends know. Tell me, will Lady Tonbridge be there? We have only called on her once, and I have missed her company very much."

"My uncle is likely to be delivering her invitation right now," he said. "And we hope to have some other friends from the musical club there, as well – Lady Julia and the gentlemen in the quartet will be invited. It will be as large an affair as my uncle has hosted in some time. Even my father is coming down – it was on his account that we have been unable to fix a date until now. We were not sure until his letter this morning when he would arrive."

"Your father – I do not believe I have ever heard you mention him."

"We are not close," he sighed. "His current living is in Cheshire, so he is but rarely in town. He never did approve of my joining the navy – although he would not speak against it publicly because my uncle supported it. As far as my father is concerned, the church was the only proper profession for any of his sons."

"Even now, when you have been so successful?"

"Fortune certainly did not change his opinion," he said. "It is possible the baronetcy has – indeed, I did not expect him to come to town for this – but I doubt his true sentiments shall ever change."

"I am so sorry to hear that."

"It is something I think of but little," he said. "I am more fortunate than many, to have at least one strong family connection. My uncle has always done all he could to further my career – it was he who saw me placed on the Iris as a captain's servant, and purchased all the items to fill my first sea chest."

"May I ask how old you were, when you went to sea?"

"I was near eight and a half."

"So young! I cannot imagine leaving your home and all you know at so young an age."

"My mother died when I was six, of fever from childbirth – the child was stillborn, a girl. Our home was never really happy again after that."

Georgiana nodded, sympathetically. "I was four, when my mother died. I remember only little glimpses of her."

"I remember perhaps a little more, but not much."

"Would it be too much to ask you why you chose to join the navy?"

"Not at all, Miss Darcy," he said. "My uncle's estate is outside of Chester, and we would always spend our summers there, all of the boys in the family. The year after my mother died, for an excursion, we went to Anglesey, for my uncle liked the notion of visiting the earldom's namesake. We went out on South Stack – it is this amazing little high rock of an island, and just after we climbed to the top, a Royal Navy frigate came round the point with nearly a full press of canvas. I do not know who she was, or what she was chasing, but it was the most beautiful thing I had ever seen. I found myself filled with longing to be on that ship, to be part of that world. I believe my uncle made a few comments in praise of the navy, and that was it, I had it in my head I wished to join the navy."

"I hope I might see such a sight, someday – it sounds so beautiful," Georgiana said. "We have only been to the more traditional watering places, so I must admit to never seeing a ship of that size under sail."

"I very much hope you shall have a chance to see it, as well. I will admit myself to be biassed, but I find there is nothing like the sight."

He left only when Mrs. Annesley began glancing up with little looks of concern; he had stayed for more than an hour, and any longer was beyond the bounds of what was proper for a morning call with most of the family out. Georgiana was startled to realise he had been there for so long.

They had conversed so easily, and on topics so intimate, that she felt more secure in thinking he could have a real affection for her, and she resolved that she must confess her affections to him soon. She would not choose the day on which to do so; she would not prepare a speech. Yet she would look for an opening, and when it came she would be bold, although the thought of it made her heart quicken painfully, and a wave of nervousness washed over her. She *must* be bold – she would not see him leave again without knowing her heart.

Elizabeth and Darcy returned not long after Captain Stanton left; they had stopped to call on the Fitzwilliams after leaving Dr. Whittling's practise. They both expressed happiness at the earl's dinner invitation – for that was an event surely worth an evening out – and regret they did not truly feel that they had missed him, for they felt his focus must surely have been Georgiana, a point Mrs. Annesley confirmed privately to Elizabeth later.

Now knowing that there would be no fear of missing his call, Elizabeth suggested to Georgiana that they go shopping, to see what might have changed in the fashions, and make any purchases that could not be done in Lambton. Georgiana agreed readily to the scheme; she had been practising the pianoforte so much over the last few weeks that she wished to purchase new music, and she would not mind visiting a modiste or two.

It was in the second shop, as they were looking at fabric, that they found themselves approached at a rapid pace by Lady Caroline Harrison, née Bingley.

"Eliza Darcy, dear Miss Darcy! I did not expect to see the two of you here in town. I had thought your whole family removed to Pemberley, along with my brother and Jane," she said. "Sir Sedgewick and I are only here for a little while ourselves before we make the journey to Hilcote. Brighton was dreadfully dull without the Regent there."

"Caroline, good morning, it is good to see you," Elizabeth managed. "We are only here for a little while ourselves as well. You may have heard from Charles or Jane that I am in the family way, so I wished to see a town physician, and I am also going to have a few sittings for my portrait."

"So you are all in town while your house guests remain at Pemberley? How very odd."

"We have given Charles and Jane leave to stay at Pemberley for as long as they need to purchase Clareborne Manor and build the new house there," Elizabeth said. "They take no issue with our needing to be away from home, and they are family anyway, not guests with hardly a connection to our family."

"Well I am glad I happened to run across you, for I had the most interesting news about an acquaintance of yours this morning. It seems your friend Sir Matthew Stanton – and my isn't he the talk of the town! – is engaged to Lady Julia Barton."

Elizabeth looked over at Georgiana, who was motionless in shock, all the colour gone from her face, as Caroline continued on, oblivious to her supposed friend's reaction: "I think all the luck in the match is on his side. I know he was elevated to a baronetcy and all, but he is after all still a naval captain. And she has fifty thousand pounds, and is the daughter of a baron. I wonder if she shall change her mind before it is all over."

"That must be merely a rumour," Elizabeth said. "He called on us this morning and said nothing of the sort."

"Perhaps he does not wish to make it known yet," Caroline said. "Which is a silly notion, given how much he is in the papers. Anyway, I had it from Mrs. Polley, and she is well-acquainted with Lady Julia."

Elizabeth took another glance over at Georgiana and knew she must get them both out of the shop immediately, rather than try to argue the point any further; Georgiana was only just holding her composure.

"Caroline, that is quite interesting news, but I do believe we must say our farewells. I promised Mr. Darcy we would be back nearly a half-hour ago," Elizabeth said. "I hope you have a pleasant journey to Hilcote."

"Well, then, farewell to you both," Caroline said, grasping Elizabeth's hands in her own and leaning closer. "By-the-bye, I think I might prefer it if you both called me Lady Harrison when we are out in society. Of course in a private gathering, Caroline would suit, but I would not want anyone to overhear anything improper in public."

"Certainly," Elizabeth said. "I know you take great care in proper address. I am sure you are most aggrieved over your slip in referring to me as Eliza Darcy. Farewell, Lady Harrison."

With the tiniest of curtseys, Elizabeth ushered Georgiana out of the shop and into the carriage.

"How can it be?" Georgiana asked, finally allowing her tears to come. "How can he – be engaged – to Lady Julia?"

"It cannot be, that is the simplest explanation. You know there are a great many rumoured engagements in town that never come to be."

"Lord Alfred's certainly came to be!"

"I will grant you that, Georgiana. But he called today, to speak with *you*, for more than an hour. Why should he do that if he had just become engaged to Lady Julia?"

"We have no notion of how long he calls on her, or whether he did before he called on us. He mentioned she was to attend his uncle's party," Georgiana said. "Perhaps they are planning to announce it there. She is very pretty – they would make a handsome couple. She was always very forward in his company – and I was not. And she has fifty thousand pounds!"

"Just because she was forward and has fifty thousand pounds does not mean he loves her, or wishes to marry her. Georgiana, I beg you would not allow yourself to believe this, or let it upset you, until you hear it confirmed by him."

Despite Elizabeth's continued attempts, however, Georgiana would not be consoled. She arrived at Curzon Street and retired immediately to her chamber. A tray was sent up for her dinner, and the tray returned untouched.

CHAPTER 11

When Georgiana's breakfast tray also returned untouched, Elizabeth made her way upstairs, nodding to Mrs. Annesley, who had remained in her room across the hall, with her door open, should her charge need anything. Elizabeth knocked on Georgiana's door, received no answer, and entered slowly.

Georgiana was there, awake and curled up on the bed. She looked flat, as though all the spirit had been drained from her, although not nearly so wretched as she had in the days when Captain Stanton's life had been in doubt. At some point, Mrs. Annesley or Hughes must at least have convinced her to change, for she was wearing her nightgown, but she looked to have slept poorly, or not at all. Elizabeth sat down on the bed beside her, and rubbed her back.

"Georgiana, you will make yourself ill if you continue on like this," she said. "It is but a rumour, and with Caroline Bingley as your source!"

"I know, but I let myself believe the news about Lord Alfred was but a rumour, and it was not, and I will not be so unprepared this time," Georgiana said. "My consolation is that he lives, for I can still remember how I felt when that was in doubt. But I must face that he may live and love another."

"Or he may very well love you, and I think that much more likely."

"I cannot help but think that perhaps he did, but when I made no show of my affections, he transferred his to another."

"I do not see when he would have had time to do that, Georgiana. You have hardly been reacquainted with each other," Elizabeth said. "I expect he will call today, as he has for the last two. Will you not dress and come down to the drawing room so you might hear him refute it yourself?"

"Oh no, Elizabeth, I cannot go. I know there is a chance he will refute

278

it, but I could not bear to hear him confirm it. I know I would break down, and I could not bear such a mortification."

"I do not think that is what you would hear, but if you will not come down, please try to get some sleep, and at least eat a little. I could not bear to see this affect your health."

"I will try, Elizabeth."

Before taking her place in the drawing room, Elizabeth went to Darcy's study, to report this latest fruitless conversation.

"Georgiana has always had a very sentimental heart," he said. "I suspected that if she ever fell in love, she would love deeply, and that does leave her very open to heartbreak."

"But we do not even know if there is cause for heartbreak!"

"There is not. I do not see how there is. I do not know why he would have come here in his condition – twice – to call on us if he intended to commit himself to Lady Julia. It is so simple – both of them seem to love each other. Why can neither of them speak of it?"

"I do not understand it. I will own that uncertainty in love is a most difficult thing, however," Elizabeth said.

"Uncertainty in love? When have you ever known uncertainty in love? You, who would turn down two marriage proposals within a span of months."

"When you returned to Netherfield, following Lydia's marriage, and called on us, I can assure you it was a most difficult uncertainty for me."

"Why else would I have returned to Hertfordshire, for any other reason than being constant to you?"

"I assure you, my heart created any number of doubts, which prevented my believing such a thing," Elizabeth said. "After I had refused you as I did, you had no reason to remain constant to me."

"None except that I love you."

"Thank God for that," she said. "But if my heart could create doubts, perhaps their hearts have as well, particularly Georgiana's, given – given her history."

"Well, I can hardly stomach any more doubts, with my poor sister's health as it is. I would be within my rights as Georgiana's guardian to call him into my study, and ask his intentions towards her. Perhaps I shall. I can tell him he must either enter into a formal courtship with her, or stop calling so frequently."

"If he is not willing to enter into at least a courtship, it would be best that he ceased calling at all. I am sure he will call today. If he is not engaged to Lady Julia, I will send him to you, and you may press him for his intentions."

"Thank you, my dear. I cannot say I would look forward to such a conversation, but it seems the best course, at this point. I cannot bear to watch Georgiana continue on with things undecided."

He did call soon, and seemed startled to find only Elizabeth in the drawing room, as he limped in, and was seated, "Mrs. Darcy, good day to you. Are the rest of your family out?"

"Mr. Darcy is in his study, attending to some correspondence," she said. "Georgiana is not feeling well, so Mrs. Annesley is upstairs attending her."

"Not well? She looked very well yesterday – I hope it is nothing serious," he said, in a tone of such innocent concern that Elizabeth felt certain the rumour could not be true.

"I believe it just a passing thing," she said.

"I do hope so – please let her know I hope to see her restored to health quickly."

"I will, thank you," Elizabeth said, and then determined she would wait no longer. "I understand there is more pleasant news from your quarter – I understand we are to give you joy on your engagement to Lady Julia Barton."

"Lady Julia! Well that is one I have not yet heard," he said. "I suppose it is more realistic, since that lady and I are at least acquainted. Ever since I returned to town, they have been attempting to see me engaged to one lady or another – it seems after capturing a French ship, I must be suitably injured, and also suitably betrothed."

"So there is no truth to it?"

"There is no truth to it at all," he said, wearily, and Elizabeth could not prevent the relief from spreading over her countenance, which he noted. "You would not tell me that your family saw any credence in these rumours?"

"We did think it odd, as you had called only yesterday and not mentioned it, however, sometimes these things are kept quiet at first," she said. "If that is the case and I have spoken of something I should not, please forgive me."

"That is not at all the case – there is no engagement between myself and Lady Julia, nor will there ever be," he said. "Miss Darcy – certainly *she* did not see any credence in these rumours, did she?"

"I am afraid she did."

Comprehension dawned on his face, and were it possible, he would have turned even paler. "Please do not tell me this had any contribution to Miss Darcy's not feeling well."

"You yourself observed she was very well yesterday – surely you can see that it did."

"I do not understand how she could believe such a thing," he said, in a tone of more emotion than Elizabeth had ever heard from him. "I do not understand how she could think there is any but her."

"Why should she not believe such a thing? You must admit you have hardly been forthcoming in the regard you have just indicated! Poor Georgiana has three times been pursued by gentlemen who turned out to be interested only in her fortune. With such a dowry as hers, how should she believe anyone would truly love her?" Elizabeth said, looking at the shock in his expression, and feeling immediate dismay that her anger at his response had caused her to betray Georgiana's confidence. "I am sorry – I have said far more than I should."

"I wish you would say more!" he cried, but Elizabeth shook her head – anything more that would be said must be said by Georgiana herself.

She saw no need to send him to Darcy, now that he had at least made his feelings known to her, but neither did she know what else to say. In the long, uncomfortable silence that followed, he finally reached inside his jacket, and pulled out a letter that was very much wrinkled and stained.

"In the navy, before we officers go into battle, we write a note to those we love, in case we do not survive. I wrote this before we engaged the Polonais, and have been carrying it since Captain Campbell returned it to my possession – I could not bring myself to destroy it. It is a letter to Miss Darcy, under cover to you, and you may well determine it is improper to do so, but I wish you would give to her – it seems the only time I have been able to express the depth of my feeling for your sister."

Elizabeth took the battered letter from him carefully, hoping deeply that inside might be the end of Georgiana's heartbreak.

"Given the circumstances, I am willing to overlook propriety, so long as you give your word as a gentleman that there is nothing improper in what you write," she said.

"I said as much in my covering letter," he said. "And I will confirm it now. If I may, I will take my leave now so that you may deliver it. I will call again tomorrow – if Miss Darcy is feeling better I would wish to speak with her."

Elizabeth opened and read the covering letter as she climbed the stairs. Its contents were unsurprising – he had already explained the custom of writing letters to loved ones before battle, and recognised the impropriety of writing to a single lady. He assured her that although he wrote of deep sentiments within the letter to Georgiana, there was nothing unchaste. He wished she would allow a dead man a little bit of leeway, but if she must read it before giving it to Georgiana, he would understand. The letter inside was in better condition, and Elizabeth clasped it in her hand as she entered the hallway and saw Georgiana leaving her chambers, fully dressed.

Georgiana had finally determined that she must meet the situation with the same resolve that had been growing within her since learning that Captain Stanton would live, and asked Hughes to help her dress. If he was engaged to Lady Julia, there would be nothing she could do, and she knew she would face the mortification of a reaction she would not be able to control. But if he was *not*, she would not go through another day without his knowing where her heart lay.

Her hopes sank, however, upon seeing Elizabeth in the hallway. If he had called – and she could think of no other reason for Elizabeth's returning upstairs so quickly – he had not called for long, and during such a short call, little else could have occurred, other than a confirmation of his engagement.

"Has he called?" she asked, trembling.

"Yes, and he confirms there is no engagement to Lady Julia. He had not even heard of the rumour, although apparently he has been the subject of so many rumoured engagements that he did not at first pay this one any mind. I suppose we would have heard of more of them if we had been taking callers."

Georgiana felt such a tremendous rush of relief at Elizabeth's words that her knees felt weak for a moment. "There is still hope!" she cried, embracing her sister. "You were right, Elizabeth, I should not have doubted him. He is so very different from Lord Alfred; I should not have compared the two situations. Oh, I cannot tell you what a relief it is to have my hopes restored."

"There is a chance you shall move beyond hope very soon." Elizabeth smiled gently, indicating they should walk back into Georgiana's room. They did so, and took up chairs in the little sitting area there. "Captain Stanton was quite upset that you saw any credibility in the rumours about Lady Julia, and that they were cause for your illness. He wondered that you could think there was any but you."

"He said that? Truly?" In a quarter-hour, Georgiana had gone from such agony to such happiness – to have a confirmation of his affections when she had only wished for more time to make hers known!

"He did," Elizabeth said. "And here is where my part in the conversation, I am afraid, does not reflect very well on me. I chastised him for wondering how you could believe such a rumour when he had not at all made his regard clear."

"Elizabeth! I am amazed you could do such a thing, but surely there cannot have been much harm done."

"Not there, perhaps, but I did also tell him that you had three times been pursued by men interested in only your fortune, and that such a history made it difficult for you to believe anyone could truly love you. Georgiana, I am so sorry – I grew angry and I betrayed your confidence without thinking."

"Oh, Elizabeth, do not worry yourself. It is nothing I would not have shared with him, if such a conversation arose, and in a way, it is a relief that you have opened the door a little for me," Georgiana said. "And anyway, I could not be upset for long at the bearer of such news."

"I have more than news to give you," Elizabeth said, holding up a slightly discoloured letter addressed simply to *Miss Darcy*. "Captain Stanton explained that it is tradition for gentlemen in the navy to write a letter to loved ones before going into battle, to be delivered if they do not survive. He had apparently written to you, under cover to myself, before the action against the Polonais."

"He thought to write to me at such a time?"

"Yes, and he has been carrying the letter since Captain Campbell returned it to him. He says it is the only time he has been able to express the depth of his feelings."

"What does it say?" Georgiana could hardly breathe; she had rejoiced in the return of her hopes, and in that letter might be, as Elizabeth said, something far beyond hope. She was afraid to wish for more, but some small part of her could not help but think that it just might contain every happiness in the world.

"I have not read it. I believe whatever is contained inside should be a private matter between the two of you," Elizabeth said, holding it out so that Georgiana could take it in her shaking hand. "He has assured me there is nothing improper beyond the general impropriety of writing to a single lady, and I am willing to overlook that in this situation. I will leave you now, and let you read your letter, but you should know that Captain Stanton intends to call again tomorrow, and hopes you will be well enough to see him."

Georgiana waited until she heard the door click closed, and even then, although she was all anticipation, she could not bring herself to open the letter quickly. Unfolding the paper, she finally saw that it had been written hastily, but still she had no trouble deciphering his hand as she read:

"My Dearest Georgiana,

"I realise the impropriety of addressing you so, and of writing to you at all, but Dearest Georgiana is what you have been to me for so long, I can hardly think of anything else at such a time.

"As I write this, we have the weather-gage (perhaps Campbell may explain what this means to you, when he delivers this) over a French seventy-four, and attempting an attack on a ship of such superior force may well be the last foolish thing I ever do in my life. Yet I know it is the proper course. The conditions are right, and I trust my crew, although they may not have been together long – I believe in them, and I hope that if you are reading this, it is following the successful capture of the ship by HMS Jupiter, wherein the captain of the Jupiter somehow came to meet his end, and not the horrible alternative.

"This is not what I wished to write to you about, however. The simple truth of things, Georgiana, is that I love you, and if I do survive this engagement, there is nothing I would wish for more than to have a chance to win your heart. If you are reading this letter, then please accept my sincerest apologies for laying such a heavy burden on you, but I must let you know that I love you, that I have for much of our acquaintance. I suppose if I had the same courage in love that I did in war, I should have told you so long ago, but I love you so deeply I could hardly speak of it, and you must know this is my greatest regret.

"I ask of nothing from you but to know that you were loved, and to forgive me for not telling you thus when you might at least have had an opportunity to respond. Please do not let this be an obstruction to you – do not spend a moment more in mourning than you would for any other friend. I would wish for your happiness more than anything else in this world, and the next.

"Yours, always,

"MATTHEW STANTON"

In its first reading, Georgiana could hardly believe the reality of the letter. She returned to the paragraph where he had told her he loved her, and read it again thrice, and only when she had assured herself of its realness did a strange dizziness envelop her. She had thought she could cry no more today, but after a first surprising sob, found herself breaking down again, although from relief and happiness, this time. He loved her, and he had told her so with every warmth of feeling, with a boldness perhaps brought on by his situation.

There could be no doubting his affections, now, to have left these as what might have been his last words to her. Georgiana shuddered at the thought of how the letter might have been delivered, by Captain Campbell, or perhaps Lord Anglesey, with the news of his death. How painful it would have been, to read such a letter, to know that he loved her but had no sense of how much she loved him. To think his love a burden to her, when even in that horrible scenario, it would have been such a comfort!

"I need not face that," she thought. "Tomorrow he will call, and I may tell him of my affections with every assurance they will be returned. Neither of us need ever be in doubt again."

The thought of his calling, of making her love known when it would most certainly be returned, sent her spirits fluttering, and it took her quite some time to feel any semblance of tranquillity. She read the letter through several times more, until she had committed much of it to memory, and was in the midst of another reading when there came another knock at her door.

"Georgiana, may I come in?" It was her brother's voice, and Georgiana rushed to wipe the tears from her cheeks. She should not be looking so poorly – not when all she felt was joy and love.

"Please do," she said.

He entered, seemed to notice the change in her countenance, and smiled. "Elizabeth told me about your letter."

"Oh Fitzwilliam, please do not be angry about it. I know it was not the most proper thing, but it has given me every reason for happiness!"

"Why does everyone assume I shall always be stern?" he asked, taking a seat near her.

"You do often look very stern, brother, but you are right," she said. "You have always been very kind to me, even when I made the most foolish of mistakes."

"I will share something with you that perhaps Elizabeth did not, and that is that I wrote her a letter even before we were engaged," he said. "There were a few things I wished to explain to her that I had not been able to in person. So you see, as she reminded me before she told me of *your* letter, I have no leg to stand on in this matter."

Georgiana laughed softly.

"So you said the letter has given you every reason for happiness?"

"Yes – he said he loved me, in no uncertain terms. It seems we have both been very much in love with each other, but unable to say so."

"I am so glad, Georgiana," he said, his voice catching. "We have been very worried about you."

"I know, and I am sorry I gave you such cause for worry – yet again."

"There was little you could do – we cannot control who we fall in love with," he said, a look of vague fondness crossing his countenance. "At least I know you shall marry with the deepest love, and a secure future, which is all I could ever have wanted for you. I will of course give my consent tomorrow."

"You believe he will make me an offer of marriage tomorrow?"

"Well I certainly hope he is not going to come here to speak to you of love without offering marriage, or at least an acknowledged courtship," he said. "If that is the case, I will have to be exceedingly stern."

"No, I suppose that would be the logical conclusion – my mind had not yet gone that far."

"You may want to let it do so before you speak with him. I would expect that being a naval captain's wife is not the easiest of lives, particularly if she is married to a captain who seems to have no fear of taking on a ship of far superior force. You should consider all that being married to him would entail before you accept him."

"I will, Fitzwilliam, I promise."

"Very good. Will you get some rest, and perhaps join us for dinner?"

"If you do not mind a very happy dinner companion, I will."

"I think we would all very much like to have a happy dinner companion."

He embraced her before he left the room, and Georgiana could not help but read the letter once more before attempting a little sleep.

By the time Darcy had returned downstairs, the portrait painter, Mr. Thorpe, had arrived, and was studiously sketching Elizabeth's features. The object of his sketch sat with her spine most rigid, attempting to keep herself still, something most difficult for someone usually so active as she.

"You were not stern, were you?" she asked, when her husband entered the drawing room, earning her a look of mild contempt from Mr. Thorpe.

"I was not stern," he said. "I was very kind, although at least now I am aware of what you all think of me, that I am the most stern man on this earth."

Elizabeth chuckled, and then looked guiltily at Mr. Thorpe, trying to rearrange her features into what they had been.

"I did, however, encourage her to think on what being married to a naval captain would entail," he said. "The letter made her exceedingly happy, but I do not know that she has thought beyond it. They would be likely to spend much of their marriage apart, so long as the war continues. Although I should not skip ahead to marriage, not until he calls."

Elizabeth had no doubt that he would call and make his offer, on the morrow. She had seen the expression on his face, and although she did not know the contents of the letter, she could guess at them, if they had made Georgiana so happy.

She thought back to her own brief separations, from Darcy, and how even these had been so difficult. He was right – she did not know how Georgiana could bear a far longer time apart from Captain Stanton. Elizabeth had not intended to fall in love with Darcy – indeed, she had put quite a lot of effort in to disliking him, for so much of their early acquaintance. Yet now she felt a new sort of relief and happiness that she had fallen in love with him, that she loved a man bound to his own estate, so that they might be together always.

CHAPTER 12

Georgiana awoke the following morning, and immediately looked over at the table beside her bed, to reassure herself that the letter was still there, that it was very much real, and then read it again, for the rush of happiness it still brought her. The course of the day would decide her fate, and she trembled at the thought of it. She would have to be the one to speak, at least at first; and although she had every expectation that anything she said should be well-received, still, she worried over how she might say it.

Her nervousness must have been apparent to all at the breakfast table; she could hardly eat, and what little attempt she did make was punctuated with a heavy clank, as she dropped her spoon, and later very nearly upset her glass of small beer. Everyone waited with her in the drawing room: it would not do for him to call and find her alone there; for propriety's sake, the private audience must be known by the family to be requested, and then granted. For Georgiana, their presence was some comfort, but it did not prevent her from fidgeting, an act usually far from her nature, as she could not focus on embroidery or a book.

Mercifully, he called early, at the very beginning of the appropriate hour, and he did not look very well. Certainly, his injuries were part of the cause, but Georgiana realised that turning over the letter to Elizabeth, and needing to wait until now for a response, must have worn on him terribly; she put herself in his place and knew how difficult it must have been to bear.

"Good morning," he said, removing his hat. "It seems we may have rain today."

They all greeted him, and made what little remarks on the weather they could, so that pleasantries might be done, and he could move on to the purpose of his visit.

"Miss Darcy, I hope you are in better health today?" He looked at her so directly, and so earnestly, that she could not help but blush.

"I am, thank you."

"I am very glad to hear it," he said. "If it is not too much trouble, I would like to request a private audience with you."

"It is not too much trouble at all," Georgiana said. As soon as she spoke, Darcy, Elizabeth, and Mrs. Annesley rose, and with little bows and curtsies, left the room as quietly as three people might. The door closed, and through it, Georgiana could hear Elizabeth's muffled voice telling Mr. Miller that no one was to be admitted to the drawing room, that the family would take callers in the conservatory.

They were alone. Georgiana felt her heart pounding as he limped over to where she was seated, sat down beside her – closer than he ever had before – and turned to face her. Georgiana shifted so she might face him, as well, took a deep, tremulous breath, and said:

"I have read your letter. You do not need to win my heart – you held it at the time you wrote those words, and you hold it now. I love you, and I cannot tell you what happiness it brought me to read that you love me as well."

There, it was said. Her speech did not go long without reward; his right hand was still clothed in a sling, but he took up her hand in his left somewhat clumsily, although with every tenderness in his grasp.

"You have just brought me every happiness, Miss Darcy," he said, his countenance that of a man much relieved, his eyes looking into hers so intently she could hardly breathe. "And you must let me apologise for all that has happened in the last few days. I did not take these marriage rumours seriously, and I cannot bear to think that one of them has caused you pain. Your sister rightly told me that I had no reason to expect it would not, when I had never made my affections clear."

"I will not say the thought of it did not hurt me," she said. "But I know it was not consciously done on your part, and I believe I must share in my part of the blame, for I also did not make my affections clear."

"There were a few times I thought you attempted to – when you came to say good-bye to me before I left for Portsmouth, particularly, but I could not bring myself to believe it, and I could not see that as the time and place to attempt to bind your heart. You know what I entered into this war wishing to do; I have been fortunate enough to have succeeded, but I cannot deny that it very nearly killed me. I did not wish to rush to an impetuous declaration," he said. "I see now that it might have been sudden, but never impetuous. I think back now about how much pain I might have saved the both of us, had I spoke then. Your sister explained a little of your romantic past, that you had been thrice pursued by men only interested in your fortune. With such a history, it is no wonder you had a fear of having your affections truly returned. It should have been me that spoke. I wish you could know how much I regret it."

"I cannot say that having been disappointed in love made me any less able to speak," Georgiana said. "I have been for much of my life what most would call shy. Indeed, I will at least give one of the gentlemen credit for making me more comfortable in speaking with gentlemen, when I first came out into society. I suppose it is something rather like the pianoforte – it must be practised. I might not have had the courage to speak to you so much when we met, otherwise."

"Do you mind if I ask if the gentleman in question is Viscount Burnley?" he asked, waiting for her confirming nod. "Lady Tonbridge gave me some understanding of the situation there. I must admit I felt a great deal of jealousy towards the gentleman, upon our acquaintance, and then anger, that he should betray you, for he must have been a fool to do so. However, his inappropriate engagement left me with a chance, which is what I so desperately wanted."

"You must credit him with more than that, for I will tell you that when I received confirmation that he was engaged, I found myself upset at the betrayal, but not at all heartbroken. That was when I realised it was you who held my heart."

"Indeed! Then although I still find his conduct wanting, I will always look upon him fondly. I feel for you, though, Miss Darcy, to have been through three such situations. I do not know how you bore it."

"Oh, but one was only a little passing thing. There was a gentleman at Lady Tonbridge's musical club who – after less than a fortnight's acquaintance – decided we were to be married. He proposed, and would not drop his suit; my brother and Mr. Miller had to escort him out."

"Did they?" he said. "I will assume he was not invited back, to the musical club."

"You know Lady Tonbridge well enough to know your assumption is correct."

"And what of the final gentleman?"

Mr. Wickham. Georgiana felt her cheeks burn, and dropped her gaze.

"I am so sorry, dearest," he said, tightening his grip on her hand. "I did not realise this one was the most upsetting to you. You need not tell me about it."

Yet Georgiana knew she must tell him about it, even if it changed his opinion of her. Now that they had each confessed the most difficult thing, she wished for every thing between them to always be honest, and that could not be so if she kept her near-elopement a secret from him.

"No, I must tell you. You should know," she said, and she proceeded to tell him of her time in Ramsgate with Mrs. Younge, of the appearance of Mr. Wickham, who had always been so nice to her as a child. Of how they had found themselves alone, frequently, and he had made love to her until she was quite convinced she was in love with him, although now that she was truly in love, she knew what she had felt back then was nothing of the sort. And then, finally, of how he had convinced her they should elope, how they had been planning to travel to Gretna Green, but her brother had arrived, and she had, already doubting that it was the right course, felt compelled to tell him of their plans.

As she talked, he held a look of shocked horror, and then, eventually, anger on his face. He said nothing, when she had completed her story, and from the lingering stony distaste on his face, she concluded that she had made a terrible mistake.

"I am sorry," she said. "I know this must lower me in your opinion. I would understand if it has changed your affections towards me."

"My affections towards *you*?" he said, incredulously, gazing at her and tightening his grip on her hand. "Oh, Georgiana, do not mistake my anger by thinking it has anything to do with your conduct. You were but fifteen! You were not out in society, and you were left alone by your companion in the company of such a man, wholly unprotected. No, if it makes any sense at all, I find my anger directed towards the past, at a man I have never met, because he might have stolen you away so that I would never have met you – stolen you away to as miserable a life as I would imagine being married to such a man would be."

"Indeed none of us need imagine," Georgiana said, feeling the warmth of relief at his statement. "He did convince Mrs. Darcy's sister, Lydia, to elope, when she was fifteen. I do not know the particulars of it – my brother would not share them, for obvious reasons – but I know there was some delay in their being married."

"So he is part of your family?"

"He is but barely acknowledged, and he was with the regulars in Newcastle before war began again, so there was quite a bit of distance between us. My brother has made it clear he is not welcome either here or at Pemberley, but Fitzwilliam would not have Elizabeth's sister ruined. I have never met her, but I feel for her, for I know how persuasive he can be."

"I am so sorry for her, and so sorry to hear you have had to suffer such events, Miss Darcy," he said. "I believe I now better understand what a curse fortune might be on a lady. You must know, if it would help my suit, I would take your entire dowry and throw it into the Thames. I have enough that we would live well without it."

"I do not consider you to have a suit," she said, feeling strangely confident. "A suit would indicate there is some uncertainty, and I do not see it, if we love each other as we do."

"I take your point with every happiness that I may," he said. "However, there are some things you must consider before I would propose marriage.

I do not have so comfortable a living to offer you as other gentlemen would. It is not a case of fortune – I have sixty-three thousand pounds, and can expect at least a little more from the Polonais, although she was so battered about she may not be bought into the service, in which case she will not bring nearly as much prize money."

"You are also a baronet," she offered.

"Yes, I suppose I am. You would be Lady Stanton."

"I will admit I find that quite appealing, although I believe I would also have seen much appeal in Mrs. Stanton."

"I suppose it is not fortune or title that should concern you, then," he said. "But I do not know how long this war will continue on. When the Jupiter is repaired, I expect I will be sent back to sea, and you would be left here to wait. It is not unusual for captains to take their wives with them to sea, and I would invite you to come with me so long as the destination and mission of the ship were not too unsafe, but I must warn you that accommodations on board are not very comfortable for a lady. You would have a space much smaller than this room as your primary living quarters, and be required to live among several hundred men, with perhaps a wife or two among the warrant officers for female company, and one lady's maid to attend you."

Georgiana had been thinking about what it would mean to be a naval captain's wife since her brother had set her mind to it, and although she could not tell him this, she could tell him of her conclusion:

"I will not say that I would have set out to fall in love with a naval captain," she said. "But I find the prospect of living without your love far worse than anything I would have to bear as your wife."

"And you understand – you do understand there is a chance I will be killed in the course of my career?"

"I do understand," she said, her eyes filling with tears. "I was – I was so afraid when we heard of the Polonais, that you might die."

He released her hand, only to use his free arm to pull her into an embrace that was not very proper, but was her every consolation at that moment.

"I am so sorry to have put you through that, Georgiana. I asked my uncle to send an express as soon as he arrived, so that any concern you might have felt would be alleviated," he said. "But you must be prepared that you may go through such an event again, and the outcome may not be so favourable."

"I would prepare myself as best I could," she said. "I do not how I would bear it, but I would rather have to bear such a thing than never have been married to you."

He took up her hand again, and kissed it, a gesture that thrilled her to her core. "That is all I could ask of you. My dearest Georgiana, will you marry me?"

The lady's answer, of course, was yes.

There was a certain order of things that was to be preserved, once marriage had been proposed and accepted. The couple emerged from the drawing room, to find Mr. Miller waiting a polite distance from the door; Georgiana needed only to request where the rest of the family had gone, so that she might join them, and partake of the happiest of embraces from Elizabeth and Mrs. Annesley, but Captain Stanton now had to request an audience with Mr. Darcy.

Mr. Miller showed him to the study, at the poor gentleman's uneven, limping pace, and sent another servant to inform Mr. Darcy that Captain Stanton had business with him, and was waiting in his study. If Captain Stanton had any fears of his reception there, they must have been alleviated when Darcy entered and, without preamble, said:

"Please tell me it is done, that the two of you are to be married."

"Indeed, we would be," said Captain Stanton, taken aback. "That is, if you would grant your consent."

"Finally!" Darcy said, reaching out to shake his hand, and, upon realising only the left was available, completing the handshake with some awkwardness. "I will give my consent readily. Georgiana's other guardian, Colonel Fitzwilliam, is fighting on the continent and will not be available to do so for some time, but I expect he would agree, and that I may speak for him."

"I thank you, sir. I must admit I had expected I would have to make my case much more thoroughly."

"Let us not stand on ceremony," Darcy said. "You must know that I inquired as to your prospects some time ago. They were suitable at the time, and since then, you have managed to acquire a baronetcy, which only benefits your suit. I will admit I was a bit surprised to learn that the discrepancy between your ages is quite a bit more than I had thought, but I am not even sure Georgiana noticed, and if she did, it was no matter to her, so I will not let it be a matter to me."

"Discrepancy between our ages, sir? I understand Georgiana is eighteen-and-a-half years of age, and as I am seven-and-twenty, there is not even ten years between us."

"I had been given to understand from one of the articles about you in the papers that you were one-and-thirty. Was it mistaken, then?"

"Ah, there is the cause," Captain Stanton said. "So far as the navy is concerned, I am one-and-thirty – my age as the navy knows it was adjusted when I joined my first ship, as I was technically too young. It is commonly enough done, I assure you."

"Well, as I said, I would not let the difference stand between you when I thought you to be one-and-thirty, so to learn that you are seven-and-twenty makes no difference to my consent, but perhaps does make my mind a little easier," said Darcy, secretly more relieved than he would let on to learn that the gentleman was several years younger than he. "You may, however, find that I am less forthcoming when we draw up the marriage articles. Recent events have made it clear that you have a greater likelihood of making Georgiana a widow than most other gentlemen she might have married. I will have to request that on the event of your death, the entire sum of her dowry would revert to her."

"Oh, as to that, I should never wish to leave her without security in life. I would give, I suppose, five thousand pounds to each of my brothers – I have two – and all the rest would go to her and our children, if we are so blessed. It would be the very least I could do."

"Well that is very handsome of you," Darcy said, admitting to himself that it was more handsome than he would ever have expected, or negotiated. Georgiana need not ever remarry, with such a fortune, should that most unfortunate event happen. "May I ask where you intend to settle?"

"I must admit, we did not discuss it thoroughly," Captain Stanton said. "I have been so long confined within the close quarters of my ships that even a London town house feels quite cavernous, and so long as the war continues, I will be required to re-join the Jupiter when she is repaired. We did discuss the possibility of her living on board, but my next assignment would need to be safe enough for me to feel comfortable with her doing so. If it is not, I would prefer to leave the decision in Miss Darcy's quarter as to the location and size of our establishment. I expect she will wish to settle in or near Derbyshire."

"Mrs. Darcy and I would be very pleased to see her near," Darcy said, not particularly inured to the idea of his sister living on board a ship of war. "You need not rush into a lease or purchase, either. You are both welcome to stay at Pemberley as long as is needed – indeed, if the war does continue and you are to be from home without her, it might be easier for Georgiana to remain with us, unless she is eager to set up her own household. The Bingleys are staying with us indefinitely, while a new house is built on their estate, so she would have friends about."

"Let us leave the decision to her, then," Captain Stanton said. "I must ask, would you have any objection to our marrying quickly? I see no need to procure a special licence – the repairs will not progress so rapidly that we cannot wait for the banns to be read – but I should very much prefer to leave England's shores with Miss Darcy's hand fully secured."

"I have no objection at all, and in fact I believe it would be preferable to all of us," Darcy said. Indeed, after months of worry, to see Georgiana settled would be a comfort to him, and holding the wedding sooner would ensure Elizabeth's ability to attend, before her pregnancy was too far along. "We shall of course have to get into the papers later, but for now I believe all I need do is give you my most hearty consent, and best wishes."

Captain Stanton spent a little time with the entire family in the conservatory before finally taking his leave, receiving congratulations from Elizabeth and Mrs. Annesley, and then discussing how the news might be shared. They all agreed that an announcement at the earl's dinner the next evening would be most appropriate, and Georgiana could not help but think of how she had feared a different announcement would be made at that event. Elizabeth requested only one exception to this plan, and that was to inform Lord and Lady Brandon early, as they were to have a family dinner with them that evening, before the Fitzwilliams left town for their estate.

Captain Stanton readily agreed to this, and was pleased that it meant that after the announcement at the earl's dinner, it might be sent to the papers (if, indeed, it did not reach them through one of the dinner guests), so that all rumoured engagements might be put to rest, and he could be congratulated on his true situation. He took his leave then, promising to call the next morning so that they might further the wedding plans.

He left behind a young lady with the happiest of countenances, and after they returned to the drawing room, Darcy, Elizabeth, and Mrs. Annesley could not help but glance up occasionally at her, so heartening it was to all of them to see her finally so happy. She remained so in the carriage ride over to the Fitzwilliams's house, and it was only the sober expression on her aunt's face that gave her even the slightest cause for worry.

Lady Ellen had greeted Elizabeth with a sort of exhausted politeness, and upon hearing Elizabeth say that she had news to share, had said: "Indeed? We have some news of our own. Please do come in, and we will tell you."

When they were seated in the drawing room, however, Lady Ellen seemed overcome, and she left her husband to speak:

"There has been a great battle, a decisive battle, at Waterloo, in the Netherlands," Lord Brandon said. "Napoleon was so thoroughly defeated by Wellington's forces, it is expected he will be forced to surrender and abdicate soon."

This was exceptional news, so far as England and the Darcys were concerned, particularly Georgiana, as it meant a much sooner end to the war than had been expected. Yet they felt there was something more the earl would say, and so none of them spoke.

"It seems the casualties were tremendous on both sides," Lord Brandon said. "We know our son was with Wellington's troops, and currently we have no certainty of whether he lives or not. We are planning to travel there as soon as we may procure passage, to see if we may find him. With so many killed, there must be an even greater number wounded, and if he is so, we will bring him home to convalesce in some degree of comfort."

The Darcys reacted with every bit of the shock, sadness, and concern they felt at the situation, and for some time discussed all that was known about the battle, and what the Fitzwilliams's trip would entail. Lady Ellen, recalling that Elizabeth's sister was in Brussels, promised to ask after her if they passed through that city, which seemed likely, and Elizabeth was nearly overcome with her aunt's kindness to think of Lydia at a time like this. It was only when they were seated for dinner that Lady Ellen recalled Elizabeth's having mentioned news, as well, and asked if she might share it.

Elizabeth froze; she looked down at her plate, clean and empty and waiting for the first course, and finally said: "It is news of a happier sort – it hardly feels appropriate to share on such an evening."

"Please, Elizabeth, any good news would be a welcome distraction right now," Lady Ellen said.

"Well – Georgiana and Captain Sir Matthew Stanton are engaged to be married," Elizabeth said.

"Oh, that is very much a comfort to me," Lady Ellen said. "We have been sorely lacking in good news in this house, and that is the best. Georgiana, please accept our deepest congratulations. We have closely followed the news of his action against the Polonais in the papers, and I could not imagine a more honourable man to marry."

"I thank you very much, aunt Ellen," Georgiana said, trying to order her response so that it might bring some comfort to her relations. "There was some time where we were very concerned for his survival of his wounds, but he is recovering very well. I hope it will be the same for Edward, or perhaps you will arrive to find him completely unscathed, and wondering at the trouble his parents went through."

She received the faintest of smiles from her aunt and uncle at this, but it was, at least, something. It was only later in the evening that she could not help but turn her mind to how this Waterloo battle should affect her and her betrothed – a quick end to the war might mean that Captain Stanton would not return to sea. Certainly neither he nor his ship were well enough to do so now, and if Napoleon did abdicate, she could not see how the Jupiter would be needed. She felt guilt over such happy thoughts, however, while still ensconced in her relations's drawing room, where they wished for the same sort of news she had longed for – news of the safety of a loved one – and she knew it was not so likely to be as forthcoming as it had been for her.

The carriage ride home from the Fitzwilliams's home was short, but made clear that London was awakening to the news of the Waterloo battle.

There was distant cheering from other quarters of town, and even in Mayfair, a great many people milling in the street, some with the gay faces of unconnected victors, others with more worried countenances, who, like the Fitzwilliams, must have feared the survival of family or friends.

When they finally reached home and retired, Elizabeth climbed into her husband's bed and sighed, "Just when it seemed we had only cause for happiness in our family, we have this Waterloo battle."

"We must not assume the worst, yet," Darcy said. "I continue to remind myself of that, and yet all I can do is worry."

"I know you two have always been close," Elizabeth said, touching his cheek tenderly.

"Yes – Edward and I spent very nearly every summer together as boys, at one estate or the other. We used to play at soldiers, he and I – and Wickham, when we were at Pemberley. We would treat the old house as a fort, and either defend or bombard it, every day," he said. "I never thought about any of us going off to a real war."

His mention of Mr. Wickham turned Elizabeth's mind to the fact that his survival must also necessarily be doubted, and she was startled at the indifference of her reaction to this thought. She might not have actively wished the man dead, but could not help but think that it might be better in the long-term for Lydia if he was. She wondered what her sister was experiencing, over on the continent in the aftermath of that battle, and hoped deeply that she had kept her promise not to go any closer to the battle-front.

"I wish there was more that we could do, other than hope for the best," she said.

"I know. I cannot bear that it will be weeks, perhaps, before we have any idea of whether he lives or dies."

"At least war may finally be at an end," Elizabeth said, laying her hand over his. "I wish more than anything that this shall be the last time we endure a wait like this."

"That is my only comfort in all of this, that it means the end of the war – I hope for good, this time. I cannot tell you how I feared the idea of Georgiana becoming a young widow."

"It is a great relief," Elizabeth said. "I do not see her bearing such an event – she was devastated enough at the thought of his death when there was no understanding at all between them."

"He indicated they would settle wherever Georgiana wished, which will likely be in or near Derbyshire," Darcy said, leaning over to blow out the candle beside his bed. "I offered to let them stay at Pemberley as long as they needed to. I must admit a certain selfishness in the offer; I am not yet ready to see her leave."

Elizabeth blew out her own candle, leaving the room in darkness. He pulled her very close, even closer than usual, and she understood his need for the comfort of her embrace. His cousin and friend possibly lost, his sister in some ways lost as well, soon to be handed over into the protection of another. At this time, it seemed that even the possibility of their own family growing was not enough of a comfort to alleviate what they would, and might, lose.

CHAPTER 13

As promised, Captain Stanton called the next morning, and although he had already heard news of the Battle of Waterloo, he was not aware of their family connection. Upon being acquainted of it by Georgiana, and of her relations's plan to travel there, he expressed his concern, and asked if he might be of any assistance to the family.

"Have they secured passage?" he asked. "There will likely be a great number of families attempting to make the crossing into the Netherlands."

"They have not," Georgiana said. "They will leave as soon as they are able to find transportation."

"Allow me to ask around, then. There must be some navy ships moving to and fro, given the substance of the battle. I should like to help in any way that I might."

"Thank you, that is very kind of you," Georgiana said. She wished to take up his hand, but could not without some degree of embarrassment. As a newly engaged couple, they were allowed some degree of freedom, but were still required to be chaperoned, and so they were sharing the conservatory with Mrs. Annesley. In such a small space, even Mrs. Annesley had difficulty making herself inconspicuous.

"Miss Darcy, would you mind if we turned our minds a bit to our own future?" he asked. "Your brother rightly pointed out yesterday that there were a few critical details that we had yet to attend to, although he did give his consent."

"Of course not. I would very much like to settle our plans."

"The first thing I wished to discuss was how quickly we should be married," he said. "For at the time I assumed I should have to re-join the Jupiter once she was repaired. Now, I am not so certain. I think it would be wise to have the banns read, but we may be able to delay the actual event if you so choose."

"If we might, I would only wish to set the timing so that we may have as many of our family and friends around us as we can – I hope deeply that group will include Colonel Fitzwilliam," Georgiana said. "I do not wish for any delay beyond that to become your wife."

"That is exactly as I would have wished it," he said. "Would you prefer to have the wedding in Derbyshire?"

"Yes, I have very little desire for a town wedding."

"Let us plan for it, then. Derbyshire is quite convenient for my uncle and the rest of my family, as well."

He then asked her where she would wish to settle, recounting what he had told her brother.

"I would very much like to settle in Derbyshire, if we can," Georgiana said.

"Then let us do so," he said. "I expect I will be at home much more than I would have been if the war looked to continue on, but still, I may receive some assignments, and I would wish you to have family near when I am from home."

"You mentioned yesterday that there might be some times when I could accompany you."

"You would wish to do that, even considering the accommodations?"

"I believe I would at least like to try it," she said. "I have seen so little of the world – I feel quite a bit of jealousy when you and Captain Ramsey talk of all the places you have been. And I think I would prefer being with you, even if the accommodations are not so comfortable, over waiting alone for you to return."

"I need not tell you how much I would prefer your company," he said, giving her so particular a gaze that Georgiana felt her heart glow.

A letter came over by servant, late in the morning, addressed to Georgiana, She knew it to be from her aunt immediately; Lady Ellen wrote with the prettiest hand. Georgiana was not sure why her aunt should be writing to her, instead of Elizabeth or Fitzwilliam, but since they were both elsewhere in the house, no one else shared in her confusion as she opened it and read:

"My dear niece,

"Your uncle and I spent our morning attempting, through every avenue we knew, to secure a passage to the Netherlands, but were not so fortunate as to find anything. It seems every family with sons in the army is attempting to make the crossing, and every ship we inquired about already has a wait list which could not be shifted, even for an earl.

"You must imagine my surprise when your betrothed called on us late in the morning. We are only a little acquainted, although I truly hope when your uncle and I return we may deepen the acquaintance. I would wish to do so merely for his being your future husband, but the service he has done our family has already very much endeared him to me.

"I believe you told him of our situation, and this has prompted him to secure a place for us on the Daphne sloop, commanded by Captain Shaw, with whom I understand you are a little acquainted. Captain Shaw does not have any private quarters he could offer us, but he very handsomely said we might sit in his cabin, and he expects it will be a quick passage, perhaps half a day, or a day at the most. We will be very limited in our baggage, we can only bring a servant each, and we must be on board at dawn tomorrow, and yet it is more welcome to us than the most luxurious berth would be in other circumstances. It is a tremendous relief to me to know that as soon as tomorrow evening we may be able to begin our search for Edward.

"I cannot praise your betrothed warmly enough. You have chosen very well, Georgiana, and you must know that right now you and he are my only source of happy thoughts. Please acquaint the rest of your family with our travel plans – I know you are dining out this evening, and so we will not be able to take our leave of you. If we are not able to return in time for your wedding, please know that I will be thinking of you both with the utmost fondness.

"Yours very affectionately,

"AUNT ELLEN"

Georgiana finished the letter with a sad smile on her face; it had indeed been a very handsome thing Captain Shaw and her betrothed had done, and yet it was unsurprising to her. They were generous men, these men of the navy, and it mattered not to Captain Stanton that the family connection, to him, would be a tenuous one until his marriage. There was a thing to be done that was in his power, and he had done it, and if it were possible for Georgiana to think of him with any more affection, she would have.

Still, although her aunt's letter had been filled with praise, Georgiana felt the full worry of its purpose. At least they need not struggle to find passage anymore, but still, to leave on such a mission! She felt her eyes fill with tears, and took a few minutes to compose herself before going to find her brother and sister, so that she could tell them of the letter's contents.

CHAPTER 14

The clergy had for so long been an occupation upon which families unloaded their younger sons that it was not unusual to find those holding its offices as dissolute men, who barely merited being called gentlemen, much less rectors or vicars. It was clear as soon as the Darcys were introduced to The Honourable Richard Stanton that he was not one of these men – indeed he seemed the opposite, a rector who believed resolutely in the true purpose of his calling. He was severe in his dress, severe in his countenance, and severe on his son – and by extension, his betrothed.

The Darcys had arrived early for Lord Anglesey's dinner, so that Georgiana might become better acquainted with the man who was to be her father-in-law. He was polite to her when they were introduced, although no one would call him kind, and she found him looking her up and down, as though he was inwardly scrutinising every aspect of her hair and dress. She imagined such a man would find them both too much in fashion, and could not help but take a step back from the father so that she would be closer to the son.

"Well, Matthew, I must admit I did not think I would ever see you settle," Mr. Stanton said. "I give you both my congratulations."

"Thank you, sir," Georgiana said.

"My son tells me you are quite accomplished," Mr. Stanton said. "You play the pianoforte, and the harp, draw and paint, and speak both French and Italian, is that correct?"

"Yes, sir," Georgiana answered.

"No doubt you read, as well. I will assume you have read the Bible, although I should always recommend another reading – you will learn much more with every reading. Have you read Fordyce's Sermons?"

301

"I cannot say I that have."

"Well, I suppose that is to be expected. You young ladies would rather read novels and swoon over Byron than read something of moral substance. Sir Matthew, you will see that you acquire both volumes, once your household is established, so that Miss Darcy may read them through."

"Yes, father."

"And what of dancing?" Mr. Stanton said. "I suppose you are one of those debutantes who is always going to balls. Do you enjoy dancing?"

"I enjoy many things, sir, dancing among them."

"Do you dance the waltz? I understand it is common here in town, now – that sinful dance. I suppose you danced it many times with my son during your courtship."

"We – we stepped out following the Marche," Georgiana said, not certain whether this should count as having danced the waltz.

"Indeed? Well, that shows some degree of propriety, at least. Perhaps there is hope for Sir Matthew yet."

Georgiana was spared any further discomfort as the other guests began to arrive, among them Lady Tonbridge, who gave Mr. Stanton a slight little curtsey, and then pulled Georgiana off to a corner of the room and took up both of her hands.

"I know I am not supposed to say anything to the greater group until the announcement is made, but I simply could not wait to offer you my congratulations. I must tell you I have been hoping for this for quite some time."

"So have I, Lady Tonbridge, and I thank you for your part in it – we would never have met if not for you."

"You may thank me for that, but you need not thank me for pulling you away from that man," the viscountess whispered, looking over at Mr. Stanton. "He is insufferable. Come, let us see if we might rescue your betrothed as well."

They made their way back over to where Captain Stanton was standing, but he was pulled away by Lady Julia before they could affect their rescue. Georgiana expected she would be filled with jealousy, watching the two of them converse, Lady Julia in what appeared to be a new, rather sheer gown, and Captain Stanton in his naval uniform, but she found she felt none; she was secure in his affections now, secure in his hand for marriage.

Instead, she felt badly for Lady Julia, who was clearly attempting a flirtation, and not making any progress, for as soon as Captain Stanton saw that Captain Campbell had arrived, he excused himself to greet his former lieutenant. Only a little later, Georgiana overheard Lady Julia speaking to her companion, saying, "Surely it will only be a little while longer before he makes an offer." It was then that Georgiana came to understand the nature of the rumoured engagement – it had come from Lady Julia herself. If her theory was correct, Lady Julia would soon be disappointed, and Georgiana found herself sympathetic to the lady's situation, despite all the pain she had suffered from the rumours of the engagement.

The time for them to go in for dinner was drawing close, and Georgiana realised that she should not have a chance to sit anywhere near Captain Stanton. Now that he was a baronet, he would go in earlier, with those who had titles, and Georgiana, Fitzwilliam, and Elizabeth would be somewhere farther down the table.

It seemed she was not the only one to have such thoughts, because Lord Anglesey appeared by her side, saying, "Lady Tonbridge and I did not like the idea of you and Matthew sitting apart at dinner, when you are only just engaged. We have a little something planned, you shall see in a moment. However, first I must go remind Matthew he is a baronet. He clean forgot he had been made earlier in the day, and tried to go in out of order at the Regent's dinner. Everyone found it quite amusing."

Georgiana smiled at the thought of Captain Stanton – who seemed to put far less import on his baronetcy than everyone else – being chided by the Prince Regent's dinner guests for forgetting his new rank. She watched as the earl whispered something to his nephew, and then made his way over to the door to the dining room.

"I believe all is ready," he said, in a voice loud enough to gain the attention of everyone in the drawing room. "I should like for us to let Miss Darcy go first, this evening, as a bride-to-be."

His statement was met with a great deal of whispering amongst all of the dinner guests not yet acquainted with Georgiana and Captain Stanton's engagement, and Lady Tonbridge waited a few moments before saying: "That is a capital idea. Please do let Miss Darcy go first."

Lady Tonbridge was the highest-ranking lady in the room, and should therefore have gone first, so her very vocal approval meant that none could disagree, even Lady Julia, who looked at Georgiana with curiosity, and perhaps a little bit of contempt, as Georgiana made her way over to take up the earl's arm. Behind them were Mr. Stanton and Lady Tonbridge, and then Captain Stanton and Lady Julia.

This order meant that Georgiana found herself sitting next to Lady Tonbridge, and across from Mr. Stanton, who in turn sat beside his son, with the earl at the head of the table. She smiled deeply at Lord Anglesey and Lady Tonbridge as they were seated, and then caught Elizabeth's eye, further down the table, long enough to see that her sister was clearly pleased at the way things had come about.

They were all seated, and Mr. Stanton would not even allow their glasses to be filled before he would say grace; the earl tolerated his brother's instructing the servants to halt with a stony countenance. As the first remove finally came out, the earl stood, looking far more pleased.

"I suppose I have piqued your curiosity by mentioning Miss Darcy as a bride-to-be," Lord Anglesey said. "So let me now tell you that in addition to celebrating Captain Sir Matthew Stanton's victory over the Polonais, and his baronetcy, we more importantly celebrate his engagement to Miss Georgiana Darcy."

Applause filled the room, as Georgiana blushed, and caught the brief expression of horror on Lady Julia's face, before the lady managed something resembling a smile. Georgiana smiled down the table, nodded, and finally gazed at Captain Stanton, who seemed as embarrassed as her, by the attention.

There were a great many things to toast, at such a dinner; it seemed a quarter-hour could not pass without someone looking down the table to Captain Stanton, nodding, and saying, "a glass of wine with you, sir." The earl stood again, later in the meal, to toast the army for the Waterloo victory, and a gentleman further down the table could not allow this to pass without also toasting the navy.

Mr. Stanton raised his glass to this toast as vigorously as any one at the table, and Lady Tonbridge, noticing this, said, "Perhaps you should have given up more sons to the navy, Mr. Stanton. It certainly has been good to Captain Stanton – a great fortune, a baronetcy, and now a very accomplished young lady as his betrothed."

"Now there I cannot agree with you, Lady Tonbridge. The navy certainly was the best choice for Matthew, as he was hardly cut out for the church, but I should always have preferred to give as many of my sons to God's work as I could."

Georgiana felt all the pain this remark must have caused Captain Stanton; she even summoned her courage to speak in his defence, but when she looked up at him, he simply shook his head no to her, and she could only give him a sympathetic gaze in return. Lady Tonbridge was right, the man was insufferable, and she wondered at the earl's inviting him here – perhaps Lord Anglesey had hoped he had changed, or at least that he would mind his manners. Georgiana had always been secure of her father's and brother's love and esteem, and the thought of growing up under such a man instead horrified her.

Mr. Stanton's statement had cast a brief silence over their end of the table. Lady Tonbridge was the quickest to recover, asking Georgiana how she got on with her practise on the pianoforte and the harp.

"Very well, I thank you," Georgiana said. "I find I have more time to practise when we are at Pemberley – we have fewer callers. I do admit to missing your musical evenings, however."

"We have missed you as well, dear. We will not have any more meetings until the little season begins again, but I beg you will come for tea some evening and play, so that I might hear you again."

"I would like that very much, thank you."

"And perhaps we may compel you to play at least one piece tonight," Lady Tonbridge said. "It might give *some people* in attendance a greater sense of your accomplishments."

The toasts continued on, and although Georgiana took only the slightest of sips at each, she had a great fear of becoming drunk. She worried even more about Captain Stanton, who had not looked entirely well when the dinner began, and was worse, now. He did not look drunk, merely tired, and she realised he would have had little time to rest, if he had been to see Captain Shaw and then Lady Ellen after he had left Curzon Street that morning.

She wished to speak with him about this, once dinner had finally wound to an end, but first she must go with the other ladies to the drawing-room, and there she found herself surrounded by those she had not sat near at dinner, wishing to offer her their congratulations and well-wishes. Even Lady Julia came by and offered a few words that were, if not sincere, at least an indication of her good manners.

When the gentlemen finally made their entrance, Captain Stanton came in even slower than his usual pace of late, and took a seat near the door, although he looked up at her and gave her an inviting little smile. Georgiana excused herself from a conversation about lace that had started some time ago with the mention of her wedding clothes, picked up two dishes of tea, and went to him.

"You have read my mind, Miss Darcy. I feel I have had too much of everything today, except for tea."

"You look very tired – are you well enough to be out here?"

"I can hardly retire early from a dinner held in my own honour. I will manage for a little while longer."

"I fear your exertions on behalf of my family this morning did not allow you enough time to rest," she said. "My aunt wrote to inform me of their plans to travel on the Daphne."

"Do not worry yourself on that account. Captain Shaw was the first person I inquired with, so it was all arranged quite quickly."

"I still cannot thank you enough for the service you did for them."

"It was nothing."

"It was not nothing to my aunt. It was the kindest thing anyone could have done for her on a most difficult day."

"Well, then, I am glad I was able to help, and I do hope to see your cousin safely returned. I know it must wear on your whole family, and particularly on you, as he is your other guardian. Are you close?"

"We were when I was younger. With the war, he has often been from home, so we do not see each other so frequently. My father selected him as my second guardian, in case anything should happen to my brother before I

came of age, but he did so before my uncle purchased his commission. I
suppose my father might have chosen differently if he had known, but I am
glad he did not – Colonel Fitzwilliam is dear to me, although we do not see
each other as often as I would wish."

"I hope I shall get a chance to become acquainted with him, and better
acquainted with your aunt and uncle. They seem like excellent company."

"They are indeed."

"I must admit to feeling some guilt in bringing you such an unpleasant
family connection, when everyone in your family is such good company,"
he said. "My father's performance this evening is fairly well typical for him.
Fortunately, we need not see him often."

"Oh, but you have not met my other aunt, Lady Catherine," Georgiana
said. "Actually, I think she and your father might get on well. Either that or
they will loathe each other, and at least that will take some of his attention
away from you."

He laughed softly, "I must meet this Lady Catherine, then."

"I sometimes wonder – " Georgiana paused; she had never told anyone
of this particular conjecture, and did not possess the courage to ask her
brother about it, but thinking about Captain Stanton's father had brought it
to the front of her mind.

"Yes, dearest?" He stared at her intently, and this gave her enough
comfort to continue.

"I sometimes wonder if my mother was like Lady Catherine – they were
sisters, after all. And my brother never speaks of her with quite the same
depth of regard as he does my father. I wonder if I would have had a very
different childhood, if she had lived, and then I feel guilty for thinking it."

"I cannot share your guilt. Any other childhood would not have shaped
your being the young lady you are today, and might not have seen us meet.
So I must be selfish, and glad your life took the path it did."

"I have never thought of it in that way," she said. "Although I suppose
there was at least one way in which she shaped my life, even if she did not
live to do so – she was very musical. The music room at Pemberley was
designed at first to house her harpsichord."

"Was it she who first favoured Scarlatti?"

"Yes, I found her old music one day, and attempted it on the
pianoforte," Georgiana said. "I hardly ever feel a connection to her, except
when I play her music."

"I think your mother could not have been disagreeable, if she loved
music so beautiful."

"I hope you are right, and although I suppose I may never know, it is
better to think what you suggest." Georgiana noticed Mr. Stanton
approaching them, and was silent, following this.

"Come, son, it is not appropriate for you and the lady to sequester yourselves in this way. I would wonder at your manners, but that you learned them from sea captains."

"Father, you are well aware that I have most often sailed under men who could rightly call themselves gentlemen."

"I see very little of your gentlemanly behaviour in the naval men I observe. Being a gentleman does not, to my mind, mix with making war for a living. How many times have you yourself violated the sixth commandment? Judgement Day shall be a long one for you, when you must answer for every man you have killed."

The earl must have overheard some of the conversation, for he approached them and said, in a quiet but steely voice, "That is enough. You may choose not to celebrate Matthew the way the rest of the country has, but I will have no more insults to him or to his betrothed in this house. Were it up to you, Bonaparte would march right into this country, and meet with nothing but prayer. I cannot believe that God would not wish us to end tyranny, and tyranny's end requires that good men must kill other good men."

Mr. Stanton's expression took on a thunderous look for a moment, as though he planned to argue, but then thought better of it. The earl held the power in his family, and his brother could not expect to cross him without some manner of consequences. "Very well, then," he finally said, and strode off.

The earl left as well, with a little nod to them, and when Georgiana looked back to Captain Stanton, she saw there were tears in his eyes, and she felt all of his heartbreak.

"I have not seen him these five years," he said. "I do not wish to ever see him again."

Elizabeth and Darcy watched the exchange between the Stantons and Georgiana from across the drawing room, and could only wonder what it had been about.

"I do not like that man," Elizabeth murmured. "I do not like him at all."

"Ordinarily I would encourage you to wait before pronouncing a judgement, as some people do seem to improve on your acquaintance," Darcy said. "However in this case, I believe your assessment is sound, and not likely to have any cause to change."

"I am not sure," she said. "My first impression of you was that you were an unsocial, taciturn man, and here we are, sitting at the very edge of the drawing room."

"There was a rather exuberant discussion of lace happening when I entered. I must assume that was your reason for seating yourself where you did. Unless – you are not unwell, are you?"

"I am fine, although I did wish to sit," Elizabeth said. "I should have rested more, earlier. Jane was right – this saps my energy far more than I would have expected."

"Let me know when you wish me to call for the carriage. It appears the guest of honour has even less energy than you do," Darcy said, looking towards Captain Stanton, who had, with Georgiana, made his way into the core of the party.

He at least did not have to remain standing for long, for Lady Tonbridge, with only slightly less authority than she would have shown in her own music room, suggested that the young ladies present honour them with some musical performances, and called on Miss Darcy to play the pianoforte first. Georgiana blushed, and demurred, but following a stern look from Lady Tonbridge, made her way to the bench first.

Elizabeth wondered what she should play, since her sister had not brought any music with her, and was startled to hear her begin one of her Scarlatti pieces, which was complicated enough Elizabeth would never have attempted it herself, even with sheet music. The musical club and the hours upon hours Georgiana had spent practising at Pemberley told here, however, for she played not only well, but confidently.

When she had finished, she rose to silence, and curtsied to them all, but it was only when Lady Tonbridge said, "My dear, you are even better than I had remembered," and began clapping, that the rest of them were driven from their stupor, and made up for it by applauding as loudly as they could.

"I once thought she would be too shy to ever perform in front of a group half this large," Darcy said, watching as his sister curtsied again, and modestly sidestepped away from the piano bench.

"I believe she is still shy, at heart," Elizabeth said. "But no one would call her a shy young girl, anymore. She will do well as Lady Stanton."

"I had thought I failed her. I did fail her, in the incident with Wickham," Darcy said. "Thank God it has all turned out well. To see her now, after the way it was following Ramsgate, it is like two different women."

"I do not think, if you asked her, that she would say you failed her," Elizabeth said, softly. "You did the best you could, to be given such a responsibility at your age."

"I could have done better."

"You shall have a chance to prove that soon enough, when you raise your own child," Elizabeth said, glancing down at her belly, and then looking up to him with a smile.

CHAPTER 15

Lord Anglesey's dinner party had broken up not long after those few young ladies brave enough to follow Georgiana's performance had taken their turn on the pianoforte, but still, it had served as a reminder to Mr. Darcy that it was not healthy for his wife to be in town.

"I have been thinking, we can begin to make plans to return to Pemberley," he said, upon her entering his study the following day. "Georgiana's matter is certainly settled, and I believe you only have one more sitting with Mr. Thorpe."

"Yes, later today. Dr. Whittling did encourage me to not stay much longer than a fortnight, and by the time we have made our arrangements, we will be nearly there. I assume Georgiana will wish to stay, however."

"I see no issue with that. All she requires is a chaperone, at this point, and Mrs. Annesley is more than capable of fulfilling that role."

"Why do we not go out and see if Georgiana is comfortable with this plan, then?" Elizabeth asked.

When they entered the drawing room, however, they found Captain Stanton was already there, and also planning to leave town.

"It has become clear to me that this is not the place to convalesce," he said. "I had three invitations arrive today – until Wellington and the army officers are returned, everyone wishes to have whatever representation from the military they may muster at their dinners and balls, and many of them are not persons I can refuse. I called at the Admiralty to request a leave of absence, and learned they are to halt repairs on the Jupiter and the Polonais, for they do not expect they will be needed. So it may be some time – if ever – before I am given another command."

"Where will you go, to convalesce?" Elizabeth asked.

"My uncle's estate – my cousin and his new bride have been there these last few weeks, and my uncle had been planning to join them in a fortnight or so anyway."

"It is outside of Chester, is it not?" Georgiana asked. "That is a very long journey in your situation."

"It is. I am not looking forward to the journey, but in the long view, it will be much better to go there."

"You might stay with us for a few days at Pemberley, if you wish to break your journey," Elizabeth said. Breaking a journey from London to Chester in Derbyshire was not the most practical of travel arrangements, but if one's betrothed lived in Derbyshire, it would suit quite well.

"Thank you, Mrs. Darcy, I would very much appreciate that," he said. "I must stay through the Prince Regent's ball, and I suspect your family may need to as well. When I received the invitation, it was hinted to me that my betrothed and her family would be there, so do not be surprised if one is delivered here. It is a private ball – at least, as private as the Regent manages to give – celebrating the Waterloo victory."

They received news of the possible invitation – and later in the day, the invitation itself, for the ball four days hence – with appropriate outward reactions. Yet inwardly, Georgiana was both thrilled and terrified. She would never in life have expected to attend a ball at Clarence House, and she wished for the presence of her aunt, who was the only person she knew who might be able to give her some indication of what to expect, and how to deport herself there. Then she chastised herself for wishing for her aunt's presence for such a frivolous thing as a ball, considering what her aunt was going through currently, and determined she would give it no more thought.

Elizabeth and Darcy, meanwhile, did not discuss it until she had joined him in his bed that evening, saying, "I suppose we shall have to delay our departure a little longer."

"Yes, I do not like it, but one can hardly refuse an invitation from the Prince Regent."

"You would not have liked it, regardless. I know how you feel about balls."

"True, but this goes beyond my general disinterest in them. A ball with that set, and with your health as it is – if there were a way to decline it, I would do so."

"Darcy, I am with child, not struck down with fever. My *health* shall survive a ball. Indeed, I would not mind dancing a few times more before I will need to stop. This may be my last opportunity for some time."

"If dancing is what you wish for, let us open up our own ballroom tomorrow morning. I am sure Georgiana will play for you, and then we may depart for Pemberley once you have danced your fill."

"We cannot, and you know it. And think of the honour to Georgiana."

"When she is married, she may attend as many balls given by the Prince Regent as she chooses."

"And I shall be stuck at Pemberley, with my poor hermit."

"You may hold as many balls *at Pemberley* as you wish."

"I will hold you to that, Mr. Darcy. You will rue the day you said it."

Now that the engagement had been announced, Elizabeth had a great deal of correspondence to attend to, and she set out to it the following morning. She had already sent the announcement to the papers, and now made out a note to Mr. Clark, requesting the banns be read beginning in the next Sunday's service. Her next set of letters was more enjoyable; she wrote to Jane, requesting she let Charles and the rest of Pemberley's staff know of the engagement, then to Kitty, asking her sister to inform the rest of the Bennets, and to the Gardiners, who had become acquainted enough with Georgiana that she felt they should be pleased by the news.

Her final letter was in some ways the most enjoyable, for of course, Lady Catherine must be informed. Elizabeth wrote what would likely be her longest-ever letter to that lady, speaking of how celebrated Captain Stanton was in town, of his baronetcy, and of their invitation to the Prince Regent's ball. She knew none of these things to be Captain Stanton's truest merits, but they were the things that would most matter to Lady Catherine. As she wrote, Elizabeth could not help but be pleased that by anyone's assessment, Georgiana had made an excellent match, but it was one that had come about through no efforts of Lady Catherine's.

She finished with enough time for a little rest before dinner, and was about to lie down when Sarah knocked on her door. "Beg your pardon, ma'am, but I wished to let you know your ball gowns are arrived from Pemberley – we had so few options for Lord Anglesey's dinner I grew worried at what should happen if you were invited to a ball. I sent for three of them; I always like the lilac silk best on you, but I wished you to have a choice."

"Thank you, Sarah, I must admit I forgot how little we packed to come to town. Were it not for you I suppose I would be showing up to the Prince Regent's ball in a dinner dress. Do you know if Hughes did the same for Georgiana?"

"She did, ma'am. Neither of you need attend dressed for dinner." Sarah looked horrified at the thought of it, and Elizabeth realised how much Sarah had grown as a lady's maid in the last year. She was no longer a young girl, unsure of whether she was doing everything right, and instead a skilled woman who took the turnout of her lady very seriously. Elizabeth would still have happily shown up to the Regent's ball in a dinner dress; she held a fondness for Sarah that had only been strengthened by her having recognised Elizabeth's pregnancy, and she felt such a fondness would survive nearly any error in her turnout.

There were two events of significance to take place before the ball. The first was a letter from Caroline Bingley to Elizabeth and Georgiana. Elizabeth had purposely not written Caroline, for there seemed no way to gracefully share the news that so contradicted the gossip Caroline had shared with them, and so Elizabeth preferred it should reach Caroline slowly, through Charles or Jane.

Caroline had, however, seen both the gossip pages and the official announcement, and wrote a letter to Georgiana and Elizabeth indicating her surprise and delight at the engagement, with only the slightest reference to having been wrong in her intelligence, and no understanding at all that she had caused a great deal of pain. She wondered would they be in town long enough to attend a dinner, and bring Georgiana's betrothed, for having a war hero in attendance would be quite the thing. Elizabeth could only shake her head, upon reading such a letter, and reply that they would all be leaving town immediately after the Prince Regent's ball, and could not fit in any more engagements.

The second event was quite unexpected to the family, although perhaps it should not have been. Elizabeth and Darcy were sitting in his study the morning before the ball, when Mrs. Annesley knocked and entered.

"I wondered if I might have a word with you, Mr. and Mrs. Darcy," she said.

"Yes, of course," Darcy said. "Please be seated."

Mrs. Annesley claimed the seat nearest her, and sitting up very straight, said, "I know we have not yet discussed such matters, but certainly Miss Darcy's marriage will necessitate the end of my employment here."

"You need not worry on that account," Darcy said. "You may take as long as is needed to find a new situation that is suitable to you, and stay with us under the current financial arrangements. It is the least we can do after all you have done for Georgiana."

"That is very generous of you, sir," Mrs. Annesley said. "However, that is why I am here so soon. I have found a new situation, not apurpose, mind you, but still, I have. A friend saw Miss Darcy's wedding announcement in the papers, and happened to mention that I should be coming available to an acquaintance of hers, Lord Epworth. He is a widower, and as he comes out of mourning, seeks to find a companion for his daughter. He wrote to me, and I visited them in my half-day, and I have found the situation to be very suitable."

"That is splendid," Elizabeth said. "We shall miss you greatly, but I am sure you shall be such a comfort to the young lady."

"I thank you, Mrs. Darcy. The difficulty of it is, Lord Epworth would prefer I begin immediately. I told him I was committed to your family through Miss Darcy's wedding, if you need me, but that I would speak with you."

Elizabeth glanced over at Darcy, and knew he was of her mind on the situation. They were for Pemberley after the Regent's ball, and would have much less need for Mrs. Annesley there, particularly with guests already in the house, and more coming. Mrs. Annesley had not sought this new position, and they could not begrudge her for wishing to take it immediately – if left to wait a month or two, Lord Epworth might grow impatient and find another companion for his daughter.

"You should take up your new position," Darcy said. "As Mrs. Darcy says, we shall miss you greatly, but I would not wish you to allow this opportunity to pass. And you will allow me to write a character for you, although you may not need it now. I would be happy to verify your time with Georgiana to Lord Epworth, if he does need me to do so."

"I thank you very kindly, Mr. Darcy," Mrs. Annesley said. "I would still wish to attend Miss Darcy's wedding – that is, if I would be invited."

"Of course you are invited," Elizabeth said. "And we will be very happy to have you there, particularly Georgiana."

"I am very much obliged to you, Mrs. Darcy. Would you wish me to tell Miss Darcy now?"

"Yes, I suppose so. There will not be a better time," Elizabeth said.

Georgiana was in her apartment, looking at the dresses Hughes had requested from Pemberley, trying to determine which might be best for the ball, when Mrs. Annesley knocked on the door.

"Please come in," Georgiana said, and upon seeing her companion, "Oh, Mrs. Annesley! Would you tell me which of these you prefer? I cannot decide."

"This always was my favourite," Mrs. Annesley said, pointing to the white silk dress Georgiana had worn for her coming-out ball. "However that is not why I have come to talk to you."

Georgiana looked more closely at Mrs. Annesley and realised that she looked quite upset. "Is something the matter?"

"I shall be leaving you, sooner than I expected," Mrs. Annesley said, and proceeded to tell Georgiana of her new situation, and how it had come about.

As she spoke, Georgiana felt her eyes filling with tears. Given more time, she would have come to realise that of course Mrs. Annesley would be leaving; Georgiana would not require a companion, once she married, and so she must necessarily lose Mrs. Annesley while she gained her husband.

"Your brother and sister have given me leave to begin my new situation," Mrs. Annesley said. "However, if you feel you still need me, I shall stay. I will return for your wedding, either way."

"No, they are right. You should go and begin your new situation with your new family. I just – oh, I shall miss you so!"

Mrs. Annesley reached out and embraced Georgiana as she had so many times when Georgiana was first recovering from Mr. Wickham's deceit, and then again during the events of the last few months.

"I shall miss you too, my dear, but soon enough you will be married, and I promise you will miss me much less after that."

CHAPTER 16

Elizabeth did wear lilac, and Georgiana her white silk gown – both of them quite thankful that outside of St. James's, court dress was not required – when the carriage stopped outside Carlton House. Captain Stanton was waiting there with his uncle, although fortunately his father was absent, and he looked a little better than he had at the earl's dinner, but not so much so that Georgiana had any expectation that she should have a chance to dance with him in the course of the evening.

Their waiting for the Darcys meant that Lord Anglesey could introduce Elizabeth and Georgiana to the Prince Regent as they came in – Darcy, it seemed, was already vaguely known to him – and Georgiana dropped into her deepest curtsey, feeling Elizabeth do the same beside her. Georgiana had seen the Prince Regent's carriage before about town, but this was the first time she had been close enough to observe him; she was surprised at how large his person was, and how unwell he looked, and made her utmost effort to avoid having these thoughts reach her countenance.

"So this is the young lady who has snared the heart of our latest baronet, hmm?" the Prince said, looking at Georgiana. "I congratulate you both. And since I have invited your poor betrothed to a ball where he may not dance, Miss Darcy, I hope he will not mind too much when I add insult to injury and ask if you will dance the third set with me."

"Of course, Your Royal Highness, I would like that very much," Georgiana said, her voice trembling, for regardless of what she said, the thought of dancing with the Prince terrified her, filling her with thoughts of how she should make some unforgivable mistake in front of such a man, and such a crowd.

They moved on, then, into a house that was even more opulent than Georgiana had imagined it would be. She had lived in the vast space of Pemberley for much of her life, but had never encountered anything in the confines of town to equal this, nor anything so ostentatious. The ceiling of the entrance-hall seemed twice as high as the one at Curzon Street, and the rooms they walked through to reach the ballroom were covered in gold leaf and the finest satins and velvets, and these materials were in turn covered with painting after painting, each so beautiful that Georgiana would have liked to pause an hour or so in each room to examine them. They walked slowly, allowing some time for study, but it was not nearly enough.

Lord Anglesey was active in politics, and within minutes of their being inside the house, had espied someone he wished to talk to, made his apologies, and departed their company. This left his nephew, as they continued on their way, to suddenly stop walking, and, as they all gathered around him, to say, in a most uncomfortable tone of voice:

"I should have thought to say this when last I called, but there will be more than a few men of looser morals than you are generally acquainted with here. Mrs. Darcy, Miss Darcy, please take care that they escort you back where they should, if you dance with them, and do not leave the ballroom without Mr. Darcy or myself. Miss Darcy, I include the gentleman who earlier asked you to dance, when I say this."

He looked at her very carefully, and Georgiana realised he meant the Prince Regent, although of course he could not say so directly. It was no secret in town that the Prince Regent had many mistresses, but the thought of his having any interest in her made her face very warm as she nodded her understanding.

"Very good," Captain Stanton said. "I do not mean to frighten any of you; it is most likely that we will all have a pleasant evening, but I would not wish to keep silent on such a thing and come to regret it later."

They were directed by servants through the house, and out into a promenade along the gardens, where an enormous set of structures had been set up, including Mr. Nash's great round "tent," which Georgiana had read about in the papers a year previously, and saw now was much more a building than a tent.

They made their way into the tent, which served as a great ballroom, and had been most elegantly decorated for the event, the floor intricately chalked. They were not there long before there came a great booming voice behind Georgiana: "Stanton! There you are! I hope we see you better."

Captain Stanton dropped into what semblance of a bow he could manage, and Georgiana followed him without knowing who she curtsied to; she could see it was another man in naval uniform, although it was that of an admiral.

"I thank you, Your Royal Highness, I am feeling a little better."

"And this must be your betrothed and her family. Will you please introduce us?"

"Of course, sir. This is Mr. Darcy, Mrs. Darcy, and Miss Darcy, of

Pemberley in Derbyshire," Captain Stanton said, then, to the Darcys, "This is His Royal Highness, the Duke of Clarence."

Georgiana dropped into another curtsey – it seemed the best action – and felt Elizabeth do the same beside her.

"It is very nice to meet you, ladies. I hope you will both give me the pleasure of a dance, perhaps the second and third sets?"

"Miss Darcy is already engaged to dance with the Prince of Wales for the third set," Elizabeth said. "So perhaps she may take the second, and I the third."

"Very good. And I see Lady Caroline Russell over there; I shall ask her for the fourth."

Captain Stanton smiled at the name, and the Duke of Clarence noticed this, saying, "Are you acquainted with the lady?"

"No, sir, for other reasons the name *Caroline* is very dear to my heart."

Captain Stanton had the misfortune to say this just as the Prince Regent was walking past him, and the Prince stopped, looking red-faced at their party, and glowering more particularly at his brother. Georgiana felt her stomach drop; she did not follow court closely, but she certainly knew that the Prince Regent and his wife, Princess Caroline, had been on poor terms for nearly the entire duration of Georgiana's life.

"Might I ask why that name is so precious to you, sir?" the Prince Regent asked. "More precious, it seems, than that of your betrothed?"

Georgiana had never seen Captain Stanton look anything approaching frightened, but he certainly looked it now, as he spoke, "I assure you, sir, not *that* precious. However, HMS Caroline was my first command as a Post Captain. I had her for five years, sir, a very lovely frigate."

Georgiana trembled in the silence that followed, as they all stared at the Prince Regent. Finally, he burst out in a tremendous roaring laughter that made others in the ballroom turn to look at them.

"A frigate! Ha, ha, ha, a very lovely frigate!" the Prince Regent said. "Well, sir, you have given me one pleasant association with the name Caroline, where before I had none. Should you like to have her again? I expect we will be laying up the ships of the line soon enough, but I think we might be able to come up with a frigate command for you, once you are well."

"I would like that above all else, sir."

"I shall mention it to the First Lord, and then you might have both your Caroline and your Georgiana," the Prince said, and then walked away, although they could hear him say, "a frigate!" and chuckle once more as he left them.

The Duke of Clarence left them as well, in pursuit of Lady Caroline Russell, and the Darcys and Captain Stanton continued across the ballroom, to a set of open seats against the wall. When they were seated, Captain

Stanton whispered to Georgiana, "Miss Darcy, if I do something else to get myself thrown in the Tower this evening, I will understand if you end our engagement."

Georgiana let out a nervous peal of laughter, felt some relief in having done so, and said, "At least the outcome was favourable, but yes, I was very worried for you there for a moment."

"Indeed, it was favourable! I do not know if he will follow through on it, but still, the prospect of having the Caroline again someday pleases me greatly."

"I hope you will not have her again *too* soon," Georgiana said.

"Of course – I requested six months' leave," he said. "I will have time to rest, and for us to have the wedding, and then we should still have a good deal of time before I would even be considered for a command."

Georgiana nodded, and smiled, but still felt that six months should go by impossibly fast, and her only hope for happiness beyond that would be the possibility of living on board with him. She could not say so, however, before the orchestra played the opening notes of the first set, and the Prince Regent and Lady Hertford walked out to lead the dance. Georgiana had not been asked for the first set; it might have been assumed that she would dance it with Captain Stanton. She encouraged her brother and sister to go dance, however, telling them she would be fine sitting there until the next set. Georgiana knew that ladies who were in the family way must eventually begin sitting out all dancing, at balls, and did not wish her sister to miss this opportunity, if it was not too late for her.

She made a successful argument; they rose, and went to join the dancers, but not until after her brother had leaned in close to her and murmured, "Will you promise to mind Captain Stanton's advice and stay with him in the ballroom?"

"Of course, brother."

In truth, Georgiana enjoyed the first set very much. The ballroom was the largest she had ever seen in town, and there were a great many dancers, but there were also quite a number of people who were not dancing, and many made their way up to Captain Stanton, congratulating him on his victory, on his baronetcy, and on his engagement and, upon learning the lady seated beside him was the one he had become engaged to, requesting an introduction. They did not all have the greatest manners, and many of the ladies were dressed shockingly forward, but they were all very kind to Georgiana, and she was moved by the way they all esteemed Captain Stanton's victory.

She hardly noticed the first set had finished until the Duke of Clarence was approaching her, and offering his arm, and she was glad to be dancing with him before his brother. That he was wearing a naval uniform made her more comfortable – yes, he was a prince, but he also belonged to the same world as all of the captains of her acquaintance.

He was a substantial man, but had a much more fit figure than his brother, and danced well. Georgiana waited for him to speak; she determined it would be best to let him set the pace of any conversation.

"So you choose to marry into the naval world, do you, Miss Darcy?" he asked, a few minutes into the set.

"Yes, sir. I will own it is not quite what I had expected when I came out into society."

"Ha! Stanton won your heart then, did he?"

"Yes, he quite did."

"You must tell me whether it was before or after he took the Polonais."

"It was before, sir."

"I honour you for it. Although I suppose you saw even then what sort of man he was."

They were separated then by the figures of the dance, and when they came back together, he spoke again before Georgiana could reply.

"The sort of man who takes on a seventy-four in a fifty-gun ship – my, what an action. I must admit I thought it lunacy until he gave a better account of the details over dinner, and even then it is a fight most captains would have passed on," he said, in a tone that indicated he did not think he himself would have passed on it. "How I wish I might have been there!"

"I did not know what to think of it at all, but that when he was assigned the Jupiter, he indicated there was little he might fight honourably."

"So he made an honourable fight where there should have been none. But I find we speak more of naval battles than might be appropriate for a young lady."

The dance separated them again, and as they came back together, he said, "Now that I think of it, it must have been you he spoke of at dinner. He mentioned a very accomplished young lady who played both the pianoforte and the harp. Was it you?"

"I do play both the pianoforte and the harp."

"It must have been, then."

Georgiana glanced over at Captain Stanton, still surrounded by well-wishers, and thought warmly of him. When she had worried he was not at all thinking of her, he had been speaking of her, and to the Duke of Clarence no less!

She had no fear of the duke trying to lead her out of the ballroom; their conversation had indicated his esteem for her betrothed, and, anyway, he knew her to be promised to the Prince Regent for the next set. He led her back to her family, therefore, and took up Elizabeth's hand.

When he came over, Georgiana took the Prince Regent's arm with a trembling hand, and let him lead her up to the front of the set. There was sweat on his forehead, and she wondered that he continued to dance when he did not seem to be well enough for it, or enjoying it.

As for her part in the dance, however, she need not have worried. The additional concentration required in leading the dance meant that he seemed to have little interest in conversation. At one point he complimented her on her dancing; she returned the compliment, although she knew herself to be far stretching the truth as she did so. Towards the end of the set, he inquired about the family estate in Derbyshire, and asked how the county was doing, and this she had no difficulty in answering.

When the dance had come to an end, she remembered Captain Stanton's warning all in a rush, but again, she need not have worried, for he said, "Come, let us return you to your family," and led her back to where Darcy and Captain Stanton were seated.

Elizabeth had quite enjoyed her set with the Duke of Clarence, but found she returned rather short of breath, and that the halt in activity brought her little relief. It was not that her pregnancy was causing any particular issue; in another ballroom, she might have been able to dance at least a few more sets. Here, however, there were so many people that the place had grown hot and stuffy, and the dancers had by now destroyed the chalk patterns, causing a great deal of dust to be stirred into the air. Elizabeth felt overheated, she longed for fresh air, and was only able to compensate with the slight relief heavy use of her fan brought.

If it had merely been her own health at risk, she might have waited, and perhaps asked her husband to bring her an ice. But the knowledge that her present situation put their child at risk prompted her to say, "I do not know how much longer I can stay in here. It is very warm – I believe I need some air."

Both Darcy and Captain Stanton looked at her with concern, although Darcy's expression extended to a depth that was very nearly panic, and Captain Stanton said, "You should go – return to the gardens. I will stay for Georgiana."

It might have been more logical for Captain Stanton to escort Elizabeth out; after all, he also was not in the best of health. Darcy, however, was worried enough about her that he took up her arm without any further thought, thanked Captain Stanton, and walked with her to the nearest exit with a most exceedingly concerned countenance.

Georgiana watched them go with her own measure of worry, and was only interrupted in her concern when she realised her betrothed had been introducing Lord and Lady Ashton, whose name she remembered eventually as belonging to the parents of the young midshipman Captain Stanton had mentioned in his first letter. Lord Ashton and his wife had a great deal of enthusiasm for Captain Stanton's victory over the Polonais, primarily because their young son had, by all accounts – including Captain

Stanton's official dispatch – fought most honourably in the taking of the Polonais, but had returned from battle with hardly a scratch on his person.

"His gun crews kept up firing at a splendid pace," Captain Stanton was saying. "I hope he shall have another chance to return to sea. He has the makings of a fine officer."

"Indeed," Lord Ashton said. "We had not expected his tenure to be so short, this time, but given he participated in the taking of such a ship, I suppose I do not know what else I could have asked for in his first outing. We would prefer he go to sea again with you, if he may."

"I would welcome him in my midshipmen's berth. I will keep you posted on my assignments, in the hopes he may join. I am on leave for the present, however."

"Your uncle indicated how particular you are about the young gentlemen you take on there. I am glad to hear he has passed muster." Lord Ashton said, turning his attention to Georgiana. "Miss Darcy, I apologise for speaking of service matters for so long. Perhaps you shall allow me to ask for your hand in the next set, to make up for it?"

Georgiana would have much preferred to remain seated with her betrothed, but gave her consent to dance with Lord Ashton with every bit of enthusiasm she could manage, and she found he desired to spend the entire course of their dance speaking of how good her betrothed had been to take his son in, how brave his son had been, in the action against the Polonais, and how much he intended to press for Captain Stanton to have another command, once he had recovered, so that Lord Ashton's son could take up his place in the midshipmen's berth.

She returned his remarks with compliments, knowing from Captain Stanton's letter that his public praise for the boy matched his private comments on his merit, and as Lord Ashton was a good dancer, enjoyed the set far more than her last.

If Darcy had been required to push a few people out of the way in order to reach the gardens more quickly, Elizabeth was fairly certain he would have. They had no such difficulties, however; they were far from the only ones seeking air at that time. Elizabeth breathed deeply as they reached the outside air, and although it did not yet bring her the relief she needed, she felt that it would soon. All of the temporary structures had taken up much of the garden's space, but soon enough they found a bench, and were seated.

"How are you feeling?" Darcy asked. "Shall I call for a physician? Surely there must be one in attendance, with so many people."

"No, I shall be fine. I am feeling better already. There was just rather too much heat and dust inside," she said. "I do not know how Georgiana can stand to keep dancing. Oh, dear – we did just leave them both without a chaperone."

"I am not very worried about the two of them – not in a ballroom so crowded as that," Darcy said. "And I doubt he would have meant to begin an attempt on her virtue by beginning the evening warning us of the morals of some of the other gentlemen here."

"Fitzwilliam Darcy, you must really trust him."

"Of course I do. I would hardly have given him my consent if I did not."

Elizabeth leaned up against him and looked around the gardens, which might have been quite beautiful, without the interruption of all of the additional buildings. They had been lit well by a succession of torches, and a number of other couples had taken the opportunity to stroll through them, or sit on the other benches. A rustling in the bushes behind them, however, indicated that not all of the couples had come outside for such innocent diversions.

"Hmm, I suppose these are the men of lesser morals Captain Stanton referred to," Darcy murmured.

"For every man of lesser morals, it appears there is a woman thus," Elizabeth whispered. "I shall no longer blush so severely over our interludes in our own house. It is our house, at least, and we are married."

"You will rue the day you said that, Mrs. Darcy."

Elizabeth laughed at his repeating her own words. "We had better make our return to Pemberley soon, then, for soon enough I shall be as large as Jane."

"And yet still as beautiful as my Elizabeth."

"You had best reserve judgement until I actually am so far along."

"If this is still my already-beautiful wife carrying our child, I feel quite confident in committing to such sentiments now."

"How confident?"

"I will lay down ten guineas that I still find you are beautiful, when you are ready to enter your confinement."

"That is possibly the most ridiculous thing I have ever heard you say, Darcy," Elizabeth said. "And I believe it must be twenty guineas."

"Twenty guineas it is. And are you truly feeling better, now?" he asked, clasping her hand tightly.

"Much better, although not so well as I will feel with twenty extra guineas in my purse."

"Then it is too bad you shall have twenty fewer guineas in your purse."

As she had danced a set each with the Duke of Clarence and the Prince Regent, Georgiana had gained the notice of all in the room, even beyond those she had already been introduced to. She returned to where Captain Stanton was seated on the arm of Lord Ashton, and wished to stay and sit beside her betrothed for the next set, for she did not like him to be here all alone except for well-wishers. However, a Sir George Wilcox approached them, was introduced by Lord Ashton, with whom he was acquainted, and asked for her hand in the next set. She looked down at Captain Stanton, wishing to stay, but he encouraged her to go and dance.

"You cannot sit all night with an invalid like me," he said. "Go and enjoy yourself."

Georgiana went off, therefore, with Sir George Wilcox, who looked to be in his middle forties, and had a great enjoyment of dancing. He danced exceedingly well, and spent most of the set asking about her accomplishments, and, as he heard of each one, praising her. Georgiana attempted to ask about his own family, but while he told her that he had a wife and two daughters, he did not seem interested in discussing any further details.

If Georgiana had spent more time in company with men such as him, she might have taken his disinterest in discussing his family as the first sign of what was to come after the set was finished, when he took hold of her hand, and said: "Have you seen the library yet? You must come and see it, if not. You really cannot come to Carlton House and see so little of it, if this is your first time here."

Georgiana felt her breath catch in her throat; even without Captain Stanton's warning, she would have felt most uncomfortable at the suggestion, but with the warning, she understood that Sir Wilcox wished the impropriety of what he openly suggested should be followed by something far more improper. They were on the opposite side of the rotunda, nearly as far from Captain Stanton as they could be, and although she looked up at her betrothed and caught his eye with a look of desperation, she realised it would be some time before he could make his way to where they were.

"I thank you for the suggestion, sir, perhaps my family and I shall go to see it later," Georgiana said, attempting to pull her hand from his.

"I believe you would enjoy it more now," he released her hand, only to put his arm around her waist, pulling her toward the nearby door. "I promise, you will be amazed. Come, let us go back inside the house, and I will show you."

There were people around them, but no one seemed to pay any mind to his improper embrace, nor Georgiana's increasing distress. She looked up at Captain Stanton and knew that he would never reach them in time; in full naval uniform, he had been required to substitute his walking stick for a presentation sword, which was useless at present, and although he moved far faster than she would have expected, the crowd hindered him.

She felt some degree of comfort that he would at least know she had been led out of the ballroom, and would follow, but then determined she should let no such thing happen. If she wished to live on a ship with several hundred men, she could not be expecting him to protect her every moment of the day. If she could not fend off Sir Wilcox, she had no business wishing to take up residence on board a frigate, and she would need to resign herself to long periods of time living without her husband.

"I thank you for the invitation," Georgiana said, digging into his toes in their thin little pump with all the weight she could put into her own heel, and as she did so, taking his hand and pulling it from her hip. "However, I must go and re-join my betrothed."

"Why I – " Georgiana did not wait to hear what he would say; she rushed off, meeting Captain Stanton on the edge of the rotunda; the next set had already begun.

"Are you well?" he asked, his countenance deeply concerned, offering her his arm, which she took up for the comfort the contact brought, careful not to put any weight on him.

"I am fine," she said, her voice too tremulous to indicate she was fully fine. "You were right in your warning. He wished for us to go off and see the library."

"You certainly seemed to bring him up with a round turn. Whatever did you do?"

"I stepped on his foot."

"Did you? I must tell you, Georgiana, that is the first unladylike thing I have ever heard of you doing, and I cannot tell you how glad I am to hear of it."

They stayed through supper – they could not be seen to leave before – but Georgiana did not dance any other dances, claiming fatigue whenever she was asked. She entered one of the supper rooms with Captain Stanton, who found some new acquaintances of his that they could sit near, ensuring their supper was mostly taken up with a recounting of his battle against the Polonais, which Georgiana did not mind at all.

Elizabeth and Darcy had remained in the gardens until some frisson in that space seemed to indicate that supper was to begin, and then followed the crowd to one of the buildings. They found themselves interrupted along the way by Lord Anglesey, who appeared seemingly out of nowhere, saying only, "Ah, Mr. and Mrs. Darcy, there you are. I should like to introduce you to Sir George Hunter. Let me see where he has got off to."

Sir George Hunter was located, not far from them, and they were introduced thusly: "Sir George Hunter, please meet Mr. and Mrs. Fitzwilliam Darcy, of Pemberley in Derbyshire. Sir George serves on the Royal Navy's Victualling Board, and given there is rather a lot of wheat required to make our ship's biscuit, I thought you should meet."

They exchanged pleasantries, and soon after that, Lord Anglesey had disappeared again, leaving the Darcys to go into supper with Sir George. Elizabeth found her husband quite engrossed in conversation with the gentleman as the first, quite spectacular removes were served, and drifted into an observation of the others around them, most quite showily dressed, and preening rather as peacocks should as they ate their supper, which amused her very much. She was feeling much better, and the supper rooms were not so overcrowded as the ballroom had been, so that she had no concerns for her health. She attempted to eat as much as she could, thinking of the child growing within her, and when she attended back to the conversation between Darcy and Sir George, they were quite on the verge of settling some of Pemberley's wheat crop on navy victuals, promising to correspond to see the matter settled.

Once they had finished speaking of business, they attempted to find topics of conversation which interested all of them, but had little else to comment on aside from the ball. This, however, provided more than enough fodder to see them through the end of supper, as a rather impossible set of towering great flummeries were brought in, each more intricately decorated than the last. Some of those present gasped as these masterpieces quivered dangerously, upon being set down on the table, but none was so devoted to art that they would not sample as many of them as they could. Elizabeth tried a few, but found herself more revived by the variety of ices that followed, the final thing she needed to soothe any lingering overheating she felt.

Elizabeth and Darcy agreed, upon leaving the supper building, that they had stayed quite long enough, and should attempt to find Captain Stanton and Georgiana, so that they might call for their carriage.

"Do you suppose we should offer him a ride home, in our carriage?" Elizabeth asked, as they made their way through the crowds milling outside, for few seemed in a hurry to return to the ballroom. "I suspect his uncle shall be here for the duration."

"I would not doubt it," Darcy said. "Georgiana did not set out to make a useful family connection, nor did I expect her to, but it appears she has. And yes, of course we should offer him a ride, and I hope he will take it."

Elizabeth glanced down at the trampled grass below her feet; she could not help but think how much more palatable marriage to her would have been at first, for Darcy, if her family possessed anyone resembling Lord Anglesey.

"I believe I know what you are thinking," Darcy said, taking up her hand and squeezing it. "Georgiana will marry for love, as I was most fortunate to do. That is worth far more than any connections."

"Thank you," Elizabeth said, reassured by his words. "Now if only we could find her."

For a few minutes more, Elizabeth despaired that they would ever find the couple within the crowd, but fortunately, they were looking for a tall man in naval uniform, escorting a tall lady in a white dress, and this combination proved quite unique. Darcy saw them first, and raised his hand so that they, who appeared to be similarly scanning the crowd, should see him.

The couples were reunited, Elizabeth's health inquired after, and answered favourably; the carriage ride offered, and quite gratefully accepted. As there were not many others leaving Carlton House as they did, their carriage came quickly. Once they were inside, Captain Stanton said:

"I must apologise for having caused your invitation here. This is an event I wish I could have borne alone."

"Nonsense," Elizabeth said. "I enjoyed my dances, and if the air had been better, I certainly would have attempted a few more. I believe they will have to stand as my last, before the child is born. And even as little as I danced, I am sure this is the sort of event that will grow even more pleasurable in the retelling."

"Elizabeth is right," Georgiana said. "I shall always be able to say I danced with the Prince Regent and the Duke of Clarence, and I cannot think of a person in Derbyshire who will not want to hear of our stories. And there were many pleasant parts to the evening."

"Still, I should have thought that a ballroom that crowded would not suit a woman in your condition, Mrs. Darcy."

"I am fine, I only needed a little air, and I expect this will hardly be the last time that happens," Elizabeth said.

Elizabeth, indeed, looked fully revived. It was Captain Stanton who seemed to have flagged as the evening went on, much as he had at the earl's dinner, and they all felt relieved that a few days would see him away from London, and able to rest.

CHAPTER 17

After her episode during the ball, Darcy was as insistent that Elizabeth return to see Dr. Whittling as Elizabeth was that it was not necessary.

"I am fine, Darcy. There is not the slightest evidence of aught being amiss," she told him. "And we leave for Pemberley on the morrow. That was Dr. Whittling's main recommendation, to leave town as soon as we could."

"Just – please see him," Darcy inhaled sharply, so that Elizabeth could see he was more frustrated than he wished to let on. "Do so for my sake, if not for your own. Your health represents two lives which are impossibly precious to me, and irreplaceable."

"I understand," she said, sympathetically, reaching out to touch his hand. "But what shall we do about Georgiana? Without Mrs. Annesley, she cannot take callers, if we are gone. You know Captain Stanton will come to call on her, and this will be their last chance to see each other before we depart – I hate the thought of Mr. Miller having to turn him away."

"What about Lady Tonbridge?"

"A viscountess might be a touch above what is required for a temporary companion, for Georgiana."

"True, but I expect that said viscountess would have no objections to spending part of the day in her own home, with Georgiana and her betrothed, particularly if Georgiana brings enough music."

"That is a rather good idea," Elizabeth said, resigning herself to another appointment with Dr. Whittling.

Georgiana's day with Lady Tonbridge, and Captain Stanton's joining them, was arranged through a set of notes passed back and forth between the town houses of all of the parties involved, and Elizabeth and Darcy deposited their sister at Grosvenor Square with a rather thick sheaf of sheet music under her arm, before driving on to Dr. Whittling's practise.

The physician listened to Elizabeth's description of overheating during the ball, as well as her promise that they were to depart for Derbyshire the morning following, and, thankfully, saw no need for as thorough an examination as he had conducted during their first meeting. He took Elizabeth's pulse, gave her a very vile draught to drink down, and encouraged her to rest as much as possible during the journey to Pemberley, and to remain there until the birth, once she had arrived.

Elizabeth, who saw all of these recommendations are reasonable, but no more or less logical than anything Jane or Sarah would have told her – excepting the draught, which very nearly made her lose her stomach – thought the visit not worth the number of guineas she knew her husband would put down for it. Still, she reminded herself of his expertise, thanked him convincingly, and reassured her husband in the waiting room that all was still well, both for her and the child, and was quite surprised by the force of his embrace, at this statement.

She held him as closely as he held her, and reminded herself to be more sympathetic, towards him, for he could not feel the progression of the child nearly so well as she could, and certainly she had given both of them more than enough cause for worry, in taking so long to become pregnant. They exited Dr. Whittling's practise, and regained the carriage, where Darcy said:

"This took far less time than I would have thought. Lady Tonbridge will not be expecting us for at least an hour more. It is not enough time for Richmond, but what say you to a turn in Hyde Park?"

Elizabeth felt a bit guilty about preying on Lady Tonbridge's hospitality, but then, based on that lady's last note to Curzon Street, which had prompted Georgiana to pack up so much of her music, felt fairly certain she was preying more upon her own sister than anyone else, and that her sister would not mind their absence at all so long as her betrothed was present.

"A little turn would be quite nice," Elizabeth said. "It shall remind me of how much more I prefer Pemberley's grounds, once we are home."

In Grosvenor Square, Georgiana found she was quite happy to be returned to Lady Tonbridge's company, although the lady had a bit more of a propensity for gossip than she had remembered. It was all good-natured, fortunately, and consisted mostly of Lady Tonbridge's reading the best items from the papers to Georgiana while they waited for Captain Stanton to call.

"Oh, look at this one. It is quite delightful – paints you in a most wonderful light," Lady Tonbridge said. "We had a glimpse of the elusive Miss G. Darcy, in attendance with Mr. and Mrs. F. Darcy, and on the arm of her betrothed, the heroic Capt. Sir M. Stanton. Miss Darcy wore white, danced with the P.R. and D. of C., and although she had no chance to exhibit on the pianoforte as she did most spectacularly at Lord A.'s dinner, we are convinced she is a conquest equal, at least, to the Polonais."

Georgiana coloured terribly, and could think of no response, but it seemed none was required of her, for Lady Tonbridge continued: "A dance with the Prince Regent and the Duke of Clarence – very nicely done for yourself, Miss Darcy. I must admit I quite miss the Regent's balls. There is nothing quite like them, but he and I – well, that was a long time ago."

Georgiana coloured again, at the thought of what Lady Tonbridge had indicated – of course the Prince Regent had a great many mistresses, but she had never thought her friend to be someone who would be among them. And yet Lady Tonbridge's comment, and her countenance as she said it, had seemed to indicate precisely that, and Georgiana could see the possibility, now that she thought on it. She had seen the painting of Lady Tonbridge, from a decade or so previously, in the hallway of the lady's house, where her friend was notably younger and of trimmer figure than she appeared now – as a titled dowager looking thus, it would not have been surprising for her to have caught the Prince's attention for at least some period of time.

There was no way for Georgiana to gracefully indicate her realisation, or her understanding of what Lady Tonbridge had just related to her. And thus, while she would have been happy enough to hear Lady Tonbridge's butler announce Captain Sir Matthew Stanton come to call at any time, presently, she was positively relieved for the distraction.

Elizabeth and Darcy were left off by their carriage, and found the park to be quite well-populated, although it was not yet the fashionable hour. Elizabeth walked along absently, happy enough to be out in the open and on her husband's arm, and expecting that there should be few, if any, acquaintances they had still in town that they would encounter here.

She was startled, therefore, to hear: "Mrs. Darcy, Mr. Darcy, how very good it is to see you!" and to find these words spoken by none other than Lady Stewart, who was approaching her on one of the paths, and gave her a most deep and appropriate curtsey.

"Lady Stewart – it is good to see you, as well," Elizabeth said, most perturbed by this turn of events, but returning the curtsey.

"I understand you were at the Regent's ball last night," Lady Stewart said, turning, so that she could walk alongside Elizabeth, along with an unidentified servant, who followed behind her. "What an event! You must give me all the details you may."

Elizabeth recognised Lady Stewart's approaching of her for what it was – a desire to know more about an event to which that lady had not been invited – and yet could not help but be amused by how her stature had apparently changed in Lady Stewart's eyes. Neither could she help this realisation's influencing her response.

"Well, it was a rather nice evening. My sister, Miss Darcy, danced a set each with the Prince Regent and the Duke of Clarence, although it is unfortunate her betrothed was not yet well enough to dance."

"Oh yes, Captain Sir Matthew – what a fine connection for your family. And I must say, so very nice to see the nephew of an earl achieve such a thing as the Polonais, instead of some no-name mushroom."

"Yes, well, we all very much esteem his victory," Elizabeth said.

"And who all did you dance with, Mrs. Darcy?"

"Only my husband and the Duke of Clarence, as it turned out," Elizabeth said. "I am in the family way, you understand, so while it was nice so have a last few dances, it was a bit of an inconvenience that we are still recovering from – it was quite warm and stuffy in the rotunda. We went to see my accoucheur this morning, to ensure all was still well, and Mr. Darcy suggested a turn in the park for some air, before we return home."

"Oh, in the family way, yes, of course, how dreadfully inconvenient, and yet, so necessary. Well, all my blessings, to you and your first-born. I hope we shall see you back in town, after the birth?"

"Yes, I suppose so," Elizabeth said. "I believe we shall take our time, in returning from Derbyshire."

"Of course," Lady Stewart said. "Well do call on us, when you are returned."

With that, Lady Stewart walked away from them, and Elizabeth could not help but say: "Has the baby made me mad, or did that just truly happen?"

"It very much did happen," Darcy said.

"So am I forgiven for your not marrying Lady Stewart's sister?"

"I doubt it, but you have perhaps proven to be a connexion which she is unwilling to give up, now, particularly given our sister's prominence in the gossip pages."

"It is strange; I had rather thought she had already given up the connexion."

"That is the flexibility of the ton, Elizabeth. Connexions may always be reforged when they are proven to be convenient, unless the cut direct has been given."

"I will admit to somewhat wishing to give her thus, when she approached me so enthusiastically," Elizabeth said.

"You are too good-hearted to do so," Darcy said. "Although you must believe referring to the Regent's ball as *inconvenient* was as deep a cut as you might have conjured, if you had intended it fully."

"I do not know that such injury was my intent, yet I cannot claim any regrets at such a thing," Elizabeth said.

"Nor should you," Darcy replied. "In fact, I rather enjoyed seeing her reaction."

"I – I must admit I did, as well," Elizabeth said, with a sideways glance at her husband confirming he was as amused as she was, by the situation.

Her chuckles were borne into out-and-out laughter, and they walked on, very much the picture of a young couple in love, even if they did not achieve the same prominence in the next day's gossip pages as their younger sister had, of late.

CHAPTER 18

In the end, Elizabeth did have her large summer house party, and it grew larger than the one she had originally imagined, for it centred on Georgiana and Captain Stanton's wedding.

The first to arrive was the groom himself, direct from London with only one overnight at a coaching inn, and looking so poorly when he arrived that Elizabeth immediately sent for Dr. Alderman. Captain Stanton protested weakly that he had no need of it, that none of his wounds was any worse; he simply had slept very ill at the inn, and the earl's post-chaise had suffered from a broken spring that the inn could not repair, so that he had been jarred about more than would have been usual during much of the course of the journey.

"I understand," Elizabeth said. "However, you would make all of us feel much less concern for your health if you were to be seen by Dr. Alderman."

"Please do," Georgiana pleaded, and if Elizabeth's concern had not fully moved him, Georgiana's did, and he allowed himself to be led off by Mr Parker.

He left behind the post-chaise, which Elizabeth had sent round to the stable to see if something might be done about the spring. Darcy was out looking at some of the farms with Richardson, assessing the latest state of the fields, but she knew he would agree they should not send it back in such a condition. For sent back she felt it must be; he must take more than a few days here at Pemberley to recover, and could travel on in one of the Darcys's carriages, although she hoped he could be convinced to remain at Pemberley until the wedding, for Georgiana's sake.

He also left behind a tall, broad-shouldered man, dressed as a servant, and Elizabeth thought he carried himself rather like the seamen who had helped defend their house during the riots, although she did not recognise him. He gaped at her for a moment when she asked who he was, then said,

"John Hawke, milady, Captain Sir Matthew Stanton's valet," pronouncing *valet* rather peculiarly.

"Very good to meet you, Mr. Hawke," Elizabeth said. "I am Mrs. Darcy, and this is Miss Darcy. Mr. Parker will see that you have all you need once he returns."

She and Georgiana returned to the drawing room, and Elizabeth knew that news must be sent on to the earl's son that he should not expect his cousin within the next few days, but that it was not so proper for her to write it.

"Georgiana, you are acquainted with the Earl of Anglesey's son, yes?"

"Only a little – I have dined with him once."

"You at least have been introduced. Would you mind terribly writing a brief note to inform him that we do not expect his cousin will be ready to continue on his journey in the next few days? That is, if you do not find the topic too upsetting."

"No, I shall write the letter."

In truth, Georgiana did find the topic upsetting, but the letter was a welcome distraction over sitting and waiting for Dr. Alderman to arrive. Captain Stanton would be put up in an apartment down the hallway where Elizabeth and Mrs. Reynolds had determined the bachelors in the house party should be lodged; it was as far as possible from Georgiana's apartment, and those planned for the other single ladies, and there was no reason Georgiana could contrive to place herself in that part of the house.

Dr. Alderman arrived, Dr. Alderman saw to his patient, and then came down to the drawing room to inform them there was no cause for worry. There were no new complications to Captain Stanton's injuries – even the shocking arm wound was healing nicely – the gentleman was still suffering the effects of blood loss, and exhaustion. A fortnight of rest, and regular consumption of Dr. Alderman's draught, should see him fully recovered.

"Come, Georgiana," Elizabeth said, after Dr. Alderman had left. "I will go with you, so you may see him. I know I would be mad to, were I you."

"Oh – thank you so much, Elizabeth."

When Elizabeth knocked on the door, they found Hawke already there, holding a draught glass. He announced them, opened the door fully, and then stood awkwardly against the wall as they made their way in.

Captain Stanton had his bedcovers pulled up as far as possible, although it was still apparent he was wearing only a nightshirt. Georgiana stayed a half-step behind Elizabeth, her face quite pink, and Elizabeth realised her sister's presence here must have felt as though it was going against all she had been instructed on over the years – to be in the bedchamber of a man, and a man not fully dressed, at that. Instruction that had likely been firmly reinforced, by Darcy and Mrs. Annesley, following Mrs. Younge's laxity. Elizabeth also realised she must have a conversation with Georgiana similar to the one her aunt Gardiner had broached with her and Jane before their wedding, and Elizabeth would need to address the topic even more delicately, for nearly all of her knowledge on the subject came from Georgiana's brother.

"Your Dr. Alderman and my surgeon Clerkwell ought to exchange notes," Captain Stanton said. "That is the most vile draught I have ever tasted in my life. Clerkwell will be quite jealous."

They all laughed, which seemed to relax Georgiana, and she took a step closer. "We were very worried about you – I am glad it is nothing rest will not cure."

"Yes, I will admit I have not allowed myself to rest so much as I should have."

"How could you, with such invitations as you received?" Georgiana said.

"Indeed. And then there was a very important matter concerning a lady that I had to attend to."

Georgiana blushed again, and said, "I hope you will consider that matter fully settled, and take the time you need to rest. We will send a note to your cousin to let him know not to expect you so soon. You will have no obligations here."

"Based on what I have seen so far, I can think of no better place to convalesce. I must thank you and Mrs. Darcy for allowing me to trespass on your hospitality far more than was expected."

"Please," Elizabeth said. "You are Georgiana's betrothed, and welcome here as long as you wish to stay. You must let us know if there is anything you or your valet need to see to your comfort."

"I will, thank you, Mrs. Darcy." He spoke wearily, and both Georgiana and Elizabeth backed out of the room, saying their goodbyes, Georgiana feeling very much relieved.

Captain Stanton did rest, remaining in his chambers for the better part of three days with little more than word from Mr. Parker that his valet said he slept, sometimes waking to eat or drink a little, and wished to communicate his particular apologies to Miss Darcy that he was not well enough to see her. After the first day, Georgiana adjusted to the strange notion that he was here, in the same house as her, although she could not see him, and went about her time as normally as she could.

As before, the pianoforte was her greatest distraction, and the new music she had purchased in London gave her a new challenge, something to fully occupy her mind. She closed the last few notes on her first successful pass through one piece, and was considering playing it through one more time, when she heard:

"That last passage was exquisite. I beg you would play it again."

It was Captain Stanton, and he so startled Georgiana that she gasped.

She turned, to see that he was standing in the doorway and looking like a man returned to something much closer to health.

"I am sorry, dearest. I did not mean to startle you."

"Oh, it is nothing – I am very glad to see you looking so much better. Will you not come in?"

"I will not. I understand your companion has left to join another family," he said, motioning to the empty seats in the music room.

"So you will listen from the doorway?"

"I will, if you will allow it."

"I am certain we can come up with some better solution," Georgiana said, rising from the pianoforte's bench to cross the room and ring the bell.

The solution she would have preferred would have been that he cross the room and embrace her and assure her that he would never again give her such a shock concerning his health, she realised, flushing. One of Pemberley's footmen was at the doorway before Georgiana could continue her thoughts in this vein, asking what the lady wished for.

"Thank you, Henry. Is there anyone else in the household who might be available to join us here?"

"Mr. Bingley is at his new estate, and Mr. and Mrs. Darcy are out riding. But Mrs. Bingley only just broke her fast, ma'am – I understand she slept ill on account of the baby kicking," Henry said. "Would you wish me to invite her here?"

"Yes, please do."

Jane entered the room some time later, at the slowest of paces, and looking wearier than Captain Stanton, who moved at something closer to his pre-Polonais pace in helping her into a seat, and then sitting himself. They all talked for a bit, but then Georgiana was encouraged to return to her practise, and attempt her new piece again.

When she had finished, she turned to face her audience, and felt her heart swell at the look of pure admiration Captain Stanton gave her. Had she missed such looks before, or had he not been so open in his countenance? She could not decide, and her conjecture was interrupted by a deep sigh from Jane, who placed her hands on her belly, looking relieved.

"I believe you will have to teach this one the pianoforte," Jane said. "This is the first time she has been completely still in a very long time."

With such motivation, Georgiana was readily convinced to play another piece, and another piece, and then another, so that eventually Elizabeth, Darcy, and Charles Bingley returned to find them all there – Georgiana still playing, Jane asleep, and Captain Stanton very nearly so, but despite his lingering exhaustion, unable to stop watching his future wife with a faint smile on his face.

Elizabeth, like the others, slipped out of the music room with her own lingering smile, and followed her husband to his study. She and Darcy barely had time to settle there, before Mrs. Reynolds knocked, and entered with the day's post.

"Beg your pardon," she said, looking concerned. "But the post just came and – well – there is a letter from Lady Brandon."

"Thank you, Mrs. Reynolds. I shall let you know later if it contains any news that should be shared with the staff," Elizabeth said, determining she should be the one to take the letter. If it contained any news of Colonel Fitzwilliam's fate, she felt she should be the one to read it first, so that her husband might be spared the shock if it contained bad news. And yet she felt a degree of hope, for if the news were bad, surely Lady Ellen would not have written in such a steady hand, if she had been able to write at all.

Mrs. Reynolds left, and Elizabeth opened the seal carefully, unfolding the weathered paper to read a short letter, delicately written:

"My dear niece and nephew,

"I wish I had more news to share with you at this point, but unfortunately, I do not. Your uncle Andrew and I had a short, safe passage, during which Captain Shaw was most kind and attentive to us, and we did manage to find lodgings here in Brussels, although at a most exorbitant cost.

"We have been searching, but thus far to no avail, although we have not given up hope. Everything is such chaos here, and the wounded have been taken to so many places, that I do not believe we have searched even a fraction of the locations where Edward might have been taken, if he was wounded. It is exhausting work, and I did not ever think I would see such a scene in my life; the number of dead and wounded continues to horrify me, and I grieve continuously to know that every one of them is another mother's son.

"We have inquired after Mrs. Darcy's sister, as well, and I am sorry to say that we have no word of how she or her husband have fared, although we shall continue to ask as we make our inquiries for Edward.

"Please keep us in your prayers, and give my love to Georgiana and her betrothed.

"Yours most affectionately,

"AUNT ELLEN"

After reading the letter, Elizabeth looked up at Darcy's distressed face, and said, "I am sorry, there is no word of how Edward has fared. Lady Ellen says everything is chaos, and they have not yet searched even a fraction of the places where Edward might have been taken."

Darcy sighed, as she handed him the letter so that he might read it himself. "I suppose it is better than bad news, but I cannot tell you how I had hoped they would find him quickly."

"I only hope they do not miss him entirely," Elizabeth said. "Surely they will be bringing some of the troops home, and I would hate for him to make the passage without knowing his parents are there, searching for him."

She did not mention the far worse alternative; she did not need to, nor could she. It was certainly plain on her husband's face, however, and she rose and made her way over to his chair so that she could embrace him. They remained there for some time, quietly, Elizabeth's chest filled with a dull, hollow worry that she felt quite certain no embrace could do away with.

CHAPTER 19

Captain Stanton improved steadily, so much so that it should have been time for the couple to set a wedding date. Yet although Georgiana was clearly pleased to see him returning to health, she said nothing of the wedding, and made her way around the house with the same subdued countenance they all held, upon reading Lady Ellen's letter. They had all been hoping that Edward would be found, well, and quickly, and the letter had intruded most painfully on these hopes with the reminder that it was very possible that he was not well, or even alive, and the news that he certainly had not been found quickly.

Elizabeth and Darcy had discussed what seemed a reluctance to move forward with the wedding from the couple, and had decided to bring up the subject when a suitable time arose. It did, one morning, when Charles had once again gone out to Clareborne early in the morning, leaving poor Jane to attempt to sleep late, following another fitful night's rest, so that only the Darcy family and Captain Stanton were in the yellow drawing room together.

"Now that Captain Stanton is doing so much better, I wonder if the two of you have thought of setting a date for the wedding," Elizabeth said, delicately, by way of opening the topic.

"It hardly feels right to do so, with Edward still missing," Georgiana said, and although Captain Stanton was silent, it was clear by his countenance that his feelings on the matter mirrored hers.

"I am sure he will honour you for such sentiments, Georgiana, but I do not think he would wish for you to delay on his account. You will only have so much time before Captain Stanton's leave runs out, and I would much rather you have the chance to spend it married."

"We still have ample time, if Miss Darcy wishes to wait," Captain Stanton said. "It hardly feels right to wed while one of her guardians is missing."

"Your position on the matter does you both much honour," Darcy said, his voice wavering. "However, if – if the worst does happen – if it has happened – you know that Edward loves you, Georgiana, and he would not wish for you to go through such a time without the comfort of a husband."

Darcy blinked a few times, but managed his speech without tears. Georgiana, however, did not, and she looked very much like she wished for the comfort of a husband, when her betrothed could do nothing but give her his handkerchief to dab at her eyes.

"May I have a private audience with Miss Darcy, to discuss this?" Captain Stanton asked, when Georgiana had recovered a little.

"You may – a brief one," Darcy said. "Mrs. Darcy and I shall wait outside the drawing room."

They stood outside waiting, a respectful distance from the door, and the conversation inside was so subdued they could hear not a word of it, although enough sound of murmuring reached them to reassure that there *was* conversation going on.

The drawing room doors clicked open softly after some time, revealing Captain Stanton; Georgiana remained seated, and it seemed that she had cried some more during their private discussion.

"We will set a date," he said. "Although far enough out that all the rest of our family and friends may join us, and perhaps even the Fitzwilliams, if Colonel Fitzwilliam is found."

"And we do not wish for a large wedding," Georgiana said. "Only those closest to us."

"I understand, although I fear some of the local families will see it as a snub," Elizabeth said, knowing that the only wedding out of the great estate for some time should have been a great social occasion for the families of the area.

"I did not think of that," Georgiana said. "I would not wish for them to feel thus, but neither of us wishes to be married in front of so large an audience."

"Perhaps we may manage an alternative," Elizabeth said, thinking through the possibilities. "I know none of us is much in the mood for a celebratory ball, but with dancing and other entertainments to occupy them, people would not focus so much of their attention on both of you, although they will all wish to be introduced to you, Captain Stanton. We might hold it a few days before the ceremony itself."

"You are right, I am hardly in the mood for a celebratory ball," Georgiana said, glancing towards Captain Stanton, who nodded at her. "Yet I also know our role in society, here. Let us hold the ball, if it means we may be married more quietly."

As the time passed leading up to the ball and wedding, Captain Stanton was finally able to go on sedate little rides around Pemberley's grounds with Georgiana, a groom following behind at a respectful distance. Phoebe, younger than Grace but not nearly so spirited, had been sent down from his uncle's estate after Captain Stanton had sent word indicating he wished to remain at Pemberley until the wedding. During one of these rides, he turned to her and said:

"I have had word from my elder brother, David, that he plans to attend the ball and wedding."

"Oh, how wonderful. I would very much like to meet him," Georgiana said. "What of your father and younger brother?"

The look on his face was so pained, Georgiana immediately regretted her question.

"My father has already responded that he is not available to attend, and I expect Jacob will follow him in this. My younger brother has always been closest to him in disposition and beliefs – he barely knew the influence of our mother."

They rode on in silence for some time before Georgiana finally said, "I am sorry to have reminded you of such a painful topic. I will not speak of it again."

"You must never think any topic closed to us, Georgiana," he said. "I will not deny that this one is unpleasant for me, but I would not withhold anything you wish to know about – not when you have been so forthcoming with me."

Georgiana felt some embarrassment, for she knew he was referring to Mr. Wickham, but also some degree of comfort, as they rode on quietly, but quite companionably, until she asked if he would tell her more about his elder brother, and that was a topic upon which he was quite happy to converse.

Much closer to the house, Elizabeth and Darcy were walking, for Elizabeth had finally thought it best to give up horseback riding, but was determined to continue spending time out of doors up until her confinement. Her stomach had swelled just slightly by now, a realisation that had filled them both with delight, although Elizabeth was perhaps more delighted that her sickness in the mornings seemed to be lessening now, as Jane had promised it would.

They were walking along the stream, and Elizabeth, feeling both tired and frustrated that she was so already, suggested they sit at the nearest of the benches that were staggered along its shore.

"Are you well?" he asked, concerned.

"I am fine, just a little tired."

"We should not have walked so far."

"This is hardly far – at least I would not have considered it so, previously."

"You are too determined to do all the things you did before, and at the same pace," he said, as they came to the bench and were seated.

"There may be some truth to that."

"I believe there is more truth to it than you are willing to admit."

"Possibly, but you know I am out of sorts when I am not able to be out of doors."

"We need not go quite so far out of doors, if we are walking, and there is always the curricle. When you are further along, we can go for drives around the estate."

"I am ready to slow my pace while walking, Darcy. I am not quite ready to be shuttled around like an invalid."

"I said when you were further along."

"Very well, then, when I am ready to be shuttled around, I will tell you," Elizabeth said.

He put his arm around her and ran his thumb leisurely back and forth across her shoulder, a movement that may have been intentional, or absent-minded. Elizabeth could not tell, but she found it very soothing, and found herself slipping into a day-dream, of the two of them sitting on this same bench some years into the future, watching their children play about them. She sighed, softly.

"You sound very content," he said.

"I was thinking of us sitting here in the future, watching our children play."

"It was terribly selfish of you to keep such a happy thought to yourself."

"I only just thought it – I would have shared it in time." Elizabeth did not mention that in her day-dream, the children were three little girls, in their summer dresses. She knew if she told him thus, he would remind her again that it did not matter to him, but she was still attempting to convince herself that it did not matter to her.

They sat quietly for some time more, before Elizabeth told him she was quite rested, and ready to return. Upon standing, however, she found herself overcome with a wave of dizziness, and grasping for his arms to steady herself.

"Good God, what is wrong?" he asked, holding her close and looking perhaps even more concerned than he had at the Prince Regent's ball.

"It is nothing, just a little dizziness – I stood too quickly," Elizabeth said. "I have had it a few times before; I know it is worse for Jane. Perhaps it will be for me, as well, as I get further along."

"Let us call for Dr. Alderman," he said, and made as though he was going to pick her up.

"Fitzwilliam Darcy, you are absolutely not going to carry me back to the house," Elizabeth said. "Let us walk back to the house – slowly, I will grant you, but still both of us walking. If the dizziness returns, you may call for Dr. Alderman, but if not, I will just go and lie down to rest for a little while."

He looked at her carefully, then offered his arm. "Very well, but we must go *very* slowly."

"And I had better not come down from my rest to find Dr. Alderman in the drawing room."

"I harboured no such thoughts."

"Yes, you did."

"Very well, perhaps I did."

CHAPTER 20

David Stanton arrived just after the Gardiners, in a modest little gig pulled by his own horse, for his living was less than fifty miles from Pemberley, easily enough accomplished with an overnight at a coaching inn, so that he and his horse might rest. This he told them only after he had stepped down out of the gig and embraced Captain Stanton, saying, "Brother, it has been far too long. Let me give you joy of your betrothal first – your victory and your baronetcy may follow."

"That is exactly as I would have it," Captain Stanton said. "May I introduce my betrothed, Miss Georgiana Darcy? Miss Darcy, Mr. David Stanton."

"Very pleased to make your acquaintance, Miss Darcy," he said, taking her hand.

"And I yours," Georgiana said, considering him. She knew from Captain Stanton that he was two-and-thirty, and he looked his age. He had lost his wife to illness three years ago, and it was clear the loss had worn on him, although he had the sort of kind, quiet, and indeed attractive countenance that made his resemblance to his brother clear.

Elizabeth and Mrs. Reynolds were still in the house, seeing the Gardiners and their children settled, so Georgiana invited him to follow her and Mr. Parker in, so that he might change out of his travelling clothes and join them in the smaller blue drawing room; she expected the two brothers might prefer some time in private before Mr. Stanton's being introduced to the rest of the household.

Georgiana found Elizabeth seated with Jane and the Gardiners, including young Susan Gardiner, perched rigidly on her chair in deference to the honour of having been allowed to sit with the adults in such a room. Georgiana gave a particular greeting to Susan, who responded with a very proper curtsey before telling her she liked her dress very much.

"I have a number of dresses that would be in your size now, somewhere in trunks in one of the attics," Georgiana said. "Would you like to go exploring while you are here, and see if you like any of those so well? They will need some alterations, to fit with the current styles, but I do not think them anything out of Miss Hughes's capabilities."

The girl looked to her parents, who nodded permission, before eagerly accepting Georgiana's invitation. Georgiana informed Elizabeth of David Stanton's arrival, then, and made her apologies for not being able to spend more time with the Gardiners, but promised that they should all be introduced before dinner.

Both brothers were already in the blue drawing room when she arrived, and as Georgiana approached, she could hear David Stanton saying, "You know, you quite wiped father's eye with your betrothal to Miss Darcy. Ever since you had enough fortune to marry, he has been saying you will take up with a Portsmouth bar maid, because *that is what sailors do*."

They both laughed, as did Georgiana, and she entered the room quickly, now that she had announced her presence.

"I beg your pardon, Miss Darcy," David Stanton said. "I did not mean – "

"It is nothing," Georgiana told him, taking the seat beside Captain Stanton. "I have met your father, and I can quite imagine it being said."

"Well, then I am glad you marry into our family with full knowledge of who your father-in-law will be," he said. "I at least do not bear the brunt of his self-righteousness – that is left to my brother here, who wisely has not been around to hear it."

"Yes," Captain Stanton said. "You at least followed in his chosen profession."

"That I did, although I would not have done so if it had not been my own preference. And I find father's and my beliefs do not align very much these days," David Stanton said, sighing. "You and our uncle will say he has made his bed and now he must lie in it, but I have fears of his being defrocked by the Church of England. He has taken up with a group which call themselves Evangelicals, but in truth they are far more radical, and his sermons are no longer what the common English man will countenance. He keeps his position thus far at our uncle's convenience, but the wrong word to the bishop and it will no longer be in our uncle's hands."

"Is it that bad indeed?" Captain Stanton asked. "I will admit he seemed very much as he ever was when he was in town, although perhaps even more severe. I did not broach any doctrinal discussions with him, however."

"I have heard that more of his pews are empty than occupied, most Sundays," David Stanton said. "It would be better for him to resign the living and leave the Church of England, and form a church where such things are appreciated, but of course he will not do that – he requires the income. I have been attempting to get him to take on a more moderate curate, who might handle some of the sermons, but thus far he will not listen to reason."

"And has Jacob followed him in his beliefs?"

"Yes, I am afraid to say, although he has at least been less radical in his public face thus far."

"I am sorry to have left you to deal with all of this. It should have been my place to help steer him back to the proper path."

"Matthew, you and I both know he would never be persuaded by you. I cannot begrudge you for having left home before the rest of us, although I will admit there were times when I was quite jealous. If he does lose his position in the Church, however, I expect we will need your help to support him. You know Jacob and I have nothing approaching your fortune."

Georgiana's back stiffened at the thought of some of Captain Stanton's hard-won fortune – the fortune he had earned in a career his father so thoroughly disapproved of – being used to support the man. It seemed her betrothed felt differently about the matter, however, when he spoke, for he first said:

"I will admit a certain delight in the thought of his living off of money from a source he so despises. However, I doubt that he would do so. He would not take a penny from me – his pride would not allow it. As you said before, he has made his bed, and he will have to lie in it. I will promise you, though, that you and Jacob will not suffer for it, if he comes to you for financial support."

There, that was more like it. Such a man who would insult his son – and her – so openly, who had caused his house to be so miserable as to prompt his son to make his own way in the world at eight and a half years of age, such a man should be required to deal with the consequences of his actions.

Further conversations with David Stanton were far more light-hearted, and Georgiana found that, like his brother, she valued his company and was very glad he had risked his father's disapproval by choosing to come to the wedding. He was introduced to the Gardiners that evening, and the Bennets the next day, whose carriage arrived with three rather sedate passengers, and Mrs. Bennet, who stepped out and immediately exclaimed, "Oh, Lizzy, it is the grandest house that ever was! How very rich you are! And Jane, how large you are grown – it will not be long now!"

Mrs. Gardiner very kindly undertook to give Mrs. Bennet a thorough tour of the house, with the patient assistance of Mrs. Reynolds, so that Mrs. Bennet was deep into one of the wings when Lady Catherine de Bourgh's carriage arrived, carrying Lady Catherine, her daughter Anne, and Anne's companion Mrs. Jenkinson. Mrs. Jenkinson murmured to Mrs. Reynolds that the journey had not been a good one for Anne, and requested they be shown to Anne's chambers immediately. Lady Catherine, however, accepted the greetings of Darcy, Elizabeth, and Georgiana, and said, "Well, where is Sir Matthew? I must be introduced."

"*Captain Stanton* is in the yellow drawing room, with some of our other guests," Georgiana said, which earned her a sly look of approval from Elizabeth as they followed Lady Catherine into the house.

When Lady Catherine had changed out of her travelling clothes and joined them all in the yellow drawing room, the introduction was requested in the singular way of that lady's, and given. Lady Catherine already knew of his particulars, but looked him up and down in very much the same way Georgiana expected her brother and Charles Bingley did the horses at Tattersalls.

They were all seated, and Lady Catherine, noticing the Gardiners, said, "Oh, your aunt and uncle from Cheapside, Mrs. Darcy – I see they are here. I do not know why they merited an invitation and Mr. and Mrs. Collins did not, when Mrs. Collins is such a particular friend of yours, and Mr. Collins has my living, and is your own cousin."

"I asked that the Gardiners be invited, Lady Catherine," Georgiana said. "We have become very well-acquainted in town, and I favour their company."

"Favour their company?" Lady Catherine sniffed, and Georgiana caught Kitty trying very hard not to laugh from the corner of the room.

"Lady Catherine, perhaps you have forgotten that Georgiana is not at all acquainted with the Collinses," Elizabeth said. "I wrote to Mrs. Collins and explained that the current house party is only for those attending the wedding, but that she is very welcome to visit at some other time during the summer."

"Well, I suppose that is acceptable," Lady Catherine said. "Perhaps I shall return for another visit and escort them, so they do not need to travel post."

Georgiana had for some time been watching the empty seat beside Kitty Bennet with a great desire to speak more closely with her friend again. When refreshments came, she took the opportunity to move there with her glass of lemonade, and was greeted with a look of open delight.

"Oh, Georgiana! I shall overlook my jealousy at your being married first to tell you how very happy I am for you. I had so hoped it would come about, and now it has."

Kitty had already expressed as much to Georgiana in her letters, but it was heartening to see her open enthusiasm; Georgiana certainly would have allowed her any amount of jealousy, to have been engaged earlier and yet married later, but if Kitty was as jealous as she said she was, it did not appear on her countenance.

"Thank you, Kitty – I am certain your time will come soon enough. The war will not last long, now, after Waterloo, and then it will be my turn to attend your wedding."

"Indeed, we shall both be naval wives!" Catherine laughed. "How wonderful that will be!"

Georgiana had not really thought of herself as such – a naval wife – although she had given much thought to what it would be like to marry Captain Stanton. Still, the man who would make Catherine a naval wife was still at sea, while Georgiana's betrothed did not know if he would have another command. Given the number of people who had promised to press for him to have another ship, though, she could not help but think that it was inevitable.

"Have you heard from Captain Ramsey recently?" Georgiana asked.

"I have – I had a letter from him two days past. He is terribly bored, although he says he would be more bored, were he captain of one of the ships of the line; the blockade feels rather pointless now, after Waterloo," Catherine said. "He gives you and Captain Stanton joy, of course – he wishes he could have returned for the wedding, but he could not get leave."

"I wish he could have been here as well," Georgiana said. She had considered reviving the Fandango with Mary, so that they could play it for Captain Stanton at least, but it felt wrong to do so with Captain Ramsey absent, given how fond he was of Spanish music. Thinking of Captain Ramsey's being absent led her thoughts to darken, as she thought of who else was absent from the house party. There had been no word from her aunt and uncle since Lady Ellen's first letter, and much as Georgiana tried to remain positive – surely no news was better than bad news – she also would not have put it past her aunt to delay the bad news until after the wedding.

The next day saw them all plagued with a strong round of thunderstorms, so that any out-of-doors activities that had been planned among the guests must be put off. Many of them chose to gather in the yellow drawing room, where conversation flowed around interjections from Lady Catherine and Mrs. Bennet as best it could. Georgiana occupied herself even more pleasantly, by pressing Kitty into her expedition up to one of the attics with young Susan Gardiner and poor Hughes, who knew where all of the dresses were stored, and suffered their stirring up a great deal of dust in their excitement.

Elizabeth saw that all of the guests in the drawing room were settled with what they needed, but then, feeling the exhaustion which had been growing every bit as much as her belly, decided not to join them immediately. She sought refuge in the library, assuming her father would be there, but finding her husband instead.

"Darcy! Where is my father?"

"He went out to Clareborne early this morning with Charles. I am glad they set out early – they should at least be sheltering in that miserable house by now," Darcy said. "I am sorry to deprive you of more favourable company."

"That is not what I meant," she leaned over, kissing his temple, and then took the seat beside him. "He has just become so much of a fixture here that is it as strange to walk in and find him missing, as it would be if one of the bookshelves were to disappear."

Darcy smiled, and looked carefully at her. "How are you holding up with so many guests, Elizabeth? You do seem a little tired."

"I expect I would look tired even if it was just us and Georgiana," Elizabeth said. "Mrs. Reynolds has everything in hand. We were expecting Lady Tonbridge and Lord Anglesey and his son and daughter-in-law today, but it is possible the weather will delay them."

"Well, I am glad you stepped away for some rest," he said.

"As am I. I will let my mother wear everyone else down for a little while, and then return," she said.

"Do not forget Lady Catherine's share in the wearing-down," he said. "I suppose I shall have to come with you."

"Yes, you shall, or we will be known throughout the county as abominable hosts," Elizabeth said, crossing the room to take up a book, and then returning to her seat.

They read, quietly, for half-an-hour, with the rain coming down in great waves outside, and frequent rumbles of thunder. Elizabeth knew that the time was coming when this would be a more frequent occasion for them; the house would empty of guests, Charles and Jane would leave for the new house at Clareborne Manor, and Georgiana would go to wherever she and Captain Stanton settled. Someday, it would just be Elizabeth and Darcy and then – God-willing – the child, here at Pemberley. Still, on this day, she found the time to be precious.

They had planned for Elizabeth's portrait to be unveiled that evening. Thankfully, it had arrived the day before the storm, escorted in the coach by none other than Mrs. Wright, who, upon seeing it safely unloaded, said she would go assist in the preparations for the ball, which Elizabeth rather thought meant she would lend her assistance as much as she could, although all the while judging whether it might have been done better in town.

Dinner came out quite well – no better or worse than it would have at Curzon Street, to Elizabeth's palate – and fortunately Lord Anglesey, Lord and Lady Stanton, and Lady Tonbridge all arrived in time to attend.

Mr. Thorpe had no interest in attending an unveiling outside of London, and so when they had all gathered in the drawing room following dinner to face the portrait in its easel, covered with velvet cloth, the honour of pulling off the cloth was left to Kitty as the most theatrical – as well as most artistic, now – among them.

The cloth was removed with sufficient drama by Catherine, and they all applauded, as they would have done no matter what it looked like. Elizabeth, who had already seen the portrait, thought it to be well-done, although perhaps a little unrealistic – certainly her features were not truly that symmetrical. The thought of everyone looking at a painting of her, and clapping, no less, she found terribly embarrassing, and she was glad when the applause ceased and they could toast the painting and then move on to other topics.

Little else was said on the painting, aside from the occasional compliment someone would come up to her and give from time to time, and of course Mrs. Bennet, who hovered around it, periodically exclaiming things such as: "My Lizzy, hanging in the great gallery of Pemberley, for all generations to see!" and "Charles, you must build a portrait gallery at Clareborne, and have a portrait done of Jane, as well!"

Only when Elizabeth climbed up into her husband's bed, and he was moving his hand languidly over her belly, as he liked to do now, did she finally learn his opinion of it.

"You have been oddly silent about my portrait, Darcy. I know you must have some opinion of it."

"It is tolerable, but not so handsome as the original."

It took a moment for his statement to register with her, and then she laughed heartily. "How long have you been waiting to say that?"

"Since well before Mr. Thorpe began."

"I should never have taught you to tease."

"I would have learned anyway, with such an example before me."

Elizabeth laughed, again – it felt rather wonderful to do so, for it had been some time since she had. The reminder of why that was struck her again, and her expression sobered, so rapidly that a far less observant man than Darcy would have noticed.

"What is the matter?" he asked.

"It just feels strange, to be laughing, when – when Edward is still missing."

"Edward loves a laugh as much as any of us; he would not begrudge you this one."

"I know, but it still feels strange," she said. "It feels strange to be continuing on, and hosting a ball, while we still have no idea of his fate. I know we do not hold the ball for ourselves, but still, I do not know how I shall make it through the evening pretending that all is well."

"I know," he said, caressing her face in a way that Elizabeth suspected was as comforting to him as it was to her. "But I am for hope, when it comes to Edward, and if we hope, we must carry on as though our hopes will be met, even including the occasional laughter."

Elizabeth knew he was right, and truly, she had no good reason to doubt in hope. In the last few years, all that she had hoped for had come to be – the discovery of Lydia and Wickham, Jane's marriage to Charles, Catherine's engagement, Captain Stanton's recovery and proposal to Georgiana, her own marriage for love, and of course her pregnancy. Nothing of substance that she hoped and prayed for had failed to come about. And yet she could not help but think that the odds could not always be so good to her, and that some day, something that she hoped for would fail to happen. She wished deeply that this latest hope would not be it.

CHAPTER 21

By the day of the ball, all who were expected had arrived, some delayed because of the weather, but still there with enough time to settle. Added to their party were Captain Campbell, and Lord and Lady Fitzwilliam, who both looked very sober, but had felt that some of the Fitzwilliam family should attend. Mrs. Annesley had sent her regrets regarding the ball, for she could only spare enough time away from her new family for the wedding itself.

Elizabeth felt the estate in its hum of activity, preparing for its largest event in many years, but knew from the looks on the faces of both housekeepers that all was proceeding as planned. Elizabeth therefore went about her morning, and then up to Sarah to be changed, with utmost calm.

She and Georgiana were the first to return downstairs – there was little joy to be had in dressing for this ball – and as Elizabeth passed the table in the entrance-hall, she realised that everyone had been so occupied on this day that they had entirely neglected the post, so that several letters sat in the little gilded box. She commented on this to Georgiana, and picked them up. The first was a letter of business for Darcy, but Elizabeth was quite shocked to find the second was from Lord Brandon. It had been misdirected – Lord Brandon's hand was quite the opposite of his wife's – and Elizabeth had only just opened it when she became aware of its purpose.

"A fine carriage coming up the drive, ma'am, quite unexpected," Mr. Parker said, rushing up to her.

"It is far too early for any of the neighbours," Elizabeth said, following him, with Georgiana close behind her.

They could see as soon as they came out of the door that the coach had the Brandon arms, and Elizabeth wished that she had noticed the letter earlier, for she had no notion of who would alight the carriage, although her heart pounded at the thought that surely they would not have come all this way to deliver bad news. Lord Brandon came out first, and then assisted Lady Ellen down. He looked much as he usually did, but Lady Ellen seemed wan, and weary, although with a certain aspect of happiness to her countenance that must certainly mean –

"Edward!" Georgiana exclaimed, for Colonel Fitzwilliam could be seen behind his mother.

"Indeed! I understand there is to be a wedding, and I have yet to give my consent!" Colonel Fitzwilliam jumped down from the carriage and embraced Georgiana, looking quite healthy.

Except – Elizabeth's breath caught, and Georgiana must have noticed by now, although she could not say anything, nor was she likely to have anything at all to say, so filled with sobs of happiness was she. Colonel Fitzwilliam had suffered the fate they had feared for Captain Stanton – there was no sling on his arm, only his now-useless sleeve, pinned to his coat.

"We found him in one of the houses that had been commandeered as a hospital in Brussels. The amputation had already occurred," Lady Ellen murmured to Elizabeth, her voice thickening with tears at the word *amputation*. "He bears it exceedingly well, though, and we are far more fortunate than many families. It was the left arm, at least, and he is quite healthy, otherwise. It is far better than I feared, at times."

Once again, Elizabeth was surprised by an additional presence in a carriage in Pemberley's drive, for when the flurry of Colonel Fitzwilliam's appearance had passed, Lydia descended from the carriage, swooned, recovered, and cried, "My Wickham is dead!"

"My God – Lydia!" Elizabeth exclaimed.

"Lord Brandon, surely you told Mrs. Darcy that her sister travelled with us in your letter," Lady Ellen said.

"I have not even had the chance to read your letter," Elizabeth said. "It was misdirected at first, and I only just noticed it with our post. But we are very relieved to see you all. Please come in and we shall sort everything out."

They all followed her into the saloon, where they might close the doors for privacy, for all the guests were to gather in the yellow drawing room to go into dinner. Elizabeth asked Mr. Parker to send for Darcy, her own parents, and Lord and Lady Fitzwilliam; for she was quickly informed that the letter to her and Darcy had covered one for Colonel Fitzwilliam's brother, meant to apprise him of the same news they had all just become acquainted with.

Lord Brandon gave his deepest apologies for the letter's delay. He had written it during the passage to Ramsgate, on the Daphne, and had posted it express from the inn where they had hired a carriage, but it seemed the proprietor had pocketed the extra money for the express, rather than sending it so. They had been certain the letter would outpace them as they returned to London for two nights, before setting out for Derbyshire. All was readily forgiven, and Elizabeth asked for a better account of how they had come to find Lydia, when Mrs. Bennet entered, followed by the others.

"Oh, Lydia! My child, you are returned to us!" she cried, embracing her daughter.

"Mama, my Wickham is dead! We searched all the hospitals, and could not find him. My poor, dear Wickham!"

With his wife and youngest daughter now openly weeping, Mr. Bennet sedately thanked Lord and Lady Brandon for looking after Mrs. Wickham, and seeing her returned to them. Lord and Lady Fitzwilliam came in, and were most exceedingly shocked to find their brother there in the drawing room; Elizabeth was surprised to see Lord Fitzwilliam, whom she had always thought quite stoic, shed a few tears at the sight of his brother, and the Fitzwilliams took some time in embraces amongst their family before they would turn their attention to the others present.

All were seated, and Lord and Lady Brandon did then explain how they had come across Lydia quite by accident, for she was searching all the hospitals as they were, and they had overheard her ask about Mr. Wickham at one place, just after they had made their own inquiries. They had asked if she was Elizabeth Darcy's sister – she was – and they had all then united in their search of the hospitals.

Colonel Fitzwilliam was found, Ensign Wickham was not. After such an exhaustive search, for they had checked every house that had been commandeered, and even the barns closer to the war front, they had been forced to conclude that he would not be found in the Netherlands, and convinced Lydia to make the crossing with them. When he was not in Ramsgate, nor in London, they had begun to suspect he had died on the battlefield like so many others.

"Lizzy, do you have any black crepe about? If not, where may it be purchased?" Mrs. Bennet asked. "My poor, poor Lydia shall have to go into mourning. We all shall."

"My God, she is right," Elizabeth murmured to Darcy. "He was my brother. At least you and I will have to go into mourning. It is too late to do anything about the ball, but the wedding – "

"I absolutely will not have Georgiana's wedding postponed by that man," Darcy said, rather more loudly than he had intended.

"And why not, sir?" Mrs. Bennet cried. "He is your family, and he has died a hero! And you shall not go into mourning for him, as is proper?"

"That man made every attempt he could to slander my name, and very nearly ruined your family," Darcy said.

Of those in the room, only he, Elizabeth, Colonel Fitzwilliam, and of course Georgiana knew of the deeper wound he had inflicted upon the Darcys, although none would speak of it. And of them, it was Colonel Fitzwilliam who finally spoke, attempting a different approach:

"Ma'am, perhaps we should wait until it is absolutely certain. It is possible there were other hospitals we did not know to search, or that he has been taken in by a farmer somewhere. Or made the crossing into some other port, and has not yet been able to get word to Mrs. Wickham. I am sure you would not wish to mourn him and then learn later he is still alive."

Mrs. Bennet seemed mollified by this argument, but Lydia was unmoved, and spoke, with fresh tears, "He is dead, I am sure of it. I know it in my heart. He would have found me if he were still alive! You all may wait to go into mourning if you wish, but I will begin now, for I know my Wickham is gone."

With this settled, the Fitzwilliams and Lydia were encouraged to go upstairs and change for the quick dinner that would be held before the ball. Elizabeth could see Lydia's spirits warring over the thought of missing the ball, for she could hardly attend if in mourning, but to her sister's credit, she held fast, and said she would stay in her apartment after dinner.

As the rest of the group departed, Elizabeth, Darcy, Georgiana and Colonel Fitzwilliam stayed behind. When the others had left, Colonel Fitzwilliam said, "I am glad Mrs. Wickham believes him dead, for in all likelihood he *is* dead, but it may take the army months to sort through everything and declare him so. I would not wish to give her false hope, but like Darcy, I will not see Georgiana's wedding postponed for that man, even if he is dead."

They left to make their way to the yellow drawing room, and were met in the entrance-hall by Captain Stanton, who was quickly introduced to Colonel Fitzwilliam.

"I heard you were returned, sir, and wished to express my happiness at the event," Captain Stanton said.

Colonel Fitzwilliam thanked him stiffly, and Captain Stanton seemed to notice the tension among the group, for he looked curiously at Georgiana. She took up his arm, and Elizabeth heard her murmur the news of Mr. Wickham's being missing, and likely dead, and of the discussion over when mourning should begin.

"I agree that we should not delay the wedding on that man's account," he said, so particularly that Elizabeth felt certain her sister had told him of her history with Wickham at some point. "How do *you* take the news, my dear?"

"I do not know how to take it," Georgiana said. "He was not a good man, and he made every attempt to use me ill, and yet I cannot say that I would wish any man dead."

They all walked on in silence, and Colonel Fitzwilliam left them to go change for dinner, Mr. Parker having offered to act as his valet, a service that would have been offered by the butler or one of the footmen for any male guest at Pemberley, but seemed particularly critical for Colonel Fitzwilliam's new situation. The drawing room already contained all but their most recently arrived guests and Mrs. Bennet, who had gone up with Lydia, and they all looked expectantly at Elizabeth and Darcy as they entered. It was clear the news of the Brandon carriage's arrival had spread throughout the house. Darcy made a brief announcement, explaining the safe return of Colonel Fitzwilliam and the additions to their party, before noting that Ensign Wickham remained missing.

"Poor fellow," Lady Tonbridge said. "We must all pray for his safe return. Mr. Stanton, perhaps you might lead us in something of the like?"

David Stanton obliged her, and then for a little while, the party relaxed into something resembling the conversation of the last few days. Elizabeth scanned the room to ensure that all were comfortable, and stopped with surprise when she saw Mary. For Mary's hair was styled without all of its usual severity, and for once it flattered her face – she actually looked quite pretty, and Elizabeth was glad to see her finally take some interest in her presentation.

The cause for this sudden interest became readily apparent, for Mary was approached by David Stanton, and soon enough the two of them were deep in conversation. Elizabeth found herself thinking back over the past few days and realised that they had often been seated together. If Mary was ever to be attracted to a man, he was precisely the sort Elizabeth thought she might go for – a quiet, conservative clergyman.

"Perhaps Mary may not wait so long to follow Catherine into marriage as we may have thought," Darcy whispered to her, watching them as well. "Captain Stanton's brother *is* unmarried, is he not?"

"He is a widower," Elizabeth said. "But I do not think such a thing would be an issue for Mary."

"We will have to watch them both more closely, if he is indeed courting her."

"I am not sure if either of them thinks of it as a courtship yet, but yes, this did rather catch me by surprise."

They were interrupted by the arrival of the Fitzwilliams, followed shortly after by Lydia and Mrs. Bennet, and Elizabeth and Darcy busied themselves with introductions for the guests who were not already acquainted, which in Lydia's case was most of the party. Lydia had, thankfully, not yet managed to acquire any crepe, but she could not receive hopes from anyone of her husband's safe return without some degree of hysterics, both from herself and her mother. Elizabeth noticed Georgiana and Captain Stanton sitting on the edge of the room, looking grave, and was glad when Mr. Parker entered and told her dinner was ready, so that she could call them all to make their entrance.

Dinner was a quick affair, but then, it had always been intended to be so, a comparably simple meal to hold them until supper. They had not attempted to recreate Lord Anglesey's trick of precedence in the dinners at Pemberley, and so as the dinner parties had grown, Georgiana found herself sitting farther and farther from her betrothed, but had not minded it so much until tonight. They had spent much time together in the last few weeks, and in three days, had the promise of so much more. Neither of them was well-situated for conversation on this evening, though, for it appeared Lady Catherine had dominated the discussion on Captain Stanton's end of the table, while Georgiana had endured the discomfort of sitting next to Lydia Wickham, who would speak of nothing but her poor husband.

It was impossible for Georgiana to turn her mind away from all the news of the day, and she still could not settle on how she felt about it. Certainly she felt the utmost happiness at seeing Edward returned – tempered, of course, by the loss of his arm. But to think of Mr. Wickham as dead, as gone from the world, was very strange indeed. She could not help but feel relief for Lydia – although it did not seem that Mrs. Wickham felt that same relief – to no longer face a lifetime married to such a man.

The gentlemen were not long over their port – in less than half-an-hour, Elizabeth, Darcy, Georgiana and Captain Stanton would need to take up their places in the receiving line as the other guests began to arrive. Yet Colonel Fitzwilliam and Captain Stanton were not among them as they returned to the drawing room, and Darcy stopped beside Georgiana to tell her, "Edward and your betrothed have gone to my study. They wished to have a private conversation, but they will return in time for the receiving line."

"Was Edward serious about giving his consent to my marriage?"

"I believe your betrothed was more serious about requesting consent than the other way around," Darcy said. "Although I do think Edward wished to speak with him; they have hardly had a chance to be acquainted. You need not fear for your wedding date, though – none of us will brook any sort of delay, whether caused by Wickham or otherwise."

"Brother, what do you feel, about his death?"

"I know the proper thing to say would be sadness, but what I feel is relief, primarily, both for Lydia, and for you."

"He no longer had an effect on me, even before I learned of his death," Georgiana said. "I hope you did not worry of his sharing the story with my betrothed. I told Captain Stanton everything, the day he proposed. I could not bear to have such a secret between us."

Her brother inhaled sharply, but said nothing, and Georgiana knew he must be thinking of what a risk she had taken.

"We played together as children, he and Colonel Fitzwilliam and I," he said. "I never could stop wondering where he went wrong. He had an excellent father, and far better expectations than most men of his station, and yet he threw them all away."

"He was not so different from Stephen Mallory," Georgiana said. "The only difference was Stephen Mallory had more fortune to dissipate."

"How do I prevent my own child from taking such a path?"

"You will raise him or her the same way you raised me, but you must remember it is not all under your control," Georgiana said, thinking of Mr. Wickham, raised by their own father after his father's death, and Captain Stanton, who had left home to be raised by others when he was so very young. By all rights, Captain Stanton should have been the one to turn out wild.

"Niece! Nephew! What are you speaking of?" Lady Catherine asked them, from across the room. "If it is the wedding, I wish to have my share in the conversation. We still have not covered all of the details, and I do not expect Mrs. Darcy – "

"Mrs. Darcy will have everything arranged to perfection, as she has this ball," Darcy said loudly, scowling at Lady Catherine, and leaving Georgiana with a reluctant look.

Everything *was* arranged to perfection, Georgiana thought as she looked down the drive with its torches blazing. This was the Pemberley of old, a Pemberley that had hardly existed during her lifetime, and she only faintly remembered, but something felt very right about it, as though the estate had been reawakened to its purpose. Elizabeth and Fitzwilliam looked every bit their part at the front of the line; Elizabeth seemed far more at ease there, although Georgiana might merely have been more attuned to her brother's discomfort, knowing that she felt much the same way he looked, regarding the crowds they would be required to greet.

Even so, with the assurance of Edward's safety, Georgiana found herself looking forward to the ball far more than she had earlier in the day. Indeed, the only thing missing was Captain Stanton, who took up his place beside her in the receiving line just as the first carriage pulled up. There followed a most intense half-hour, as the guests filed past all of them and must be continually introduced to Captain Stanton, and then give their best wishes for the wedding. There were gentlemen who wished to speak about the Polonais, and ladies who remembered Georgiana as a little girl, going about the estate with her mother, and could not believe she was all grown up and about to marry, and they all wished to speak of these topics at length.

Georgiana was already quite tired when they finally entered Pemberley's vast ballroom, but felt her spirits lift at the prospect of dancing, and even more at the prospect of her first partner. For she and Captain Stanton were to lead off the dance; he was unsure how long it would be before the lingering soreness in his leg and arm became bothersome, but he felt confident in being able to make it through the first set, at least.

"Now *you* must tell me if the pain is too much and we must step out," Georgiana told him as they made their way to the front of the ballroom, and bowed.

"We are leading, my dearest. If we step out, they will all follow, and that will be the end of the dance."

Georgiana giggled at the thought of it. "You are sure, then, that this will not be too much?"

"I shall be fine," he said. "But let us not choose a reel, if you please."

They bowed to the room, and began. Georgiana watched him carefully, but saw no sign of stiffness, and eventually relaxed, allowing herself to enjoy the dance.

"So did Colonel Fitzwilliam give his consent?" she asked, when they had settled into the figures.

"He did, almost immediately."

"You were gone for a while, though," Georgiana said, before they separated.

When they had circled and come back together, he said, "Waterloo was a most horrific battle, Georgiana, and in addition to his more visible loss, Colonel Fitzwilliam also lost many of his comrades-in-arms."

"But he seems just as he ever was."

"He does not wish to worry his family."

"But he would speak of it to you? He is barely acquainted with you."

"We have both known battle. Life in the army and the navy may be quite different, on the face of it, but there is not so much difference in the fighting, and the loss."

"Will you promise me something, then?"

"What do you wish me to promise?"

"That you will never hold back for fear of worrying me."

"I will promise you that," he said, clasping her hand tightly before they separated again.

As the dance continued, Georgiana gained a better idea of who the other couples were. There were, of course, the married couples, although with Elizabeth choosing not to dance this evening, Darcy had obliged Lady Catherine. Lord Anglesey and Lady Tonbridge had danced together, Kitty Bennet and Captain Campbell, and Mrs. Bennet and Charles Bingley. Mr. Bennet had no interest in dancing, and Jane and Anne had retired with Lydia following dinner; Jane would begin her confinement immediately after the wedding, unless her health required her to do so before. Georgiana saw Mary Bennet last, dancing well down the floor with David Stanton, and looking quite a lot happier to be at a ball than Georgiana had ever seen her.

It seemed Captain Stanton had made the same observation, for he said, "Miss Bennet and my brother have been spending quite a lot of time together, and now they dance the first set."

"I think it could be a good match. Do you?"

"I do, now that I see them together. He has not written me of any ladies since he came out of mourning. Perhaps he is finally ready, and Miss Bennet is the only lady of my acquaintance who might engage him in the sort of conversation about theology he enjoys."

Georgiana had promised the second set to her brother, and he came over to claim her hand soon enough. They danced quietly; she did not wish to broach their conversation of earlier, for it seemed far too heavy a topic for a ballroom, and then he was handing her over to Lord Brandon.

Elizabeth approached Lady Ellen as Lord Brandon was leading Georgiana to the floor, and Darcy had gone over to where Colonel Fitzwilliam and Captain Stanton were sitting.

"Aunt Ellen, these last few weeks must have been exhausting for you," Elizabeth said. "It will likely be a late night – please do not feel as though you need to stay through the whole of it."

"Oh, I believe I shall stay through the whole of it," Lady Ellen said. "There is nothing I needed quite so much right now as a fine English ball, after seeing the results of so much savagery."

"I cannot even fathom the things you must have seen."

"I was surprised at how quickly I became desensitised to it all. It is not as though I have not known death, but this was at a scale you cannot comprehend without seeing it," Lady Ellen said. "Constant streams of carts filled with the injured, and many of them so far gone I do not see how they could have survived. And as we got closer to the front, the smell, oh – "

Here Lady Ellen reached into her reticule and pulled out her smelling salts, taking a strong whiff of them, which disturbed Elizabeth quite thoroughly, for Lady Ellen was not the sort of woman to usually have need of salts.

"At least you found him," Elizabeth said. "I cannot tell you how worried we were, and how happy we are at his return."

"Yes, I cannot bear the thought of what it would have been, to return without him," Lady Ellen said. "I feel so badly for your poor sister, that she had to do so."

"I cannot thank you enough, for your care for her. I know she can be – difficult, sometimes."

"She was not difficult at all," Lady Ellen said. "She had no more or less fortitude than I, in such a terrible situation, and she had a far more difficult outcome to deal with."

Georgiana danced every set before supper, for no gentleman of close acquaintance would see her sit out a dance. It was such a contrast to the

Prince Regent's ball, to dance with her cousin Andrew, Lord Anglesey, Captain Campbell, David Stanton, and Mr. Clark, all men she knew and trusted, and to be within Pemberley's vast but comfortable ballroom.

She would have been fully happy on the evening, but for two things. The first was that Captain Stanton sat out most of the dances, although he had danced a set with Kitty when he noticed she was without a partner. The second was that Edward did not dance at all, and spent much of his time sitting in the far corner of the ballroom, often talking with Captain Stanton, or Darcy. There were sights that cheered her, however. Georgiana had never seen Mary Bennet dance more than three sets at a ball, and yet she had continued dancing right through the supper set, which she danced with David Stanton. And there was Lady Ellen, who danced several sets and looked impossibly elegant, considering how exhausted she must have been.

They were now well past the supper set, and Georgiana stood beside Elizabeth and her brother during a break in the dancing. Georgiana admired Elizabeth, who had not danced, but had been a most active hostess, considering her condition. Now, however, she looked quite tired, and indeed the hour was growing late.

"I believe we will make this the last set," Elizabeth said.

"I had been hoping the last three sets would be the last set," Darcy said.

"This is Pemberley's first ball in a great many years, Darcy. You know we cannot leave them thinking it was underdone."

"Very true. No one could complain of such a thing now."

"Will you help me go around and let everyone know this is the last dance, and it is to be a waltz?"

"A waltz? Elizabeth, you forget we are not in town."

"The waltz must make its way to the country someday, Darcy. It may as well be now," Elizabeth said, turning to Georgiana and giving her a little wink.

It was for her! Georgiana tried to keep from smiling openly. Of course Elizabeth had remembered that embarrassing night; of course she had remembered that Georgiana and Captain Stanton had never finished this dance.

"You will scandalise the county," Darcy said, although his countenance showed he was not entirely serious.

"Most of these families spend time in town. They will hardly consider it a scandal. Now, will you help me make it known?" Elizabeth said, then, turning to Georgiana. "You had better go find your partner."

Georgiana looked about the room to find Captain Stanton, and saw he was still in the corner, speaking with Edward. She approached them shyly, not wishing to interrupt, but they both noticed her right away.

"Miss Darcy, there you are," Captain Stanton said. "How have your dances been?"

"Very pleasant," Georgiana said, suddenly unsure of what to say, for she very much wanted to dance, but did not wish him to feel he had to, if he was not well enough for it.

"Is it time for the waltz, then?" Captain Stanton asked.

"It is. How did you – "

"Your sister filled me in on her plans earlier. I have been sitting out more dances than I might have otherwise, to ensure I would be ready for this one."

"She had this planned all along, then."

"I cannot say how long she had it planned," Captain Stanton said. "But I know she apprised me of it after the first set."

He offered her his arm, and they were about to make their way to the floor, when Kitty Bennet came up to them, looking quite resolute.

"Why yes, Colonel Fitzwilliam, I will dance the waltz with you."

"I did not – I cannot – " he sputtered, quite taken aback.

"Come, a young, healthy man like yourself cannot spend an entire ball without dancing," Kitty said, holding out her hand. "And you know I am an engaged woman, so you need not fear me."

"Miss Bennet, I will assume you have noticed that I only have one arm, now."

"You still have two legs. We will manage," Kitty said firmly, still holding out her hand. Finally, Edward extended his, and they followed Georgiana and Captain Stanton to the floor.

"She may have done him more good there than an entire evening's worth of talking," Captain Stanton murmured to Georgiana, when they had distanced themselves a bit from the other couples.

"Do not discount your own help," Georgiana said. "But yes, although I dearly wish Captain Ramsey could have been here, I think perhaps he was not meant to be, because Kitty was meant to – well, be Kitty."

They both laughed, but Georgiana began to feel that the attention of much of the ballroom was focused on her, and glanced around to see that it was so.

"They look to us to lead," she whispered, feeling her face grow warm at the attention.

"Well, then, lead we must," he said, placing his right hand upon her shoulder, and taking up her hand with his left hand, to ready them for the Marche.

When the music began, they progressed around the ballroom, and it was impossible not to sense how many in that space watched them. It was a bit of a relief when they transitioned to the Pirouette. Georgiana arched her arm over her head, to join her hand in his, and there was no pain this time, only a little thrill deep inside her at the closeness, as his hand pressed against the small of her back. Georgiana gazed into his eyes, as the dance

361

required and she would have wished to do anyway, and blushed at the thought that in three days they would be man and wife, and even closer than this.

She was quite pleasantly surprised to find he was very good at this dance; it required good timing and rhythm, something they each had earned through years of musical experience, and something which was not lost among those who were not dancing, for the couple was much commented on.

They wound their way down the ballroom, and Georgiana gazed at her betrothed with all the joyfulness she felt, all the chaos and news from earlier in the day quite forgotten, and she found his countenance mirrored every bit of happiness and tenderness that she felt. They did not speak, but they danced just as two people who were very much in love should dance.

Elizabeth stood at the edge of the empty ballroom, the candelabra in her hand barely lighting what had been so brilliant an hour ago. It was two in the morning, and yet she could not bring herself to retire.

She fingered the pendant of her newest necklace, and thought back to the waltz, and how although a part of her had longed to dance, she had also enjoyed standing beside her husband, watching a progression of couples that quite delighted her. There were, of course, Georgiana and Captain Stanton, her primary purpose for including the dance. But there had also been Kitty and Colonel Fitzwilliam, who had been required to change positions to accommodate for Colonel Fitzwilliam's arm, and so appeared to the opposite of all the other couples in the ballroom, but otherwise managed quite nicely. There were Lord and Lady Brandon, who had waltzed as those who were veterans of many a season, although Lady Ellen could not help but look over at her younger son occasionally with a look of deep contentment on her face. And there were Mary Bennet and David Stanton, who would not waltz, but stood at the edge of the ballroom, deep in conversation.

"There you are," said the giver of the necklace, stepping up close behind her and wrapping his arms around her so that he could rest his hands on the slight little bump of her stomach. "Surveying the scene of your latest triumph?"

"I would hardly call it a triumph."

"I shall. It will be the talk of Derbyshire for some time."

"Well certainly, given we scandalised the county." Elizabeth teased, in saying this – in truth, although they did not make up her fondest memories of the ball, she had felt a certain happiness on the evening in seeing all of the local families enjoying themselves so, particularly those who had gathered around her aunt Gardiner in order to reminisce. And rather more of them than she had expected had taken up their place in the waltz – it had helped that many of the older couples had already been lured off to the saloon, for the tea and final little kickshaws served there.

"I will own that they do not seem to have been very scandalised," he said. "And even if they were, it would have been worth it, if just for Georgiana's countenance."

"It is so wonderful to see her so happy – and they are not even married yet."

"Indeed, and I know the event will be complete for her now, with both Edward and I there to give her away," he said. "And what of you – are you happy?"

Elizabeth had an easy answer to this question, and it was not only caused by seeing Colonel Fitzwilliam returned to them. She had spent so much time at the beginning of her marriage sacrificing herself for her sisters, and she still felt it was worthwhile – even Mary had her chance, now – but now it was time to turn to her own happiness, and her own family, and she looked forward to the events that were to come with a great deal of joyful anticipation.

"I am," she said, covering his hands with her free hand. "I am so very happy to be Mrs. Darcy."

"I am more happy you are my Elizabeth," he said, leaning to kiss her shoulder. "Now come to bed, my darling Elizabeth."

AUTHOR'S NOTES

All of the noble titles used within this story were either extinct during the Regency, or are entirely made up, and any resemblance of any of the names within to actual people is entirely coincidental, with the exception of brief, fictitious encounters with members of the royal family. Specific to the royal family, in 1814 (the year in which this begins), Princess Caroline, the Prince Regent's wife, moved to Italy, so I assumed only the Queen would be receiving.

The Prince Regent's ball is fictitious in itself, although based on others held at Carlton House, and hopefully at least architecturally accurate, as the rotunda mentioned was built the year before and would still have been there. Amazingly, although it has been moved, it still stands today on Woolwich Common. The waltz described in this story is the Regency version of this dance, which underwent many changes before the Victorian era, where it became something much more like the dance we know today.

More specific to the main characters, I have chosen to make Colonel Fitzwilliam's father the Earl of Brandon, rather than of Matlock; while making him the Earl of Matlock is popular, for having been mentioned in the 1996 miniseries, it is not part of the original novel's canon. Similarly, Colonel Fitzwilliam himself is not given a first name in the original novel, and I have used Edward, rather than the more popular Richard.

The Duke of Bolton's first son uses the courtesy title of a viscountcy that would previously have been earned by the family; while it might more commonly have been a marquisate or earldom, it is entirely dependent on what titles would have been earned by the family before the dukedom, and to avoid confusion, I did not want a third earl within the story. The two sons of earls in this story, because they are in families lacking a second title, would have the precedence of viscount, with their surnames used in place of the courtesy title. Again, this was done to avoid the confusion of introducing additional titles.

All of the main naval ships listed (excepting the Foudroyant), were real ships with careers that were not so exceptional, while some ships with lesser roles have entirely made-up names. A number of authors, Jane Austen included, have based career-making events for their naval captains off of Lord Cochrane's capturing of a frigate in the sloop-of-war HMS Speedy. In seeking something a little different, I had Captain Stanton capture a 74-gun ship with a 50-gun ship. While not based on an actual naval action, particularly one of Napoleon's Hundred Days, I believe under the circumstances, as written, it would have been realistic (or at least as realistic as the existence of a Mr. Darcy), although it would have had no impact on the outcome of the war, with Waterloo soon to come.

The reward of a baronetcy for the victorious captain would also have been realistic, and indeed, my closest model for Captain Stanton was Sir Philip Broke, the gentleman captain of HMS Shannon, who was made a baronet for his victory over the USS Chesapeake. Coincidentally, Broke attended the Portsmouth Naval Academy at the same time as Jane Austen's brother, Charles. Meanwhile, Richard Stanton's Judgement Day comment is based in part on comments made to Edward Pellew (another frigate captain, of HMS Indefatigable fame) by his grandfather.

I have tried to stick carefully to the canon established in *Pride and Prejudice*, with the exception of some of the events listed in the final chapter (namely, Georgiana's and Kitty's fates), and of placing the events of this story a year after they should have occurred based on what is commonly thought to have been the timing of the original novel. The events of the Corn Bill Riots and Napoleon's Hundred Days were as real and as intertwined in terms of their timing as they appear in the story. I did perhaps rush the naval build-up in order to pace the story properly, but then again, I can hardly see how preparations for returning the fleet to sea did not begin immediately, although the Admiralty may not have been public about them.

I have done research in numerous sources for this story, but wish to call out the following books as having been particularly helpful: *Our Tempestuous Day: A History of Regency England*, by Carolly Erickson; *Georgette Heyer's Regency World*, by Jennifer Kloester; *Fashion in the Time of Jane Austen*, by Sarah Jane Downing; *Jane Austen and the Navy*, by Brian Southam; *All Things Austen: A Concise Encyclopedia of Austen's World*, by Kirstin Olsen; *Jane Austen in Context*, ed. Janet Todd; and *Jane Austen's Country Life*, by Deirdre Le Faye.

And of course, in addition to Austen, I am indebted to Patrick O'Brian, Frederick Marryat, C. S. Forester, and many others who have so vividly recreated the naval portion of the Georgian and Regency eras.

ABOUT THE AUTHOR

Sophie Turner lives in the Washington D.C. area, where she works a wholly unrelated day job, reads a tremendous amount of historical fiction, and dreams about living in Britain. She blogs about her writing endeavours at sophie-turner-acl.blogspot.com.

Made in United States
Orlando, FL
11 October 2024